Touches of Austen, Books 1-3

Touches of Austen, Books 1-3

A Touches of Austen Boxset

LEENIE BROWN

LEENIE B BOOKS
HALIFAX

Cover design by Leenie B Books. Images sourced from Deposit Photos and Period Images.

Touches of Austen (Books 1-3) © 2021 Leenie Brown. All Rights Reserved, except where otherwise noted. All of the titles in this book bundle have been previously published as single titles.

ISBN: (ebook) 978-1-989410-83-7 (print) 978-1-989410-84-4

Contents

Her Secret Beau

Dear Reader,

To those who know me, it is no surprise to hear that I am a fan of Jane Austen's work. I have written many stories in her universe which play with her characters and plot lines. However, the collection of stories you hold in your hand is not in her universe. Instead, this bundle of books contains the first three stories in my *Touches of Austen* Collection of Austenesque stories.

Each story in this series features original characters and plots that have only just been touched in some way by the influence of Jane Austen and her classic plots and characters.

In this three-story collection...

- *His Beautiful Bea* contains nods to *Mansfield Park,*
- *His Darling Friend* pays subtle homage to *Emma,* and

- *Her Secret Beau* has touches from *Northanger Abbey* in it.

In some of these stories, the influence of Jane Austen's well-loved novels is readily seen while in others, you may need to look more closely. And then, along with the intentional nods to Miss Austen's work in each story, there will also be some which are purely serendipitous.

If you are an Austen-lover who can't help but see the world through Jane-coloured glasses and would like to share your observations about which elements in these books you thought were Austen-inspired, you can do that in my *Touches of Austen Readers Group* on Facebook.

Happy Reading!

His
Beautiful
Bea

Helping her capture the gentleman she loves just might
break his heart.

Chapter 1

Graeme Clayton's pretty neighbour, Beatrice Tierney, blew out a breath, settled back against a tree in Stratsbury Park's garden, and attempted to find a comfortable position in which to read. Graeme pushed off the garden wall against which he had been leaning as he watched Bea and walked in her direction

The weather was warm, but not unbearably so, and the shade cast by the sprawling canopy of leaves above Bea surely provided a pleasant respite from the rays of the sun. That was good. Bea did not do well when she became overly warm. Hers was not the strongest constitution. Illness seemed to like her just as much as everyone else did.

A blessed, cooling breeze occasionally fluttered the hem of her skirt and attempted to turn the pages of her book. Graeme could just imagine how that would begin to annoy Bea soon enough. She did not like to have her reading interrupted by anyone or anything. Of course, it was not the breeze that was going to put a stop to her reading.

She darted a glance in the direction of her cousins, Felicity and Grace Love. Her lips twitched with displeasure as she turned her attention back to her book. It was an interesting expression, but not unexpected since the elder Miss Love, Miss Felicity Love, had claimed the attention of Graeme's younger brother, Everett.

From the time Bea had met Everett, she had followed him around with a particular look on her face that spoke of her adoration. It was not an obvious expression. It was simply an unmistakable softness in her eyes and the tipping up ever so slightly of the corners of her mouth.

Bea brushed away a fly that was meandering a path across the words she was attempting to decipher just as Graeme cast a long shadow across the page, causing her to look up to see its source.

"Is it a difficult passage?" Graeme chuckled as her lips puckered into a deeper scowl.

He knew very well that Bea was not short on intelligence. She might be quiet, verging on the edge of overly reserved and gentle, but it was not due to lack of intellect. In fact, when she did open her mouth to speak on any subject, her comments were impressively well-thought-out. He knew that she studied things — mulling them over and over, assessing them from every possible angle, and then, and only then, having decided she had a good grasp of her ideas, her thoughts on a matter *might* be shared. Equally as often as not, however, she would merely smile softly, raise a brow, and remain silent. It perplexed him how she could keep her opinions to herself so often. He had a devil of a time keeping his tongue from saying exactly what was in his head.

She was not the only one of the two of them who observed things to assess the lie of the land. Graeme was an expert in observation himself. For instance, today, for the past twenty minutes, he had been watching Bea. She had sighed and shaken her head often, her lips had pursed, her brow had furrowed, and the pages of her book had not flipped in all that time. She was contemplating something, and he was rather certain he knew what it was.

He took a seat next to her on the ground and,

giving her shoulder a nudge with his, repeated his question, earning him a very pretty scowl. However, as quickly as the scowl had formed on her lips, it melted away into the pleasant expression she wore in company when she would rather be elsewhere but did not wish to offend.

She was about to deny there was any issue at all — much as she always did. Others were permitted to be displeased and out of sorts, but Bea never allowed herself to be so — at least, not in company. One had to look for more subtle clues as to how Bea was really feeling, but that was just one of the things that made her uniquely his Bea.

"No," she began her denial, just as he had predicted she would, "the passage is not difficult. I was just distracted by the excellent weather."

Graeme, who was not content to let the situation pass so neatly, snatched her book out of her hands. It might be entirely possible to provoke her into revealing the truth of what he suspected.

"Your distraction has nothing to do with my brother?" he asked as he snapped the book closed on her marker.

Ah, there was her look of panic — a slight widening of the eyes and a sharp, though quiet, inhale of breath. He had obviously hit on the very thing which she was valiantly attempting to conceal.

Though they were only neighbours, Bea and her brother, Maxwell, had spent so many hours in company with Graeme and Everett that Graeme felt he knew the Tierney siblings almost as well as he knew his own brother. Well, "only neighbours" was perhaps not the most accurate way to describe who the Tierneys were to the Claytons.

Captain Tierney and Sir Herbert Clayton had been friends since childhood, and when the captain had come into some money — enough to buy a small estate for his family — he had settled on Heathcote which was not more than four miles distance from the western boundary of Stratsbury Park. And in such a manner had begun a closer friendship between their families. They had spent many days and evenings in one another's company during that first month after the Tierneys' arrival at Heathcote.

And then had come the day when Captain Tierney had been required to return to his ship. He had called on his friend Sir Herbert the evening before his departure and extracted a promise to care for

Mrs. Tierney and his children if something unfortunate should befall him. As fate would have it, the unfortunate did befall the captain, and he had never returned from sea.

Bea had borne the news with far more fortitude than Graeme had expected to find in one so young and female. It was then that he had taken a greater liking to her. She was not like the silly girls he had met over the years. She was unique in her quiet strength and resolve and so very unlike himself that he found himself compelled to attempt an understanding of such a person. His reward had been a comfortable friendship that allowed him access to the Beatrice others looking on would likely not suspect existed.

He nudged her shoulder again. "I do not believe it was the weather disturbing your reading," he whispered. "Are you positive your distraction has nothing to do with my brother?"

Bea shrugged.

Seeing he was not likely to get more of a reply from Bea than that, Graeme switched tactics and pressed on. "Miss Love is very pretty. How old is she now?"

Bea heaved a sigh. "Felicity is nineteen, just as I am, and Grace is seventeen."

"Are they both out?" he asked, moving her book away from the hand that attempted to reclaim it. He was not leaving this spot today without finding out if his suspicions about Bea's feelings for his brother were correct.

"Yes," Bea's lips stretched into a thin smile. "I have been regaled with the delights of the season several times since their arrival a fortnight ago."

Graeme shifted, placing the book on the grass next to him and stretching out his legs.

"Will you be going to town this next season? I could make a good number of introductions for you, and even with your modest dowry, I believe, we could find you a suitable husband."

He had not even finished speaking before her head was shaking back and forth.

"You will not go? I thought Max said he had put aside enough to give you a bit of a season."

"I do not wish to go. I have no desire to endure the crushes about which my cousins have told me. I prefer our small assemblies here."

"I imagine it will be harder to find a gentleman worthy of you here, but I have not been to an assembly in some time. Perhaps there is someone who has already captured your heart?" He tipped his head and studied her face carefully, looking for any indication that there might be a gentleman she already preferred.

The signs he sought were there — the slight blush on her cheek and the lowering of her eyes — but he chose to ignore them and continued on.

"There is always Bath. I would assume the crowds there are not so great as they are in London, and Mother has been forever begging father to take her there. I am certain she would enjoy taking you along. She does enjoy your company."

Bea ran a finger absent-mindedly along the chain that held a pendant Graeme knew contained a lock of her father's hair. Between that action and the way in which she had pulled the corner of her bottom lip between her teeth, he knew she was considering the possibility of going to Bath. However, as fascinating as that fact was, it did not help him discern her feelings about his brother. So, he circled around to Everett once again.

"Everett is planning one last go of the season before he takes up his position."

Bea nodded. "I know."

There was an interesting sadness to her tone.

"Unless, of course, he finds a lady before then. Perhaps Miss Love will be capable of finally snaring him."

There it was — a small, sad, fleeting frown. It was true. Beatrice Tierney was in love with his brother — the fortunate clod. Hailed as the more studious of the two Clayton brothers, what Everett possessed in the ability to apply himself to his studies and excel, he lacked in his capacity to see the subtly obvious before him. However, Graeme would contemplate how his brother could have missed recognizing Bea's preference for him later. Right now, he needed to make Bea smile.

"Many have tried to bring him up to scratch, you know, but none have succeeded. He is a handsome devil — much like his older brother."

Bea chuckled. "He is, at least, humbler than his brother," she chided.

"So, you do not deny that the Clayton brothers are handsome?" Graeme teased.

Bea rolled her eyes. "I am not blind," she said with a light swat to Graeme's arm.

"Neither am I," Graeme retorted.

Bea's brows furrowed in confusion.

"I am not speaking of being blind to my own comeliness." He smiled at her. "For I assure you that I know precisely how fetching I look." He winked and then chuckled as she once again rolled her eyes. It was always a joy to provoke her just enough to elicit a small response such as he had just received.

"I see many things clearly. For instance, I can see that Miss Love and Miss Grace are attractive and well-skilled in all the arts required to capture a husband." He shrugged. "There are many such ladies in London, who, if they wish for a desired outcome, will do their best to achieve it no matter the ploys and scheming necessary."

He nodded in response to her wide-eyed questioning look. "A fellow has to tread carefully. However, that is not all I see clearly."

"It is not?"

"No, it is not." He crossed his arms and leaned against the trunk of the tree, his shoulder resting lightly against hers, and his arm wishing to wrap around her and pull her close to his side as he had done when she was just a girl. However, she was no longer a mere child, and he was not her brother, so unless he wished to get scolded and have her dash away, neither of which would assist his cause, he refrained.

"I also see the way you look at my brother, and frankly, he is a fool to ignore you. I would not ignore a lady of beauty and good character such as yourself if she was to look at me so longingly." He pressed his lips together to keep from chuckling at the quick breath she drew. He had shocked her just as he had planned.

"I do no such thing," Bea refuted weakly.

"Lying does not become you, my beautiful Bea."

"Do not call me that. I am not beautiful."

He peeked over at her. Her cheeks were aflame as he knew they would be.

"My dear, if there is one thing I know, it is beautiful women, and you are definitely beautiful – beguiling, even, when you blush so prettily." He reached out a hand and grabbed her arm to prevent her from jumping to her feet and running away. Bea did not like compliments of her person or actions. She preferred to fade into the background — to act without recognition or praise, qualities that would serve a parson's wife well, but also qualities that made it easy for a numbskull, soon-to-be parson, like his brother to overlook her.

"Now," he said, holding her arm firmly as she tried to pull it out of his grasp, "as I have said, I am of the belief that my brother is an idiot and Miss Love is a grasping...," he cleared his throat, "something that is not appropriate for a lady's ears."

Bea's eyes grew wide, and her head tilted as she looked out toward where Felicity was talking in a very animated fashion to her sister while clinging to Everett's arm.

"I saw both her and her sister in London," Graeme whispered near Bea's ear.

"Then, why did you ask me if they were both out?" She gasped as his lips brushed her cheek when she turned her head.

He smirked and shrugged. "I am a cad and wished to hear your opinion of them."

"Which I did not give," she pulled on her arm again, finally freeing it from his hold.

"Oh, but you did," he replied. "Your tone and the shortness of your replies told me all I need to know. You are not pleased with them — or more precisely, you are not pleased with Miss Love since she is the one who has enchanted my brother."

"I have never enjoyed my cousins," Bea refuted. "We have little in common. They like fashion and soirees while I prefer books and domestic pursuits. However, you have never been home when they visited before so you would not know how very unalike we are."

He chuckled. "Deny it if you must, but you are jealous." He climbed to his feet and extended a hand to her.

Bea looked at his hand warily.

"Come. You cannot sit here the full day. Mother will wish to know you took some exercise. She worries about you."

Bea's brow furrowed as she studied his face. "You will not say shocking things, and your lips will not touch me?"

A hint of mischief touched his smile. "You know I am constitutionally incapable of not saying something shocking at some point, but I shall refrain from touching any part of you other than your fingers with my lips."

Bea sighed and shook her head, but a touch of amusement curled her lips into a small smile as she placed her hand in his and allowed him to help her to her feet.

"Good heavens," he muttered as he pulled her upright, "if my brother does not marry you, I might. When you smile like that, it is difficult not to wish to break my promise to confine my lips to just your fingers."

He winked as her mouth dropped open. "As I said, I am constitutionally incapable of not being shocking." He tucked her hand into the crook of his arm.

He was teasing her, of course — at least, partially. She was both beautiful and beguiling, but if she were not so obviously lovesick for his brother and if she were not Bea, his friend and the closest thing he had to a sister; he would be hard-pressed not to consider her as the next Lady Clayton.

Chapter 2

Laughter and whispers wafted on the breeze that blew through the open garden doors at the far righthand side of the blue drawing room at Stratsbury Park later that day. Grace and Felicity were gathered with Everett and Graeme near the piano at the opposite end of the room.

Beatrice began, once again, to read the page of the book which lay open before her. How many times has she tried to read this same page while sitting in the garden? She should likely turn back a few pages and begin reading there, for though the words from the pages had passed through her mind, not one of them had made an impression.

If only Felicity were not such a flirt, and if only Everett had ever seen Bea as more than his friend's little sister, then, maybe, this day would not be the drudgery it was turning out to be. Maybe then, she would be able to read without distraction. It was not as if she was only capable of reading in a silent room. She was proficient at reading in the sitting room at Heathcote while her brother and mother had a discussion. However, the idea that Everett was so taken with her cousin had rendered her powerless against distraction or worse, victim to it.

"You are a fair sight to see," Max Tierney said as he plopped down next to her and flicked her book. "I am surprised you have not finished this yet. I half expected you to be ready to peruse the library for another to replace it before we leave today, but you have more than half of this book left to read."

Bea smiled at her brother. He was not a great reader. He preferred being out of doors and being busy to sitting and reading. However, he was the dearest and best brother for whom a lady could wish, and he found her love of reading to be something about which to be proud. She had heard stories from her mother and Lady Clayton about how challenging it was for some book-loving ladies to find husbands. Apparently, whether it was true or not, according to Lady Clayton and her mother, social convention promoted ladies who preferred more sociable pursuits. Thankfully, Max was not one of those sorts of gentlemen, and there was hope that whomever her sister-in-law ended up being, she would be a lady with more than feathers for brains.

"I promise I shall not disappoint you," she replied. "I have completed my book of poetry and would like to replace it, and Sir Herbert has already promised me that I can borrow another from his library. Will you help me choose a new book?" She knew his answer before he said it. The library at Stratsbury Park was not so dear to him as it was to her.

Max shook his head and laughed. "Not likely. My knowledge of poetry is limited."

Of course, he would assist her if she truly needed him to, but she knew that he knew she did not require help finding something to read. The most help she might require would be reaching a shelf.

He stretched out his arms, resting them on the back of the sofa with one wrapped around her shoulders. "I know a few poets and poems, but not a vast array. You would do better to ask Everett or even Graeme. They would know more."

Even in his refusal he was offering his help. She

could not fault him for his care of her at present. "Then, if I require assistance, my dear brother, I will ask one of them and not you."

"I will be eternally grateful."

She laughed softly as Max squeezed her shoulder. "Did you enjoy your walk?" she asked.

Everett and Max, accompanied by Felicity and Grace, had left the garden at one point, and had meandered down some path in the wilderness. Graeme had suggested that he and she follow, but Bea, who, due to the lingering effects of a childhood fever, tired more easily than most ladies, had thought it best to return to the house since there was a full afternoon of entertainment and dinner yet to come.

Graeme had not been disappointed and readily acquiesced, admitting that he preferred not to hear the babblings of flighty females in his own garden. Apparently, listening to such ladies in London was acceptable if one was at a ball or some other function. However, in the privacy of one's own estate, such activities should be avoided as much as was possible. Yet, despite his objections to such things, he would have suffered them for her sake. For all his taunting and teasing, he was very caring. She was blessed to have been left in the care of such good men by her father. Of course, neither Graeme nor Max had been men when her father had died.

"I wish you had joined us." Max rubbed her shoulder as he often did when he wished to soothe her. Apparently, he knew that she was not pleased to have been left behind.

"You did not seem inconvenienced by my absence. In fact, you did not even bother to ask me to join you." She pursed her lips, and her brows furrowed. Max was one of the few people to whom she ever spoke so freely. "I am surprised you even remembered I was here."

Max tugged her closer and kissed her head. "Oh, come, now, Bea. You were pleased to sit and read. Do not tell me you would rather have listened to our cousins regale you with stories of their adventures in town."

She shrugged. It was not the fact that she had been left to return to the house that bothered her, as that was her preference. It was the feeling of being utterly forgotten – that is, she had felt forgotten by everyone but Graeme.

"Still struggling with that passage, I see." The very gentleman about whom she had been thinking perched himself on the arm of the sofa. He nudged her leg with his. "Slide over so I can sit properly before Mother lectures."

Bea peered up at him. Graeme was another person to whom she felt comfortable being less than accommodating and often spoke as freely with him as she did with her brother. "There is room beside Max."

"I do not wish to sit next to Max and have his arm draped around me. Slide over." He batted his lashes. "Please." He chuckled when she made a small, exasperated sound.

Oh! He was trying. Why he found it so enjoyable to provoke her beyond the bounds of propriety at times was beyond her. It was nearly, but not quite so, exasperating as her delight in his taunting. However, she knew that he was the sort of gentleman who was playful with his friends, and she liked being counted as his friend. It was likely that in which her delight was founded.

"Very well." She nudged Max, who moved over, pulling her with him as Graeme slid down the curved arm and into the corner of the sofa.

"She needs a new book of poetry," Max said, leaning around Bea to talk to Graeme. "I have told her to see you or Everett if she needs help choosing one."

Graeme once again snatched Bea's book from her. "She has not even finished this one. Why ever would she need another?"

"My book, if you would," Bea said, holding out her hand. "And that is a novel, not poetry."

Graeme smiled and with a small shake of his head, tucked the book between his leg and the arm of the sofa. "Reading is for when you are alone." He tilted his head and looked at her with a teasing glint in his eye. "Unless, of course, you would like me to read to you."

"Are you courting my sister?" Max asked with a laugh.

Between his kissing her cheek earlier – which Max did not and would not ever know about – and Graeme's offer to read to her now, the question seemed a good one, except for one particularly important thing. This was Graeme. Graeme was nearly a brother to her. A handsome, completely-not-related-to her brother. She studied his profile. It was not all sharp edges, but it was not soft curves either. There was a definite manliness to it that she was certain helped him charm ladies in town. The

way he often refused to be clean shaven, preferring to have a bit of a shadow of a beard was quite
becoming. Perhaps, she decided on such an exam-
ination, *dear friend* would be a better classification
for Graeme than nearly a brother was. After all,
a lady could find a brother handsome. However,
finding him somewhat desirable was wrong, and
Bea could not deny that she was comfortable
admitting that Graeme Clayton was desirable.

"Gentlemen can read to ladies without courting
them," Graeme retorted. "Have you never read to
your sister?"

"I prefer to read to myself," Bea replied before
her brother could.

Max read to both her and their mother at times,
just as her father had done. It was a lovely tradition,
but when she wished to thoroughly enjoy a book
by rereading and pausing to ponder things, such as
now, she would rather do the reading herself.

"If you would kindly return my book, Mr. Clayton."

Graeme ignored her request, for, as it turned
out, he had come with one of his own.

"Miss Grace has proposed playing whist. They
will need a fourth to complete their set."

"I thought they were going to play the piano," Bea said in some confusion. Was that not why Felicity was sorting through music and batting her lashes at Everett? Her cousins certainly did flit easily from one thing to another!

"No, there shall be singing and playing after dinner. They are only selecting their pieces now," Graeme explained. "So, do you wish to be their fourth? I said I would ask."

"They would far rather have Max," Bea assured him.

"No, I asked Everett which Tierney he would like me to ask to join them, and he specifically asked me to inquire of you, not Max."

"Oh," was the only reply Bea gave for a moment. The idea that Everett should request her was rather pleasant even though she knew it was her ability to pay attention to the game better than her brother did which recommended her. No matter the reason, he had preferred her, and she would be happy with that. It was a step in the right direction after all. "I suppose I could endure one round."

"I thought you might," Graeme whispered with a wink.

She shook her head and pleaded with her eyes

that he would not say anything more. It was bad enough that he had managed to extract a confession about her admiration of Everett from her earlier. She did not need her brother knowing that secret, too.

"Please, allow me to escort you to your table, my lady," Graeme said as he stood and extended his hand with a flourish.

Relief washed over her. He would keep her secret. She should have known he would. He had always been trustworthy. Some lady, someday, was going to be truly fortunate to have him for her husband. Of course, that day was likely a long way off, for Graeme was, by his own admission, in no hurry to leave being a bachelor behind.

Chapter 3

"Miss Abernathy's playing was such a delight," Grace placed her card on the table.

For the pitiful little attention that the young woman was paying to her cards, she was playing as if she knew what she was doing. Surprisingly.

"But then the harp is so beautiful when played well," she continued as play passed to the next player. "Do you not think so, Beatrice?"

"I imagine it is. However, I have not had the pleasure of hearing a harp. Sadly, there are none of my acquaintances who play it."

How did she keep the tone of her voice sounding as if she were genuinely interested in what Miss Grace had to say?

Grace clucked her tongue. "Such a pity," she murmured.

According to Graeme, the pity was the way Miss

Grace could talk about any subject for an extraordinarily long period of time. Miss Love had only to mention a topic and her sister was sure to have some story about it. For the most part, it seemed that Miss Grace was simply a chatterbox until she ended the discourse with a question about it to direct to either Everett or Bea.

"Perhaps," Bea agreed. "But then, I guess I will only ever be able to say how great a pity it is once I have heard a harp played as skillfully as you have described it."

Ah! There was his clever and not-altogether-pleased Bea. Graeme glanced around the group. No one, except perhaps for Max, appeared to know that Bea was being anything more than utterly kind. Not that Bea was being unkind, per se. It was just that her frustration with her cousins was beginning to fray her equanimity.

"And what about you, Mr. Everett Clayton, what do you think of the harp?" Grace asked.

And just like that, the attention shifted back to his brother.

Everett studied his cards, clearly oblivious to the ploys going on beside and across from him by the sisters Love. "I have always found the song of a harp to be a most ethereal one." He lay his selection and took the trick. "That is six for Miss Love and me," he said with a smile for Felicity, who sat opposite him. "Four more and we win."

"We are a very winning pair, are we not?" Felicity dipped her head and smiled as she asked it.

"Indeed, we are," Everett replied, his smile growing slightly.

Oblivious to the ploys did not mean he was unaffected by them. The blundering sap.

"I have not had this much success at whist since the last time that your cousin and I played our brothers at Christmas. Do you remember that?" Everett turned to his right and directed the question to Bea.

"I do. We were delightfully successful, much to our brothers' disappointment."

Bea's sweet smile and happy expression were lost on Graeme's unobservant brother because he had turned his eyes back to his cards after a quick return of Bea's smile. It was unlike him to be so inattentive. Graeme had seen many a lovesick swain become so in the presence of the lady whom they favoured, but he had honestly never expected it from his normally stalwart, rule-abiding brother.

"I think Bea and I could take the lot of you," Graeme grumbled. He was sitting just behind Bea and to her left, between her and his brother, and he was not at all pleased with the progression of the game at present. And it had nothing to do with who was winning or losing.

Bea was supposed to have partnered with Everett. That was the plan. However, before Graeme could convince Bea to take a spot at the table, Miss Love had weaseled her way into being Everett's partner. And for the entirety of the game thus far, the comments had been about this gown or that carriage, as well as several soirees that were absolutely *the thing!* She had directed the conversation to nothing that was of interest to either he or Bea, and from the look on Max's face, he was equally as disinterested in the Miss Loves' social calendar. It was enough to make Graeme's head spin and his blood simmer since it appeared that each story was specifically designed to show Bea at a disadvantage.

"Oh, then we shall deal you in at the next hand. I am certain my sister would not mind surrendering her seat to you for one round, would you dear?"

Felicity turned to her sister with what Graeme classified as the most patronizing of smiles.

Grace blinked and looked first at Graeme and then her sister. There was definitely more innocence to Miss Grace than there was to her sister, for Graeme, who had made it a bit of a sport for himself to observe chits in the ballroom for their small unspoken conversations, did not miss the slight tip of Felicity's head toward Bea and her pleading eyes that flicked in Everett's direction.

Apparently, though Grace had yet to discern it, Felicity found Bea to be something of a threat. This was good, Graeme supposed. It likely meant his brother had spoken about Bea and had not forgotten her completely when faced with the fawning and flirtatious Felicity.

"Most happily," Grace replied with a smile that was given a moment too late to be genuine.

"Very good then," Graeme said, settling back and crossing his arms, "pay attention to what is being played, and do not leave me in a place where it will be impossible to make ten before my brother does." Graeme ignored the scowl Everett gave him, as well as the flustered gasping noise Grace made.

"Mr. Clayton does not like to lose," Bea said.

She was trying to cover his rudeness. She was a peacemaker at heart. Ruffled feathers were things she could not abide without some attempt to smooth them.

"He is rather intense when he plays," Bea continued. "It was not at all a pleasant evening when Mr. Everett Clayton and I beat Mr. Clayton and my brother."

"I should say it was not," muttered Max, who was sitting diagonally across the table from Graeme and between the two Miss Loves. "Graeme can be rather blustery when he is in a foul mood."

"And are you as blustery as he?" Grace lay a hand on Max's sleeve.

"Mind your cards," Graeme growled.

"None is so blustery as Mr. Clayton," Bea answered, turning to give Graeme a small teasing smile that caused him to catch his breath and swallow instead of retorting.

Good heavens, his brother was a fool!

"I, on the other hand, do not care if we win or lose," Bea continued, "as either way my book shall be returned when our game has concluded." She pressed her lovely lips together. Likely to keep from looking even the smallest bit triumphant about reclaiming her beloved book.

Graeme raised his left brow. "She jests. Bea enjoys winning just as much as I do. It is just that she is incapable of being anything less than gracious."

Idiot! he shouted in his mind while glaring at his brother. He doubted Miss Love contained two ounces of the good-natured temperament Bea possessed.

"You speak of my cousin very familiarly." Felicity gave Graeme a look that questioned his true relationship with Bea – or perhaps she was just hoping to push Bea in his direction and away from Everett.

Whatever her purpose in questioning his use of Bea's name was, it was not going to sway him from his goal. He would be dead and in his grave before he let a chit like Miss Felicity Love outwit him.

"My brother likes to flout social conventions when he can," Everett replied, once again laying his card, and taking the trick.

"I see no need for such formality with good friends of long-standing." Graeme stretched out his legs and purposefully bumped his brother – the idiot's – leg with his foot. "How old were you when you arrived at Heathcote, Bea?"

"Can you not figure that out yourself?" Max asked with a chuckle. "I would think you could since you know how old you were then, how old you are now, and how old my sister is. It is not a complicated calculation."

Graeme shrugged. "I prefer to allow Bea to save me the bother of such things." And he wished to give Bea an opportunity to speak about something of substance while highlighting the previous claim she held on both his and his brother's attentions and affections. It was likely that Everett would miss the point of the lesson since he was once again smiling at Felicity, but perhaps that lady would feel a small jab of something. Graeme did not care what the discomfort was named so long as Miss Love felt it. She had given enough of her own pokes and taunts over the course of the game.

"I was nine, Max was fifteen, as was your brother — no, that is not correct. Mr. Everett Clayton had just turned sixteen, and you were..."

Bea's lips curled into a small smile, and she tapped her lip with a finger as if she actually had to strain to remember his age.

The bumbling blockhead! Graeme's foot bumped his brother's once again as Graeme uncrossed and re-crossed his ankles. If Everett would pause for even one moment and take his eyes off his cards or Miss Love and looked — really looked — at Bea and the way her lips pursed into a perfectly kissable pucker before she decided she had calculated Graeme's age appropriately, there would be no way Everett could continue entertaining Miss Love when such a beguiling creature as Bea sat beside him.

"I believe, Mr. Clayton was an extremely ancient seventeen, were you not? Your birthday is in May, and we had arrived in March, just at the end."

"There is no fault with your memory," Graeme replied. "But do mind your cards."

"She only had to take her mind off them because you could not subtract ten from nineteen," protested Max, who was once again laughing at Graeme, not that it bothered Graeme in the least. He preferred not to be taken too seriously. Serious times would be his eventually, but they were not his lot just yet.

"It is not that I could not do the calculation. It is

that I did not wish to do it," Graeme replied. "The other one," he whispered to Bea.

"Are you cheating?" Everett asked.

"I am merely attempting to assure myself of a better position from which to beat you."

Everett turned toward his brother, who was still leaning over Bea's shoulder, whispering in her ear. His brow furrowed as he took in the way the two were cozily positioned.

"Yes," he said slowly as if distracted, "but are you cheating?"

Graeme smiled at his brother's expression. It was good to see him finally taking notice of Bea, even if it was only because Graeme was nearly cheek to cheek with her.

"Mr. Clayton –"

"Graeme," Graeme hissed in Bea's ear.

"Mr. Clayton," she said firmly, "does not cheat. Cheating is for a much weaker sort of man, is it not, Mr. Clayton?"

Graeme nearly forgot himself and gave her cheek a brushing kiss when she turned her head, but he caught himself in time not to embarrass her. He could have withstood the teasing he would have received, but he would never do anything to harm Bea.

"Indeed, it is. I do not play games of shifting and shadows." At least not often. He straightened and smiled at Miss Love. That lady seemed the continually shadowy sort.

He had heard her name bandied around his club as coquettish and a likely candidate to be lead astray in some dark corner. In his opinion, she was not the sort of lady after whom a soon-to-be-parson should be chasing. No, Everett would do better with a lady of Bea's quality. He should probably take his brother aside and inform him of the things he knew about the lovely Miss Love, and perhaps he would — after their guests left. For now, he would continue as he was, attempting, with little success, to get his brother to notice Bea while enjoying spending so much time at her side.

Chapter 4

Bea sighed as she watched a drop of rain trail down the windowpane. Usually, she did not mind rainy days, for after her work was done, she would sneak up to the old schoolroom where she could paint, read, or simply sit at the window and watch the world get washed clean of the past and made ready for the new growth that would follow the rain. However, today, she would be expected to help entertain her cousins, and both Grace and Felicity had already grumbled several times about not being able to go on the picnic that had been planned.

The sky was growing darker, and the light for working on her stitching was fleeting, so Beatrice tucked the sash she wished to add to her yellow dress back into her workbasket. Michaelmas and its assembly were yet six weeks away. There was no need to strain her eyes to adorn her dress when there would be an ample amount of sunny days between now and then to complete the pattern she had begun.

"Oh, la," Grace said dolefully.

Bea closed her eyes and drew a calming breath in preparation for whatever complaint she was about to hear. Then, she fixed a smile on her face as she lifted her eyes from her workbasket to her cousin.

"I had such hopes of visiting the meadow," Grace rose and walked to the window where Bea sat. "Mr. Everett Clayton described it so well that I am certain I have never seen anything so lovely in all my life."

"We picnicked there the last time you were here." Bea kept her voice soft in an attempt to mollify some of Grace's disappointment and hopefully, prevent another declaration about how hideous it was that it was raining on a day when the delight of a picnic was anticipated.

"Oh, but I am certain it has changed so much in two years that I shall not recognize it. Things are that way, you know," Grace pulled her eyes away from the greyness of the day and turned them toward her cousin. "When you see them all the time, you forget how much they have changed and how delightful they can be." She sighed and sat down next to Bea. "I am certain I shall find it much altered."

Bea could not help smiling at the forlorn look on Grace's face and the wistful tone of her voice. She sounded very much like a young girl, and Bea found she could not fault Grace for being unable to contain her disappointment as she should. Grace was, after all, merely seventeen, and not all ladies matured so quickly as Bea had, especially not ladies who still had both their mother and their father to dote on them.

"Beatrice likes to paint on rainy days," Mrs. Tierney offered.

Bea could tell by the tightness of her mother's expression that having young ladies around who were not averse to grumbling and complaining was beginning to wear on her. Neither Bea nor Max had ever been the sort of children to carry on about a disappointment for long.

"There are supplies in the schoolroom." Mrs. Tierney suggested, her smile softening as she looked at her daughter. "Although Beatrice has not had a lesson in almost two years, I cannot bring myself to redo the room just yet, and so it remains, waiting to be used on days like today."

Bea caught her frown before her mother could see it. Her father had insisted that the schoolroom be made up specifically for Bea, and she was loath to share it. It was her room, her bastion of solitude. However, she knew sharing her personal refuge would benefit not only her cousins but also her mother, and bringing pleasure to her mother was not something Bea would refuse to do. Therefore, with more excitement than she felt at the prospect, she agreed with her mother and insisted that her cousins join her in painting.

"Max will return soon," Mrs. Tierney added encouragingly. "I am certain he would be willing to sit for a silhouette or a portrait."

This brought a delighted squeal from Grace. "Felicity is the very best at taking likenesses. Mr. Bailey complimented her on her work all the time when she was at school and even used one of her pieces to demonstrate how a likeness should be done."

To Bea, it appeared that, according to Grace, Felicity was always the best at one thing or another. Felicity's samplers were the best and most elaborate. Felicity knew just the right ribbon to add to a hat to make it the envy of her friends. Felicity had the best taste in gowns and music. It was most frustrating! Bea sighed softly and directed her frustration to carefully organizing her work basket before tucking it away and leading her cousins to the schoolroom and seeing that they had everything they needed to be entertained.

Then, as Felicity and Grace chattered about some roses that were prized for their colour, Bea got out her landscape and set out her own painting supplies.

"Oh, those are lovely," Grace said, coming to look inside the wooden box of brushes that had been a gift from Lady Clayton to Bea on her last birthday. "These are nearly as nice as the ones Miss Abernathy has, Felicity." Grace turned to her sister. "Come, take a look. You will like them."

Felicity's left brow rose, and her lips pursed in an expression that declared she certainly could not be bothered to cross the room to look at a set of anything.

"A brush is a brush. It is not the tools that make the artist great but the technique the artist uses and the talent she possesses. I tell that to Amelia —

Miss Abernathy —" she explained to Bea, "all the time. And truly, Grace, it is not as if Amelia can paint better because of her brushes. She possesses no talent. Her work is still dreadful. It is fortunate she is so skilled at playing the harp and dancing, or she would be in a sorry state. What man would wish to marry a lady with no accomplishments whatsoever?"

"One who wishes for her thirty thousand, I suppose," replied Grace, causing both herself and her sister to titter.

"Is Miss Abernathy someone from your school?" Bea asked in an attempt to participate in her cousins' conversation.

"Oh, she is my dearest friend," Felicity said. "We were in school together, and now we attend all the soirees together. We are nearly inseparable. In fact, I have missed her dreadfully these past weeks."

Bea tipped her head and studied her painting, deciding both where to put some flowers and how her cousin could speak as she was about Miss Amelia Abernathy and yet claim to be her particular friend. This was why it was challenging to participate in discussions with her cousins. Their ways were so foreign to her. "When will you see her again?"

"Oh, in a fortnight. When we leave here, we are to travel to her father's home in Kent for a house party. It will be very exciting. We might even both find a husband while we are there," Felicity replied.

"If we both still require one," Grace whispered with a knowing smile.

Felicity's cheeks coloured as she glanced at Bea and then gave her sister a sharp look.

Bea picked up her brush and attempted to ignore the implication of Grace's words. Everett had been most attentive to Felicity for the past five days since their first introduction. He had walked with her, played cards with her, sang while she played the piano, and even taken Bea's book of verses to read to Felicity.

Bea made a show of concentrating on the flowers she was planting in the garden on her canvas, and said, "A house party will be exciting, I am sure."

"Oh, indeed!" Grace exclaimed before beginning a litany of things that she just knew would happen at this party. This, in turn, led into another recital of many of the interesting bits of gossip from the season. This meandering stream of stories, which were of great interest to the Misses Loves and of little interest to Beatrice, continued until there was a soft tapping at the door and in walked Max, followed closely by Everett and Graeme.

A story about an unfortunate gentleman who had been rejected twice by the same lady ended abruptly and was replaced with excited exclamations of greeting and cries of how dreadfully dull the day had been without the gentleman for company.

"Did you miss me?" Graeme asked Bea. He had wandered away from the shrill voices of the Misses Loves and had found his way to the corner where Bea was working.

"It is a fine representation," he said as he studied her painting. "You are becoming quite proficient in landscapes, which means you will soon have to move on to other things such as handsome neighbours whom you missed."

He had missed her. As he settled himself against the wall just behind her and to her left, he had to admit how pleasant it was to be greeted by her smile. He had been restless all day, but here, he finally felt at ease.

Bea chuckled. "Did I miss you?"

"Oh, you did," Graeme replied with a smile. "I hear it was quite dull around here without me."

Beautiful blue eyes filled with amusement met his.

"Most dreadfully, but if you do not believe me, you may ask Grace."

How his brother could prefer anyone to Bea was baffling.

"There is no need for her to repeat it. I heard her quite well when we arrived," he replied with a laugh.

"Bea," Max kissed his sister on the cheek in greeting. "I have put the thread you wanted into your workbasket, and this is the book you wished to borrow." He placed it on the table next to her. "Everett apologized for not returning it when he was finished reading it yesterday."

"I did not realize he needed to apologize to you," Bea said with a raised brow.

So, his brother's actions were beginning to vex the ever-patient Bea? Graeme turned his eyes toward his brother to watch him as he was still being regaled by the Miss Loves about something.

"He was not apologizing to me, ninny," Max said. "He was sending his apologies to you."

"He could not walk across the room and make them himself?" Graeme's voice was thick with contempt. "I shall speak to him," he promised. His brother had been raised with better manners than he was currently demonstrating and the fact that it was Bea whom he was treating so poorly made it a far greater offense in Graeme's mind. Bea was not just some lady. Her care had been entrusted to their father.

"There is no need," Bea assured him. "I am certain Everett will remember to speak to me at some point."

Graeme nodded toward his brother, who was still engrossed in whatever it was that Felicity was showing him. Their heads were bent together over something. "Has he been like this the whole time I was gone?" Graeme had left two days ago to visit a good friend and help him with the purchase a horse and had only returned that morning.

"Like what?" Max asked. "Swooning at my cousin's feet?"

"Yes, that," Graeme replied, "and doing it to the exclusion of all else."

Max shrugged.

"Yes." Bea's answer was soft and worryingly resigned.

"We expect a happy announcement any day now," Max said with a laugh.

Graeme glanced at Bea, who was applying herself to her work with fierce determination. It was a sign that she was not at all happy. He had worried that leaving Stratsbury was a bad idea, but he had promised Shelton that he would accompany him to get that horse. Now, Graeme knew that he had been correct, and the person he had hoped to help see happy was far from it.

"It has not progressed to that in so short a time, has it?" he asked.

Bea lifted one shoulder and let it fall.

"Are you well, Bea?" Max asked, finally noticing his sister's distraught look.

Bea's smiled as brightly as she could at him. "I am well. Rainy days tend to make me quiet. You know this, and you must also remember that I have been listening to our cousins all day. My ears are weary."

It was more than weary ears. It appeared his dear

friend had a weary heart as well. Had she truly given up all hope where Everett was concerned?

"Do you need a rest?" Max pressed. "Graeme, Everett, and I can entertain Felicity and Grace while you go lie down."

"I am well," Bea insisted. "Mama will call for tea now that you are home, and I shall stay behind to work up here. A few moments of silence and my spirits shall be restored."

Graeme doubted that last bit, and from the look on Max's face, her brother was not convinced either.

"If you are certain," Max agreed uneasily.

"I am."

"Very well. Then, I shall see if tea is being made ready and return. Shall I fetch you a cup?"

"That will not be necessary," said Graeme. "I will bring her one when I get mine." He tipped his head and raised a shoulder in a half-shrug in answer to Max's startled look. "I, too, find your cousins grating, and I might not be able to refrain from speaking harshly to my halfwit brother. Therefore, it might be best if I invade Bea's solitude."

While it was true that he had no desire to listen to the Miss Loves, he also did not wish to leave

Bea. He needed to see her smile. He turned toward her and placed a hand on his heart. "I promise to invade your solitude quietly."

An actual smile, not a forced one, curled Bea's lips while delight shone in her eyes, and Graeme knew in that instant he would promise just about anything to see that expression always on her face. She was a dear friend, after all, and he always wished to see his friends happy. Therefore, it was only natural that he should feel so about Bea, or so he told himself in an attempt to reason away the startling thought.

"Are you certain you are not courting my sister?" Max asked with a grin. "I would not mind, you know."

Bea rolled her eyes and shook her head.

"I do not think she would have me," Graeme said with a smile on his lips and an odd ache in his chest.

"Well," Max said as he turned to leave, "if she ever changes her mind, you have my permission to court her, and I am confident I could persuade Mother that you are not a complete reprobate."

"Lying is not becoming," Graeme said to Max's back.

"You are not a reprobate," Bea said.

"I am not?" Graeme pulled a chair over near her and sat down. "It is very disappointing to hear I have not succeeded since I have tried so hard to be one."

"No gentleman with a heart so good and kind as yours could ever be termed a reprobate." Bea looked over at him and seeing him sitting in a chair that was designed for someone much younger and shorter than he, giggled. He could not blame her. He was certain he did look ridiculous since his knees were nearly as high as his chest.

"There are other chairs," she suggested.

"Not over here," he answered. He was not leaving her side until he was required to gather their tea. "You think I am kind?"

"I do."

"I shall have to work on that," he muttered in a lighthearted tone.

"Please do not." Bea turned towards him for a moment. "I like that you are kind — and honest and occasionally polite." Mischief twinkled in her eyes.

He shrugged. "I will allow it to be so, but only

TOUCHES OF AUSTEN, BOOKS 1-3

if you promise not to tell anyone else. We rogues have an image to maintain."

"I promise to not say a word," Bea agreed with a laugh.

"Everett," Graeme called, "you should come see Bea's picture. It is nearly complete, and I think she has captured the meadow nearly to perfection."

He heard Bea's small, displeased gasp. She would likely be rather put out with him for drawing attention to her work and complimenting it. But her painting was good, and his brother had yet to even extend a polite greeting to her. And that last fact was one Graeme wished to see corrected immediately. He was not unaware of the hurt such neglect had caused Bea.

"You are painting the meadow?" Grace asked.

"I am."

"Has she truly captured it?" Grace turned to Everett.

"I said she did," Graeme muttered.

"A few more flowers, and it will be very like how I remember it," Everett said with a smile. "It is very good."

"Thank you," Bea murmured.

"She was also grateful to have her book

returned." Graeme tapped the book that lay on the table and glared at his brother.

"Was that your book that Mr. Everett Clayton was reading to us?" Felicity asked.

"It is not mine, but it is one I had borrowed and had not finished reading," Bea explained.

"I am sorry I forgot to return it," Everett said with a sheepish grin.

"I am happy you did not forget longer," Bea replied. "I am looking forward to finishing it."

An odd sense of pride swelled in Graeme's chest at her words, and he felt a desire to congratulate her for not just brushing the apology aside with an "It is of little significance." He knew from the way her cheeks flushed that replying as she had done was not easily accomplished.

"I thank you for being so understanding," Everett replied, shifting as if he were going to lean against the table and begin a conversation.

"Let me take your likeness," Felicity suggested, placing a hand on Everett's arm and drawing his attention away from Bea. "I am very good at it," she coaxed.

"Oh, she is," Grace assured and then, as they moved away, continued on with the same information she had shared with Mrs. Tierney about the instructor who used Felicity's work as an example to instruct others.

"He is an idiot," Graeme grumbled. "So easily led by a pair of fine eyes and ample —" Graeme coughed as he realized what he was going to say about Felicity's figure was perhaps not appropriate to be saying to Bea.

Bea smiled sadly. "I am beginning to agree."

It had indeed come to that. She was giving up on Everett.

"Ah, but they will be leaving in...what? Surely, it is soon."

As disappointed as he was with his brother, he could not help but push his frustration to the side and attempt to lift her spirits. He truly did not know what he saw in his brother. She deserved better. She deserved someone who would not ignore her or place her behind another.

"Ten days," Bea said with a sigh.

"And then, he will return to himself," Graeme said it hopefully, but he knew that ten days was a long period of time when desires were stirred, and hopes, such as Miss Love appeared to have for his brother, were ignited.

Bea nodded, though to Graeme it appeared she was only placating him to leave the subject of Everett behind, and continued mingling small white and yellow flowers with the blue ones that were already in the scene.

Chapter 5

For two days, the clouds prevailed in the sky, spitting out the occasional burst of rain — sometimes soft and gentle and other times as if someone in the heavens had kicked over a mop bucket. The greyness of the days and the dampness of the ground kept Bea and her cousins indoors.

For those same two days, Heathcote was blessed with the presence of the Clayton brothers. One came to sit for and fawn over Felicity, and the other, to watch and grumble.

So it was on the day when the skies finally cleared, the cloudless sky was greeted by Beatrice with some relief, for now, they could take their drawing and painting into the sunshine where Grace's exclamations of delight over the drawing her sister was doing could reverberate off of the trees and flowers rather than the walls of the schoolroom, which had become to Bea a very con-straining room with so many people of a talkative variety to fill it.

Then came the joyful day two days later when the ground was declared to have sufficiently dried out, and it was decided they would pack up their art supplies, along with a picnic lunch, and finally seek out the meadow Grace so desired to see.

On this morning, as her cousins eagerly awaited the arrival of the Claytons, Bea handed her bag of drawing supplies to her brother, who stored them in the carriage next to the picnic basket.

"Are you not bringing your paints?" he asked.

Bea shook her head. "I prefer to draw when in the meadow and paint when in the house." She drew in a deep breath and released it with satisfac-tion. "It is a beautiful day, is it not?"

"I will not argue that," Max replied. "I am pleased to see you looking so happy. I dare say you were beginning to look a bit wane by last evening."

Bea wrapped her arm around his and walked with him back toward the house.

"Today, I shall be able to find a quiet spot," she said, laying her head against his shoulder for a moment.

She loved moments of solitude. They refreshed her as nothing else could. Usually, she would find a few moments each day to steal away to the schoolroom, her bedroom, or some corner in the garden, but since her cousins had arrived, finding both those moments and any place that was not invaded either by person or voice had been nearly impossible. There had been a few times of refreshment during their visits to Stratsbury when she was left to herself in the garden or in the library. However, they had not ventured from Heathcote in four days, and Bea's equanimity was wearing thin.

"Whatever the reason, I am glad to see your improvement. Perhaps we will be able to arrange the drives so that you can even enjoy a bit of quiet while travelling. You look tired."

Bea sighed. "I am. I must admit I have not slept well, but I suspect today will help with that as well."

Lying upon her bed at night had been the only place where she had been able to contemplate the events of the day, which was as necessary for Bea as eating or getting fresh air. However, her ruminations had not all been of the particularly pleasant sort. There was no denying in her mind that things were progressing between Felicity and Everett to a point from which there was no turning aside of affections. And so, she had begun to prepare herself for the inevitable disappointment.

She tugged gently on her brother's arm, causing him to stop. They were nearing the house, and she needed to speak to him where her cousins could not hear. Her heart seemed to leap into her throat, but there was something she needed to ask him — no matter how distressing his answer might be.

"I have listened to our cousins speak endlessly of their desires to marry." Her cheeks grew rosy. It felt wrong to be asking what she was, but, she reminded herself, it was only information for her own sake and not gossip that she sought.

Max tipped his head. His brow furrowed in question. "I do not plan to ask either of our cousins to marry me if that is what is worrying you. I know Grace has batted her lashes at me and all that, but I have not developed a fondness for her."

Bea smiled. She had been wondering about that, almost as much as she had been wondering about Everett's intentions. "They have spoken most frequently of Felicity's hopes." The fingers of her free hand ran back and forth along the seam of her gown nervously. "Does she hope in vain?"

Her brother's cheeks puffed out for a moment before he blew out a breath. "Everett has not mentioned his intentions, but he seems smitten."

She swallowed the disappointment that rose at such a statement. After all, she had known it was not just a trick of her mind making her see how enamoured Everett was with Felicity. "Do you expect him to offer for her?"

Max shrugged. "I am not certain, but I would not be surprised should it happen." His eyes narrowed as he studied her face. "You do not still like him, do you?"

Max had found Bea's diary about four years ago and had read her confessions of love for Everett Clayton.

Bea shrugged.

Max sighed and pulled her into his embrace. "Do you wish for me to speak to him?"

"No," Bea said with some force. "He must not know."

Max released her and, placing her hand in the crook of his arm again, began a short circuit of the drive rather than returning directly to the house. "I could –"

"No," Bea interrupted. "I only wished to know so I can prepare myself."

Max stopped and stood for a moment, silently shaking his head. "If I had known you still harboured feelings for him, I could have arranged things, made comments, promoted you." His eyes shimmered when he turned to her. "You know I would do anything to see you happy and protect you from harm."

She nodded. Her lip trembled at seeing such emotion on her brother's face. "It is why I could not tell you," she whispered. "I am not the sort of lady who schemes and steals her way into a gentleman's affections."

"Ah, Bea." He wrapped an arm around her shoulder, and they continued walking. "Perhaps he is merely infatuated and having a bit of a flirt. It is a rather pleasant thing to be the object of a lady's attention."

"Perhaps he is," Bea agreed. "But I fear that even if it is just a passing fancy for him, Felicity seems determined to ensnare him."

Her brother blew out a breath. "I shall warn him if I can."

"Thank you," Bea wrapped her arm around his middle and squeezed him tightly. "Even if he is never to love me, I would hate to see him taken in." She sighed. "However, there is the possibility that Felicity might actually love him in earnest. Perhaps you should not say anything."

"I will only plant a seed of caution. I shall not accuse our cousin of anything heinous."

Bea squeezed him again. She was fortunate to have such a brother to whom she could speak so openly and who cared so well for her. Not everyone was so blessed.

"Here comes Clayton now," said her brother, nodding toward the road.

"Two carriages?" Bea asked in surprise. "Could they have not ridden together? And when did they get a curricle?"

Max waved vigorously at the approaching vehicles. "That is Shelton's curricle."

"Who is Mr. Shelton?" Bea asked a bit breathlessly. It seemed Max had forgotten she was still holding his arm, for his strides had lengthened, and she had to scamper to keep up.

"A friend of Graeme's — the fellow he went to visit about a horse. You remember that, do you not?"

"Max, please. Could we please assume a more sedate pace?" She pulled on his arm.

"My apologies," he muttered as he slowed.

Thankfully, they reached the steps before either vehicle, and Bea was given a moment to bring her breathing back under control before having to make any greetings.

~*~*~

"She's quite the beauty, is she not?" Roger Shelton eased himself down next to Graeme, who was seated a short distance away from Bea.

Graeme had wanted to sit with Bea as she drew, but since that would likely mean Shelton would follow suit, he did not. He knew how Bea enjoyed drawing in quietness, and Shelton was not the quietest of gentlemen.

"Which one?" Graeme asked, sparing only a glance at his friend before returning his eyes to his book, which was propped in such a way that he could appear to be reading and yet steal glances at Bea.

She had looked well earlier, but yesterday, her

features had been drawn and tired, causing him to worry that she was becoming unwell. Bea would never admit such a thing until it was beyond what was acceptable and the apothecary would have to be called. As odd as it was to imagine, he wished she was the sort of lady who complained, but she was not.

"The one on your brother's arm."

"Ah, Miss Love. Did you not meet her in town at the Abernathy's soiree?"

Shelton snapped his fingers. "That's it! I have been attempting to place her all day. She is Amelia Abernathy's friend." He tipped his head. "I am surprised she did not latch on to you instead of your brother. I heard she was looking for money."

Graeme shrugged. "I heard the same, but I was not here when she arrived." He shifted and closed his book. "She had my brother well enchanted before I appeared. Not that I would have allowed her sort to cling to me anyway."

"Her sort?' Shelton asked with a laugh. "When did you become so discriminating in your tastes? There was a time when a pretty face and a pleasing figure was all that was needed to catch your interest."

"Not if they were the sort to cry compromise, which she is. Besides, I do not like her — not even well enough for a dalliance."

Shelton's brows rose. "Your brother seems to like her quite well."

"I also do not like that," Graeme replied firmly. "I have warned him, but you know Everett."

Shelton nodded. "He tends to think he is always right."

"Precisely so."

"Do you think he genuinely likes her?"

Graeme sighed. "Yes. I have considered the possibility." As much as he wished with all his heart that Everett was merely being duped, he could not deny that his brother seemed truly besotted and not just a complete fool. He stole a look at Bea. He had still not reasoned out how his brother could prefer Miss Love over Bea.

"She's a pretty thing as well," Shelton whispered as he indicated Bea with a nod of his head.

"Why are you whispering?" Graeme demanded as a quiver of irritation at the comment settled in his gut.

"I do not want her brother to hear me say such

a thing. He seemed rather protective of her when I was introduced."

Graeme chuckled. "Your reputation precedes you, my friend. Any brother with half an ounce of sense would be protective of a pretty sister around you. I swear you reek of charm and seduction."

Shelton shrugged. "I do, do I not? But then so do you — or at least you used to. However, there is something different about you today. You are shunning pretty girls and keeping watch over her." Again, he indicated Bea with a nod of his head. "Is she special?"

Graeme smiled and nodded. "She's Bea."

"I do not follow."

"Her father and mine were good friends since childhood, and to make a long and tediously boring tale short, ten years ago, when Bea was nine and Max was sixteen, their father, Captain Tierney, moved them to Heathcote. He left shortly after they were settled and never returned — killed by the Spanish or the French. It is hard to tell the nationality of a bullet. My father had promised to care for the captain's family if such a thing happened."

"So, she is like a sister?"

Graeme shook his head. "No, not a sister. A friend." A very dear friend, he added to himself. "She likes my brother," Graeme blurted. "She has for some time." He huffed. It was a sound of exasperation. "I have attempted to draw his attention away from Miss Love to Bea, but he is too besotted." He shook his head. "He is going to break Bea's heart, and I could throttle him for it."

Shelton's eyes were wide, and his eyebrows raised in surprise.

"Bea is quiet and all that is good. She is kind and helpful. She never wishes for praise but always wishes to please. She would make a perfect parson's wife, but my brother is too stupid to recognize her worth."

"Are you certain you do not think of her as a sister? For you speak like a brother or –" Shelton tilted his head and studied his friend. "You love her."

Graeme's brows furrowed, and he shook his head in disbelief. "Of course, I love her. She's Bea." He moved to rise, but Shelton's hand on his arm stopped him.

"No, not as a friend. She's the one you spoke about when you visited, is she not?"

Graeme blew out a breath and turned to face his friend. "Bea loves my brother, and I only wish to see her happy." No matter how the idea of his brother marrying Bea irritated him! She deserved better than a dolt who had to be convinced of her worth rather than recognizing it of his own volition.

Shelton nodded his head slowly as if he were considering what Graeme was saying, but Graeme knew better. Shelton was reasoning things out, piecing things together, and drawing conclusions. A gentleman did not survive as somewhat of a rake and be generally well-liked, as Shelton had, without a keen mind.

"She loves my brother," Graeme repeated.

It had been foolish of him to speak to Shelton about a lady whom he found enchanting but was unavailable. However, his tongue had been loosened by alcohol that night after they had ridden out to purchase Shelton's new hunter, and the things that Graeme had been pondering since the evening he had nearly kissed Bea during that blasted card game had come spilling out. He had been wise enough to leave out names, but still, he knew Shelton was no fool.

"Do you truly wish to see her happy?"

Graeme looked at Shelton warily. "Yes."

Shelton smiled. "Then, capture her heart before your brother can break it."

The hairs on the back of Graeme's neck bristled. The smile Shelton was wearing was calculating. He had seen it before — often right before some poor chap was about to be fleeced or lose his lady.

"I consider myself the charitable sort," Shelton continued, "and I am approaching that age where a wife will be expected. I could save her heart from harm."

Graeme's eyes narrowed. "You will stay away from her," he growled.

Shelton chuckled, clearly enjoying taunting his friend. "Will you call me out if I do not?"

Graeme folded his arms and smirked in return. Shelton knew that Graeme would never call anyone out because it was, for one thing, illegal, and for another, Graeme was not the best shot nor all that adept with a sword. So, to use a duel as a threat would be of no effect. However, there was a threat that Graeme knew would shake Shelton. "No, I will shoot your horse."

Shelton chuckled again. "Very well, I will not

risk my horse unless I see it is necessary to do so."
He rose. "However, I think I shall see what Miss
Tierney has been drawing — just in the way of
being friendly and all. Would you care to join me?"

"Did you say you were returning home tonight?"
Graeme asked hopefully as he scrambled to his
feet.

Shelton shook his head. "No, your mother said I
may stay the week. She is a dear, is she not?"

"I promise you I will shoot your horse," Graeme
grumbled as he followed Shelton over to where Bea
was sitting.

Chapter 6

"Have a go, Miss Tierney." Mr. Shelton held out his racket to Bea. "Miss Grace has already outdone me three times. I am quite fatigued." He smiled and wiggled the racket in invitation. "Your brother says you are quite good at this game."

"Go on, Bea," Max encouraged, as he dropped onto the bench next to his sister. "Neither Shelton nor I have been able to beat her. You are our only hope to dethrone Grace as queen of the shuttlecock."

"Can Grace and Felicity not play each other?" Bea asked. She had been riding earlier that day, and, with the weather being so warm, she was feeling the first pangs of a headache. A rest would likely drive those pains way while a vigorous game would not.

"Felicity will not play anyone who does not bear the last name Clayton," Mr. Shelton grumbled.

"No matter how loudly anyone bearing that name protests," Max added.

Bea had heard Graeme's grousing. "It does appear that Mr. Clayton is in a rather foul mood."

Max chuckled. "I am impressed that he has not yet stomped off in a huff."

Mr. Shelton eased down onto the bench beside Max. "He'll endure for as long as he feels there might be a hope of victory. Loss never sits well with him — a loss to a lady sits even less well."

Though Max had informed Bea about Mr. Shelton's reputation for charming ladies, he seemed to her to be a gentleman of worth for he had treated her very respectfully and he showed such fondness for his friend. Anyone who was a particular friend of Graeme's could not be a complete ne'er-do-well, for Graeme did not abide fools and charlatans.

Max took the racquet Shelton still held and passed it to Bea. "One game," he begged. "Losing to a female does not sit well with any gentleman, and begging his sister to take up his defense is not easily done. Please, take pity on us and defend our honour." He clasped his hands in front of him and turned doleful eyes to her.

"You are pitiful." Bea laughed as she rose. "I shall do my best to restore your honour." She curtseyed deeply to the gentlemen on the bench. "I do hope there is a reward for such valiant behaviour."

~*~*~

The shuttlecock bounced off the lawn. Everett had missed hitting it, and once again, Felicity had won a point.

Since the method of play, as set forth by the Miss Loves, required whoever had dropped the shuttlecock to bow out of the game and be replaced by the third person standing at the side, Graeme took the racquet his brother handed him and, with a sigh, prepared to enter the game.

The same process had been followed in the second group, which had been made up of Shelton, Max, and Grace until Shelton and Max had deserted him. He would have gladly joined them in departing if he could have done so without admitting utter defeat at the hand of a lady like Felicity Love. Had he been playing against Miss Grace, he could have born the defeat, but there was something about Miss Love that provoked him to the

point of caring that she would be named the ulti-
mate victor.

"Beatrice," Grace cried warmly.

Graeme looked in the direction Miss Grace was.
There was Bea with a racquet in her hand. This
game just might become fun if Bea was playing.

"Have you seen how many times Felicity has
retained her racquet?" Grace asked.

"I have, and my brother and Mr. Shelton have
begged me to play in their stead. I understand they
have been unsuccessful in causing you to surren-
der your racquet and hoped I might do better."

Graeme guffawed. "Do not tell me that Shelton
and Max wish for you to defend their honour?"

"Men are such delicate creatures." She wore a
teasing smile. "Their spirits are so easily crushed,
and their moods so easily fouled –" one eyebrow
arched "– that one must do all one can to protect
them."

"We are not delicate creatures," Graeme
protested. His mood was foul, he would not deny
that, but he was not a delicate creature. *He* had not
quit the game. "Do you hear her, Everett? Bea is
condemning all men just because Shelton and Max

are not up to the challenge of winning. Shocking, is it not?"

Bea's cheeks turned rosy at his teasing, but she did not shy away or attempt to turn the conversation. She was in the game to win.

Everett chuckled. "No, it is not so very shocking, considering it is Bea."

"Whatever do you mean?" Bea asked with feigned innocence.

"You may be quiet and bookish, but you are also devilishly determined once you have set your mind to a task. She is a fearsome opponent, Miss Grace," Everett warned.

How could his brother know such things about Bea and not love her for it?

"Bea?" Grace's eyes were wide. "I cannot imagine her being anything but sweet and obliging."

"Oh, she is that," Everett assured. "Bea is one of the sweetest and most obliging ladies you will ever meet unless she has a mallet or a racquet in her hand."

"Or a set of cards," Graeme added. Bea's eyes lowered as they often did when people talked about her in any flattering fashion. It, much like the teasing smile she had turned on him just moments ago, was one of the many expressions that he found particularly charming about Bea. "And it was Bea who rounded the tree first this morning on our ride," he added.

"She beat Shelton?" Everett asked in surprise. He had not gone riding with his brother, Shelton, and Max because Felicity was fearful of horses. Instead, he and she had remained behind at Stratsbury with Grace who was to act as a chaperone for their walk through the gardens and down the lane.

"Just, but beat him she did."

"He was being gentlemanly," Bea argued. "I am certain he could have won if he was only riding against other gentlemen."

Graeme and Everett both laughed at that.

"Shelton is rarely a gentleman," Graeme said.

"I cannot believe that. He has been all that is proper whenever we are together."

A disturbing thought crossed Graeme's mind. There was one time when Shelton would play the gentleman and allow a lady to win at anything.

"I assure you that it is true. He dislikes losing just as much as you do."

He glanced over to where Shelton was conversing with Max. Shelton had best not be attempting to win Bea's affections.

"We have just met. He was likely trying to make a good first impression. The next ride might be different."

"The next ride?" Graeme's head snapped back around to the group gathered around him.

"Yes, the day after tomorrow, if the weather holds, we are to meet for a ride. Max thought two days of riding in a row might be too much for me." Bea added the last part quietly.

Graeme scowled. Shelton had not mentioned such an arrangement to him. He would make certain he was also part of that ride. Shelton was not going to woo Bea without some interference.

"Must we discuss riding any longer?" Felicity asked. "Can we not play?"

"We have no one to take the place of whoever drops the shuttlecock," said Grace.

"Oh, I had only planned on playing one game," Bea explained. "The weather is warm, and my head is a trifle sore."

Graeme eyed her carefully, looking for any signs that she was unwell. The fact that Bea had mentioned any matter, whether trifling or not, was, in his opinion, a reason to worry. She looked well enough.

"The winner of your game could play the winner of ours," he offered. "That is if Bea thinks she can tolerate two games."

Grace gasped indignantly. "She has not won yet."

"Oh, but she will," Graeme muttered. Then, he turned to Felicity. "What say you, Miss Love? If you win this match, which I am not saying you will, are you agreeable to playing Bea," he smiled and, after a short pause, added, "or your sister."

"And the winner of that game could play me," Everett added.

"I will gladly play you," Graeme said to Everett.

"You?" Felicity tittered. "You have not done very well at beating me yet today, and to play your brother, you shall not only have to beat me but also either Beatrice or Grace."

"Ah, but, to this point, the prize was not to play Bea," he replied.

Bea rolled her eyes. "I am beginning to regret agreeing to play for Mr. Shelton and Max."

"But you have agreed," said Everett. "The winner of your match will play the winner of this match, and then that person shall play me."

"And then we shall have tea and lounge about until it is time for dinner," Graeme added.

"Very well," Bea said, turning to Grace. "You may hit first."

They took their places, but instead of both teams playing at the same time as they had before, Graeme insisted that he and the others watch Grace and Bea play before playing their own match. Felicity only grumbled slightly before allowing that Everett was likely correct in agreeing with his brother. Graeme was just thankful that he could arrange a short rest period for Bea between games, and he was pleased to be able to watch her play, for her naturally retiring nature was replaced by determination once she entered the game.

The shuttlecock flew back and forth. Both ladies ran this way and that to hit it back to their opponent. However, after several minutes, the shuttlecock hit the ground and the round was over.

"Did I not say she would win?" Graeme could not help how the pride he felt at Bea's accomplishment coloured his tone.

Her flushed cheeks deepened in colour, and she

dipped a curtsey in acceptance of his praise before taking her seat on the lawn next to Grace and Everett.

"Wish me well," Graeme said to her as he rose.

"May the best player win," she replied.

He could tell by her expression that she expected him to be annoyed that she had not sent him off to be victorious. But instead of kissing her lips, which were puckered to hold back her smile, as he surprisingly felt compelled to do, he merely bowed to her with a flourish and said, "Indeed, he shall."

Much to his delight, her smile spread across her face at his actions, and he entered this match against Felicity with more interest than he had for any game he had played yet today.

When play began, Grace and Everett cheered for Felicity to win, as Graeme expected. Bea, on the other hand, held her peace until he narrowly escaped missing a volley. Then, she clapped her hands and shouted a well done.

Delight buoyed his spirits, and he gave the shuttlecock a resounding thwack, sending it flying out of Felicity's reach. He turned and bowed to his audience of three.

"Miss Tierney," he said, extending his hand, "I believe this game is ours."

"So, it is," Bea said as she allowed him to help her to her feet. Then, she took her place and play began. It was not a short game. For though Graeme was finding it challenging to keep his eyes where they should be, since Bea was far more delightful to look at than some feathered object, he managed to school himself well enough to send many return-ing volleys.

"Oooh," Bea cried and went sprawling on the grass with the shuttlecock lying just in front of her racquet.

Graeme's breath left him in a whoosh. Dropping his racquet, he hurried to her side.

"Blast," she muttered as she pulled herself up to a sitting position.

"Careful! Do not rush in rising." He knelt next to her.

She huffed. "I am well. I am not happy, but I am well." She brushed at a few bits of grass that clung to her.

She was not well. If he had to guess how she was feeling, he would say she was put out that she had lost and likely embarrassed. Added to that, landing on the ground as she had surely hurt and... "Your arm is bleeding." Graeme pressed his handkerchief to the scrape just below her elbow on her right arm. "You should have let that one pass," he chided softly.

"And let you win?" She brushed at a tear that had escaped the blinking confines of her eyes.

"I won anyway," he said softly. He was rewarded with the small smile he sought.

"Is she injured?" Max appeared at Graeme's shoulder. "It was a spectacular move," he added as he crouched down next to his sister.

Graeme chuckled. "It was a very graceful leap." He lifted his handkerchief to examine her scrape. "We should see that this gets cleaned and dressed. Hold this." He once again pressed the cloth firmly against her still bleeding arm until her hand came to cover his. Then, he slipped his hand out from beneath hers and grabbed her right arm above her elbow as Max took her left arm, and together they helped her rise.

Bea grimaced as she rose, and she favoured one foot. She had hurt herself more than she was willing to admit. Why could she not complain just a bit?

"Did you turn your ankle?" Graeme swept her into his arms without waiting for her reply. He was not about to allow her to attempt walking and injure herself further.

"Yes," Bea admitted, "but I am certain I can walk."

"You should not walk on it," Graeme replied.

"And that means that you must carry her?" Max asked, his eyes registering his shock at Graeme's holding his sister.

It had only seemed natural for Graeme to gather her into his arms when he saw her lips clench and her brow furrow as she tried to stand. Now, however, he supposed it did look odd that he should be assisting Bea, instead of allowing her brother to perform the duty.

"It is my doing," he explained. "I shall see her to the house as penance." He waited, not breathing for a moment, until Max gave his approval. Graeme would have allowed Max to carry Bea if Max had insisted, of course, but he would not have been happy about relinquishing her. It felt good to have her here in his arms — exceptionally good — and, if he was to be honest with himself, it felt as if this was the place where she belonged.

Perhaps Shelton was correct. Perhaps he did need to win Bea's heart — not to protect it from being broken, but to protect his own heart from such a fate. Indeed, he could not imagine allowing another man — not his brother or even hers — rendering the service he was currently providing, for he could not countenance the idea of her in the arms of another — not now, not ever.

"I can walk," Bea protested. "My ankle is only a little sore. If you allowed me to lean on your arm, I certain I could make it to the house without a problem."

"And how are you going to lean on my arm when your hand is required to press a cloth to your wound?" he asked as he began toward the house.

"I could tie the cloth around my arm."

He shook his head. "No, you must allow me to be the gallant knight."

She sighed. "I feel foolish."

"You should not," he answered, tightening his hold on her and pressing her closer to him. "You have saved me from playing another game."

She leaned her head against his shoulder. "You could have allowed me to win. Then you would not have had to play another game."

He chuckled. "I rarely allow anyone to win."

She laughed at the truth of his words. Anyone who knew him, knew that Graeme played to win — nearly always. There had only been a few times when he had willingly lost to his mother when playing cards.

"And you see where that gets you," she said. "Either playing more of a game which bores you or carrying foolish females around the garden."

"First," he replied, "I do not find the game as dull as the company I was forced to keep while playing, yourself excluded, of course. And second, I do not carry foolish females — ever. Had a foolish female fallen, I would have very ungallantly begged someone else to carry her or sent for a footman."

"Thank you. You always know what to say to make me feel better." She smiled up at him from where she rested against his shoulder. "You should know that the only other people who can do that are Max and my father."

He bowed his head in acceptance of her word. "I am honoured to be in such company." He gave her a squeeze. "And just like them, I would do anything to protect you."

Her head rubbed against his shoulder as she

nodded. "I know," she whispered, and then silence fell comfortably around them as the truth of Graeme's statement settled into his heart and, he hoped, into hers as well.

Chapter 7

Two days later, Graeme scanned the garden at Heathcote for Bea as he rode alongside Max and just behind Shelton. Today, Bea's mother had said she would be able to do more than sit on a sofa in the sitting room or a bench in the garden, and he knew she would take advantage of the freedom. She was not one who liked to be confined, but she also not a disobedient daughter.

Her mother was not known to coddle her children, but she was also not the sort who foolishly flouted precautions, especially when it came to Beatrice. Having nearly lost her daughter to a fever when Bea was just eleven, Mrs. Tierney stuck firmly to all prescribed restrictions, and a turned ankle that showed signs of bruising required, according to Bea's mother, a full two days of rest with little walking. Mrs. Tierney would not confine

Bea to her bed, but she would not have her hobbling about — not even with a cane. Bea was to rest with her foot on a pillow.

Ah! There she was, near the hedge, walking slowly and with a noticeable limp.

Shelton looked over his shoulder and smiled at Graeme before doffing his hat and greeting Bea. "Miss Tierney! I missed our rematch. I am confident I could have been victorious today."

The man was incorrigible! He had taunted Graeme about his carrying Bea to the house the day of the shuttlecock tournament and had not stopped being an annoyance ever since.

Bea hobbled over to the hedge which bordered the side of the garden and faced the path to the stables just as a groom came trotting up with a second at his heels.

"My mother was insistent that I should not ride, or I would have accompanied Max."

Shelton swung down from his horse. "I am certain it was a wise decision on her part, but yours was an absence which was felt most profoundly. May I join you for a walk around the garden?"

"I am only allowed one more circuit before I must sit and rest my foot."

"Then one escorted turn around the garden it will be." Shelton handed the reins of his horse to the groom and headed to the small opening in the hedge just a few feet away. "Do not move. Stay just where you are," he called as he went. "I shall be there directly."

Graeme's eyes narrowed as he watched Bea smile and welcome his friend.

"You look out of sorts," Max said as he dismounted.

"Do you not worry about how charming Shelton is being with your sister?" Graeme gave his horse's neck a pat before allowing a groom to lead him away.

"I see no harm in it. He will be gone in a few days, and I doubt he can do much damage in so little time." He smirked at Graeme. "Are you jealous?"

"No, I am not jealous. I am just well acquainted with my friend and his ways." It was not a complete lie. He was well acquainted with how Shelton conducted himself with females. It was, however, a complete and utter untruth that he was not jealous. He did not like the way Shelton was smiling at Bea or causing her to giggle. That was Graeme's job. He was the one who was supposed to tease her into a smile and shock her into laughter.

"He is flirting with Bea and not some more easily duped young lady," Max replied.

His flirting with Bea was the point! It did not matter that Bea was more sensible than most ladies. Shelton knew that Graeme cared for her, and yet, the infuriating chap flirted despite that fact. Not that he was about to share any of those details with Max. Therefore, he clamped his teeth together and attempted to glare a hole through his friend as he followed Max through the hedge.

Thankfully, Shelton and Bea would not be allowed to walk so companionably for long and he would not be the one to have to rouse suspicions further by being the interference. It was likely the first time since meeting them that Graeme was happy to see the Love sisters approaching from the house.

Everett was, of course, at Felicity's side. He had once again cried off riding to spend the morning with the ladies. For once, Graeme did not censure him for doing so since he, himself, had wished to do the same thing.

"Mother said she would have breakfast set out

on the terrace," Bea said as Max greeted her with a kiss on her cheek.

"Have you eaten?" He fell into step next to his sister.

"No, I was waiting for you, and you know I like to have some sort of exercise before breaking my fast. Even if that exercise is a very short and slow hobble around the garden."

"How is your ankle today?" Graeme flanked Shelton since both places next to Bea were already taken. "Is it enjoying the exercise as much as you are?"

Bea grimaced. "It is protesting loudly, but you must not tell my mother. I cannot bear another day of sitting."

"Bea may *prefer* to sit and read," Max said, "but she does not like to be *required* to sit and read."

That was excessively true. Bea was often in the company of a book. However, he had heard her grumbles over the years about the books her mother had prescribed as ones all young ladies should read. She had read them, but she had not enjoyed doing so.

"Who won the race today?" Felicity asked.

"I did," said Shelton, lifting his chin, puffing out

his chest, and looking for all the world like the most pompous of gents.

The pose, however, was affected with a whimsical smile and air, for though Shelton was confident in his own abilities and person to the point of being obnoxious, he possessed not an arrogant bone in his body. It was this brashness, mixed with his natural charm, that made him popular with so many females.

Graeme's scowl deepened. It was a further reason that Bea should not be leaning on Shelton's arm.

"These gents were miles behind me," Shelton continued, looking at Graeme and raising a taunting brow while a smirk played at his lips. "I had half expected to be done with my breakfast before either of them rounded the tree and turned back to Heathcote."

"I should think not!" Max argued. "Graeme nearly overtook you at one point, and I was not so very far behind him."

"How exciting!" Grace chirped. "To the victor must go the spoils; therefore, Mr. Shelton shall have the first muffin!" She hurried over to the table that had been set out and lifted the cloth from the bowl of muffins, keeping the bowl in her possession until Shelton had seen Bea seated and taken his own seat. Only then did Grace hold out the muffins to him with a bit of a flourish, and after he had selected a nice plump cake from the top of the pile, she replaced the cloth and seated herself next to him.

Bea's lips twitched, and she shot a knowing glance toward Graeme. Grace had been arranging things so that she could be seated near Shelton ever since the day after their picnic — the day when she had played shuttlecock with him. It was obvious to anyone who was paying the smallest amount of attention that Grace was interested in capturing the gentleman's notice.

"Mr. Everett Clayton has been invited to the Abernathy's house party. Is that not the best news?" Grace said as she carefully sipped tea from her cup.

A breeze tugged at the cloths covering the food on the table as if it wished to make a plate of breakfast for itself. Bea's eyes turned toward Everett, whose cheeks had grown the faintest bit rosy.

"Is this good news?" Graeme asked his brother pointedly, not caring that it flustered him. His heart did not know whether to rejoice at the news or be saddened. If his brother were gone, Graeme could have Bea all to himself and perhaps convince her of his worth. However, he also knew that if Everett were delighted to attend a house party, he was very likely fully lost to Felicity. Such news would make Bea unhappy, and Graeme could not bear the thought of her being unhappy even if it would lead to his own happiness.

"It is not bad news. A house party is always a good time," Everett replied.

Graeme glanced at Bea and was relieved to see that she did not appear to be distressed by his brother's reply.

"Yes," Shelton agreed with a sly smile, "house parties can be a grand time as long as you avoid the true purpose of them."

Grace blinked. "Whatever do you mean?"

"He means he enjoys flirting but not enough to be leg-shackled," Graeme supplied.

Bea hid her smile behind her cup. It was good to see that he had shocked her into amusement.

"You do not wish to marry?" Grace asked as if such an idea was the most ridiculous one in all the world.

"Grace," Felicity chided softly, though her eyes, unlike her tone, appeared eager to hear Shelton's answer to Grace's question.

"It is not that I do not wish to marry. I just do not wish to marry now," Shelton said, picking a morsel of cake off his plate and popping it into his mouth. "There is plenty of time for marriage when I am older."

A bird song rang out from a branch of the tree overhead.

Shelton looked up. "Even the creatures agree, you see," he added with a smile.

Graeme settled back to watch the interaction between Shelton and Miss Grace. However, the reply to Shelton's comments did not come from the expected source.

"Do you fear it? Or is it just the giving up of freedom that keeps you from the marital state?" Bea's hand flew to her mouth. "Forgive me. That was most improper."

Graeme saw her cheeks redden. "Thinking aloud?" he asked. It was an unusual thing for Bea to speak without thought, and he could imagine how mortified she must be. He also wondered just how interested she was in his friend's marital state.

She nodded.

"So, Shelton, what is it?" Graeme asked. "Fear or freedom?"

"You do not need to answer." Bea shot Graeme a look of displeasure.

Graeme shrugged. "I am curious to hear his answer," he said with a smile. Perhaps if he could be more improper than she, it would lessen her mortification. However, from the look on her face, he was not certain that it was a good plan.

"I have no qualms about answering as long as every other person at the table answers as well," Shelton said. He held Graeme's gaze as if in challenge before looked at each other person gathered at the table. Having received assurances of participation from Max, Everett, and the Miss Loves, he turned to Bea. "And you, Miss Tierney? Will you answer?"

"I will start if you wish."

He waved his right hand in a fashion to encourage her to continue.

"I am kept from the marital state by the lack of an offer," she said with a smile.

"Do you have a beau who should be making this offer?" Shelton inquired.

Bea shook her head. "No, sadly, I do not."

"But you are not opposed to the idea of a beau or marriage, then?"

"No, Mr. Shelton, I am not. However, I do not wish for just any gentleman as a beau or husband. The gentleman, who wishes to marry me, must be of a good moral character and be someone I could love and respect and who would return those same feelings to me."

Shelton's eyes slid to Graeme and then returned to Bea. "That is very wisely said, Miss Tierney. I, too, would wish for love and respect in marriage."

"Yes, but that is not what keeps you from it, is it?" Graeme prodded. He did not like the way his friend was smiling at Bea nor the way Bea's eyes had dropped to her plate.

"No, it is not," Shelton replied, shooing a fly away from his cup of tea before taking a sip. "I believe the question was if it was fear or freedom that kept me from marrying." He turned to Bea. "Would either of those keep you from marriage if there were a gentleman wishing to make an offer?"

"You are not offering, are you?' Max said with a grin.

"No, no, no. I am not ready to marry anyone

even if she is as lovely as your sister or cousins. I was merely posing a question of interest." His eyes slid from Max's face to Graeme's. "For curiosity's sake." He smiled at Bea. "I have not offended you, have I?"

She shook her head. "No, I am not offended, nor am I so entrenched in my freedom, such that it is for a lady under the authority of her mother and brother, to refuse an offer if extended by a gentleman of good moral fiber, who would show me both love and respect." She gave Shelton a pointed look, and Graeme smiled at her temerity.

"Yes, yes, that is true, a young lady's freedom is not the same as that of a gentleman," Shelton acknowledged before Bea continued her answer.

"I do not fear marriage to such a man."

"Well said, Miss Tierney. Now, I shall answer." He took a sip of his tea and then drew a breath. Apparently, he was going to answer honestly. A flippant response would have slipped from Shelton much more easily.

Graeme looked from Shelton to Bea. Shelton was not the sort to be anything but open with those he regarded as friends. He must hold Bea as a friend.

"Both fear and freedom keep me from seeking a wife at this particular time in my life," he said. "Being a husband and father comes with great responsibilities, to which, to be blunt, I am not certain I feel equal." His lips curled into a smile. "And then, I do enjoy my freedom. My time is mine to a large extent, as is my income." He shrugged. "It is not perhaps the best of answers, for it certainly does not show me to best advantage, but there it is."

Bea tipped her head and, much to Graeme's annoyance, smiled sweetly at Shelton. "Perhaps it does not show you to good advantage amongst a group of your peers, but to us ladies, it is a very good answer."

Shelton's brows furrowed. "It is?"

Bea nodded. "You view your family as a responsibility not to be taken lightly. You know that your sole claim to your time and money, as well as other freedoms, will need to be abandoned for the well-being of a wife and children. That is very commendable, is it not, Grace?"

"Oh, indeed, it is," Grace agreed, her head bobbing up and down vigorously.

"And I suspect, as my mother would say," Bea

continued, "when the right person comes along, it will not feel like a loss of freedom but the gaining of a great treasure, and your fear of failure will pale when compared to your fear of losing that lady."

Graeme would gladly give up his freedom rather than lose Bea. His eyes turned to his brother who seemed to be interested in the conversation but not overly affected.

"That is exactly what she would say," Max agreed.

Shelton was quiet for a moment. "I had not considered it in such a light. You are incredibly wise, Miss Tierney. I almost wish I were making you an offer."

"You do not," Bea said with a laugh.

He smiled and shook his head. "No, you are right, but it is not because there is anything lacking in you."

"I hope one day there will be another who agrees," she said softly.

He patted the hand that lay on her lap. "I am certain there will be." His eyes fell once again on Graeme. "Mr. Clayton, what say you?"

"I say Max is next."

Max laughed. "My answer is short. I am not fearful of marriage. I have cared for a mother and sister for some time now, so I do not feel completely unprepared. However, I do enjoy the limited freedom I have and have not met the lady who makes me wish to be parted with that freedom." He turned to Graeme. "Now it is your turn."

Graeme did not like the twinkle in Max's eye. The fellow had been teasing him about courting his sister and being jealous of Shelton, and now that they were speaking about marriage, he was fearful that Max would ask if he wished to marry Bea. How would he answer that? To lie and say he did not wish it might cause Bea to think he did not care for her. However, if he said he did wish to marry her — as he did — and she did not wish to marry him, as she likely did not since she was in love with his brother, their friendship would be broken.

"I need only to find the lady who will accept me," he said.

"You do not fear it?" Grace asked.

Graeme shook his head. "No, I fear loneliness more."

"Are you sure you still need to find the lady?"

Shelton asked with a grin. "Surely there is one who has made you think of loneliness?"

Graeme shrugged. "I did not say I had not found a lady I wish to marry. I said I needed to find one who would accept my offer of marriage." He forced his eyes to stay focused on his friend rather than allowing them to shift to Bea.

"You are in love?" Bea asked in surprise.

His eyes met hers as he nodded. "I believe I am." His heart did not know whether to ache or rejoice at the disappointment he read in her expression. Perhaps there was some hope that she could be swayed from loving his brother to loving him.

Chapter 8

The evening air settled in, cool and refreshing, as the sun began to dip toward the horizon. Bea once again found herself sitting in the garden while the others wandered along the paths at Stratsbury. Tomorrow morning, Felicity and Grace would be leaving for the Abernathys', and with them, would go Everett and Mr. Shelton — one to attend the house party and the other to his own estate. At the moment, each gentleman had one of her cousins on his arm.

Grace had been undaunted by Mr. Shelton's answers yesterday morning. In fact, it appeared as if she had taken them as a sort of challenge — a call to arms in disabusing the gentleman of his concerns about being ready for marriage and coaxing him to give up his love of the freedom that bachelorhood afforded.

Bea had made it to the middle of the garden before her ankle's protests had overcome her determination to complete the circuit. Graeme had offered to sit with her while the others walked, but after a few moments of persuasion by Bea, he had continued walking and talking with Max.

She smiled as he turned ever so slightly to look back at her. He was very attentive — he had always been so. Being the eldest of the group of boys by one year, he had always made certain she was safe — even if it meant opposing Max. Max had bristled at the idea of anyone thinking he did not care well enough for his sister, but he had also recognized when Graeme was determined and knew that to push him would only result in a fight — one that Max was likely to lose.

Bea leaned against the back of the bench on which she sat sideways with her legs stretched out on the length of the seat. As she rested her head on her hand, she considered the changes that were to occur in the near future. Her familiar little group was about to splinter and shift.

She closed her eyes and allowed herself to feel the disappointment of Everett's being lost to her. She tried to remember what it was about him that had first drawn her interest, but she could not. She had always just preferred his more serious nature. He had spent many hours reading as a boy and been teased mercilessly by Graeme for doing so. They had that in common.

Graeme had always teased her about her love of reading as well. She shook her head and chuckled. It was not as if Graeme did not read. He did, and he enjoyed the activity to an extent, especially if he could read the piece of literature aloud and in a dramatic fashion. He was more lively than Everett — more like Max in that respect, or her father.

She wrapped a hand around the necklace her father had given her. Even after nine years, she still missed her father dreadfully. Would she ever have a pendant to replace the one he had given her? She sighed. Presently, it seemed unlikely, but the future was unknown. There might yet be someone who would claim her heart as her father had done to her mother's. How she longed for someone to love her in such a fashion. She allowed herself one more bittersweet moment of contemplation about her father before turning her thoughts back to her group of friends.

Everett would be gone. He would marry Felicity

— it was obvious that he would –, and then he would take up his living and begin his own family. He would be near — just down the road a mile or two. However, he would have responsibilities that would keep him busy and away from such frequent gatherings as this.

And Graeme? She bit her lip as she considered him. Who would be sitting here with him? Who was it that he loved? She blew out a great breath as the pain of that thought threatened to crush her. She should have known he would find a lady who would capture his heart, but neither he nor Everett, who had been in town for the season with Graeme, had mentioned anyone in particular. That absence of comment had made the announcement of his being in love quite shocking. If she had been given some indication that her friend was to leave her, she might have been able to face such news without this sadness.

She shook her head and brushed a tear away from the corner of her eye. She was being foolish. He would still be here at Stratsbury. It was not as if he would be truly leaving. His duties were here. However, he would not be so free to meet her in the morning for a ride, and his arm, when strolling in the garden, would always be claimed by someone else.

Change was inevitable. Bea knew this to be true, but the truth of the fact did not make the acceptance of the changes to come any easier.

She, herself, would one day be expected to marry. She knew she could not live forever with Max, no matter how much she wished it. Her brother would eventually take a wife, and there would be new Tierneys to occupy the chairs in the schoolroom and fill the bedrooms at Heathcote.

Max had set money aside for her to have a season, and though she did not relish the idea of going to town, she knew she would have to endure it — for his sake. She was practical enough to know that her greatest chance of securing a good husband would be in those crowded ballrooms of town.

"You promised the rest would be refreshing, but I did not expect you to sleep."

Bea jumped, and her eyes popped open at Max's comment. She had not heard anyone approaching. "Where are the others?" she asked.

"Graeme grew weary of listening to Grace," Max replied with a laugh.

"She never stops speaking," Graeme muttered.

"Shelton can suffer without us bearing witness to it."

"You are a strange friend." Bea swung her legs off the bench and accepted Max's help in rising.

"Shelton would do the same," Graeme said in defense of his actions. "Are you tired? Did we wake you?" Care drenched each word he spoke. It was endearing.

"No, I was not sleeping, although I cannot honestly say I am not a trifle fatigued." She smiled sheepishly at him. "I do not say it to complain or to disparage, but I am looking forward to the quiet that shall be restored to Heathcote on the morrow."

Graeme chuckled. "Then, you are well?"

"You looked distraught," Max prodded.

"I was merely pondering life," Bea replied. "We are on the cusp of a new place in our lives. We are children no longer."

Max wrapped an arm around his sister's shoulders. "No, we are not children, but the future does not need to be bleak."

"Oh, it is not; I am sure. Many good things will happen. I am only grieving what has been." She rested her head against Max's shoulder. "I have decided to go to town for the season."

"You have?" Graeme asked in surprise. "But you do not like large crowds."

Bea sighed and nodded. "You know me well." Very well. Perhaps better than anyone else. "However, if I am not to be a spinster and a burden to my brother, as well as a disappointment to my mother, I will have to endure the masses."

"Mother will be pleased to hear it," Max said, "but I will not mention it to her until after our cousins have left. I do not wish to listen to their peals of delight and have things twisted in such a fashion that we end up having to take a house with them for three months!"

"I would rather be a spinster," Bea said between giggles.

"I would rather that as well," Max agreed with a shudder. "But it will not happen. You are not the sort of lady to go unloved. Indeed, you have never lacked for a partner at an assembly."

"You are my brother, so you tend to see me in a better light than others."

"No, he has the right of it," Graeme said. "And I

have several seasons of ladies with whom to compare you. You shine as brightly as any of them."

"Are you certain you do not wish to court my sister?" Max asked with a smirk.

"This is the thanks I get for supporting your claim?" Graeme cried and appeared, curiously, to be somewhat flustered. "May I not say something flattering without an ulterior motive? Or are you just desperate to be rid of her?"

Max laughed. "I would gladly keep her forever, and I suppose it is not fair to continue to tease you about such things. But you must know, I would be happy to give her to you — not because I wish to be rid of her, but because you have always cared so well for her. And you do suit each other. Your less serious nature balances well with Bea's tendency to ruminate and draw terrible conclusions. Oof," he blew out a breath as Bea's elbow made contact with his side. "You do tend to think of the direst result," he protested.

"I consider the consequences so that I can avoid the direst results," Bea protested.

"She has a point," Graeme agreed. "She saved us from disaster more than once."

Max could not deny it, for even though Bea was

a good number of years younger than either her brother or Graeme, she had been the one to point out what devastating results some of their boyhood plans might have had.

"I would like to retire to the library for a while," Bea said as they approached the house. "My cousins are departing tomorrow, and I shall once again have time and quiet in which to read."

"I will inform your mother," Graeme said, "and I will come to collect you when she says I must."

"Try to convince her that an hour would be perfect."

"I promise nothing, but I will do my best," he said with a bow before leaving her and Max to find their way to the library.

"You do not need to stay with me," she said as they reached the door. "I shall be well, and I promise not to climb any ladders. The books I wish to read are all within reaching distance with my feet flat on the floor."

"You will not be lonely? You have just spent time sitting alone in the garden. I feel guilty leaving you again." And he did look as if he felt a great deal of guilt. Her brother liked to have a good time, but he was not one to shirk his responsibilities without feeling the weight of such an offense.

"I asked you to leave me in the garden, and I am asking you to leave me now. You should not feel guilty for doing as I request." She placed her hand on his cheek. "You are an excellent brother." The comment earned her the smile, as well as the solitude, she sought.

She hobbled to the far end of the library to where a group of chairs sat near a window that had been opened to take advantage of the evening air. The book of verses she wished to read was on the shelf just to the left of the window. She located it and another that stood beside it on the shelf and took them to the chair closest to the fresh air. She lit the lamp on the table as the light from the window was fading, and she would need greater light by which to read. With a sigh, she settled into the chair, tucking herself into the corner of its wing and propping her feet on the footstool that stood in front of it.

Thus she sat, engrossed in the poet's descriptions of the peak district for many minutes. Indeed, she had read several poems before her attention was drawn to the window and a rustling and whispering just below it.

She sat quietly, straining to hear what or who might be outside. A giggle floated softly into the room, followed by a low masculine voice, and then silence. As noiselessly as she was able, Bea crept to the window and peeked out to see which of her cousins was in the garden.

She quickly covered her mouth with her hand to catch a gasp as she spotted Felicity and Everett wrapped in what appeared to be a rather passionate embrace. Her heart jumped and skittered to a quicker pace, but it did not ache — not as she expected it should. Everett was lost to her as she had expected he was, but the realization of such a truth did not bring tears to her eyes or a sensation of being crushed as she had feared it would when the inevitable could be denied no longer. Curious that.

She returned to her book, but her mind would not contemplate the words on the page. It instead wished to consider why her heart had not been more affected. Perhaps it was that she had prepared herself well enough for this moment, or perhaps it was that she did not actually love Everett Clayton with the sort of love that drove one to slay dragons and best knights.

There was a bit more rustling outside the window and fading giggles that spoke of Felicity being returned to the house. How the two lovers had been able to escape the house when there were so many eyes to watch them was puzzling to Bea.

"Everett."

Bea leaned her head toward the window.

"I have been looking for you," Graeme said.

Ah, so Everett and Felicity's absence had not gone unnoticed.

Bea closed her book and stacked it atop the one on her lap. She should move to a place where she would not be tempted to listen to the conversation outside. She placed her books on the table and picked up the lamp, but she did not move as the discourse below her caught her ear.

Graeme apparently knew what his brother had been about in the garden and was scolding him. Her lips curled into a smile. It was rare for Graeme to scold Everett about impropriety. Graeme had often been the receiver of such chiding.

Bea moved the lamp to a table near another set of chairs and returned to retrieve her books.

"So you never thought of Bea as more than Max's sister?"

Bea paused and waited to hear Everett's reply to Graeme's question. She knew she should not listen, but her curiosity would not allow her to do what was proper until she heard his response.

"No, never," Everett replied.

Bea's breath caught. It did hurt a bit to know that her love, such that it was, had never been returned and had never had a hope of being requited. But the pain was the just result of doing as she knew she should not. Bea moved quickly away from the window but not rapidly enough to miss Graeme's next words.

"Neither have I..."

Tears gathered without warning, and a crushing weight threatened to squeeze every last ounce of breath from Bea's chest. This was the pain she had expected to feel when she had seen Everett and Felicity together. This was the pain of love being ripped from her heart. She drew a deep, shuddering breath and blew it out as she clearly realized what her heart had been attempting to tell her over the past few days.

She loved Graeme.

She drew a second breath and released it slowly as she blinked against the tears which accompanied the knowledge that he did not love her in return. She pressed one hand against her aching heart and rubbed her forehead with her other hand, attempting to quiet the throbbing that was beginning behind her eyes. She needed to go home. She needed to climb into her bed and have a good cry. She needed to be away from here and away from him. So, gathering herself as well as she could, she doused the lamp and quietly slipped out of the library, leaving her books and her heart behind.

Chapter 9

As he waited in Heathcote's drawing room the next afternoon, Graeme flipped through one of the books he had found on a chair in the library at Stratsbury last night when he had gone to collect Bea at the appointed hour. He had been a few moments late in going to the library since it had taken him longer than expected to find Everett and have a particular, and rather important, discussion with him. Yet, Graeme had been surprised to find that Bea had not waited for him, and he was even more surprised when he had discovered she had left her books behind. It was very unlike her and had caused him no little amount of unease.

However, beginning with Shelton cornering him and forcing him to admit his heart was well and truly lost to Bea, Graeme's day had been unsettling, but not in a truly unpleasant way. That is it was not unpleasantly unsettling until he had found these books where Bea was supposed to have been. Most of the day had been spent in nervous wondering. First, he had wondered if he would destroy his friendship with Bea if he mentioned his growing attachment to her. Then, after hearing her say she was going to London for the season and knowing that the must mean she had given up on his brother, he had felt anxiously hopeful when approaching his brother to make certain there would be no danger of damaging their relationship when he made his plans to marry Bea known.

Graeme closed the first book and began paging through the second. He had intended to speak to Bea last night to see if he might have some chance of winning her before she hied off to London in search of another. However, she had been gone before he had gotten the opportunity. All that had been left of her presence had been these books. He snapped the second book shut just as Max entered the drawing room.

"She is resting."

"Is she terribly unwell? I should have never asked her to walk in the garden with me." Graeme ran a hand through his hair. He had been worried about

Bea ever since he had returned to the drawing room last night and heard that she had been taken home in a state of ill-health. In fact, he had slept very little last night as a result, and he had not been able to focus on anything today.

Max's head was tipped and his eyes roamed Graeme from head to foot.

"I look a fright." There was no use in denying it. He had not shaven, his hair was rumpled, and his cravat was somewhat askew.

"You are. I dare say I have never seen you in such a state outside of when we are in London and have been out excessively late." Max nodded his head toward the door. "Come to my study. Bea will likely be down for tea in a few minutes, and I will ask her if she is feeling up to seeing anyone, although I cannot imagine her refusing to see you even if she is unwell."

"It was not the walk in the garden," Max continued as the two friends walked the short distance down the hall to Max's study.

"It was not?" That was somewhat of a relief.

Max shook his head. "I do not know what caused her to become unwell." He waved to the chairs in front of his desk in an invitation to

Graeme to be seated. "All I know is that she came flying out of the library so quickly that I had to catch her to keep her from falling when she knocked into me. I had been on my way to check on her for Mother's sake."

"And you have no idea what was the cause? None at all?"

"No. I questioned her about what might have made her feel so unwell, but unless she took a chill from the open window, I do not know what it was."

Graeme placed the books he carried on the desk. "It was not overly cool last night."

"No, it was not." Max picked up the top book and turned it over in his hands.

"I believe she left those behind in her haste."

Max picked up the second book and turned it over in his hands just as he had with the first book. He gave his friend a curious look and then returned his attention back to the two books on his desk. "I am not sure she will want these. She said there was nothing she wanted at Stratsbury."

Graeme expelled a breath as if he had been punched. Nothing she wanted at Stratsbury. He ran a hand through his hair again. He had known

it was a possibility that she would refuse him, but...
he had hoped.

"That is just how she said it as she rubbed her
head and fought tears. It was very odd. I asked if
she had not found the book for which she was
looking — which we both know is an impossibility
because she knows Stratsbury's library so well —
but she merely shook her head and repeated that
there was nothing at Stratsbury for her." Max
tipped his head again, and his brows drew together
as he looked at Graeme. "You do not look much
better than Bea did last night."

"I did not sleep well. I was worried about Bea."

Max leaned back in his chair. Silence engulfed
the room, save for the light tapping of Max's fingers
on the edge of his desk and the steady keeping of
the time by the clock.

"Are you certain you do not wish to court my
sister?" he asked without so much as the slightest
twitch of his lips or twinkle in his eye. Though
Max was a year younger than Graeme, he appeared
to be much older as he slipped from Bea's older
brother to her father-figure. "You seem to care for
her very much."

He did care for her — more than he thought he

could ever care for anyone. He scrubbed his face as he blew out a breath. He was weary, so very weary from not having slept and from worry.

"I want to marry her," he blurted. Rising from his chair, he paced to the window, attempting to ignore Max's startled expression. "I love her."

"You love Bea?"

"I do." With all that was in him, he loved her.

"I know I have teased that you might, but I never imagined it to be true."

"Neither did I." Graeme glanced over his shoulder and smiled sheepishly at Max. "I guess I knew I had always cared for her, but I thought it was only because she was your sister and a friend."

"What changed?"

Graeme shrugged and turned to lean against the window frame. "My brother is an idiot."

Max laughed. "That is not a new revelation to you. You have been saying so for years."

"Yes," Graeme agreed with a grin, "but when he took up with Miss Love and ignored Bea, he sunk to a new level of idiocy." He shook his head. "The more I attempted to get him to realize his stupidity, the more I began to wish he would remain as he was. I did not wish for him to have Bea, but I persisted in my attempts because I wanted Bea to be happy."

A flash of yellow outside the door, which Max had left partially open, caught Graeme's attention, halting his confession.

"Bea," Max called. He held a finger to his lips while looking at Graeme and tipping his head toward the far side of the room.

Graeme nodded his understanding. He would remain silent and hidden until Max wished for him to reveal himself.

Bea must have come to the door, without entering the room, for the door only opened marginally more than it had been open.

"Graeme brought these for you." Max indicated the books on his desk.

"I will collect them later."

"I think now would be better." Max's tone was demanding, which was unusual for him.

Bea crept into the room as if she did not wish to claim the book on the desk but was also unwilling to defy her brother's wishes.

"Graeme had hoped to call on you." Max was very intently focused on his sister as if he were attempting to decipher something. "He was concerned about you when you left in such a flutter."

"I do not flutter." Bea folded her arms, and Graeme could just imagine the glare she was giving Max.

Max stood. "Last night you fluttered, but you are correct. It is very unlike you. Are you feeling better now?"

"Yes. Thank you," she replied after a moment's pause. She was hiding something.

"Then, you would not be opposed to entertaining a guest?"

Again, there was a moment's pause before Bea replied. "Has Mother invited someone to tea?" She shifted uneasily.

Max's lips twitched. Apparently, he also knew that his sister was attempting to play coy. He shifted his attention from Bea to Graeme. "No, I asked you to stay, did I not, Graeme?"

"Indeed, you did."

Her hand flew to her chest and a small squeak escaped her. "Well, then... I suppose I should go see that things are ready," she said without so much as glancing in Graeme's direction and acknowledging his presence.

"No, you should have a seat." He pointed to one of the chairs in front of his desk before he came around that piece of furniture and perched himself on the edge of it while his sister sat down in front of him.

"Would you like to tell me what it was in particular that made you so unwell last night?" he asked.

Bea shook her head. "No."

Graeme's eyebrows rose. Bea rarely refused outright to do as her brother asked.

Max crossed his arms and smiled. "Am I to understand then, that it is something which you wish for neither me nor Graeme to know?"

Bea said nothing.

"And it happened when you were in the library," he continued as he rubbed his chin.

Bea fidgeted. Max was fairly good at deducing things when his mind was set on discovering what he wanted to know, so Graeme could understand her discomfort.

"You told me that the window was open, and you were sitting near it. However, you do not seem to have caught a chill."

"Your books were not near the window." Graeme took the seat next to her.

She gave him a fleeting glance. "I moved away from the window after –" She snapped her mouth closed.

"After what?" Max asked.

Bea shook her head.

Max's focus did not shift, and the two Tierney siblings sat in silence for a short time just looking at one another until the stalemate ended with a huff from Bea.

"There were people in the garden," she admitted, "and I did not wish to pry into their business by listening to their conversation."

Ah. Graeme's heart sank. "Everett and Miss Love?"

Bea spared him another fleeting glance as she nodded.

"I am sorry they upset you." Perhaps she was more attached to his brother than he had suspected yesterday.

"Why would their being in the garden upset you?" Max asked.

"It is not their being in the garden but rather what they were doing in the garden," Graeme explained softly. There was no need for to Bea relive what had caused her pain.

"What were they do—"

"They did not upset me," Bea interrupted Max's question. "I am not a fool. I knew Everett preferred Felicity, and it is not as if I have never seen anyone kissing before. It happens frequently enough at assemblies."

"Felicity had just returned to the house before you came crashing through the hall. Are you certain they did not upset you?" Max asked.

Graeme watched Bea's expression carefully. She looked exasperated but not as if she were trying to avoid the topic of Felicity and Everett. She must truly not be attached to him.

"I had a headache, my ankle hurt, and there was a tightness in my chest. Can I not have such without it being brought on by emotional distress?"

"You can," Max agreed. "In fact, you have had such on several occasions – often resulting in your being in bed for two days, and Mother threatening to call the apothecary. Neither of those things has happened and..." One eyebrow arched as he gave Bea a pointed look. "You cried."

He held her gaze for a moment longer before pushing off his desk. "I will see if the tea is ready, and Graeme, you can see my sister to the drawing room in ten minutes. There is a matter I wish to discuss with my mother." He gave a nod to Graeme and left before Bea could mount a protest.

She twisted her fingers in her lap.

Graeme could not for the life of him figure out why she was so ill-at-ease with him. They had always had a comfortable relationship – until today.

"Thank you for bringing the books." She glanced at him.

"It was my pleasure. I must say I was surprised to find them and not you in the library."

"My apologies. I was not well."

"I had hoped to speak to you about something rather important." He smiled at her when she looked up at him. He would know if he had a chance with her or not before he left this room today. "I was late arriving because I had to speak to my brother first." He ran a hand through his hair and then rubbed both palms on his knees. Breathing was becoming difficult, and his heart was drumming an uncomfortably rapid beat. "I needed to ask him about his intentions regarding Miss Love and his opinion of you."

She closed her eyes. "I know," she whispered. "I heard."

"You heard?" Graeme shook his head against the lightness he felt as his heart seemed to climb into his throat. Had she run away because she heard his confession to his brother about his love for her?

She nodded, daring only to dart a quick look at him. "I did not mean to hear. I was moving away from the window and your voices carried."

Could the world look any bleaker? "I have no hope then?" The words clawed their way out of his mouth, bearing jagged bits of his heart in their grasp.

Bea's brow furrowed as she turned her full attention to him. "Forgive me, but I do not understand. Hope of what?"

Graeme drew a breath and released it. He would survive this – just barely most likely – but he would survive. "Hope of your ever returning my love."

Her eyes grew wide and her mouth opened as if to speak. However, when no sound came out, she closed it again.

Seeing her confusion and finding some hope in it, he continued, "I love you. Is there any hope that you could ever love me in return?"

Bea shook her head, and her mouth opened and closed once more before she found her voice. "You love me?"

The small glimmer of hope he had found moments ago began to burn brighter at the sound of wonder in her words. "Did you not hear me say as much to Everett?"

Slowly, she shook her head from side to side. "You said you had never thought of me as anything other than Max's sister."

Joy split Graeme's face with a smile. He had hope. She might yet accept him. "You did not hear it all."

"I did not?"

"No." A chuckle of pure relief bubbled out. "I asked Everett if he had ever thought of you as more than Max's sister because I needed to know if he would be hurt if I declared myself to you. And he said –"

"He had not," Bea supplied. "And then, you said that you had not either." She blinked at the tears which made her eyes shimmer.

Graeme took her hands in his and slipped off his chair to kneel before her. "I had not considered you beyond that until recently while I was trying to help you win my brother's affections. I kept comparing Miss Love to you and questioning how my brother could prefer someone who was so much..." He searched for the word to describe Felicity but could not come up with one and so settled on, "Less than you. I envied that you loved Everett."

Her eyes still shimmered, but her lips smiled happily.

"Then, when Shelton came and paid attention to you, I cannot describe how jealous I was. I knew then that I did not want another man to claim you." He shrugged. "But you loved my brother."

She shook her head. "I did not love him. I only thought I did. I was infatuated with his pleasant manners and his serious nature, but I do not believe I ever truly loved him." She looked down at their joined hands. "I knew it the instant I saw him kissing my cousin. My heart should have shattered, but it did not. It pinched with disappointment, but the disappointment did not crush me as I knew it should." She peeked up at him. "It did not crush me as *your words* did. I love you. Not Everett. Only you."

Elation washed over him. "You love me?"

Bea nodded. "I do."

"Enough to marry me?"

Again, Bea nodded. "Yes."

"You will be mine?"

Bea laughed as she nodded a third time. "Forever," she assured him.

Forever. She was his, and he was hers. He wanted to sweep her into his arms, but he hesitated. "May I kiss you?" A stolen kiss on the cheek was one thing. A kiss such as the one for which he longed seemed to require her permission.

Bea did not nod for a fourth time. Nor did she once again tell him yes. His always proper and simply lovely Bea leaned forward and pressed her lips to his before saying with a playful smile, "You shock me with your reserve. I had not thought you capable of such."

He rose from the floor and pulled her to her feet. "I did tell you that I was constitutionally incapable of not being shocking, did I not?"

Her lips were still smiling with amusement in the most beguiling way. "Indeed, you did, Mr. Clayton."

"Graeme," he corrected as he pulled her into his embrace and lowered his head to kiss her.

"My Graeme," she whispered against his lips.

"My beautiful Bea," he replied before claiming her lips with a kiss that was deep and passionate, mingling their souls, declaring his troth, and engraving her on his heart forever.

His Darling Friend

Friend

He's known her for her whole life, but he's never thought of her like this until now.

Chapter 1

Roger Shelton slumped down on the cream-coloured settee in the far corner of the Abernathy's drawing room next to a pretty young lady whom he knew would not bat her lashes at him or smile coyly as all the other eager young women at this house party seemed wont to do. Not that he blamed them, of course. He would make a fine catch if he were ready to be caught.

"Why must we attend these things?" The petite blonde next to him whispered.

"Because neither you nor I are married, and our parents wish to be rid of us," Roger replied.

How often had he heard his mother bemoaning his unmarried state to her mother, who would return her own tale of woe about having an unwed daughter? It seemed to be a frequent bent in nearly every conversation when their two families gathered for tea, dinner, or whatever excuse either her mother or his could conjure for themselves to be together.

"Perhaps your mother would like to see someone take over your care, but my father is not anxious to send me packing," his companion retorted.

Roger chuckled. He enjoyed these moments of unfettered banter with his friend. She would speak openly to him, for she wanted nothing from him. Not a kiss, not a dance, not a marriage – with her, he was free to be himself. Even if that often led to her scolding him.

"Is that so, Vic? Then why do you suppose your father gave me this." He withdrew a small packet from his pocket and handed it to her. "I was to deliver it to you here with the accompanying message that he trusts your decisions but would like to meet the chap before the vows are read."

With a resounding thump, Victoria Hamilton's right hand connected with Roger's chest, causing him to exhale quickly. She was not one to pull her punches as some chits might. She did not care one jot if Roger thought her less than delicate, and he liked that about her.

"He said nothing of the sort. You are the worst

liar – no! I cannot say that. I know you to be a very good liar – but in this, you shall not deceive me."

"It was worth a try," Roger admitted, rubbing the slightly sore spot on his chest where she had hit him.

He had known she would not believe him. Her father was too kind to tease in such a fashion, and he was in no rush to see his darling daughter given away to anyone.

"Your father did give me that package for you. That is the truth. As is the fact that my mother suggested I take a good turn through the ladies of the room looking for more than pleasant curves and a willing smile."

"You are dreadful!"

Roger placed a hand on his heart. "I promise you she said that very thing. Mother is not known for her delicacy when chiding me." In that way, Victoria was a lot like his mother. "There was also something in her diatribe about grandchildren before she turned her toes up." He shot a devilish grin at his friend.

"Do not say it," Victoria hissed.

It amused him how her expression was appropriately appalled at the mere thought of what he was about to say. She did know him well. Of course, her expression would not prevent him from continuing.

"Mother was not pleased when I suggested that producing children did not require a marriage license."

"You did not!" Victoria shook her head. "Of course, you did. I can nearly hear you saying it."

"I am wounded."

"By the truth?"

"No, by the thought that you think I would –" A severe glare stopped his words.

"Are you or are you not, Roger Shelton, the charmer of ladies, the stealer of kisses, the seeker of pleasure?"

He could not refute her statement, so he did not. He simply sat quietly and waited for her to continue.

"None of that embarrasses you as it should," she muttered. "Did you get your hunter?"

Apparently, the discussion of his ill behaviour was at an end.

He nodded and extended his feet out in front of him, crossing them at the ankles and making himself very comfortable. "Clayton helped me."

"Mr. Clayton?" she asked with a smile that caused him to raise a brow in question. "He is pleasant," she retorted with a huff. "Naught else."

"That is good to know since I do believe he is getting married. At least he seemed on the point of proposing when I left Stratsbury Park, and I dare say the lady was only waiting for him to ask. She'll accept him, happily."

"Indeed?" Her tone was filled with delight.

"Thanks to my assistance."

Victoria blinked, and her mouth dropped open for a moment. "I beg your pardon?" she asked incredulously.

Was it so impossible to believe that he would help a friend in such a way? He supposed it likely was. He was not known as the sort of gentleman who looked for ways to be snared. But then, he was setting the parson's trap for his friend and not himself, so it really should be more believable.

"I may have pointed out to Clayton how he and his neighbour Miss Tierney would suit each other quite well."

"You?" There was not a single ounce of belief in her tone. "You helped a fellow charmer make a match?"

Ah, that was why she was so disbelieving. It was not just any gent he had helped. Graeme Clayton was nearly as much a rogue as he himself was. Roger shrugged and puffed out his chest a bit. "I have always been very good at reading people."

She shook her head.

Why did she have such a difficult time believing that he could do anything good?

"I assure you I am. How else have I remained a bachelor for so long when there are so many who would trip over each other to be my bride." He winked at her, and she rolled her eyes, just as he knew she would.

"I am certain I could find a match within the assembled hopefuls. Not for myself," he clarified. "I am not in any hurry to be married, but several gents seem eager and, yourself excepted, there is not a lady here who is not hoping to snare a husband."

"I am not the only lady who does not feel a need to rush to the altar," Victoria retorted as if he had affronted her most grievously, but there was a small curl of her lips that told him she was not entirely put out with him.

He leaned toward her. "Marrying at three and

twenty would not be rushing," he muttered near her ear.

"Oh, good heavens, you have been talking to my mother, have you not?"

Roger nodded. "Why do you not marry?"

"Why should I?"

"Do you really wish to live with your brother and his wife?"

Victoria expelled a great sigh but said nothing. Roger knew very well that Victoria did not like the new Mrs. Hamilton and had been quite delighted to hear that her brother and his new wife would be spending a great deal of time in town or at a rented cottage near the sea when the weather got too warm to abide London.

"Why do you not marry?" she asked instead of answering his question.

"I do not marry for quite noble reasons, or so Miss Tierney says."

The brow over her left eye rose skeptically. "And what pray tell are your noble reasons?"

Roger folded his arms and looked at her — his dear friend who did not believe there was a noble bone in his body. "Do you not think me capable of being honourable?"

Her lips pursed, and her brow furrowed. "It is not that you are incapable of such," she said after a full minute of silence. "You know that I have always told you how honourable you could be. You have the potential to be a very fine gentleman who is sought after for more than his looks and a bit of fun."

Her cheeks coloured slightly as she said those last words. Impropriety of the sexual nature always made Victoria blush when she referenced it. She was as proper as he was improper. She might not agree with all of society's strictures, but her behavior was always impeccable. She assured him that it was possible to both disagree and still adhere to the rules. He was not certain he believed her.

"If you think me capable of being honourable, then why do you question so vehemently as to whether or not my reasons are noble?"

She expelled an exasperated huff. "Because I see little evidence of your nobility when it comes to the fairer sex." The blush on her cheeks deepened a shade. "And I did not question you vehemently. I questioned. That is all."

Roger's lips tipped up on one side. "I will only

tell you my reasons after you have told me your reasons for not marrying."

Her eyes grew wide, and she shook her head. "I cannot."

"Cannot or will not?"

"Will not."

That answer stopped Roger from any further prodding. They had not had any secrets – or at least not many secrets – ever. They had shared nearly everything with one another growing up, and it bothered him that she would choose now to decide she would keep something so interesting from him.

"I would not tease you," he offered.

"I know you would not, but..." She sighed and shook her head. "I would feel too foolish."

She did not trust him. She said she thought him capable of nobility, and yet, she did not actually trust him. It stung as much as if she had slapped him. He drew a breath and released it.

"Very well," he said, "then, I shall not tell you mine. You may write to Miss Tierney to discover them if you wish, but I shall not tell you."

"I have hurt you," she said softly as she placed a hand on his still folded arms.

Feeling very much like a petulant child, he

merely shrugged and changed the subject – somewhat.

"Who shall we see matched?" He would prove to her in some way that he was capable of thinking about marriage in a serious fashion.

"I really could not say," she replied. Her brow was furrowed. "Are you well? I did not mean to – "

"Perfectly," he cut off her apology. He did not wish to hear it at present. "I am perfectly well."

He was not. His closest friend in all the world had just told him in so many words that she did not trust him. However, he was not about to admit to it.

"I say we spend a day considering who might complement whom at this gathering, and then I shall begin." He leaned close to her and nudged her shoulder with his. "If you would be so kind, I should rather appreciate it if you would attempt to discover which sort of gentleman we might match with Miss Grace Love."

"Why?"

There was that skepticism again.

"She knows my reasons for not wishing to marry since we played a little game when I was visiting Clayton, and rather than heeding the fact that I have no desire to marry, she has taken it upon herself to follow me around and attempt to prove my reasons are not insurmountable." He lowered his voice. "Frankly, I do not trust her. She is very marriage minded and only seventeen." He shuddered.

"Far too young to be attached to an old man such as yourself?"

"Far too flighty. And I am not old. Might I remind you that you are only four years younger than me?"

"Younger is the important word," Victoria said with a laugh that always lifted his spirits — even when he was put out with her. "I shall see what I can learn about Miss Love."

"Thank you." Roger pulled a second small package from his pocket and after rising handed it to her.

"What is this?" She turned the item over in her hands.

He smiled. "Did you really think, my darling friend, that I would not remember your birthday as I always have?" He winked and then giving her a bow, left her so that she could open his gift in private.

Chapter 2

Victoria should have known Roger would not forget her birthday even if she were not at home. He never had. Not once in all the years she had known him, whether he was at home, school, or elsewhere, had he ever forgotten. No matter where he was, there would always be a gift for her on her birthday.

She knew what would be inside the package even before she untied the lavender ribbon that held it closed. The colour of the ribbon never changed because, while her friend might be a charming rake who sported a devil-may-care façade, he had a secret sentimental side to him, and he knew that lavender was her favourite colour.

Victoria wound the ribbon around her finger and, then slipping it off in a neat little bundle, she put it in her pocket. She would incorporate it into something she wore later. She always did, and Roger would always try to guess how she had used it. It was part of the tradition which never changed, just as what was inside was also unchanging.

Girls like flowers and pretty things like butterflies. That was what Roger had said the first time he had presented her with a birthday gift when she was eight and he was twelve. His sketches had improved since then.

She lifted the carefully cut pasteboard card from its wrapping. This year's gift was designed as a calling card might be. On the left-hand side of the card, there was a delicate daisy with its petals drooping down and slightly damaged, and a butterfly, perched on the center with its wings folded, and then on the right, in eloquent writing with several swoops and swirls, in place of her name, it bore the words: "My Dearest, Darling Friend."

Roger Shelton was a trial at times, but then, at moments like this, she remembered just why she loved him as she did. A more loyal friend could not be found. He bore her scolds with great aplomb and seemingly sought out such lectures, for why else would he share some of his exploits with her?

She scanned the room. There he was, watching

her from across the drawing room where he was just entering into a conversation with some gentlemen. She smiled at him and pressed the card to her heart. His replying look of pleasure was perhaps the best part of his gift. She sighed. He had such potential to be a much-sought-after gentleman – and not as he was now, but for proper reasons.

"What is that, Miss Hamilton?" Miss Grace Love, the very person Victoria was to seek out, plopped down on the settee.

"A birthday gift from a good friend," Victoria replied, tucking the card away before it could be examined by the young lady next to her.

"From Mr. Shelton?"

There was perhaps too much curiosity in the young lady's tone. Miss Grace almost sounded a trifle jealous.

"Yes," Victoria replied. "We are neighbours, and our parents are great friends. He brought me a few things from my father as well."

"You are friends of long-standing then?"

Victoria nodded. Her companion's tone had shifted from one of jealousy to hopefulness.

"He had said, when we were at Heathcote

together – that is my cousin's home — that he was not going to attend this party."

"He does try to avoid gatherings like this," Victoria assured her.

It was rather unusual to see Roger in a setting such as the Abernathy's House Party. He preferred soirees with gardens, alcoves, and a few less-observant chaperones. Soirees were events where one might glide in a few moments late and leave as early as was needed. However, at a house party, all gliding in and sneaking out was taken note of, and should any young lady and young gentleman be absent at the same time, rumors of compromises and wedding were sure to race ahead of the young couple's return to the room.

"It is pleasant to see him," Miss Grace said.

If words could be sighed, Miss Grace's pleasure at Roger's presence had been, and Victoria could see why Roger was hoping to rid himself of the young woman's attentions. Grace oozed what Roger would call the toxic fumes of the death of a bachelor, who would most likely not go to his final resting place, meaning his marriage chamber, willingly. Victoria felt her cheeks heat at her thoughts. He was shocking even when he was not present.

"I was surprised by his arrival." She looked at her companion. "He is not here to find a wife."

"Oh, I know," Grace assured her. "But he might change his mind."

"I very much doubt it. There is no delicate way to say this, but I would have you be warned. Mr. Shelton's reputation is not... well... it is not good. He is a charmer, who is looking for some fun and not a wife. He will flirt, but he will not offer marriage."

"Do you wish to marry him?"

Victoria blinked. That was a very forward question. "I... I... I do not have any intention of marrying just yet."

"You do not?" The question was accompanied by a look of utter horror. "But do you not fear being thought of as on the shelf?"

"Not yet." In a year or two that might become a concern.

The young woman next to Victoria gave her a perplexed look as if such a thing were too difficult to comprehend.

"I should very much like to marry," Grace said with some feeling.

That was not a great revelation to Victoria, but

it was a good opening to discover information she could use to keep Roger unfettered. "You are so young. Why would you wish to marry so soon?"

Grace pulled her lower lip between her teeth and leaned closer to Victoria, lowering her voice to a whisper when she spoke. "Well, you see, my sister is soon to be married so remaining at home would be dreadfully dull without her."

"Is that the only reason?" It was not a very good one in Victoria's opinion.

"No, I also love children and should find great pleasure in decorating my own home without my sister telling me how it should be done."

Decorating one's home and being rid of one's sibling were also not good reasons to marry. A house could only be decorated so many times, and siblings? Well...

"In my experience," Victoria said, "older sisters will still tell you how things should be done even after both they and you are married. I have seen it."

"Felicity will be too busy with her parsonage," Grace assured Victoria.

"That is happy for her then."

"And me," Grace added.

"Quite so," Victoria agreed. No matter how

much she wished to dissuade the young woman of her ill-thought-out notions, it was not Victoria's job to do so — if it was even possible. Her task was to discover what sort of gentleman Miss Grace Love might consider for a husband.

"Aside from my friend, who has just arrived, have any of the other gentlemen caught your eye? You need not worry about telling me, for I assure you that I am only here because my mother requires me to be. I will not try to steal any of the gentlemen here away from you."

"Oh!" Grace blew out a breath as if something of great importance and effort had been asked of her. She obviously took the duty of finding and securing a husband quite seriously.

"Let me see." Once again, she drew her bottom lip between her teeth as she studied the gentlemen in the room. "Mr. Ainsley has very nice eyes. They crinkle when he smiles as if he feels the expression throughout his whole being. It is good to find a man who can feel so deeply, do you not agree?"

Victoria nodded. "A feeling husband is a good thing. I should like someone who could commiserate with me on things."

"Mr. Ramsey is..." She sighed.

"He does cut a fine figure," Victoria agreed.

"And so tall."

"That he is," Victoria agreed. Mr. Ramsey was likely the tallest and broadest gentleman in attendance. "A lady would feel well protected with him by her side."

"Oh, she would."

Victoria pressed her lips together at the near desperation in Grace's tone. "What of status and fortune? Do you prefer a title? Or do you wish for an estate in a particular location or of a certain size? Would a home in town be desired?"

"I had not thought about the size of a man's estate, although I had thought a home in town, even if just rented for the season would be quite nice."

"If you enjoy the season, that is a must. But what of a title?"

Grace shrugged. "A title would be nice, but truthfully, it is not necessary. As long as he has a sufficient income to be comfortable – even after children are born."

"One must not forget about the children or their education," Victoria agreed.

"Yes, yes, their education must be the best. My

parents spared no expense on my or my sister's education. We are both very accomplished." Victoria's companion lifted her chin as she said the last part.

"Then you will wish for a gentleman who values such things."

"Without a doubt, but what gentleman would not?"

Victoria grimaced. "Mr. Shelton," she whispered. "He is much more of the philosophy that education can be found in play and leisure. His children would, of course, have a governess or tutor, but he is not favourably disposed to sending them away." She shrugged. "I believe he did not enjoy his own schooling and thinks it can be accomplished in a better fashion than what he experienced."

"Indeed? Well, that is most shocking!"

"I agree." It was a lie. Victoria liked the idea of being able to instruct her daughters, should she be so blessed as to have any, in a great variety of subjects – even those not considered useful to the female mind. "However, since you are so accomplished, you might do well in such a situation. I am certain you could teach your children many things – music, art, language, reading, and so forth."

"Me? Teach my children?" Grace's lashes fluttered. "I had not considered I should have to do that."

"You would find it unpleasant then?"

"Intensely." She sighed. "But Mr. Shelton is so perfect."

"Dashing, wealthy, a good conversationalist, and even an excellent dancer," Victoria said in support of Grace's statement. "But then there is also his penchant for pleasure which could cause an issue."

"Oh, no! He has said it will not."

Victoria's brow furrowed. "He has said what?"

Grace scooted closer to Victoria and turned her head to look directly at her companion. Then, in a low whisper, spoken in such a fashion that her lips moved very little, she said, "He thinks he is not ready to marry because he knows that when he does, he will have to give up his freedom since being a husband comes with great responsibility. He does not take such things lightly."

"He said that?"

Grace's head bobbed up and down.

Victoria looked across the room to where Roger

was deep in conversation. Did he consider marriage so seriously? There still was no evidence of such a thing.

She shifted and the corner of the card in her pocket poked her leg and her conscience. Roger treated friendship with great respect. It would stand to reason that he would also treat a wife in the same fashion. He taunted his mother – and hers – but he was always true to his word to them both. No wonder he had sounded so hurt earlier.

"There is still the matter, however, of educating your children, and that is a difficult thing to overlook. So, what if you and I attempt to discover what Mr. Ramsey and Mr. Ainsley think on that subject?"

"You would assist me?"

"I would." Victoria would do anything to keep her friend from an unhappy match, even if it meant assisting this young woman in finding a husband.

"That is so generous of you. My mother is excessively busy with Felicity. We expect there to be a happy announcement from that front in the near future, so I dare not pull Mama away from such a thing. But..."

"You would also like your chance at happiness?"

Grace nodded vigorously. "I would like that so very much."

"Well, then," Victoria said, rising and extending a hand to her young companion, "shall we take a turn around the room and see if we can discover some happiness?"

Chapter 3

Roger skirted the edge of the room. Their host had announced that there would be an impromptu musical exhibition in two hours time, and since he had no desire to be pressed into singing or some such thing, Roger was making his escape as quickly as he could.

"Mr. Shelton, do you sing?" Miss Grace stepped into his path.

"He does not like to sing in public." Victoria's look was apologetic.

She had likely attempted to keep Miss Grace from approaching him with her plan to conscribe him to a musical display.

"But it would be so delightful to have him sing while I played."

Could the young woman look any more forlorn without actually pouting? Roger did not like sulking misses. He did not like flighty, fidgety misses. He did not like misses who clung to a fellow or followed him around without invitation. There were a great number of misses he did not like, and house parties seemed to be where they gathered to perfect their evils. Due to the attentions of several hopeful misses, the afternoon had been trying to say the least. He was only staying for a few days to humor his mother. Then, he would sneak off to some friend's home which was free from females seeking to snare him.

"I have never sung with anyone playing except for when required to do so for my and Miss Hamilton's parents."

Victoria's eyes narrowed just as Grace chirped with delight. "Then, perhaps Miss Hamilton could play, and you and I could sing."

"No," he said at the same time as Victoria.

"I do not sing duets," he continued.

"And I do not wish to perform. I hope to only enjoy the music," Victoria added.

Roger would be sorry to not hear his friend sing or play. She was not without a good bit of talent. However, he also understood her desire to not be paraded in front of all the gentlemen here as if she were actually interested in marrying one of them. She was not. She had said so.

"Did I hear talk of a duet?" Mrs. Abernathy had turned from the direction in which she was headed to join Roger's unfortunate group.

"No," Roger answered while Grace said "yes."

Mrs. Abernathy laughed. "It cannot be both yes and no. It would be excellent to hear some gentlemen lending their voices to our production." She held up a hand as Roger opened his mouth to refuse to sing once again. Her other hand waved a set of gentlemen towards her.

Much to Roger's dismay, the three gentlemen obediently responded by joining them.

"I have had the notion that some duets would be just the thing for our musicale. I am certain there is at least one or two of you gentlemen who would be willing to assist me in this," Mrs. Abernathy said.

The suggestion was met with silence and an eagerly expectant look on Grace's face.

"My Amelia is playing the harp, of course. However, she can also play the piano very well, and I am certain it would not tax her too much to prepare two numbers." The lady smiled and straightened the cuff of her sleeve. "She is very accomplished."

There was a lilt to her voice that suggested the gentlemen gathered around her should consider her daughter as an excellent choice for a wife – because she could play more than one instrument, which was ridiculous in Roger's way of thinking.

His left eyebrow rose as he shared an amused look with Victoria. How often had they discussed what he considered an accomplished wife to be? Not once in all of those discussions had the necessity of playing both the piano and harp arisen as requirements for Mrs. Shelton.

"Miss Hamilton and Miss Grace could play for two of you and..." her eyes searched the room. "I am certain we could find someone to pair with the remaining gentleman."

"I am not playing," Victoria said softly. "I am certain my skills are not prepared to be put on display with such short notice. I am dreadful about practising, you see." Her cheeks flushed, and she glanced uneasily at the gentlemen of the group who were not Roger.

Roger's brow furrowed. Why would she care what those gentlemen thought of her lack of practice? Had she set her cap at one of them? The thought caused his scowl to deepen, though he knew it could not be true. She had declared she was not ready to marry.

"I am certain you must have one song that is familiar enough to play," Mr. Carlyle said with a smile.

"I am afraid I do not," Victoria replied, returning his smile.

"A simple piece could be practised with time to spare," Mr. Carlyle pressed much to Roger's annoyance.

Victoria had said she did not wish to play. Why could it not be left at that? Why must this... this... popinjay attempt to persuade her to do what she did not wish to do? He folded his arms and glared at Carlyle.

"What of Miss Grace," he said. "She was eager a moment ago to have someone sing with her."

Carlyle shrugged and looked to his friends.

The rude dolt! That man was not good enough for Grace – for whom Roger only cared a trifle –, and a far cry from even touching the edges of good enough for Victoria. Carlyle was one gentleman at whom Victoria would not set her cap if Roger had anything to say about it – which he would make certain he did.

"How about you Mr. Ainsley?" Victoria asked.

Roger stopped glaring at Carlyle long enough to notice a speaking look pass between Grace and Victoria. Mr. Ainsley, was it? He had seen the two ladies conversing with several young bucks during the past hour and a half. One of them had been Ainsley.

The eyebrows on the gentleman being questioned flew upwards as his eyes grew wide. "I am not opposed to singing."

"Will you sing with Miss Grace playing?" Roger asked.

The gentleman looked as if he wanted to loosen his cravat. Poor fellow to be put upon as he was being. Not that Roger felt too much pity for him, for the removal of Grace and the probable match that could be made was worth the gentleman's unease.

"Yes, yes, of course," Mr. Ainsley muttered.

"Excellent!" Mrs. Abernathy cried. "That is one duet arranged. Now, about Mr. Carlyle, Miss Hamilton."

Oh, for heaven's sake! Did no one understand the words *I am not playing*?

"I am sorry," Victoria said with a small shake of her head.

"Then, perhaps my Amelia would suit, Mr. Carlyle?"

The man did not look as if he wished to be suited by anyone, save Victoria. He gave Victoria one more pleading look.

"I will see what I can find," Victoria said.

She was going to play for the fool? Roger snapped his mouth shut.

"Then there is only Mr. Shelton and Mr. Walcott who need accompanists."

"No, it is just Mr. Walcott," Roger inserted. "And if he were to sing while Miss Abernathy played, all your troubles would be at an end."

The lady before him gave him a cajoling look. "Mr. Shelton, you simply must sing. I can tell you must be very good at it for when you speak there is such a melodious quality to your voice."

"No," Roger said. "I have already told Miss Grace that I have only ever sung with Miss Hamilton playing, and since she is already playing for Mr. Carlyle and requires time to practice for that performance, you will just have to do without me. However, I promise to applaud loudly for Miss

Grace, Miss Hamilton, and, of course, your daughter. It will be a great pleasure to partake in listening to all the musical selections." He bowed and made to leave them.

"Then, Miss Hamilton simply must play for you, and I shall find another lady to assist Mr. Carlyle."

Roger shook his head. "Oh, no, Madame. I could not do such a thing to Mr. Carlyle. He worked so hard to acquire Miss Hamilton. It would be a grave injustice to snatch his prize from him." Even if it would make Roger feel quite happy to cause the gentleman some discomfort after the way he mulishly pursued Victoria. "On this, I will not be moved," he added to his host.

Mrs. Abernathy scowled, but only for a moment. Then, her ever-pleasant smile – the same unflappable smile every good hostess wore – found its way back onto her face.

"I shall applaud the loudest," Roger assured her.

"Wait," Victoria said before he could slip away. "I had wished to speak to you." She turned to Mr. Carlyle. "I will join you, Mr. Ainsley, and Miss Grace in the music room as soon as possible."

The scowl Carlyle wore was satisfying, and with a small flourish, Roger extended his arm to his friend, and the two slipped out of the room to find their way to the garden.

"I have spoken to Miss Grace as you requested," Victoria began. "And you were correct that she is determined to marry – excessively determined. However, I believe I have convinced her that you are not perfect."

"She thought me perfect, did she?" Roger chuckled. He knew he was far from perfect, though he also knew he did cut a fine figure and had very charming manners — most times.

"He is perfect," Victoria said with a sigh while batting her lashes.

Roger laughed outright at that. The foolish actions of a young debutante became even more ridiculous when demonstrated by a lady as refined and sensible as his darling friend. "Which imperfection did you expose to her?"

They rounded a hedge and began down a path bordered by delicate flowers on one side and a great expanse of lawn on the other. There were a few couples making use of the lawn to sit and, Roger assumed, practice their musical numbers.

"Several," Victoria replied.

Roger pulled his eyes from observing the couples on the lawn to look at her. She was grinning broadly.

"However, Miss Grace did not seem to think your penchant for female companionship would be a problem for a wife."

"It would not be," Roger agreed. His time to be carefree was now and not when he had a wife and family.

"I was not aware of how seriously you viewed taking a wife." Her head dipped. "I am sorry. I should have considered how loyal you are to your family and friends, but I did not."

She had obviously heard his reasons for not wishing to marry. It was gratifying to hear her praise of him. Miss Tierney had praised him for his reasons when he had shared them at Heathcote that morning, and it had been quite pleasant to hear. However, it was far more gratifying hearing it from Victoria than it had been from Miss Tierney or would be from anyone else for that matter, for Victoria knew him best.

"The one item which Miss Grace could not reason away, however," Victoria continued, "was your view on educating your children at home. She is not keen to take on the task of education even if she is highly accomplished. Therefore, you will need to be adamant about a wife being an integral part of your children's education if you wish to keep her unfavourably disposed to pursuing you."

"Noted." That would not be a hardship, for he *was* adamant about his wife, just like himself, being involved with the development of their children's minds. "And have you discovered the gentleman with whom we might match her? Is it Ainsley?"

Victoria nodded. "He is one candidate. She also finds Mr. Ramsey appealing, and we discovered over a very long hour and a half of speaking to various gentleman that Mr. Yardley is not without his charms."

"Yardley, Ainsley, and Ramsey. Well done." He smiled at her. He had known she would not fail him. She never did. "And did you discover any gents who captured your fancy, my lady?"

She rolled her eyes just as he expected she would. However, her reply of "no" was not as quick in coming as he expected. It was almost as if she were pausing to consider some fellow before making her decision. Or perhaps, she was hiding the truth from him. That would make two secrets she held and would not share with him, and he did not like it one bit.

"I should go practice."

"Yes, we would not wish to make Carlyle wait," Roger grumbled.

He did not wish to return Victoria to the house. He wanted to make another, longer circuit of the garden with her at his side, but he would see her to the music room as she requested merely because she had requested it. Then, he would make his way to his room and while away his time lying on his bed, alone, with a book. It sounded dreadfully dull, but it was also the one place he knew he would not be called on to escort some lady on a walk or be expected to take part in empty conversations. How many times could he describe his estate? Or tell a lady which horse in his stable was his fastest or favourite?

"How long are you staying?" Victoria asked as they ascended the stairs to the music room.

"I had hoped three days at most, but if we are to see Miss Grace happily settled..."

"You do not think you can manage the feat in three days?" She teased.

He shook his head. Miss Grace did not appear to

be the quickest study and persuading a gentleman into marriage could prove to be tricky if the gentleman did not wish to be persuaded. Roger would have to discover which of the three candidates Victoria had mentioned was most eager to be settled into his future. As he considered these things, he and Victoria walked in companionable silence to the music room door.

"I am happy to have you here," she said.

He held the door partially open but closed it at her admission. "Why do you not yet wish to marry? I believe you have already heard my reasons."

She shook her head. "I just cannot tell you. I assure you that if I did, I would be embarrassed beyond recovery."

"Will you ever tell me?"

She drew in a breath and released it slowly as a maid scurried past them. "Maybe on the day I marry, for then it shall no longer matter."

He scowled. It was not the answer he had hoped to hear. He had thought she might tell him if they were at home. He had not thought she would make him wait so long as until her wedding day – which she had admitted was not something she was seeking to have happen any time soon.

"Perhaps I shall just have to find you a husband," he teased, though his heart was not truly in it. "Since that is the only way I shall ever know your secret." His heart was feeling rather bitter about that.

"Please, do not. I beg you."

He ignored the fear in her tone and continued on his teasing path. "Is there no one here who could charm you from your single state?"

Again, she unexpectedly paused before replying. "None who would have me."

Were those tears in her eyes? Bitterness fled and regret filled its place in his heart.

"I apologize. I have gone too far in my quest to know your secret, but we have shared so much." He wanted to wrap his arms around her and hold her close so that she could feel his remorse for causing her discomfort.

"One day," she whispered. "One day, perhaps we can share this secret as well."

He nodded and opened the door slowly. He would have to accept that for now.

"Are you well?" he asked as she passed him to enter the room.

"How can I be anything but well when you are here?" she said lightly.

He shook his head. "Seriously, Vic, are you well?"

"I would be better if I did not have to practice the piano, but yes, I am well. You have not upset me."

Perhaps he had not upset her, but his own heart was far from settled as he turned to seek the safety and solitude of his room.

Chapter 4

Victoria settled into a chair next to the piano and shuffled through the available sheets of music looking for a song that was familiar.

"Is my brother treating you well?" Diana Berkeley whispered as she took the chair next to.

Victoria glanced up from the pages she held and smiled at Roger's older sister, who had agreed to be her chaperone for this house party so that Victoria's mother would not have to attend. There was a young Berkeley boy who would be visiting Roger's mother, and since Mrs. Hamilton did not yet have any grandchildren, she had wished to help Mrs. Shelton enjoy her grandson.

"He always does," Victoria replied before turning her attention back to the sheets of music she held.

"What about that one?"

Victoria shook her head. "I am forever getting the timing wrong in the middle. If I were just playing, I could fudge my way through it, but that is not possible when someone is singing." She sighed.

"Is something amiss?"

"I do not wish to play."

"Then, why are you?" Diana was a lot like her brother in not bowing to the demands of others. If Diana had not wished to play. Diana would not have played.

Victoria shrugged.

"You felt guilty," Diana said.

It was not a question. It was a statement of fact. A very accurate statement of fact.

"I would not have told your mother."

"I have no doubt that Mrs. Abernathy would have seen to that duty for you. I could see it in the way she arched her brow at me when prodding me to play for Mr. Carlyle." Victoria lowered her voice and lifted a piece of music to hide behind as she whispered. "I confess that I was also fearful of how Mr. Carlyle would portray me to the other gentlemen."

"Are you considering any of them?"

"Not presently," Victoria replied. "However, one

must not paint herself as unyielding when she does not have the advantage of youth on her side."

She lowered the piece of music she had used as a shield. "I shall have to marry eventually, and I have not met every gentleman here. Most I have seen at one function or another in town, but I have not had an opportunity to converse with any of them. It would be foolish to hinder my chances over a piece of music."

"But I thought you were intent upon –"

"Yes, well," Victoria cut her off before she could finish her comment, "that is as likely to happen now as it has always been."

"You are not giving up hope, are you?"

"What do you think of Mr. Ainsley?" Victoria asked, ignoring her friend and chaperone's question.

"Does this mean you are giving up hope?" If Diana was anything, she was persistent. "Do you like Mr. Ainsley?"

"He is a very nice gentleman, but I am not asking for myself. Miss Grace, who has, as I understand it from Roger, spent some time at Stratsbury Park attempting to sway your brother from his single state, seems to think Mr. Ainsley might be a better alternative as a husband."

"Oh!" Diana's eyes grew wide as understanding dawned on her. "I have only heard good things about him from the other chaperones. His finances are good. His country estate is not lacking. He does have the care of his mother, but she is a dear lady – or so I have been led to believe. One can never be too certain with these chaperones. They might be trying to rid themselves of an unwanted prospect instead of speaking truthfully."

"This whole marrying business is a bit of a nightmare if you ask me. Does anyone truly know who she is marrying when she agrees to be wed?" Victoria shook her head in disgust. It was the part of the season she liked the least. It was difficult to discern the true intentions of anyone when a proper front must be displayed at all times. The length of a dance or a call in a drawing room was not enough time to learn much about someone. Topics were kept to the mundane and safe. One must not venture into areas of discussion that were of much substance.

"One does if she does not rush into it. Berkley and I knew each other for nearly a year before we were betrothed. Be patient. There is no need to have the thing decided by the end of this party. Unless, of course..." She smiled knowingly but did not finish her thought. She did not need to finish it, for she knew precisely where Victoria's heart lay.

"I have sung this one before." Mr. Carlyle, who was holding a sheet of music, had approached them. "'The True Lover's Farewell'," he said, presenting her with the music.

Victoria shook her head. "I am afraid I have never played that song." She picked up the music which lay on top of the pile on her lap. "This one I know quite well."

"'The Ash Grove'?" He eyed the piece. "It seems simple enough."

"It is not complex. Mr. Shelton and I have performed it several times. It is one of my father's favourites, and so he requests it often. I doubt I shall stumble at all while playing, for I shall be able to listen, and my fingers will just do as they have learned to do."

"It is a favourite of your father's, you say?"

The way Mr. Carlyle's eyebrows rose in curiosity caused Victoria to wonder if she should not have just accepted the new piece he had presented her.

His look was too calculating. It was as if he were considering how he might use this to impress her father or some such thing.

"And do you also like this song?" he asked.

Very much so, especially when Roger sang it. Mrs. Abernathy had not been wrong in her assessment of Mr. Shelton's ability to sing. However, that was not what she wished for Mr. Carlyle to know. She wanted Mr. Carlyle to know as little about her as possible, so she said, "It is a very pleasant song."

From the smile he wore, she knew he was satisfied with her answer.

"Then, it shall be perfect. Do you think we might try it now?" He motioned to the piano.

Victoria tamped down her irritation about having to play anything at all, handed the remaining sheets of music to Diana, and took her place at the instrument. The things one had to endure to please one's mother!

Thirty minutes later, once Mr. Carlyle, who was as exacting as she had imagined him to be, was satisfied with both his performance and hers, Victoria was allowed to quit her spot at the piano.

"Of all the frustrating, arrogant men!" she complained in a whisper to Diana. "Did you hear him instructing me on how best to play?"

Diana linked her arm with Victoria's. "I did. You bore it quite well." She glanced over her shoulder to where Mr. Carlyle still stood near the piano, singing the song to himself. "I rather think he might be considering you."

Victoria shuddered. "Please, do not accept any offers from him for anything. I shall take to my bed or be taken home early with a horridly contagious disease if necessary. I cannot abide such an imperious person!"

Diana chuckled. "Perhaps you should refuse to do as he says next time you meet so that he will know of your disgust of his fussiness. You gave him no reason to think you were anything but pleased to perform as directed. It was really not like you."

"He is the biggest gossip, Diana! I have heard him making mince of more than one lady."

"And if he were to say one bad thing about you, I would only need to tell my husband or my brother, and the man would be sorry for having ever even *thought* of you in a light that was not positive." She gave Victoria a stern look. "Do not let him lead if you do not wish to follow. That is it. Plain and simple."

Victoria sighed. Diana was correct, of course.

"If I had not heard him denigrating Miss Deighton last season..."

Diana gasped. "Is he the source of her troubles?"

Victoria nodded.

"Does my brother know this?"

"I could not say."

"I would think he does not if he allowed you to spend time with such a gentleman."

"Diana, I am nothing more than a friend to Roger. It would seem very strange if he did not allow me to spend time with other gentlemen." There was no reason for Roger to stand guard over her as if she were his.

"Little more than a friend," Diana scoffed.

Victoria gave her a pointed look, and she said no more.

Grace waved to them as they stood by the door and then turned to say something to Mr. Ainsley before hurrying over to join them. Neither Victoria nor Diana could leave without her. It would not do to leave a young woman alone in a room with two gentlemen and no chaperone.

"He is simply wonderful," Grace said when they had entered the hall. "His voice is divine. I am certain I could listen to him sing for hours, although he is perhaps not as good as Mr. Carlyle. You were very fortunate to have acquired such a good partner." She sighed. "And his care for how you played. I found it very touching." Her hand rested on her heart.

"I found it tiring," Victoria said. "He was condescending and overbearing."

"Then, you do not like him?" Grace looked at Victoria as if there were something wrong with her. "He is so handsome."

"I wish for more than a pretty face," Victoria replied. "I want someone who will treat me with respect, and I fear the only person Mr. Carlyle respects is Mr. Carlyle."

"How did Mr. Ainsley treat you?" Diana interjected.

"He was very kind. He asked after my comfort many times, and he excused all my mistakes while encouraging me to try again."

"You see!" Diana cried. "That is how a young man should treat a young lady. Mr. Ainsley is the sort of gentleman one should seek. Even if his eyes are not as deep a brown as Mr. Carlyle's and if, in terms of stature, he does not tower over any of the other men, his character sounds as if it is all that it should be."

"Do you really think so?" Grace asked eagerly.

"Yes," Diana answered firmly. "I have no doubt in my mind that Mr. Ainsley could make a fine husband for some young lady."

That seemed to make Grace think quite well of herself if one could judge such a thing from the lift of her chin and the smile on her lips.

"Do we still need to discover more about Mr. Yardley or Mr. Ramsey?" Victoria inquired.

"Hmmm." Grace's brow furrowed.

"I think it is a good idea if we do," Diana answered. "One does not select a hat without trying several, and I dare say it would be foolish to not consider the other gentlemen," she held up a finger, "unless, of course, your heart is engaged. Then, we must not waiver from our objective."

They stopped in front of the door to Victoria and Diana's room.

"Come," Diana said, "we will refresh ourselves and discover your heart's intent in our room." She opened the door. "I will send a message to your mother so that she does not worry about where you are. She was quite pleased to allow me to keep watch over you. I am certain she will not mind if I continue to do so."

Grace entered the room behind Diana. "Oh, I am sure she is far too busy with my sister. Felicity does like to sneak off at times." The young girl plopped down on the window seat. "This is an excellent view!"

"Yes, well," Diana said, "Victoria is not without a substantial fortune. An excellent view is expected."

Grace blinked as she turned to Victoria. "I had no idea you were an heiress."

"I would not say heiress," Victoria countered.

"I would," Diana said in a loud whisper. "But Victoria does not like to speak of such things. She finds them vulgar."

"I do not! I just think that a lady should be valued for more than the amount of money attached to her name."

"I am certain she should be, but that would not have gained us such a spacious room with such an excellent view."

"It really is a beautiful garden," Grace said.

"Mother, Felicity, and I have a room that overlooks the drive. It is the same room we use whenever we are visiting Miss Abernathy. She and Felicity are particular friends, you see."

"Pull the bell, please, Victoria," Diana said as she took a seat at the desk near the window. "This message must get sent to Mrs. Love straightaway. We would not wish for her to worry that her daughter has gone missing."

Victoria moved to do as requested while Grace set forth on an explanation of how her mother rarely worried about her. It was Felicity, it seemed, who was the cause for concern.

"And she was found in the garden – alone with Mr. Everett Clayton. She is fortunate that Mother was not there or the scolding that she would have had to endure would have been great indeed!" Grace leaned forward and whispered. "She was not wearing her bonnet, and her cheeks were very rosy when she returned to the house. She will not tell me what she was doing, but I am not so stupid as she thinks. I have heard what happens in dark corners of gardens."

To Victoria, it looked as if the young lady was

quite interested in what happened in those dark garden corners.

"Proper young ladies do not find themselves alone in gardens with gentlemen." Diana's tone was firm but gentle.

"Oh, no, of course not." A smile tipped the right side of Grace's mouth. "Unless she wishes to marry the gentleman."

Diana put down her pen. "Not even then," she said sternly. "It is a dangerous game your sister plays. A gentleman who is trapped is not a gentleman with whom it will be easy to live after the vows have been said."

"And then there are those gentlemen who will refuse to offer," Victoria added.

Grace gasped. "Are there really such gentlemen?"

"Sadly, yes," Diana said. "My brother would be one, I should think."

"Your brother?"

"Mr. Shelton," Victoria explained.

"Mr. Shelton is your brother?"

It was unlikely that the girl's eyes could grow any rounder than they were.

"He is, indeed. And I know for a fact that he

would not do what would be expected if he thought he had been trapped. He has a very peculiar notion of what is and is not honourable, and since a lady trapping a gentleman is not honourable, it justifies the gentleman in refusing to offer for her."

"But she would be ruined!" Grace cried.

"Most certainly," Diana agreed, "but such is the consequence for her duplicity. That is what he would say."

"I can hear him saying it," Victoria agreed.

Grace's mouth hung open for a full half minute before she snapped it closed. "And he wishes for a wife to help educate his children?"

Victoria nodded.

As Grace shook her head, a look of utter aghast bewilderment suffused her features, and Victoria knew, beyond a shadow of a doubt, that Roger was safe from the machinations of Miss Grace Love.

Chapter 5

"Good day, brother dear," Diana said as Roger took the chair next to her in the Abernathy's music room. "How have you been keeping yourself?" She lifted an eyebrow and gave him a teasing look.

He looked around the room before ducking his head closer to her ear and whispering, "I have been reading."

"Indeed?" There was a hint of laughter in her tone. "Mother will not be best pleased to hear you are secreting yourself away with a book when you should be looking for the future mother of her grandchildren."

"She has you for that," Roger returned. "Would you be increasing again?" He darted his eyes around the room once again as he whispered the question. "It would be a wonderful thing if you were since Mother would be too distracted with your health and all things infant to pay much attention to my single state."

"Really, Roger! You are going to have to come to the point someday, and you are not growing any younger, although the debutantes seem to be."

Roger sighed. "You mean they are growing younger, sillier, and harder to abide."

"That is precisely what I mean. I do not understand how some gentlemen can wait to marry until they are well into their thirties and seem content with a frivolous young thing." Her eye narrowed when Roger smirked. "You are incorrigible! There is more to marriage than the marriage bed."

"Why must you also assume I do not take the role of husband seriously?"

"Because you rarely appear serious about anything."

That was true. He could not fault her logic. He did like to sport a devil-may-care attitude. It was so much more enjoyable than being dour and somber.

Her shoulder bumped his when she leaned closer to ask, "Who besides me has accused you of not taking the role of husband seriously?"

Roger scowled as he watched Victoria speaking to Carlyle.

"Victoria," he muttered.

How she could countenance a popinjay like Carlyle with such equanimity as to smile and look interested in whatever the man was saying was beyond him!

There were times to be polite and times to be disinterested. This was a time to affect an air of indifference. A lady did not present herself as attentive at a house party unless she wished to encourage the suit of a gentleman. There were far too many who were thinking very seriously about marrying at a gathering such as this for an appearance of attentiveness to any gentleman to be thought of as anything less than an incentive to pursue the obliging lady. Paying such marked attention, as Victoria seemed to be doing presently, was akin to drawing forth a ravenous lion by placing an injured and bleeding animal in front of it.

"I thought you enjoyed music," Diana said.

"I do."

"Then, you might wish to stop glaring as if you want to run through the next person to step up to the piano."

Perhaps he did not wish to gravely injure the *next*

person to perform, but there was Carlyle. Roger would not mind seeing that gentleman properly laid out on the lawn with some sort of wound.

"Mr. Carlyle has a lovely voice." Diana had followed Roger's glare and found the object of his discontent. "He is singing 'The Ash Grove' since Victoria is so familiar with that piece of music."

Roger's scowl deepened. That was the song he sang with Victoria.

"He was particularly interested to hear that the song is a favourite of Mr. Hamilton."

Roger eyed his sister skeptically.

"I did not tell him that. Victoria did." She sighed. "I think he is quite smitten with her, but then who could blame him. She is not flighty, she behaves just as a proper young lady should, and she is well-dowered. I know I am prejudiced, but Miss Hamilton is one of the best choices at this party."

"I would not argue with you about that," Roger muttered. "But *he* is not the best choice of gentleman." He turned his full attention back to his sister. "She could do far better than him."

Diana blinked. "How so?"

"He thinks far too well and too often of himself."

"An air of arrogance is not always a bad thing,"

Diana refuted. "He is confident. Confidence is a good quality to have in a husband."

"No," Roger grumbled. "He is not merely confident. He thinks of no one save himself. Would you have Victoria tied to a gentleman who does not consider her an equal or of enough importance to see to her needs ahead of his?"

Diana studied Mr. Carlyle for a moment before replying. "I suppose I would not, but if he is who makes Victoria happy, then who am I to stand in her way?"

"Her chaperone," the words rumbled from him.

Could his sister seriously not see what was wrong with a match between Carlyle and Victoria? He would expect such a thing from his mother, but he had always thought Diana to be more sensible than their mother when it came to making matches.

"As her chaperone, your job is to ensure she makes a good connection – one which will bring her the most advantage. And you know I do not speak of money or position. This is Vic. There are a good many things more important than riches and titles when seeing her settled."

His words had earned him the full attention of his sister.

"And what, pray tell," Diana asked, "is more important than a secure financial future?"

His eyes narrowed. "Her heart – as if you do not know." If he did not trust his sister as completely as he did, he would think she was leading him down a merry path.

"And Miss Grace? Do we wish to consider her heart as well when we are scheming?"

"As long as her heart is not set on me, you may do anything you wish with it."

She was nowhere near Roger or even looking in his direction, yet he could feel the disapproval of Victoria at such a statement. He sighed.

"It would, I suppose, be best if we took care not to damage the young lady's heart."

There. Surely, that would satisfy both his sister and Victoria.

"Mr. Ainsley seems a good candidate. He was quite attentive to Miss Grace while they were practising, and he seems a respectable sort of fellow. I shall do my best to encourage them to spend some time together if I can," his sister whispered.

That was good. He turned to say something of that nature to his sister.

"And then, I shall have to decide upon someone to recommend to Victoria since you do not think Mr. Carlyle will do."

"Victoria is in no hurry to marry," he protested.

His sister raised a skeptical brow.

"She said so."

"What a lady says and what she truly thinks are not always the same."

Roger crossed his arms. "Vic is not one of those ladies."

"If you say so," his sister whispered as the first young lady took her place at the piano.

He did say so. He knew so. Victoria always told him what she thought – often more directly than was entirely proper. Of course, that was typically because he had provoked her to it. He shook his head. No. If Victoria were intent upon finding a husband, she would have said something.

His eyes narrowed as Carlyle leaned toward Victoria and whispered something.

"If it must be done, then choose anyone but Carlyle," he whispered to his sister.

"Will you help me?"

He shrugged. Could he help her? He had no desire to see Victoria marry just yet. He enjoyed her friendship too much to wish her taken from him. Oh, he would still be allowed to visit her, but it would not be the same as meeting on a nearly daily basis.

"I will consider it." That was the best he could offer his sister at present. No, that was not the best he could do. "Present your ideas of who might be a good option to me before you say anything to Victoria. I will vet them. No fortune hunters. No gentlemen who care more about their horses or jacket than anything else. And no scoundrels."

Victoria deserved only the best husband.

Roger joined in the polite applause around him and settled back to listen to the next selection while discounting each and every gentleman in attendance as not good enough for his darling friend.

~*~*~

"There are lemonade and sweets set up in the garden," Mrs. Abernathy said when the last musician had risen from the piano.

"Oh, how fortuitous," Diana exclaimed. "I had expected the gentlemen to scuttle off to some activity while we females would be left to stitch in the drawing room. And that is not conducive to making matches. I really do not know why more hostesses do not plan an abundance of activities to keep the ladies and gentlemen together at these things." She rose and took her brother's arm. "How are sparks to be ignited if the individuals whom we wish to have matched are kept apart? It seems very backward to the purpose of a house party. Would you not agree?"

"I would not dare to disagree," Roger replied with a smile. "However, I must say I enjoy the times of separation, for often the chaperones are not as attentive in those moments, and... well... ladies can be persuaded to steal away for a few moments."

She swatted his arm. "Really, Roger! You are a rogue."

"Only because I am not yet ready to marry," Roger refuted.

"Over there," Diana pointed to the left with her fan. "Mr. Carlyle is absconding with my charge." Her lips twitched.

Roger wished to argue with her that it was not truly absconding if they were all headed to the same place, but he did not because it was far more important to him that they reach Carlyle and Victoria quickly. The less time Victoria spent alone with that gentleman, the better.

"Mr. Shelton, Mrs. Berkeley," Miss Grace called to them.

Roger groaned at the delay the young lady posed.

"Was it not the best afternoon of music ever?" she cried when they approached.

"Oh, it was amongst the best I have attended," Diana agreed. "You sang beautifully, Mr. Ainsley."

"Thank you." He smiled at Grace. "My accompanist was quite good."

"Delightfully so," Diana said.

"To be sure," Roger muttered as he attempted to see through the door to the garden and catch a glimpse of Victoria.

"Miss Hamilton played beautifully, as well," Mr. Ainsley continued. "Simple songs are often the most enjoyable."

Roger eyed the gentleman. Was he complimenting Victoria while he had Grace on his arm for any particular reason? It would be a very shabby thing indeed if Ainsley were flattering another lady with hopes of securing some support from her chaperone while in the presence of a lady such as Grace who so obviously admired him.

Roger took a moment to imagine skewering the gentleman with a pointed question regarding his intentions. The thought of Ainsley squirming at such a question cause Roger's lips to tip up with amusement even as he once again attempted to see Victoria through the open garden door while his sister went on and on about favouring simple musical selections over grand arias.

"I think there is a time and a place where each is best," Miss Grace said. "Do you not agree, Mr. Shelton?"

Roger returned his attention to his group. "I could not say as I was considering the refreshment to be found in a glass of lemonade rather than attending to your conversation."

"Oh!" Grace cried. "Do not let us detain you any longer."

"Thank you." He really could not get out to the garden quickly enough.

"Join us," Diana invited. "I really should find my charge and congratulate her on a job well done."

It took very little time to find Victoria when they finally reached the garden. Pleasantries – tiring pleasantries – were exchanged along with congrat-ulations from one lady to another and back.

"Mr. Carlyle, your performance was divine," Mrs. Abernathy cooed as she came to inspect the table upon which the refreshments were laid. "We really should have you sing with my Amelia when next there is an opportunity. Her abilities would highlight yours so well."

"I am not certain I can give up Miss Hamilton. She was very accommodating, and I would not wish to snub her."

A fine, gallant, yet not entirely so, response, Roger thought as he hid his scowl behind the rim of his glass.

"Do not let me hold you back," Victoria said.

Roger's scowl turned into a smile at her words.

"I am certain I have played the only song I would feel comfortable playing," Victoria continued. "Therefore, if Miss Abernathy is willing and there is another time to display your musical talent, please do not let me stop you from doing so."

The cad took her hand! Roger wished to yank it away from him!

"Are you certain? I should not wish you to think my admiration fleeting."

Why would she smile so pleasantly at such a statement? Did she not know that doing so was far too encouraging to the likes of Carlyle? Unless... it was not possible. Victoria simply could not mean to encourage Carlyle.

"I am positive, Mr. Carlyle."

Roger sighed softly in relief. At least she had not said something like *I could never think your admiration fleeting.* Her answer — a polite response without being indulgent — proved his point. She was not interested in snaring Carlyle.

Mrs. Abernathy clapped her hands. "Excellent. One evening after dinner we will have to have some music. It will be imperative." She turned her eyes on Roger. "Perhaps you will favour us with a song, Mr. Shelton?"

"No," Roger replied between sips of lemonade. "I have no intention of singing."

"Oh, I am not easily dissuaded, Mr. Shelton. I shall work on you until you agree."

"It will never happen," Roger replied with a smile. "I am quite a stubborn old goat."

Victoria's lips pressed together, but her eyes were laughing.

Mrs. Abernathy shook her head. "That is what

all gentlemen think at one point or another, but few truly are as stubborn as they declare. I shall not be discouraged, Mr. Shelton."

Thankfully, she turned away from him to Mr. Carlyle.

"Now, Mr. Carlyle. If you would be so good as to lend me your arm, we shall tell my Amelia the good news. She was quite taken with your singing; I assure you."

Carlyle gave Victoria an apologetic look but extended his arm to Mrs. Abernathy and allowed her to lead him away.

Roger took another sip of his lemonade. Perhaps if Mrs. Abernathy could dispose of Mr. Carlyle and his *admiration*, then Roger might be persuaded by gratitude to favour her with a song.

Chapter 6

"Mr. Clayton!" Grace greeted the gentleman with great animation as she and Victoria approached him.

Mr. Ainsley had excused himself from Grace's side some minutes ago, and Roger was being a dutiful brother and escorting his sister as she followed behind her charge and Miss Grace Love.

"Miss Grace," Mr. Everett Clayton replied with a small bow.

"You must meet my friend, Miss Hamilton," Grace said. "And her chaperone, Mrs. Berkeley. She is Mr. Shelton's sister. And, of course, you know Mr. Shelton. Is it not exciting that we are able to be together here just as we were when I was at Heathcote?"

"Indeed, it is." The gentleman's reply was accompanied by a polite smile but not one which spoke to Victoria of him genuinely being delighted to be where he was at the moment.

Grace looked around as if something were missing. "Where is my sister?"

Mr. Clayton's smile wavered. "With your mother and Mrs. Abernathy, I believe."

"Well, then, you must join us," Grace offered. "We are not a big party, but a stroll through the garden and the wilderness beyond is much more pleasant when accompanied by friends. Is it not, Mr. Shelton?"

"Not particularly," Roger grumbled, earning a swat of his arm from his sister. He scowled at her. "Did you wish for me to lie?"

"Yes," Diana replied. "There is a time and a place for abject honesty. This is not one of them."

"You and mother," he grumbled under his breath.

"I think it can be a wonderful thing to be surrounded by friends," Diana said to Grace. "And I am certain Roger is happy to see you again, Mr. Clayton." She raised an eyebrow at her brother.

"Of course, I am not disappointed to see you, Clayton," Roger admitted. "That was not my meaning."

"Then was your meaning that you preferred not to be in company with us ladies?" Victoria knew she likely shouldn't ask such a thing, but the opportunity to unsettle Roger when he had been what she would consider to be rude was just too tempting to ignore.

Roger pressed his lips together and looked at his sister. "Of course not," he lied.

Victoria knew he was lying for he said the words with that particular smile he wore when he was avoiding being scolded. She caught her breath as the smile slipped into something more calculating and grimaced even before he opened his mouth, for she knew that whatever was going to be said was designed to be shocking.

"I find wandering in the wilderness with ladies – or, more precisely, *a* lady – to be a particularly enjoyable pastime. So much can be learned about life and nature during such a stroll." He batted his eyes three times at Victoria, daring her to scold him for his innuendo.

"Do you collect flowers and leaves and press them in books?" Grace asked.

There was nothing but innocent curiosity in her expression. Oh, the girl was in desperate need of education before she was ready to seriously consider marriage. Victoria sent a pleading look to Diana, while Mr. Clayton attempted to recover from a sudden coughing spell.

"My brother is not speaking of proper pursuits," Diana said softly.

"Then, of what is he –" Grace's question stopped abruptly. Her eyes grew wide as her cheeks flushed a brilliant red. Apparently, she had deciphered Roger's meaning.

"He is very wicked to speak of such a thing in the presence of ladies," Victoria assured her young friend. "He is an absolute scoundrel."

Roger had the decency to look somewhat censured.

"He just has not yet found the right lady with whom to walk and behave appropriately," Diana added. "It is how it is with some gentlemen. They are nothing but rogues and rascals until they find a reason to be otherwise. Quite often it is a lady who compels such a change."

"Yes, yes," Grace said quite seriously. "Mr. Shelton has said as much himself."

"When did I admit to such foolishness?" Roger demanded.

"Why at Heathcote! Do you not remember our discussion about why you did not wish to marry?"

"Indeed?" Diana said with much interest.

Roger's expression twisted as if he had been poked by a hot iron.

"Oh, yes!" Grace continued. "Mr. Shelton fully intends to give up his current ways, which I now understand to be excessively improper, when he marries. However, he is not ready to do that just yet. And my cousin, Miss Tierney, said that he would no longer fear giving up his freedom when he met a lady who claimed his heart and caused him to fear losing her more than he feared losing his reprobate lifestyle." She batted her lashes and gave Roger a pointed look.

Victoria bit back a smile. It appeared that though Miss Grace tended to ramble on at a fairly rapid pace, she was not without the ability to hide a reprimand within a pleasantly delivered bit of information.

"So, Clayton, how are you finding this gathering?" Roger, who looked eager to leave their current topic of conversation, motioned to the path ahead of them, indicating they should walk on. "Is it all you had hoped?"

The gentleman's polite smile was back. "It is difficult to say since we have only been here a short time. However, the music this afternoon was delightful."

This set Grace on a course of admiration for all the musical selections – *again*. Victoria smiled and nodded just as she had the first two times when Grace had shared her raptures about the musicale.

Indeed, it was Grace who bore the greatest share of the conversation as they continued down the path, past the grand old tree with a bench beneath it, around the loop where the path turned at the stream, and back to where the others were gathered on the lawn.

Victoria was excessively relieved when Diana suggested that Grace should make certain her mother was not missing her.

"My ears are weary," Roger muttered as he dropped onto the lawn next to Victoria when Diana and Grace were well away from them.

"Miss Grace does possess a great talent for conversation," Victoria agreed.

"Her sister is little better," Mr. Clayton, who had joined them, added.

Victoria looked at her companions uneasily.

"I thought you and she were destined to be married," Roger said easily as he leaned back and propped himself up on his elbows.

"Are you certain you wish to discuss this here?" Victoria inserted. This seemed like a conversation that should be held between gentlemen when they were far removed from ladies.

"It is not a secret," Roger replied. "I am certain Miss Grace has mentioned Miss Love and Mr. Clayton's attachment." He looked toward where his sister was walking with Grace. "She must have said something. I cannot imagine her keeping silent about such a thing."

"Well, yes, she has mentioned it," Victoria admitted, "but it was done in the privacy of my room and not in the garden."

"How many were in your room?" Roger queried. "Three people?"

Victoria nodded.

"Then, the only thing different between Miss Grace telling you about her sister and Mr. Clayton's attachment and my mentioning it now is our location," he concluded before turning back to Mr. Clayton.

"I thought we were destined to be married as

well," Mr. Clayton replied. "However, I had little competition at Stratsbury Park. My brother would not give Miss Love a second look, and Max was her cousin. So, I was the logical choice, you see." He blew out a breath. "However, at a house party with so many gentlemen of fortune, as this party has, a clergyman's living seems to lack the polish necessary to hold her attention."

"Has she broken off with you?" Victoria whispered.

Mr. Clayton shook his head. "Not yet, but I expect it."

"That is dreadful!"

"Is it?" Mr. Clayton asked. "Or is it fortuitous? I hardly know, although, presently, I will admit that I find it rather dreadful."

"Of course, you do," Roger assured him. "But that does not mean it will always be as it is now. She might just be having a bit of fun and will realize that no one else measures up to you."

Mr. Clayton shook his head. "Graeme warned me about her. Apparently, she was quite the flirt during the season. I thought my brother was just being my brother." He shrugged.

"I helped Graeme secure his current lady, you know," Roger said.

Mr. Clayton laughed. "Did you? I cannot say that I noticed."

"That is because you noticed nothing aside from Miss Love when I was at Stratsbury Hall," Roger retorted. "However, a little flirting with Miss Tierney and the threat of pursuing her myself were what brought him to the point."

"That is how you arranged a match?" Victoria shook her head. "I fear that does not make you a matchmaker at all."

"It most certainly does!"

"And are you going to flirt with Miss Grace to make Mr. Ainsley take notice?"

"You are attempting to match Miss Grace with Ainsley?" Mr. Clayton asked in surprise.

Both Victoria and Roger nodded.

"Good luck to you both," Mr. Clayton continued, "I hear he has a beauty back home who will not be out until next season, but he has promised to wait for her."

"No!" Victoria cried. "Are you certain?"

Mr. Clayton nodded.

"Then, what are we to do? Miss Grace finds him

very attractive as a possible suitor." Of all the rotten luck! Victoria looked to Roger for an answer, but he only shrugged and shook his head.

"There were some others she mentioned," Victoria said after a few moments of silence. "How did you not know this?" she demanded of Roger. "You were supposed to find out things about the gentlemen she listed."

"And when have I had the opportunity?" Roger argued. "I spent the time you were practising with Carlyle in my room and then I have been with you, my sister, and Miss Grace ever since."

He had a point. "Very well, I will allow you that," she said.

"You would not trade the elder sister for the younger one, would you, Clayton? Miss Grace is a bit of a chatterbox, but she seems trustworthy, if a trifle naïve."

"A trifle?" Victoria muttered, causing Roger's left eyebrow to cock in question, though he said nothing.

"I am afraid I cannot oblige you in such a fashion," Mr. Clayton answered.

"Are you certain?"

"Really, Roger!" Victoria exclaimed. "The gentleman's heart is not free at present to consider anyone."

"My apologies, Clayton."

"I am not offended."

Roger flopped back onto the grass and placed his hat over his eyes. "You will keep me safe from marauding females if I fall asleep, will you not?"

"Perhaps," Victoria replied.

Roger lifted his hat and looked at her. She smiled in return, and he once again put his hat over his eyes. She would not let anyone accost him – at least, not anyone he did not wish to have accost him. The thought of him finally choosing someone to be his wife pricked her heart.

"You would not consider a parson, would you, Miss Hamilton?"

"No, she would not," Roger said from beneath his hat.

"I think I can speak for myself," Victoria retorted. "I am not opposed to the profession, but I am not certain I am best suited for the position of parson's wife. However, if I were to find myself enamoured with a gentleman who was destined to be the caretaker of a parish, I am certain I would be able to find my footing. After all, I am not unfamiliar with serving the tenants on my father's estate. I would imagine being a parson's wife would be somewhat similar in some regards?"

"Most likely," Mr. Clayton replied with a nod.

He looked so forlorn. She had yet to meet Miss Grace's sister, but Victoria was certain she would not like the young woman. How could any lady toy with the heart of a gentleman who seemed as pleasant and obliging as Mr. Clayton?

"I am certain that, in time, you will find the right lady to fill the role of Mrs. Clayton," she assured him. "And," she added with a whisper, "I would not discount Miss Grace just because her sister has treated you ill. Grace is talkative, but she is the sort of young lady whom I do not mind claiming as a friend."

"You are very kind, Miss Hamilton."

"That she is," Roger muttered from under his hat.

"And I would be happy to count you among my friends as well, Mr. Clayton, so if you are in need of a partner for a game of cards or for a dance or some such thing, I do hope you will consider asking me."

Roger's hat lifted from his eyes, but Victoria

ignored him, choosing instead to smile at Mr. Clayton, who was thanking her for her offer.

If jealousy could work on Roger's friend, then maybe, it could also work on him. She would not toy with Mr. Clayton. She was not the sort of lady to do such a thing. However, marriage could not be put off forever, and before she began searching in earnest elsewhere, she needed to know if she had any hope in securing the heart of the gentleman who had held hers for most of her life.

Chapter 7

"We will start from the top of the table, of course, with Amelia." Mrs. Abernathy waited for her daughter to join her where she stood near the door to the drawing room in which all the houseguests were gathered to wait for dinner.

"Shall we see who it is who will dine with you?"

Miss Abernathy said an eager yes as her mother shook a bowl containing several small pieces of paper. She swirled her hand inside the bowl and pulled out a name. "Oh! How delightful! Mr. Carlyle."

The gentleman straightened his jacket, crossed the room, and offered his arm to Miss Abernathy, whose waited only until her daughter and Mr. Carlyle had left the room before looking around and calling Victoria forward.

Of all the inane ideas! Roger crossed his arms

and leaned against the wall near the window. The woman was obviously assigning gentleman dinner partners at random, but she was proceeding through the ladies based on status. Victoria was well-dowered. It was not something she published nor was it a fact she kept secret. He glowered at two gentlemen who had started whispering when Victoria's name was called. He did not like it. His friend did not need any fortune hunters scampering after her.

"Mr. Clayton," Mrs. Abernathy said.

Roger blew out a breath. It could be worse. She could have been stuck with Carlyle or one of those whispering gents.

Lady after lady was summoned forward and gentleman after gentleman was assigned as a partner.

"Is this not the best?" Grace said as she took Roger's arm. "It is such a surprise! I do like surprises."

"I do not," Roger replied.

Grace giggled. "I will admit I had hoped I would be assigned someone different."

"I hear Ainsley has a chit waiting for him at home," Roger whispered.

Grace's smile slid into a frown. "Does he indeed?"

"I have not asked him, of course, but that is what I have heard. We should proceed with caution."

She tipped her head. "What do you mean *we*?"

That had not been well-thought-out. He had forgotten that Miss Grace was not in on the scheme to see her married. "You seemed fond of him, and I had thought to help you in securing him."

"That is very kind of you, Mr. Shelton."

"Think nothing of it. Anything for a friend of Miss Hamilton."

"She is very nice," Grace said as they waited for the remaining couples to enter the dining room.

"The best," Roger replied, looking down the table to where she sat across from Miss Abernathy and next to Everett Clayton. She was smiling and leaning her head toward Clayton to hear what the fellow was saying. Truly, she needed to learn some restraint. Such open interest even for a chap thought by many to be firmly secured by Miss Love was not wise. Tongues would wag, and chaperones would scheme.

Grace touched his arm. "Are you fond of her?"

He nodded. "We have been friends for longer than I can remember. My first memory of our friendship was when I brought her a toad and placed it in a teacup on this little table that she had which she would lay out all properly with a cloth and imaginary biscuits."

"A toad!" Grace giggled. "And what did she do?"

Roger chuckled. "She nodded her head in greeting and instructed Mr. Brown – that is what she named him – that he was not to spill his tea or eat all the biscuits. And then, she proceeded to instruct me with the same rules and scolded me for my dirty hands. She has been scolding me ever since."

Grace giggled but pressed her lips together as Mrs. Abernathy entered with her husband and took her place.

"My hands are clean, I assure you," Roger whispered to Grace as a bowl of soup was placed before him.

"I shall have to thank Miss Hamilton for having taught you such good manners," Grace teased.

He glanced down the table at Victoria once again. She had taught him many things over the years. Was there ever a better friend that anyone could have? She leaned toward Clayton again. Roger caught his scowl before it could form and turned back to his soup.

"If she is such a good friend," Grace whispered, "why do we not attempt to find her a husband? Every young lady needs one eventually."

"She does not wish to marry just yet," Roger answered.

"But she does look very pretty sitting next to Mr. Clayton and talking as she is. I know he has his heart set on my sister, but..." she let her words fall away, replacing them with a simple shrug.

Victoria looked pretty no matter who was sitting next to her or whether she was talking, being silent, or scolding him. Roger applied himself to eating his soup and attempted to keep his eyes from wandering too often down to where his friend sat.

"There are other gentlemen."

Grace did not seem ready to give up the idea of seeing Victoria matched with some gentleman at this party.

"Not Mr. Carlyle, of course," she added quickly. "He was very demanding when they were practising, and Miss Hamilton said that such behaviour indicates a gentleman who will not be an attentive husband." She slurped a spoonful of soup. "And every lady wishes for an attentive husband, do you not think?"

Roger nodded his head as he scooped the last spoonful of soup from his bowl. It was a small comfort to know that Carlyle was not someone Victoria admired, no matter how much the gentleman had seemed interested in her earlier.

"Tell me, Miss Grace, what do you wish for in a husband? If I am to help you find one, I must know a thing or two about what you would prefer."

"But," she protested in a whisper as her soup bowl was taken away, "we have not settled on a match for Miss Hamilton."

Roger had no desire to settle on a match for Victoria. The very idea of her marrying anyone made him wish to refuse the venison placed before him, and, if anyone knew him as well as Victoria knew him, they would know that venison was among his most favoured foods.

"I believe since she is not so desirous to marry as you are, it might be best if we decide upon a match for you before we attempt to arrange something for Miss Hamilton."

"Do you truly think that would be best?"

"Yes." He was very sure of it.

"Very well," Grace said, and, while Roger savoured his venison and occasionally glanced in Victoria's direction, Grace enumerated all the qualities she wished for in a husband.

~*~*~

"She actually cares about how she will be treated and not just how he looks or what style of architecture his house is," Roger said later to his sister. He blew out a breath. "She is not completely without sense." The fact still surprised him. He had not, to this point, thought that Grace possessed any great amount of substance, and he still did not think she possessed much. However, she was not without some depth.

"She also informed me that Mr. Carlyle is not a good choice for Victoria, which I believe I already told you, but I think it is good that you have the information from more than one source."

"Mr. Clayton would be better," Diana agreed.

That was not what Roger had meant. His brow furrowed. The two – Clayton and Victoria – had spent a great deal of time together this evening.

First, there had been supper, and then, there had been cards.

"He is not available," Roger said as he watched Victoria take a turn of the drawing room on the man's arm.

"Not yet, but I have heard rumors that he might be... and soon."

"Where did you hear this?" If it was from Victoria, it was news that was no better than Roger already knew.

"A couple of the other chaperones were discussing it in hushed tones earlier. It seems Mr. Walcott or Mr. Ramsey might be more to Miss Love's liking." She leaned close enough to her brother that her shoulder pressed into his. "Their incomes are substantial."

That information seemed to match nicely – unfortunately so – with what Clayton had said. How did Miss Grace have a sister who was so calculating and cunning? The two ladies seemed to be exact opposites, yet he had heard Grace praise her sister as if Felicity were a goddess capable of no wrong. He shook his head. The chit was more than a trifle naïve just as Victoria had insinuated earlier today.

"Mr. Ainsley's heart is not unfettered," Roger said, his mind still focused on the better of the Love sisters. "I have mentioned it to Miss Grace."

His sister's eyes grew wide.

"Clayton says the gentleman has a lady waiting for him at home. She is not yet out, but there seems to be some sort of arrangement."

"Since he is here, his mother must either not be in favor of the match, or she is unaware." Diana sighed. "Neither speaks well of him, in my opinion."

"His mother might be unreasonable. Remember how our mother was when you were first out. There was not a gentleman in all of London who was deemed good enough for her daughter. Even Berkley struggled to win Mother's approval."

"But he has it now."

"Because he has provided her with a grandchild," Roger muttered.

Diana jabbed him with her elbow. "She liked him before Thomas was born."

"But you must admit she likes him even better now."

Diana chuckled. "She does, and her admiration of him will only grow as our family does." She shook her head at Roger's teasing smile. "No, I am not increasing." She flicked open her fan. "Not that I am avoiding it," she added.

Roger laughed out loud at that. His sister may pretend to be shocked by his improper behaviour, but she was not so far removed from it herself. On two occasions in their lifetime, he had come across her in the garden late at night sneaking into the house just as he was sneaking out. Of course, she had been out to go swimming while his purpose was not so innocent. However, the truth of the matter remained, she was not so flawless as she might like to appear.

"Now, if I wish to keep Mother happy..." She scanned the room. "Who here would meet her expectations for you?"

Roger shook his head. "Leave off, Diana. I am not here to find a wife."

"Humor me," she cajoled. "Discussing possibilities with you is a great deal more fun than discussing them with the other chaperones." Again, she flicked open her fan. "Not one of them has yet mentioned any physical attributes – only fortunes and estates. A secure future is a good thing, do not get me wrong, but truly, one must think about whose bed she will be warming to do her duty."

Roger shook his head and chuckled. "And is that why you chose Berkley?"

Her cheeks flushed. "I was not unaware of how warm his bed could be when we married," she whispered.

Roger turned startled eyes to her. "Indeed? I am not the only rake?"

"I do prefer the term rake to what Mother would call me, but no, I did not warm bed after bed, my dear brother."

"Only Berkley's?"

She shrugged. "Only once... or twice. But that is not what we were discussing, and you will not mention that to Mother. Ever. Or I will have Berkley hurt you."

Roger chuckled. "I would not dream of telling Mother unless greatly provoked."

"Now, how many of these ladies capture your fancy?"

Roger looked around the room. There were lithe figures as well as pleasantly curved ones. There were ladies with golden hair and those with tresses of toffee and chocolate. There was even one beauty who wore her flaming locks very well. Some were tall and would be able to nearly look him in the eye without rising onto their toes to do so, and then there were those who would be perfectly sized to snuggle into his side and listen to his heart. Nearly all of them had fair complexions, even if their beauty varied by degrees. There were several whom he should be attempting to charm, for they had very kissable pouts. However, not one of them made him pause long enough to seriously consider her. He shook his head.

"The same number who would meet with Mother's approval," he said in answer to his sister's question.

"One," Diana said.

"No, none," Roger corrected.

Diana gave the smallest shake of her head before tipping it toward the door to the garden. "One," she repeated.

Roger's eyes followed her head tip. There, standing at the door, was Victoria.

"You said you would allow me to present any possible matches for her to you for approval, and I am."

Him? Marry Victoria?

"Think about it," Diana whispered before rising and leaving him to do just that.

Chapter 8

Victoria's morning ride had been as delightful as any ride through the countryside could be. The sun was shining in a nearly solid blue sky as only a few clouds were dotting the expanse above. The air was fresh and not at all close. The only thing which had dampened the enjoyment of the exercise had been that it was entirely too short. Well, maybe that was not the only thing which had not met with Victoria's satisfaction. There had been one thing — or rather, one person — missing.

"Have you seen Roger today?" Victoria had slipped into the library and had taken a seat next to Diana on a sofa.

"He said good morning to me," Diana replied, looking up from her book. "He was dressed to go riding. I assumed he was going with the group."

"He was not with us." Victoria pulled her lower

lip between her teeth. He could be anywhere. He had spoken of escaping after a few days of being at the house party when he first arrived, but then, when they had decided to help Grace find a match, he had said he would be required to stay longer. "Did he leave?" she whispered behind her book.

There was worry in the wide eyes that met Victoria's question. "I will ask."

Victoria put a hand on Diana's arm to keep her from rising. "No, please do not. He may have wished to slip away unnoticed, and I should hate for him to become the topic of gossip due to my curiosity."

"It is not as if his absence will not be noted and remarked on," Diana argued. "It is best to know now if we shall have to endure such whispers."

Diana covered Victoria's hand with her own. "I will only be a moment, and I shall be as discreet as possible." One of her eyebrows arched. "I should like to know if my little brother is fulfilling his duty to his mother or not."

Victoria could not help smiling at Diana's stern tone. Diana would likely lecture Roger about his disappearance, but she would not tell their mother. The two had always kept each other's secrets. It was a far different sort of relationship that they had than Victoria had with her older brother. He had often found it necessary to tell their mother or father if he found Victoria doing something she was not supposed to be doing. Not that those moments were frequent. Victoria did not like to stray outside of the rules too often. She did not always agree with the guidelines in which she was to live, but she did not wish to be found wanting in any way. Therefore, she suppressed her displeasure and behaved as was expected.

Of course, both her mother and father were not severe in their adherence to societal expectations, and that did make for a great deal less displeasure on Victoria's part. Unlike some in the upper circles, her parents were welcoming of new arrivals – even those who had made their fortune rather than inheriting it. And while Victoria had had all the proper education a young lady should receive from a governess, her parents had also encouraged Victoria to learn all she wished to learn on any subject she chose.

Neither her father nor her mother had ever kept her from exploring books on flora and fauna nor had they kept her from reading her fill of novels.

Had she been the sort of lady given to excessive imagination and dramatics she might have found her reading materials restricted, for her mother could not and would not abide anyone who was melodramatic.

Sense should always rule over sensibility, according to Mrs. Hamilton, and in that way, Victoria was much like her mother. It was why she could sit here now, wondering where Roger was, without feeling to great a need to go to the window and watch for him — even if one could see the entry from the second window on the wall facing the front of the house and it had a very inviting chair near it. She would remain where she was and apply herself to her purpose for being in the library.

Victoria opened her book and picked up the lavender ribbon used to hold her place. This had been the ribbon Roger had given her when she was twelve and had just discovered that one could like a neighbour boy much more than one might like a brother. She smiled as she remembered the discussion she had had with Diana about that very thing.

Obviously, there was no way Victoria was going to ask for an explanation from her mother about why her heart seemed to race and her cheeks flushed when Roger smiled at her. Nor was she going to reveal to her mother that, occasionally, Roger kissed Victoria in her dreams. However, Diana, who was a very wise seventeen at the time, had seemed the best person to ask. She was, of course, facing her first season, and so she knew so much more about gentlemen and hearts and the dreary feelings that permeated a young lady's very soul when a favoured gentleman left to attend school.

Diana had insisted upon Victoria telling her who the young man was who had captured Victoria's affections, and Victoria had feared that Diana would not approve of her liking Roger. However, on that account, Victoria had been most assuredly wrong for Diana had actually been quite delighted with the idea that one day they might be sisters.

Of course, even now, Diana still hoped one day they might be, but if Victoria were completely honest with herself about Roger – something she had been attempting to be more and more lately – she would have to admit that the possibility seemed less likely than it ever had. Roger still treated her as a special friend, but he never attempted to flirt with her or kiss her. He never had. In fact, he had never even seemed to feel it awkward to embrace her on occasion. It appeared as if Victoria was little different than Diana in Roger's eyes.

"He has not left," Diana whispered as she smoothed her skirts after returning to her spot on the couch. "He is just gone off by himself. He does that you know."

Victoria nodded.

"And from a quick look in the drawing room and a glance into the garden, it appears there are no young ladies missing from our party." She shrugged when Victoria looked at her in surprise. "It is Roger."

Could three words spoken with a tone of regret cut a heart more deeply? It was a good thing Victoria was not given to dramatics, or she might take herself off to her room to have a good cry over the idea of Roger seeming to prefer every lady to her. Or so it appeared from the way he spoke of the debutants in town and the ones he had met while at school.

"To be fair," Diana continued almost as if she could read Victoria's mind, "it has been some time since I have heard any scandalous whispers regarding my brother. I had hoped it was a sign that he was finally coming to the point, but..." she let her thought trail off.

Victoria had hoped the same when she saw him arrive at the Abernathy's, for he had immediately asked about her location. She had heard him. However, he had only arrived to deliver presents to her from himself and her father. He was merely seeing to the well-being of a friend. He was good at that. She had heard him speak of a few close friends and how he was going to help this one or that one with some project. She sighed. He had even helped one become engaged. Yet, he seemed none too willing to consider marriage himself.

"Are there any gentlemen here whom you might recommend?" she asked Diana.

"Besides my brother?"

Victoria nodded as she swallowed the sorrow that rose at the thought. "I must start considering other possibilities."

"Are you certain? You are only three and twenty."

"Only?" Victoria said in a scoffing tone. "I am a veritable old maid compared to the rest of the hopeful ladies here. I dare say the next oldest is a very ancient nineteen."

"No, no. Miss Hannington is twenty."

"That is still three years younger than me," Victoria argued. "So, you see my point."

"Not completely," Diana insisted.

"I doubt I will be invited to many more of these parties."

"That is not a bad thing," Diana whispered. "I have never understood the appeal of a house party. There are eight gentlemen here – eight! Out of the hundreds that live in England, you and the others are expected to consider making a match with these eight gentlemen because their parents are friends with Mr. and Mrs. Abernathy, or they are relations like Mr. Danvers.

"I must admit that Mrs. Abernathy has not chosen paupers. I think Mr. Clayton might have the smallest income, and his is not unreasonably low. However, that is not my point. My point is that there are only eight gentlemen here. And," she leaned closer and gave a look around the room before continuing, "there is no guarantee that any of them will capture your heart. A healthy income is important, but so is your heart." She gave Victoria a pointed look as she said the last bit. "Do not sacrifice it for some imagined duty which you think must be performed before you are five and twenty."

"I have been waiting for over ten years for my heart to gain the gentleman for whom it longs. Perhaps it is time to pack that desire away with the toys in the nursery as something from childhood that is not to accompany me into adulthood."

Diana looked truly pained at the comment. "Consider other gentlemen if you must, but do not give up on him just yet."

Victoria wove her lavender ribbon in and out between her fingers. She did not wish to lay her love for Roger aside. Indeed, she was not sure she could.

"You know he was not pleased to have Carlyle sing with you," Diana whispered. "And last evening, he did not seem happy about how much time you spent with Mr. Clayton."

Victoria tipped her head and looked at her friend. "Then, you think there is hope?"

Diana nodded.

"Very well. If you think there is hope, I shall not despair just yet." No, she would not despair. She would keep doing as she had begun yesterday. She would spend time with Mr. Clayton and a few of the other gentlemen to see if she could provoke some sort of response from Roger.

With that settled, and with only a small concern left about where Roger was, she turned her mind back to the book on her lap and the Dashwood sisters' plight as they entered London with the hopeful, matchmaking Mrs. Jennings. She wished them well, for this business of finding a husband could be a dreadful ordeal designed to crush the very soul of a lady who loved where love seemed not to be readily returned.

Chapter 9

"I will require him again in a few hours time." Roger handed the reins of his horse to a groom.

Then, as he pulled off his gloves, Roger walked behind the stable and down a small path to the pond. He tossed his gloves on the ground and removed his jacket before tossing himself under a tree. Picking up a small twig from the ground beside him, he threw it into the water. However, it did not create a very satisfying splash. With a sigh, he hauled himself up from his spot and went to gather some rocks – smooth ones which would skip across the water.

Once he had a small pile of ammunition in his hands, he returned to his place and began the task of seeing how many times he could skip each rock. Focusing on such a task and counting the hops across the pond, he hoped, would be just the sort of absorbing trivial activity which would rid his mind of the fear that had settled into it last night.

"I thought I saw you ducking behind the stables."

Roger looked up to see Diana's husband, Benjamin Berkley, approaching.

"I did not see you," Roger admitted. To be honest, he had seen very little on his ride from the Abernathy's to his home. His horse knew the way, so there was very little need to steer the animal, and so, Roger had found himself lost in his thoughts.

"I was under the impression that I was not going to see you for another week, at least," Berkley said as he sat down next to Roger.

"You aren't," Roger replied.

"And yet, here you are."

"I needed to get away from all those females." It was mostly the truth. He needed to find a place away from a *particular* female so that he could try to sort out his thoughts.

"That is understandable. How is my wife faring?"

"She seems to be enjoying herself. She has taken

a second young lady under her wing since Victoria is not challenging enough."

Berkley laughed. "That does sound like Diana. She does like a challenge, which is likely why she was willing to take me on."

Their mother had not liked Benjamin Berkley for good reason. The gentleman was not the most sedate fellow. He liked to have fun, and his fun had come in a great variety of forms before he had met Diana.

He was an excellent horseman and still found an occasional race to be something he could not resist. He had also been a great gambler at his club, though not in the usual fashion. He had not tossed away more than a few coins at a card table. Instead, he had found great delight in betting on challenges posed to him by his group of friends. One such challenge had included stealing a kiss from one of the patronesses at Almacks. He had managed to kiss the lady's cheek and, then, had found himself promptly banned from the establishment, much to his satisfaction as he claimed his winnings.

Thankfully, Diana had seemed to have a calming effect on him, for, from the time he started courting Roger's sister, Berkley rarely found himself acting rashly. And since the arrival of his son, he had become nearly decorous – nearly but not quite.

"A guinea says I can skip this rock further than you."

Roger shook his head. "I am not interested."

"Not even if I do it with my left foot against the tree. Like this." Berkley stood and placed his foot flat against the trunk of the tree at about knee height.

"You cannot skip a rock standing like that."

"I think I can," Berkley retorted.

"I am not taking your money, nor am I giving you any of mine."

"Then, let's make a different agreement. If I can skip the rock – not if I can skip it further than you, but just if I can skip it – you truly do not think I can?" he asked in response to Roger's look of disbelief.

"No, the angle is all wrong."

"You might be right, but then again, you might be wrong."

"Very well, if you can perform this feat, what do you require in payment besides my admitting that you were right?"

"You must answer one question."

"What question?" Roger eyed his brother-in-law skeptically.

"No, I will not tell you. You must agree to an unknown question, which should not be too hard to do unless, of course, you are hiding something?"

Roger tossed a rock and watched it hop three times before sinking beneath the water. There were things that he wished to keep secret, but then, if he admitted to hiding something, he knew Berkley well enough to know that the man would attempt to discover whatever it was. Roger looked at the awkward way Berkley was standing with his foot still against the tree. Surely, there was no way that he was going to be able to skip a rock.

"I accept."

"Hand me a rock. Pick the worst one for skipping."

As if Roger was planning on giving him the best rock to use for such a purpose! Roger was not unskilled at playing games of chance, and he knew that it was always best to have the odds in one's favour even if it meant arranging things to best advantage.

"You could not find a worse one?" Berkley scoffed when Roger handed him a round craggy rock that fit in his hand so that he could conceal it in a fist but only just. A large and uneven rock such as that was not for skipping — lobbing at the head of an enemy perhaps but not skipping.

"I was only doing as instructed."

Berkley shook his head. "Only because it suits your purposes," he said with a laugh.

"Precisely," Roger admitted.

"It only needs to skip once for me to win."

Roger nodded. "It is not the number of skips but the mere occurrence of, at least, one skip." His lips quirked into a smirk. "However, more than one skip would be more impressive."

Berkley's eyebrows rose as he considered that while Roger hoped the suggestion would cause him to throw the rock with too much force in the wrong direction.

"One question per skip?"

The man was proficient at twisting things. Roger shook his head.

"Very well, but I might be able to skip this more than once."

"You might," Roger agreed.

Berkley huffed, hopped his right foot into position, swung his arm out to the side, and snapped the rock into motion.

If the blasted thing did not bounce once but twice off the water! Roger shook his head. He should have known better than to enter into a bet with Berkley. There were very few challenges the man had never won, but this one had seemed such a sure loss.

Berkley removed his foot from the tree and turned with a grin to Roger. "Why are you here? And do not tell me about needing to get away from females. I want to know if it is because a particular female is chasing you and you do not wish her to do so, or if there is a particular young lady who has finally captured Roger Shelton."

Roger clenched his jaw and shook his head. He should have known that the one question Diana's husband would ask would be the one question that he did not want to answer.

"Ah ha! It is a particular young lady."

"You sound a bit like your wife," Roger grumbled.

"Well, we have been hoping for some time."

"Hoping for what? Roger asked. "That I would marry?"

Berkley nodded. "But not just marry."

Roger cocked his head and looked at his brother-in-law in confusion. "I do not follow."

Berkley shook his head. "I cannot say. I have promised."

"That does not make any sense."

"Tell me who she is. What is the name of the lady who has sent you running?"

"No, it is enough that you know there is one."

Berkley scowled. "Do I know her?" he asked as he took a seat next to where Roger was once again sitting.

"I am not telling you."

"Then, tell me why you are running away from her."

Roger drew a calming breath. How did his sister manage to endure such a persistent fellow?

"If I had to guess," Berkley said in a more serious tone, "I would say you are feeling a lot like I did when I met Diana. The thought of taking on a wife and family..." He shook his head. "Terrifying. Worse than sneaking through the fence at old Tenley's house. He had this gardener with one eye, who was a crotchety old fellow – worse than Tenley. Anyway, I survived. Neither the gardener nor his wolfhound ever caught me." He blew out a breath. "And so far, I have survived being both a husband and a father, though the thought of raising my son does still give me palpitations. However, I do not need to do it on my own. I have Diana, and she did survive having you as a brother." He nudged Roger with his elbow and chuckled.

"You are right," Roger admitted. "What do I know of responsibility?"

"Far more than you realize." Berkley shook his head. "A gentleman with a father like yours and who is still on speaking terms with that father knows more about responsibility than he might like to admit."

"I am not my father."

"None of us are. However, there is enough of him in you that you know that taking a wife is a grave responsibility. Your father is not unlike mine."

"But how do I know I can be the gentleman she deserves?"

"Do you love her?"

Roger nodded.

"Does she love you?"

That was the heart of the matter. He did not know if Victoria loved him. He shrugged.

Berkley picked up the second to last rock and sent it skittering across the pond. "Can you see her with anyone else without wishing to send that fellow to some far off desolate land to live in exile?"

"No."

Roger had wanted to physically harm Carlyle, and while he had refrained from thinking of doing away with Clayton simply because he was the brother of a good friend, Roger had wished the man would decide to leave the house party or be found in some compromising position with Miss Love so that he could not present himself as a possible suitor for Victoria.

"Then make her love you. Go back to that blasted house party and charm her out of her stockings – figuratively, not literally." He cast a sidelong grin at Roger. "Unless, of course, that helps your cause."

"As you did with Diana?"

Berkley shrugged.

"She told me," Roger admitted.

"Did she?"

"Yesterday, and I am not yet over the shock."

Berkley laughed. "You were shocked by such an admission? I highly doubt that."

"She is my sister."

"Precisely. You are not the only Shelton to have an improper bent."

Roger chuckled. "That I knew. I just did not realize it ran so deeply with my sister. And I would have been quite delighted to have remained ignorant."

Berkley laughed again. "Are you going to show your face in the house?"

"I came to retrieve a jacket."

"You could have sent a servant."

"A servant would not have been able to provoke my mother."

"You are not going to say that to her, are you?"

Roger rose as he nodded. "That is the very thing I have planned to say in response to her protest that I should not have come to retrieve that jacket."

"You mean the jacket you do not really need?"

"That is the very jacket."

"Come. You can see your nephew and take a report back to my wife about all the things she is missing."

"She cannot leave any sooner than Victoria

does," Roger said as they began their way across the lawn to the house.

"Yes, but she will be more eager to return when the party is done. And I am very eager to have her return." He drew and released a deep breath. It was a sound of longing — one which Roger's heart felt and understood.

"I am likely going to run afoul of my wife and possibly Miss Hamilton, but..." Berkley stopped speaking and looked as if he were not certain he should continue. "However, if the lady who has captured your heart is the one whom Diana and I hope you will finally notice, then, I feel I must, as a service to my fellow man and brother, relieve some of your anxiety and tell you that I do not think your suit would be refused."

Roger's brow furrowed. Was the fellow speaking about Victoria? Was that why he might find her put out with him for having spoken to Roger?

"I can say no more than this." Berkley looked around the garden before leaning a bit closer to Roger and whispering, "she has loved you for years."

Roger stood stalk still. "Victoria?"

Grinning, Berkley clapped Roger on the shoulder. "You did not hear that from me. I will deny it vehemently. Now, come along. We have a child to see and an imaginary jacket to retrieve."

"Victoria loves me?"

"Why do you suppose she has not yet married?" Berkley gave Roger a shove to start him walking.

It was an action for which Roger was grateful, for it was as if his brain could not think of anything but those three words *Victoria loved him*.

"Is that truly why she has not married?" Roger asked when his mind was able to conquer things such as walking and speaking.

"You did not hear that from me either," Berkley said as he opened the door to the servant's entrance. "I will deny it vehemently."

Chapter 10

The evening breeze stirred the curtains in the drawing room. Dinner was over, and the card tables were being set up. From the chair where Victoria sat, she could see Grace and her sister, Felicity, standing on the lawn talking with Mr. Clayton and Mr. Ramsey. Grace's features were all animation as she attended to the conversation.

Oh, to be young and hopeful. Victoria remembered the excitement she had felt during her first season. Every event was new. Every gentleman was a possibility – well, not an actual possibility for her heart was already lost to her friend – but an imagined one. And there had been the ever-present hope that some new dress or hairstyle would be the one which would finally capture Roger's attention.

Victoria turned her eyes back to the room. Roger

had still not returned from wherever he had gone. There had been much-whispered speculation at dinner. Some thought he had bored of the party and left. Others thought perhaps he had been asked to leave after some indiscretion – not that they had heard of any particular reckless behaviour, but he did have a reputation for dalliances. At least one lady had sighed wishing that she was the cause for his removal from the party.

"It is far too excellent an evening to spend inside, Miss Hamilton." Mr. Carlyle stood before her. "Would you be so kind as to allow me to walk with you around the garden?"

"I had not thought to move from my chair until required to play a hand of some game," Victoria replied with a smile. She would not be opposed to a walk in the garden with Diana or Grace or even Mr. Clayton, but she had no desire to encourage Mr. Carlyle.

"I promise we will not go far. Just to the rotunda and back."

"My chaperone is not here to accompany me."

"We will be in the open. No one would frown on us for walking side by side in clear view of everyone."

"But I really should let Mrs. Berkley know where I am."

"I saw her not two minutes ago standing in the garden, just outside the door, speaking with Mrs. Love."

Victoria glanced out the window. The rotunda was not all that far from the house, and there were no trees or bushes to obstruct the view. "Very well. I shall walk with you, but only after I have informed Mrs. Berkley and asked her if she would like to join us."

She placed her hand in his outstretched one and allowed him to first assist her in rising and then to escort her to where Diana was speaking with Mrs. Love.

"Mrs. Berkley," Carlyle began when the ladies had paused their conversation and looked his direction, "Miss Hamilton has given me permission to escort her to the rotunda and back if you will allow it."

Diana gave Victoria a questioning look.

"I thought you might like to join us," Victoria said.

"Oh, if you are wanting company, Felicity is a great walker," Mrs. Love inserted. She stepped away from them slightly and called, "Felicity," while waving her handkerchief.

Victoria's smile tightened on her lips so that she did not visibly cringe at the action.

"We older ladies would much rather sit or stand and watch you younger ladies, would we not, Mrs. Berkley?"

Before Diana could do more than open her mouth to speak, Mrs. Love was once again calling to her daughter.

"It would be such a fine thing for a group of young ladies and gentlemen to walk without us. Oh, good," she said as her daughter approached. "Felicity dear, Mr. Carlyle and Miss Hamilton are looking for people to join them on a walk to the rotunda, and, knowing how fond you are of walking, I naturally suggested you would be delighted to join them."

Felicity looked from her mother to Mr. Carlyle and then to Victoria. She smiled at Mr. Carlyle, but, when she looked at Victoria, she raised a brow as if she wondered why Mr. Carlyle would wish to walk with her. "Of course, I would be pleased to join you, Mr. Carlyle." She batted her lashes.

"Did I not say she would be happy to join you?" Mrs. Love beamed at her daughter.

"I shall return with an escort," Felicity said before hurrying back to her sister and the two gentlemen she had been talking to before her mother had called her.

"If I know my Felicity, you will also be joined by Grace as well as Mr. Ramsey and Mr. Clayton. Felicity does seem to be a favourite amongst the gentlemen," Mrs. Love whispered before tittering behind her fan and declaring that such a thing was entirely too improper to say, but a mother could not help her delight at seeing a daughter so well-received. She placed a hand on Diana's arm and added, "The number of soirees to which we had invitations during this past season was nearly overwhelming. She was very popular."

"How fortunate for you," Diana said.

"Are you certain you do not wish to walk with us?" Victoria asked Diana.

"Oh, you are too kind, Miss Hamilton, but we shall take our ease on that bench over there until you return," Mrs. Love answered, causing Diana to scowl briefly.

"I think Mrs. Love desires my presence," Diana answered.

"It does seem that way," Victoria agreed softly.

"And I suppose I would like to be close to the house and easily found should my brother return," Diana added.

"Oh," Mrs. Love said in an eager whisper, "I should like to know the true reason for his disappearance."

She was not alone in that wish. Victoria wanted to know the same thing. However, Victoria was not the sort of lady to say such a thing in front of others. If she and Diana had been alone, she would have said the same thing, but seeing as they were not, she held her tongue, which seemed to be a skill Mrs. Love seemed not to possess. How Grace had grown into the sweet, though naïve, young woman she was still baffled Victoria. She could see where Grace got her fondness for filling the air with a constant stream of words, but neither Mrs. Love nor Felicity seemed to possess the sweetness that Grace had.

"Did I not tell you?" Mrs. Love said with no little amount of excitement as Felicity approached.

Victoria caught herself before her eyebrows

could rise in surprise for Felicity did not have her hand on Mr. Clayton's arm but rather on Mr. Ramsey's.

"Mr. Carlyle, we are all ready to proceed to the rotunda," Felicity declared.

Victoria caught Grace's eyes and sent her a questioning look. Grace shrugged one shoulder and smiled a sad half-smile, while Mr. Clayton looked resigned.

The poor man was not only being thrown over but in a very open and grand fashion. She would have to speak to Roger. Mr. Clayton needed to find someone other than Miss Love to court. No amount of beauty was worth being treated poorly! Why the gentleman would do much better to pursue Miss Grace!

It had been said in jest when they were all gathered on the lawn yesterday, but as Victoria considered it now, it was not a deplorable idea other than it would mean Mr. Clayton would have to see Miss Love on a regular basis. That was not something Victoria would be able to countenance, and she imagined it must be the same for gentlemen. How did anyone, regardless of gender, watch the person whom they thought they had loved – or perchance did love and still loved – happily attach themselves to another without losing their equanimity.

"I apologize. I was woolgathering," Victoria said when she realized Mr. Carlyle had asked her a question.

"I was merely wondering if you were fond of walking."

"Oh, yes. I rather like it."

"Do you have a particular path that you walk when you are at home? I know I tend to ride in the same direction each morning unless I make a conscious choice to take a different route," Mr. Carlyle said.

"Does that mean you prefer riding to walking?"

"I must admit that I do. There is nothing quite like feeling the rush of the wind and the power of the beast on which you are seated when the horse is thundering along some field."

"I would have to agree. That is a very intoxicating feeling."

Mr. Carlyle looked at her in surprise. "You allow your horse to gallop?"

Victoria nodded. "Trotting is no way to win a race."

Her companion looked taken aback by such information. "You race?"

"Occasionally, yes."

His lips turned downward as a startled, yet curious expression settled on his face. "Neither of my sisters will allow their horses to do more than trot. They claim it is far too dangerous and unladylike."

Unladylike? While Victoria would like to take exception to being referred to as unladylike, she paused and considered that being thought so by a gentleman like Mr. Carlyle might not be so bad a thing. It might just stop him from pursuing her at all, which would please not only Victoria but also Felicity if the way she kept looking over her shoulder at Victoria was any indication.

"Dangerous or no, I still maintain it is the only way to win a race."

"I am not certain I have met a lady who races horses," Mr. Carlyle muttered.

Or perhaps, he had just not met any who would admit to racing.

"But we were speaking of walking, were we not? Before I was distracted by your preference for riding," Victoria said.

"Yes, yes, we were. I believe I had inquired if there was a particular path you favoured."

"There is," Victoria replied with a nod. "But I must say it is not actually at my home. It is at Mr. Shelton's. We are neighbors, and our parents are good friends," she explained, not that she thought Mr. Carlyle did not already know that — no matter what sort of feigned look of surprise he wore. "On their estate, there is a path that winds down from the stables to a frog pond and then through a small stand of trees before opening into a sheep's pasture. It is not a very long walk, but it has such a variety of scenery that makes it most enjoyable. And, if one wishes, a stop at the pond to listen to the frogs is..." she sighed, "peaceful. Absolutely peaceful."

"It sounds charming. Do you walk there alone?" There was a particular tone to his question that hinted at wishing to know if Roger were a rival.

"Not always," Victoria replied. "Over the years, I have, at times, walked there with Mrs. Berkley – though less after she married than before, of course – and when Mr. Shelton is home, he will, on occasion accompany me." And capture at least one frog whom he would address as Mr. Brown and ask him how he had been keeping himself and if he still attended tea parties. Her lips tipped up at the thought. Roger would be an excellent father. His children would never want for entertainment. She caught a sigh before it escaped her as she considered that she might have to watch him entertain children who were not hers.

"And do you visit your neighbors often?"

Victoria nodded. "My parents and the Sheltons are great friends. We are in each other's company to some degree several times a week. My mother will call on Mrs. Shelton, or Mrs. Shelton will call on my mother. And when Diana and I were young, we spent a great deal of time playing together and being tormented by her brother."

"Then, Mrs. Berkley is very nearly like a sister to you and Mr. Shelton, a brother."

Victoria smiled. "Nearly." But not quite. Mrs. Berkley might be a sister, but Roger was not a brother. He was her friend, her very dear friend, who had captured her heart.

"Oh!" Felicity cried. "There was a rock. Oh, dear! My ankle turned." She limped on her left foot and leaned heavily on Mr. Ramsey's arm, pressing herself against him as she did so.

"You should sit down," Mr. Clayton said. "It is a fortunate thing we have reached the rotunda."

"Indeed, it is!" Felicity agreed. "Would you help me take a seat on the steps?" She asked Mr. Ramsey.

Mr. Ramsey eagerly assisted her.

Felicity held her foot out in front of her and twirled it this way and that while whimpering softly.

"This is very unfortunate!" Grace declared. "I heard Mrs. Abernathy just today speaking to Mama about the ball she is planning, and you love to dance."

"Oh!" Felicity brightened. "I am certain my ankle shall be well by then."

"If it is not, I shall dance with every gentleman for you," Grace volunteered as she crouched down to rub her sister's ankle.

Felicity's lips curled slightly as if displeased before she turned her look of disdain into a grimace. "Do be careful, Grace. And I am certain that with just a bit of rest, I shall be able to dance every dance."

"If you are not able to dance, there is always the chance of a stroll in the garden," Mr. Carlyle said.

Felicity ducked her head and blushed but not before Victoria saw her cast an uneasy glance at Mr. Clayton. "I do enjoy gardens."

"Indeed," Mr. Clayton muttered. He turned and looked back towards the house. "They will likely start playing games soon. We should head back."

"But I had hoped to see the far side of the rotunda," Felicity said with a small pout.

"You do not need me for that," Mr. Clayton said. "I find I have had my fill of *gardens*."

Victoria's eyebrows rose. It appeared Mr. Clayton had reached his limit for endurance. She could not help but feel somewhat happy for him.

"Do you wish to return to the house, or will you stay with your sister?" Mr. Clayton asked Grace.

"Umm," Grace looked uneasily at her sister. "It would be rather unkind to make Mr. Clayton return to the house by himself."

"Then you must accompany him," Felicity said. "I am certain Mr. Carlyle and Mr. Ramsey will see me safely returned. My ankle is feeling much better already. I think it was only a small turn and likely will only bruise with no other ill effects." She straightened, lowered her foot to the ground and held a hand out to Mr. Ramsey to help her rise. "Do not tell mother I have hurt myself. I would not wish for her to worry."

"Oh, goodness no! Of course, I would not wish for her to worry either."

And with that, Grace took Mr. Clayton's arm, and they left Victoria precisely where she did not wish to be — at the rotunda with Felicity, Mr. Ramsey, and Mr. Carlyle.

Chapter 11

Roger slipped into the Abernathy's library and made his way to the liquor cabinet. A bottle of port stood at the ready surrounded by several glasses.

For the past two nights, several of the gentlemen in attendance had claimed the library as a haven of sorts where they could escape the festivities in other portions of the house.

"There is a bet going on about you."

Roger turned from the sideboard, carafe of port still in hand, and eyed Mr. Yardley, the only other gentleman in the room. "About my absence?"

Mr. Yardley nodded as he rose to join Roger. "Apparently, some did not expect you to return." He handed his empty glass to Roger to be refilled. "I would not have returned," Yardley muttered. "Blasted house parties were designed to torture us, gentlemen. I am certain of it. I have five sisters at home. I do not need to be sent to a house brimming with young debutantes to let me know I need to marry. Between my sisters and my mother, I have constant reminders."

He picked up his glass. "However, I would like to have all five of my sisters here so I could see them married off. Then, I could find a quiet place to ruminate at least once during the day."

"So you would not be interested in a wife who has a talent for talking?" Roger asked.

Yardley snorted. "Heavens, no!"

"I imagine that once they are all married, you will be able to take the place of your sisters for your mother then?"

The man peered over his glass at Roger, his brow furrowed. "How do you mean?"

"I assume your mother is used to having five females with whom to converse, is she not?" Roger unbuttoned his jacket and relaxed into a chair across from Yardley. The man was one of the gents Grace had listed, and since the man was used to talkative women, perhaps he might be amenable to considering Grace – with a little persuasion.

Yardley nodded. "Go on."

"When all your sisters are finally married off – are they younger or older?"

"The youngest is just turned fifteen."

"Well, then, it will not be long until all of them are married, I would imagine."

"I would hope," Yardley muttered into his glass before taking a gulp of its contents.

"And when they are all settled at estates which are likely too far away for daily visits, your mother will need someone with whom to discuss fashion and recipes and the like. Of course, she might have enough neighbours to suffice, and you will be left to yourself." Roger bit back a smile at the look of horror on Yardley's face. "Not many neighbours?"

"Only three, and they are worse than my sisters for gossip!"

"I suppose a quiet wife would be willing to listen to your mother and likely agree to everything she says."

The look of horror on the face of the gentleman across from Roger deepened.

"Or," Roger swirled his drink, "you could choose a wife who is not so very quiet but is sweet and likely to question things. I would imagine such a lady would spend a great deal of time keeping your mother occupied, but, well, there is no way around it, you would still be subjected to a degree of chatter. However, the volume of two ladies cannot be as great as six."

Yardley drained his glass and placed it, with a loud thud, on a table he could reach from his chair. "And do you have a particular lady in mind who fits these qualifications?"

Roger took a slow sip of his port. "Perhaps. Is your mother kind?"

"Exceptionally."

"Are you opposed to a young wife?"

"First season?"

Roger inclined his head in an affirmative response. "Soon to enter her second."

Yardley's brow furrowed while he scratched his jaw.

"You are not so very old," Roger prompted. "You are what? A year older than me?"

Yardley shrugged. "Twenty-seven."

"The same age then."

"Does she have feathers for brains like so many do?"

Roger shook his head. "She does not seem to

be excessively bright, but she has potential for growth."

"So she wants guidance?"

Roger nodded. For all that Grace thought she was well-accomplished, she had spent too long in her sister's shadow to have learned anything of real value. Oh, she had no doubt learned to flirt and speak about inanely trivial things, but he sincerely doubted that she had learned how to think for herself. Simply being removed from her sister's influence would be a boon to her.

"Who?" Yardley demanded.

"Miss Grace Love."

For a moment, Roger thought Yardley's eyes might pop out of his head.

"That coquette? Does Clayton not want her?"

Roger placed his glass alongside Yardley's. "No, no, that is Miss Felicity Love. I would take a wide berth around that one, and Clayton would do well to be rid of her. Grace is her sister."

Yardley's brows were still lifted as he shook his head.

"They are as alike as a rainy day and a sunny morning," Roger assured Yardley. "I dare say that

Miss Grace received all the sweetness in that family while her sister got none."

Yardley still did not look convinced that he should consider Grace.

"She will likely not thank me for this, but Miss Grace has mentioned that she finds you attractive. Therefore, persuading her to accept an offer should not be too challenging should you think, after getting to know her, that you would rub along well together. She is no pauper."

"I had heard that," Yardley muttered. "Carlyle and Ramsey mentioned it in relation to the elder Love chit. Both are looking to make improvements to their estates."

"And you? Are you looking to improve your estate?"

Yardley shook his head. "I am looking for some-one to be the mother of the heir to my estate."

The right corner of Roger's lips tipped into a sly smirk. "It would be no hardship to attempt such a thing with Miss Grace. She is not so thin as some and perhaps a trifle shorter than I might prefer, but she is not without some very pleasing curves."

Yardley chuckled. "And, from what I hear, you are well-versed in such things."

"Was," Roger said. He had noticed the fine figures of several ladies in attendance, but not one of them had appealed to him as they once would have. To be honest, for some time now, he had not found as much enjoyment in studying the female form as he used to. He had pondered that thought for a while as he sat in his room discussing marriage and family with Berkley, and, on his ride back to the Abernathys', he had come to understand that it was because he craved something more. *Someone* more. He did not just want a pretty lady to charm and seduce. He wanted a friend – a most beloved friend. Someone who would not only warm his bed but who would also tease him out of a bad humour and encourage – and even scold – him to making wise choices.

"Why do you not pursue her if you think she is so tempting and sweet-tempered?"

Roger shook his head. "My desires lie elsewhere."

"Miss Hamilton?"

"Yes." There was no point in denying it, for he intended to make his preference known as soon as he could find a few moments alone with his friend. He pulled at his left sleeve. He knew that Berkley had told him Victoria was favourably inclined towards him, but still the thought of presenting himself to her in such a way made him uneasy. She deserved so much better than he had ever been. However, in his mind, there was no man in the world who was truly good enough for her, and so, it was just as well that he present himself to her rather than some other undeserving fool.

"I had thought so," Yardley cried. "That is why I put my money on you returning – especially with Carlyle sniffing around her purse strings."

Roger tipped his head and studied Yardley. "I beg your pardon?"

"I told you. Carlyle wishes to improve his estate, and everyone knows Miss Hamilton has the heaviest purse."

Was that the reason the fellow was pursuing Victoria?

"Miss Abernathy is just as well-dowered," Roger said.

"But Miss Abernathy is a trifle more difficult to pry away from her mother's side long enough to *convince* her that she should marry him."

Roger's heart hammered in his ears. "What do you mean?"

Yardley chuckled. "Surely, someone with your reputation must know how one goes about persuading a lady."

But this was Victoria. She was not some lady. She was... Victoria. He rose. It was perhaps best if he showed his face tonight rather than waiting until morning as he had thought to do.

"They are playing cards in the drawing room," Yardley offered as Roger reached the door.

"Do you wish to play and perhaps observe Miss Grace?" Roger asked.

"No, I would like to stay right where I am in undisturbed bliss and most likely getting properly foxed."

Roger pulled the door open to find the very young lady about whom he had been talking standing in the hall with Everett, attempting to persuade him to play cards.

"You have returned!" she cried in delight when she saw him.

"Indeed, I have, Miss Grace," he said as he cast a significant look at Yardley, but Yardley only shook his head and remained seated where he was.

"Is there alcohol in there?" Clayton asked.

Roger moved out of his way and allowed him to enter the library.

"My sister has been abominably rude," Grace whispered. "And I think he is giving her up," she added after taking a peek inside the library.

"Is he?" That seemed a development of no little significance, and Roger could understand why Everett was in search of some libation. Were Roger not in desperate need of finding Victoria, he would take himself back into the library and attempt to help the fellow through it with a few encouraging words and by refilling his glass as needed.

Grace nodded as she poked her head around Roger so that she could see inside the library again. "Mr. Clayton," she said, "please do not drink too much. You will only feel dreadful in the morning."

"I will only drink as much as is needed," he assured, lifting his glass in salute to her words.

She marched into the room and added in a low voice. "She is not worth casting up your accounts and feeling as if a battalion of soldiers is using your head for their parade. Oh, good evening, Mr. Yardley. Are you not going to play cards?"

He shook his head.

"And do you have as good an excuse as Mr. Clayton?"

Yardley opened his mouth and then closed it.

"He does not," Roger said, earning a glare from Yardley.

Grace's brow furrowed and her lips puckered. "Are you a bore, Mr. Yardley?"

"A bore?" he cried. "I should think not. I am a rather interesting fellow."

Grace shook her head and sighed. "I am afraid that is not true, for all the interesting gentlemen are playing cards – save, of course, for those who have been treated very poorly by my sister."

"There is no chaperone in here," Roger warned.

"Oh, goodness!" Grace cried and scampered to the door. "I forgot in my concern for Mr. Clayton. You do not suppose I am ruined now, do you? That would be quite horrid."

"I am absolutely certain your reputation is still intact," Roger replied with a chuckle. "And if it is not, I am sure one of us gentlemen would do right by you."

Grace shook her head. "Not you. Your sister told me. You will not be tricked into marrying no matter what might happen to a lady's reputation because of her scheming." Her brow furrowed. "Of course, I was not scheming. I did not mean to trick anyone into marriage."

"I am certain you did not," Roger assured her as he closed the door to the library.

"It is not that I would not consider it, which is likely not right for me to do, is it?"

"No, it is not. Or I imagine that is what my sister would say." Roger offered her his arm, and they began walking toward the drawing room.

Grace glanced back over her shoulder. "Mr. Yardley is very handsome, is he not?"

"I suppose he must be if you say so," Roger replied.

"And poor Mr. Clayton." She sighed. "I quite like him. I did from the time we arrived at Heath-cote. However, as Felicity pointed out, she is older, and so it is she who should marry first."

Roger stopped walking. "And you gave him up for her?"

Grace shrugged. "I had not lost my heart to him." She glanced back at the library door. "And I thought my sister had." She shook her head. "But apparently, she has not, for she is at the rotunda with Mr. Ramsey likely letting him kiss her."

"But I thought you thought Mr. Ramsey was of interest."

Again, Grace shrugged. "I did, but..."

"Your sister is older?"

Grace nodded.

"She deserves to be an old maid," Roger muttered. "Is she at the rotunda alone with Mr. Ramsey?"

"No. Miss Hamilton and Mr. Carlyle are with them."

Roger pulled Grace across the drawing room in his hurry to reach the window. "I do not see them."

"That is because Felicity wished to see the far side of the rotunda." She blew out a breath. "So she can kiss him," she added in a disappointed whisper.

"Do you wish to go to the rotunda with me?" Roger asked.

"Why are you going there?" Grace hurried behind him toward the garden door.

"Because I am not going to allow Mr. Carlyle to kiss Victoria."

Grace blinked. "Do you think he will?"

Unfortunately, Roger did. The backside of the rotunda was the perfect secluded place for a gentleman to attempt a seduction. He stopped just outside the garden door and pulled Grace off the path. "Do you remember how we were talking about finding a match for Miss Hamilton?"

Grace nodded.

"And can you keep a secret?"

Again, Grace nodded.

"I have found her a match."

"You have? Who? Is it Mr. Yardley?"

Roger blew out a breath as he shook his head. "It is me. She is the one who I fear losing more than I fear losing my freedom."

"Oh, that is the most delightful thing!"

There was no mistaking Grace's delight for it was evident in her excited whisper and the quick clap of her hands as well as the smile on her face.

"Then, we must hurry," she said as she took his arm and stepped back onto the garden path.

Chapter 12

The evening breeze ruffled the hem of Victoria's dress. It was a pleasant enough evening to be out in the garden, or it would be if she had been in the garden with anyone other than her current companions. She glanced back at the house one last time before following Felicity around the rotunda.

"Oh, a path!" Felicity cried.

There before them was a narrow path that wound down the hill and into some trees.

"Would you like to see where it leads?" Mr. Ramsey asked.

"No," Victoria replied before Felicity could say a word. "We are to return to play games. Your mother will be worried, as will Mrs. Berkley."

Felicity rolled her eyes and giggled. "You do not need to accompany us. You may stay right here with Mr. Carlyle. I am certain he would not feel it an inconvenience to wait here with you while Mr. Ramsey and I explore this little path. I am sure it would not take long."

"No longer than necessary," Mr. Ramsey said with a wink for Felicity, who blushed and ducked her head while peeking up at the gentleman at her side.

"I am not allowing you to go wandering down a path with no chaperone." Victoria held Felicity's gaze.

"You are such a prude." Felicity smirked at Mr. Ramsey. "Whatever do you expect us to do while we are out of your sight?"

"It is most improper, and I shall not be a party to your ruin."

"What Miss Hamilton says is true," Mr. Carlyle said. "It would not be right for us to allow either of you to play so recklessly with Miss Love's reputation." He turned to Victoria. "I think we ought to accompany them."

"We are expected back. We told our chaperones that we were going to the rotunda and back."

"And we are at the rotunda," Mr. Carlyle replied, "and when we return, we will be back. I see no untruth in what we said even if we take a short stroll down this path."

Victoria gaped at him. He saw nothing untrue in his story? "To the rotunda and back did not include to the rotunda and then a little further and back." She folded her arms and glared, in turn, at each of the others who were with her.

"Then, we have no option but to wait here for them to return."

"We have the option of them not taking a walk down that path." Victoria pointed to the path down which Felicity and Mr. Ramsey were already walking. "Of all the deviant and deceitful things!"

"There is no harm done," Mr. Carlyle cajoled. "We can still see them."

"And when they reach the trees, Mr. Carlyle, then what?"

Victoria descended to the path. She shook her head and huffed attempting to clear some of the anger she felt at being placed in the situation in which she found herself. Miss Love was horrid. Simply and utterly horrid. There was no other word for her. She treated her sister poorly and ignored the gentleman who was courting her while blatantly flirting with another. And then there was

Mr. Carlyle who saw nothing wrong with what was being done?

"I promise you that I shall never agree to walk with you in the garden again," she said, allowing her displeasure to bubble over.

"Not even when we marry?"

Victoria stood stalk still and turned slowly toward Mr. Carlyle. "I beg your pardon?" She was certain her ears must be playing tricks with her mind. He certainly could not be presuming that she would marry him!

"I was only wondering if your never walking with me again was to be confined to this house party or if it extended to when we were married."

She had heard him correctly. "We are not marrying."

He smiled. "I think we are. We are quite good together. Your piano playing mixes well with my singing. You are lively and thoughtful – just what I prefer in a lady."

"Piano playing and liveliness? These are the requirements for your wife?"

"They are but two."

"No." She shook her head to emphasize her point. "No, I will not marry you."

He caught her hand. "Please, Miss Hamilton? I can give you more reasons if you give me time to consider them, but surely, you feel the attraction between us."

He was mad. That must be it. There was no attraction between them. She merely tolerated him because she had not wished to be rude.

He lifted her fingers to his lips.

"Mr. Carlyle, I will thank you to unhand me this instant. I feel nothing akin to attraction to you, and I have no desire to marry you."

He dropped her hand and shrugged. "What will the others say?"

Disquiet settled around her chest, pulling it tightly in on itself, forcing out what breath she held in her lungs. "What will who say?"

He waved his hand back toward the house. "The others." His lips tipped up on the right side. "We have lost sight of Miss Love and Mr. Ramsey, and they have lost sight of us."

"You would lie?"

His brow furrowed though his smile did not fade. "Lie? About what?"

She looked down the path toward where Felicity should be but was not. Then, she turned toward her companion, dipped a curtsey, and said, "Good evening, Mr. Carlyle," before heading back toward the rotunda. She needed to be back in the safety of the house. She cared not what happened to Felicity at the moment. The girl had made her decision, and she could face the consequences. Victoria was not prepared to be forced into marrying Mr. Carlyle.

"Miss Hamilton," he called after her, "the damage is already done, do you not think?"

She stopped at the top of the steps to the rotunda. Looking down at him where he stood on the ground below her, she shook her head. "Damage or no damage. I will not marry you, Mr. Carlyle." She held up her hand as he began to ascend the stairs. "No, Mr. Carlyle, you must remain here in case, Mr. Ramsey cannot carry Miss Love to the house by himself."

His brow furrowed. "I do not understand your meaning."

"Her ankle."

"It is not injured."

"Oh, I am certain you are quite correct about that." The little vixen had been walking far too quickly down that path for her ankle to have been even slightly injured. It was a ploy. Nothing more. An act to rid herself of Mr. Clayton and her sister so that she could have Mr. Ramsey all to herself.

"However," Victoria continued, "she did say it was injured, and I feel it is only proper that I seek help for her."

"But, she does not wish to worry her mother."

Victoria laughed. "Of course, she does not, for that would not give her the opportunity she is now taking to be alone with Mr. Ramsey, and, I am certain, Mr. Ramsey is happy to help with any subterfuge that would lead him to where he is now, doing what he is likely doing." She smiled at Mr. Carlyle's surprised expression. "I have been friends with Mr. Shelton for far too long not to know how these assignations go."

"Indeed?" Mr. Carlyle's brows rose before a smirk crawled across his lips. "And how precisely do you know?"

Victoria's cheeks flamed at his insinuation. "It is not how you imagine. He merely likes to shock me with stories." That was probably not helping her cause. "It matters not. You must stay here, and I will inform Mrs. Love of her daughter's injury."

She spun on her heels and hurried around the rotunda.

She should not have been hurrying quite so quickly, for it was her haste which made her lose her footing on the bottom step of the rotunda.

She brushed the dirt from her palms. They would likely bruise, but the skin was not broken, no matter how much the stinging wanted her to believe it was. Her dress, however, was not so fortunate. There was a small tear at the bottom where her foot had caught it as she had risen from the ground after falling. She sighed as she noticed there was also a green stain from the grass on her left hip.

She dashed a tear from her cheek. This was nothing about which to cry. A little pain was not worth the tears. However, returning to the house as she was would be worth a few tears if Mr. Carlyle chose to tell tales, for those tales would be much easier to believe when coupled with the state of her clothing.

She would take the less direct path to the house. The one that would take her to the side where she could then slip around to the front. It would be easier to sneak in and up to her room without being seen if she approached it in such a fashion.

Oh! Her knee hurt, but she was not about to lift her skirt to check it until she had gained the privacy of her room.

Thankfully, the only person near the front of the house when she entered was Mr. Clayton, who was making his way up the grand staircase with a rather full glass of what appeared to be port in his hand.

"Miss Hamilton," he greeted as she made to pass him.

"Mr. Clayton."

"Your dress is looking worse for the wear."

"As are you," she returned with a smile. His cheeks were flushed, and his gaze wandered, and if Victoria were to guess based on how her brother looked when he had indulged too much in alcohol, Mr. Clayton was well on his way to being foxed.

He chuckled. "I am not feeling it, though I suspect I will tomorrow, and it will make for a long ride home."

"You are leaving?"

He nodded. "It seems best. Miss Love is off in the garden with Mr. Ramsey."

"Yes, I know."

He blew out a breath and offered her his arm. She thought about not taking it until he swayed. Then, she considered how taking his arm was a good way to ensure his safe arrival to the hall above them.

"You will be missed," she said as she helped him up the stairs.

He snorted. "Not by many. House parties." He shook his head. "Dreadful things."

"Indeed." Victoria could not agree more with his assessment.

"No need to stay where I am not welcome," he added.

Victoria pointed him in the direction of his room and stood at the top of the stairs watching for a few minutes to make sure he was far away from any danger of falling down the stairs before she turned and went to her room, where she sat on her bed and examined her somewhat bloody knee.

She had to agree with Mr. Clayton — going home did not seem so bad an idea.

She rose and rang the bell for her maid before going to the washstand to pour a little water into the basin for washing her hands.

"Would you send for Mrs. Berkley," she said

when her maid entered. "And then I think I shall retire for the evening."

"Right away, miss."

Victoria removed her shoes and pulled off her stockings. They were dirty and torn but not beyond repair. Once her knee had been washed, she began the work of undoing her hair while she waited for her maid to return and help her with the unfastening of her dress.

"Blast," she muttered. She had put Roger's lavender ribbon in her hair tonight in case he came back. She had foolishly thought that if he saw it, he might realize how much she cared for him. And now, that ribbon was missing. It had likely fallen out when she fell. She should have woven it into her hair rather than just using it as an adornment on her comb.

"Is something wrong?" Diana asked as she came into the room.

"I fell," Victoria turned so Diana could see her knee.

"Oh, my dear, how did that happen?"

"I was attempting to get away from Mr. Carlyle as quickly as I could." She shrugged. "I should have been more careful."

Diana wore a horrified expression as she crossed to where Victoria sat. "What happened?"

Victoria shook her head. "I will tell you, but not now. Right now, I need you to tell Mrs. Love that her eldest daughter has sneaked away down a secluded path behind the rotunda with Mr. Ramsey. She twisted her ankle earlier, and so Mr. Carlyle was good enough to stay in case there was a need for his assistance in returning her to the house."

The eyebrow over Diana's left eye rose. "Mr. Carlyle was good enough to do that?"

"That is what you are to tell Mrs. Love."

"And then, you will tell me all?"

Victoria nodded. She would gladly tell her friend all that there was to tell, after which she would ask Diana to take her home.

Diana gave her one more concerned look before exiting the room and leaving Victoria to the care of her maid.

Chapter 13

"Where is Victoria?" Roger demanded.

Three people were descending the steps to the rotunda when Grace and Roger reached it, and not one of them was Victoria.

"Victoria is it?" Carlyle smirked.

Roger glowered at him. "We have been friends our whole lives. Now, where is she? Miss Grace said she was here."

He was not opposed to hitting a popinjay such as Carlyle if needed. In fact, he'd be rather pleased to do it. However, now was not the time for such things no matter in which direction his feelings ran on the subject.

"Oh, she was. I assure you she was." Grace clutched his arm more tightly. "She was right here when I left."

"I do not doubt you," Roger assured her. "What

is that?" he asked as, out of the corner of his eye, he noticed Miss Love stooping to pick something up off the ground.

"My, you are a suspicious fellow this evening, Mr. Shelton." Miss Love spoke in a sweet, teasing tone; however, Roger was not in the frame of mind to politely endure teasing. He rarely was when the source was a conniving female such as Miss Love.

"And your cheeks are rather flushed, and you have a few tendrils of hair out of place." He added a smile and fluttered his lashes much as she had done a moment ago. He chuckled when she gasped as if affronted. "That will not convince me of your innocence. I know full-well the advantage that a secluded location such as the far side of the rotunda and the path beyond can give to those who are hoping to avoid propriety for a few minutes."

"There is a path behind the rotunda?" Grace asked, leaning her head to the side as if attempting to look around the stone building in front of them. "How do you know?"

"I have seen it," Roger answered. "I always make myself familiar with all potential traps and routes of escape," he added. "I do not intend to marry until I decide to marry."

"To avoid a trap?" Carlyle said with a laugh. "Do you not mean devise a plan to take advantage of the seclusion such a spot affords?"

Roger affected a nonchalant shrug. "Not unlike what you and Ramsey were about."

"We were only seeing the other side of the rotunda," Carlyle assured him with a hint of anger in his voice.

"Yes, well, a seduction is much more effective if there is a lady to seduce," Roger quipped, causing the gentleman's eyes to narrow. Drawing out Carlyle could be an exceptionally satisfying prospect.

"I was not alone," Carlyle replied. "Miss Hamilton was willing to keep me company."

He felt Grace grasp at his arm, as he moved to close the distance between himself and Carlyle. "Where. Is. She?" He enunciated each word slowly.

"She returned to the house," Ramsey put forward.

"Yes, yes," Carlyle agreed. "But not until *after* she informed me of how well you have taught her about assignations."

As much as Roger wished to hit the man, he

refrained, allowing himself to only give Carlyle a good shove that sent him stumbling backward. "She is a good friend. I would be careful how I spoke of her if I were you."

"Is that so?" Carlyle taunted. "Exactly how good a friend is she, Shelton? We all know your reputation with the fairer sex."

"Mr. Shelton." Grace was at his elbow. "Please, do not hit him."

"Why not?" He pulled his arm away from her. "Even you must know what he is insinuating about Victoria."

"I do, and it is most improper. But think of the explanation that will be required if Mr. Carlyle returns with a black eye or bloody nose." She looked at Carlyle and added, "Not that he does not deserve both."

From the vehement tone she used to say that last bit, it appeared to Roger that there was some fire hidden within Miss Grace Love. Hopefully, she would learn to use that fire when dealing with her sister, who was smiling behind her fingers as if what was happening was the most amusing things she had ever witnessed.

"Do you find me entertaining, Miss Love?"

Roger asked. "Or do you find it diverting when someone accuses another lady of impropriety?"

Felicity gasped. "You are very forward, Mr. Shelton."

"And you are a conniving wench, Miss Love."

"Mr. Shelton!" Grace scolded.

"She is. You have seen how she has treated Mr. Clayton."

Grace shrugged and nodded.

"Mr. Clayton, who," he glared at Felicity, "happens to be the brother of my very dear friend."

"It was not right what she did, " Miss Grace said.

"Indeed, it was not. You are far more sensible than your sister will likely ever be, Miss Grace. Shall we return to the house?" Spending any further time with Ramsey, Carlyle, and Miss Love seemed a poor idea for it would only lead to him being less and less able to rein in his temper and would do nothing to help him find Victoria.

"Mr. Ramsey is not good enough for you," he whispered as he and Grace began to walk back to the house. "You deserve far better."

"Thank you," Grace muttered sadly.

They walked silently for a few moments, and with every step, Roger became more and more indigent about whatever had transpired at the rotunda – and not just because of what Carlyle had implied about Victoria.

The bulk of his anger lay with Miss Love. Had she not schemed to steal away with Mr. Ramsey, Victoria would not have been put in a position with Mr. Carlyle which was awkward enough for her to say anything as shocking as what Carlyle had implied she had said about seductions. Victoria did not say shocking things to anyone but him – and then, it was only because he had pushed her to the point of doing so.

Added to that sin was the abominable way in which Miss Love had treated Everett – and her sister. He glanced sideways at Grace. How could an older sister take advantage of a younger sister in such a fashion? Was Miss Love completely incapable of loving anyone save herself? He was about to inquire of Grace how she could abide such a sister when they were approached by Mrs. Love.

"Have you seen Felicity? Is she well? Why did you not tell me your sister was injured?" she demanded of Grace all in one breath.

"That is likely because she is not injured," Roger replied.

"But I have received a report that she is!"

"She did turn her ankle, but she said that it was nothing and that I was not to worry you about it," Grace said.

"She was not favouring either ankle when we saw her just now. However, her hair was a bit disheveled, and her cheeks looked rather pleasingly pink, which I would assume was due to the few stolen moments with Mr. Ramsey and not any particular injury."

Mrs. Love's eyes grew wide, and she turned once again to her youngest daughter. "Did you know your sister was planning to sneak off?"

Grace shook her head. "Not completely."

"What do you mean not completely? Either you did or you did not?"

"I knew it was likely and that it was what she wished." Grace's head dipped.

"Then, you did know."

"Yes," Grace whispered, "I knew all too well when she sent me back with Mr. Clayton. Until then, I was not entirely sure."

"Mr. Clayton is not with her?"

"No, he has given up on her," Roger said, "as any sensible fellow should."

Mrs. Love gasped.

"She has treated him very ill, madame."

"Has she indeed?"

She was questioning the fact? How could she not see that it was true beyond a shadow of a doubt?

"She ignored him while flirting with others and this after spending some stolen moments with him in the garden at Stratsbury Park." He motioned toward the rotunda. "And tonight, she has schemed to do the same thing with Mr. Ramsey without taking care whatsoever to hide it from Clayton, who is not happy about being rid of her at the moment, but he will be."

"Can all this be true?" She looked as if she was about to faint dead away.

"Yes, Mother," Grace answered.

"And you have helped her conceal this?'

"She asked me to."

"With all due respect, madame," Roger interrupted, for he did not wish to stand here discussing Grace's role in all of this when he needed to find Victoria, "I believe it is your eldest daughter who deserves your ire at present. I will return Miss Grace to the house."

Mrs. Love tipped her head and gave him a questioning look. "I have not seen you all day, and now you are here with my daughter. Why is that?"

Roger blew out a breath, but before he could say anything, Grace replied for him.

"He was looking for Miss Hamilton. He has only just arrived back from...where were you?"

"I went home."

"He has only just arrived back from his home and needs to speak to Miss Hamilton most urgently. So, I was helping him find her."

"We were never outside the view of the house, madame."

"Nothing untoward happened?"

"I would never treat your daughter so ill. Nor would she allow it."

"I would not?" Grace asked.

"No, do you not remember what you told me earlier when we were discussing Mr. Clayton?"

"Oh! Right!" She shook her head as she looked at her mother. "Mrs. Berkley told me that Mr. Shelton would never be tricked into marrying anyone. He would leave them ruined – not that he would ruin them, that part would be done by the lady's scheming – rather than be forced into marriage. And I would not be foolish enough to be ruined."

Mrs. Love wore a perplexed expression. "I think that is good?"

"Most admirable," Roger assured her. "Now, if I could return Grace to the house and find Miss Hamilton."

"Yes, yes," Mrs. Love still wore a bewildered expression. "She is in the house, and, from what I heard before Mrs. Berkley found me, Miss Hamilton was seen to be on her way upstairs with Mr. Clayton."

Had the woman said what he thought she had said?

"Why was she on her way upstairs with Mr. Clayton?" Grace asked.

Mrs. Love shook her head. "How should I know? However, it does seem rather improper."

It most certainly did! Roger gave Grace's arm a tug. "I think we should walk rapidly."

"If it would not cause a stir, I would suggest we run," Grace said as she scampered to keep up with him. "In fact, if you wish to run, I can find my way back to the house on my own."

"No, I told your mother I would see you there. I am a man of my word."

"For a gentleman with your reputation, Mr. Shelton, you are most shockingly noble."

Roger chuckled and thanked her. He had never taken advantage where advantage was not given. He was not a swindler – not even when it came to kisses. And while he had enjoyed every garden and alcove interlude of which he had been a part, and he was not opposed to presenting the suggestion of impropriety, not once had he stolen anything. However, all of that was in the past. Presently, he had only to find Victoria and persuade her to marry him and make him the happiest of all men.

"You!"

Roger stopped just inside the door to the drawing room as a red-faced gentleman approached him.

"May I be of service?" he asked warily. He had not seen Mr. Upton at the house party before this, but he knew him from town. The man was a rash, hot-headed man.

"Roger!"

He turned to see his sister hurrying toward him. It seemed he was not destined to make a quick and quiet entry.

"Where have you been?" Diana asked.

"With my sister," Mr. Upton said just before his fist made contact with Roger's chin.

Chapter 14

Roger staggered backward, rubbing his throbbing chin. "I went home," he said to Diana.

"Home?" Mr. Upton scoffed. "Not according to my sister."

"I swear I have not been with your sister," Roger said, dodging another punch before dropping his shoulder and charging the man, sending them both to the floor.

"You'll marry her!" Mr. Upton struggled to toss Roger off of him.

"I will not marry a liar." Roger sat on Mr. Upton and held the fellow's wrists. "And if your sister is the one who has told you that she was with me, she is most certainly a liar. I was at home. You can verify that with my mother, my father, and Mr. Berkley, as well as his infant son."

"Get off me!"

"Not unless you give me your word that you will not attack me again."

Mr. Upton struggled for a moment longer before assuring Roger that he would not hit him.

"Now," Roger said after he had risen, straightened his jacket, and smoothed his hair, "might we find a place to discuss this in a more gentlemanly fashion?" He rubbed his chin. A cold compress would be most welcome.

"The library," Mr. Upton suggested.

"A proper choice." Roger turned toward the door. "And bring your sister," he called over his shoulder.

"I would also like to speak to you." Diana followed him from the room. "However, I must go up to my charge and tell her that someone has spread a vicious rumor about her and Mr. Clayton."

Roger shook his head. "Vicious rumors seem to be the thing this evening."

Diana raised an eyebrow at him and scowled. "And if you had been here instead of dashing home, none of them would have started."

Her words smarted nearly as much as his chin. "I had a good reason to be gone." He caught her elbow before she could make her escape. "I spoke to your husband."

"About what?"

"Your hopes for me."

She tipped her head, her brow furrowing.

He blew out a slow breath as Mr. and Miss Upton joined them. "I will tell you more later. Just know that I wish for the same." He released his sister's elbow and motioned to the library. "After you."

"Diana," he called to his sister before he followed the Uptons into the library.

She turned toward him.

"I'm sorry."

She stood looking expectantly at him.

"For making a mess of things."

She smiled at him.

"You will tell Victoria that?"

She nodded.

"She is not with Clayton?"

Diana sighed and walked back to him. "It is a rumour. She is in her room. She fell – I believe while trying to avoid Mr. Carlyle."

Carlyle had caused harm to come to Victoria? Could fury cause a gentleman's heart to explode from beating too rapidly? He rubbed his chest. He was likely to discover the answer. "I should have injured him when I had the chance!"

Diana patted his cheek. "Later, dear. You have people waiting for you." She tipped her head toward the open door in front of which he stood.

He gave her a small smile and then, drawing a breath, joined the Uptons and a sleepy Yardley in the library where he crossed to the decanter of port and poured a small amount into a glass.

"Yardley, I am disappointed. You have not emptied this carafe."

"There is only so much one man can consume. Clayton did a fine job helping me consume that much." He glanced at their companions. "Should I leave?"

Roger shook his head. "There is no need. In fact, you might find this entertaining, and I would appreciate a witness should Mr. Upton decide to accost me again." Roger rubbed his chin.

"You hit Shelton?" Yardley asked Upton.

"He has ruined my sister." Upton stood behind the chair in which his sister sat.

"He has?" Yardley asked in surprise.

"No, he has not," Miss Upton protested.

"But I heard you say he," Upton stabbed the air in Roger's direction, "stole away to be with you."

Miss Upton's look of mortification deepened. Roger was confident that if the chair were to burst into flames and consume the young lady with it, she would not be coming back as a disgruntled ghost except perhaps to torment her brother.

"You did not hear everything." Her voice was barely above a whisper.

"I heard enough."

"No!" Miss Upton sprang from her chair and turned on her brother. "You never hear enough. You only ever hear what you wish, and you never stop to consider or verify if what you have heard is true."

"I... I... I... I do," Upton sputtered.

"No, you do not. Do you know how many perfectly acceptable gentlemen have not called on me because you have heard something and assumed the worst? And now this! Why are you even here? Was not our aunt a good enough chaperone? Were you afraid I might actually make a match before you could ruin it?"

Roger leaned against the sideboard and nursed

his glass of port while watching the Uptons with interest.

"I am ruined!" Miss Upton dropped back into her chair and covered her face with her hands, her shoulders rising and falling in shuddering silent sobs.

"Why are you here?" Yardley asked Miss Upton's brother.

"Grandmother has taken ill and is not expected to survive the week."

Miss Upton gasped, and her sobs became audible. Roger's heart clenched at the plight of the young woman.

"I have been sent to see that all is well in here," Mr. Abernathy said as he entered the library. "My wife was fearful that one object or another might be injured in your discussion." He gave Roger a quizzical look with a tip of his head toward Miss Upton.

"Her grandmother is gravely ill," Roger replied. "And her brother is an idiot."

"I am sorry to hear it," Mr. Abernathy said. "Will you need to take your sister home?"

"Yes, sir," Mr. Upton answered. "I fear that my

mind is not right at the moment. It seems I heard something which was not what was said."

"Distressing circumstances can cause such to happen. Might I inquire what you heard that was not right?" Mr. Abernathy asked.

"My sister was speaking with your daughter when I arrived, and I heard my sister say that Shelton had stolen away to be with her." He shrugged. "I do not know what the rest was about. I apologize for arriving at a conclusion without all the facts. To both of you," he said, turning to look at Roger. "You would not consider marrying my sister, would you?"

Roger shook his head. "I am afraid I would not. Not that there is any particular deficit with your sister."

"Miss Upton," Mr. Abernathy said, "are you able to tell me about what you and my daughter were speaking which led to this unfortunate misunderstanding?"

"Miss... Love," she managed between sobs.

"What about Miss Love?" Mr. Abernathy pressed.

Miss Upton drew and released a breath as she

dried her cheeks with the handkerchief her brother had given her.

"We... had heard... a rumor that she had set her cap at... Mr. Ramsey." Her eyes were fixed on the handkerchief as she now twisted it in her hands as she gained control of her emotions. "He is very handsome and has a good fortune, unlike Mr. Clayton, who is only handsome and possesses a moderate fortune. Well, you see." She paused. "She had told Miss Abernathy 'I wish he would be like Mr. Shelton and steal away to be with me all day.' I was shocked, of course, and gasped just as my aunt joined us and made me repeat it to her." She sighed. "Which was just as my brother appeared."

"And decided to seek me out," Roger said.

Miss Upton nodded her head. "But I did not know that is what he was doing until he charged across the room at you. Can you forgive me?"

"Of course. As long as we do not have to marry," he replied with a wink.

She smiled.

"Was that the extent of my daughter's gossip?" Mr. Abernathy did not sound at all pleased.

Miss Upton nodded. "The only other thing that

was said before Mr. Shelton entered the drawing room was said by my aunt. She told us that Miss Love would not be best pleased to hear that her offcast – meaning Mr. Clayton," she clarified, "was seen going upstairs with Miss Hamilton."

"Did she say where she heard that?" Roger asked.

"No, she did not. I am not even certain if she heard it or saw it. I was going to ask her, but my brother..."

Roger nodded his understanding. "Miss Hamilton is in her room with my sister. She is not with Mr. Clayton. However, I heard the same thing from a different source."

Mr. Abernathy shook his head. "This is a fine mess, is it not?"

"Indeed," Roger agreed.

"I am almost sorry I have spent the whole evening in the library," Yardley muttered.

"I will speak to both my daughter and my wife." Mr. Abernathy turned toward the door which was flung open before he reached it.

"You cannot marry her." Victoria with a robe wrapped tightly about her and her hair hanging down her back in a braid paid no attention to the others in the room or her chaperone who was attempting softly to tell her that she should return to her room.

"I am not going to," Roger said.

"He is not?" Victoria asked Miss Upton.

"I said I was not." Roger folded his arms and raised a brow at her.

"I was only double checking," Victoria argued. "Where have you been? It is not right to leave without telling your sister or your friends where you have gone."

"I was at home."

"That is what I said," Diana inserted.

"But why? Why would you leave without telling me?"

Roger glanced around the room. "Please get the details of this correct when you share it," he said to the others, "I am not unfamiliar with scandal, but Miss Hamilton is new to it."

He took her hand and pulled her a step closer to him. "I went home to think. Mr. Brown sends his greetings."

"You went to the pond?"

He nodded. "I had something to consider. Recently, it had been pointed out to me that there was a lady in attendance at this house party who would make a very good match for me."

Her brow furrowed. "Why was she a good match?"

"Yes," Diana inserted, "I, too, would like to know that."

Roger glared at his sister briefly before turning his attention back to Victoria. Diana knew perfectly well why. The broad grin she wore confirmed it.

"You choose to ask why and not who?"

"I will ask who after you have told me why," Victoria retorted. "It is not polite to question how I question."

He chuckled. Even here when things were higgledy-piggledy, she scolded him. There had never been any pretense between them.

"Very well. Then, I shall answer why. She is a good match because I love her, most dearly."

Victoria's eyes grew wide. "Who?" Her whisper seemed to take a great deal of effort.

"You, my darling friend, you."

"Oh." She glanced around. "I think I require a chair."

"I'll not let you fall," Roger assured her, pulling

her into his embrace. "Unless, of course, you refuse me. Then, I shall let you gracefully drop to the floor."

She laughed. "Refuse you? What am I to refuse?"

"My offer of marriage."

"And why would I do that? I have loved you for years."

"But what about your reason for not marrying?" he teased.

She shook her head. "It is no longer a reason. For it was only a lack of an offer from you which kept me from marrying. But what about your reason?"

He squeezed her more tightly. "What is there to fear if my best, most beloved friend is my wife? I would rather lose anything other than you."

Her smile in response was all the answer he needed, but just to clarify for their audience, he asked, "You will marry me then?"

"Gladly. Most happily. With pleasure."

"You found her!" Grace cried from the door to the library, causing them both to turn toward her. "I was looking for you, Miss Hamilton, to tell you that Mr. Shelton was looking for you."

"She found me," Roger answered. "And has

saved me from a miserable life without her by accepting my offer."

Grace clapped her hands. "I had hoped so since you are holding her most improperly."

Victoria laughed along with Roger.

"We really do need to see her well-matched," Roger whispered to Victoria.

"Indeed, we do," Victoria replied.

"But not before we cause a bit of a stir." He gave her his best wolfish grin.

"And how shall we do that?"

"I think it must begin with a kiss." He bent his head to touch her lips with his. Then, he pulled back just a nose's-breath, and whispered, "I love you." After which, as any good rogue would, he claimed her lips once again in a deep, passionate kiss that sent shivers of delight through him and, to his great satisfaction, caused her to melt into his embrace and twine her fingers in his hair.

At that moment, he knew that his future would be perfect, not because there would never be any struggles or heartache, but because Victoria would be at his side both as his wife and his dearest, darling friend.

Her Secret Beau

Beau

With a sister like she has, keeping her suitor a secret is a must.

Chapter 1

Grace Love was not the sort of lady who sat along the wall during dances. She was not the sort of lady who stayed at home when there was an outing to the park. She was not the sort of lady who avoided any sort of fun. Or, at least, she had not been such a lady until now. And all it had taken for Grace's world to change had been one house party.

Through narrowed eyes, she watched the progress of her sister's hat as the carriage Felicity was perched in made its way down the street.

"Grace, dear, do not spill your tea on that chair."

"Of course, Mama." Grace pulled her attention back to the sitting room in the townhouse they were renting for the season and away from her traitorous sister.

"Is it not wonderful that Mr. Ramsey has followed Felicity to Bath?" Mrs. Love had crossed to the window to almost, but not quite, peek out of the window. She stood so that she was concealed by the drapery while she attempted to look down the street.

"Of course, Mama." Grace knew that her mother was hopeful that this match would take for Felicity since the last one had not and the circumstances surrounding the dissolution of that match had not placed Grace's sister in a favourable light.

Therefore, every effort was to be made on Felicity's behalf. One did not cry off an attachment to very many gentlemen before she was marked as a lady to be avoided at all costs.

The tea in Grace's hand had lost its appeal. She forced one last sip of it before discarding her cup to the table next to her chair.

Felicity's reticence to commit to just one gentleman had completely shattered any hope Grace had of a wonderful season, for, to help her sister, Grace had been required to give up half of her new dresses and was to accept only a fraction of the invitations she received. Next year could be hers. Once Felicity was married. Until then, she was relegated to the position of a lesser relation – a toadeater. Her lips curled in disgust.

She rose from her chair. "I think I shall go up and read."

"You are a good sister." Her mother favoured her with a pleased smile from where she still stood, almost peeking out of the window. "Who knows, if this drive goes well, you may have a season after all."

"Of course, Mama." Grace forced a smile to her lips. How had she thought her sister was all that was good? How did one live her whole life with another person and not realize that the person sharing your maid was horrid?

Filled with morose thoughts and dashed hopes, she trudged up the stairs to her room. She had thought at one time it would be wonderful to be Felicity, for her sister seemed so cunning, so self-assured, so worldly-wise — and it was not as if her sister was not all those things. She was. It was just that she used them to promote herself at the expense of others – including her own sister.

Grace flopped on her bed and stared at the ceiling. She had very little desire to read. She had only used reading as an excuse to avoid the hopeful effusions of her mother, which she knew would follow Felicity's departure and would not cease until Felicity returned and could add to the chatter about her good fortune.

Was Mr. Ramsey not the most handsome man ever? Was she not the most fortunate creature in all the world? Grace rolled her eyes at the imagined declarations of her sister. Of course, Felicity would say all this with a sigh and an affected wistful look.

Her sister was fortunate. She was fortunate not to be forcefully betrothed to the man who had taken her for a drive since he and she had been in the garden alone for some time at the Abernathy's house party. And as far as Mr. Ramsey being handsome was concerned – well, any lady who cared to cast a glance in Mr. Ramsey's direction could decipher he was an Adonis. In fact, it was Grace who had first pointed that fact out to her sister when they had arrived at the house party.

"I said it because I was considering him," she told the orange ball of fluff that curled up at her side. "You know, Philomena, I was also the one to suggest that Mr. Clayton would make a good catch. His living is not small, and he has such a gentle spirit." She sighed as she ran her hand through her cat's fur. "I should not have said a word. I should have kept all my thoughts to myself, for if I had not said anything, perhaps, I would be installed in a parsonage or be driving with Mr. Ramsey now." She huffed. "And I would be riding in Hyde Park, not in Bath, for I would not have put my reputation in danger."

Philomena mewed her agreement, and Grace rewarded her with a scratch behind her ear.

Before the end of the Abernathy's house party, everyone had heard of Felicity's walk to the garden pavilion with Mr. Ramsey and Mr. Carlyle. That bit of interesting and potentially scandalous news had grown in interest once it was discovered that Mr. Clayton had gone home with his hopes dashed. It did not help either when Felicity, who was unaware of the betrothal which had happened in her absence, attempted to begin a rumor about Miss Hamilton's hair ribbon being in Mr. Carlyle's possession after they had spent a few private moments together.

"Grace."

Grace pushed up onto her elbows and looked toward her bedroom door as it opened slowly.

"You are not reading!" her mother cried, coming into the room.

"I could not ignore Philomena," Grace retorted.

"No, I could not do that, could I, sweetling?" she said to her cat, who once again mewed in agreement.

Her mother gave her an appraising look. "Your time will come. There is no need to sulk overly much because your sister must be put forward. Indeed, your time might be sooner than expected." Her eyes lit with excitement.

"I do not see how," Grace grumbled. "What if Felicity decides someone else is better than Mr. Ramsey as she did with Mr. Clayton?"

Mrs. Love pushed Philomena to the side and took a seat on the bed. "Oh, she will not. She cannot be that stupid."

Grace was not sure she agreed. Stupid was giving up a kind gentleman like Mr. Everett Clayton for a handsome gent who carried himself with a trifle too much assurance. One could not possibly be so attractive as Mr. Ramsey and not know it. At the thought, it occurred to Grace that perhaps she should be happier that her sister had been stupid, or she might find herself tied to that very Adonis-like gentleman who thought too well of himself.

No, she scolded herself, that was bitterness talking – although — Mr. Ramsey had been willing to sneak away in the garden with Felicity when everyone knew that Felicity and Mr. Clayton were nearly betrothed, so maybe it was not bitterness but truth?

"Have you heard a word I said?"

Grace blinked and looked at her mother. "No?" Had her mother been speaking?

"I thought not, for I expected you to be far more excited than you are at such wonderful news."

Grace's brow furrowed. "What wonderful news?"

"You received a letter."

"You opened it?" Grace cried when her mother handed her an unfolded letter.

"I am your mother."

"But it was mine." Just like the three new gowns hanging in Felicity's wardrobe were supposed to be in her wardrobe but were not.

"And I have given it to you."

"But you read it first. Now the news is not as special."

"Oh, I think it is."

"It cannot be since I did not know of it first," Grace retorted before turning her eyes to the missive she held.

"The Sheltons are coming to Bath with your cousin, Bea."

"Mama! You should have let me read it!"

"I am letting you read it, but the news is so exciting. They have asked if you could join them at the house they are renting. It is just outside of town, but not far. You know how Bea is about crowds of people. I suspect that is the reason."

Grace's eyebrows rose as she read the invitation. She knew that Mr. Shelton and Miss Hamilton, who was now his wife, liked her despite her "trollop of a sister." She fought to keep her lips from curling in amusement at Mr. Shelton's description of Felicity. However, it still surprised her that she would be asked to join them as a special guest. After all, Mr. Graeme Clayton could not much care for the family of the lady who had injured his brother.

"I wonder if Mr. Everett Clayton will be with them?" Part of her hoped he would be, while the less vengeful, more logical side of her brain hoped he was not. While she would find it quite delightful for Felicity to have to wonder about whether Mr. Clayton was sharing his tale with the other gentlemen in Bath, Grace would also feel dreadful about Mr. Clayton having to see her sister flirting with Mr. Ramsey.

"Oh, I should think not. He is not mentioned, and I truly think he would be if he were coming with them." Her mother shook her head. "He is best off in town, far from here."

"Far from Felicity," Grace muttered.

"I would not say such, but yes," her mother said. "It is better to not be reminded of one's disappointment."

"There is that," Grace agreed.

"And he might harm Felicity's chances. I cannot believe you hid her behavior from me for so long."

Grace closed her eyes. She had been through this with her mother more than once already. "I did what Felicity asked. I will not make the same mistake." Ever. Nor would she lose another gentleman to her sister. Ever.

"I know you will not. You are a good girl." Mrs. Love patted her youngest daughter's leg. "And now you will not have to sit around watching your sister have fun. I am not so blind as you might think. I know you are unhappy, and I cannot blame you. But your time will come."

"Of course, Mama."

"You are a good girl." Her mother patted her leg once more before rising to leave the room. "I will send your maid to help you pack."

"Mama, there are yet two days until they say they will call."

"One cannot be too prepared," her mother said as she left the room.

Yes, one could be. If one's clothing was all in a trunk when she needed to wear some of that clothing, one would most definitely be too prepared. Grace flopped back on the bed and reread her letter.

"I wonder if they would allow you to join me?" she asked Philomena. "I will ask." She sighed and smiled – not just with her lips but with her whole being as she contemplated being in company once again with Miss Hamilton – no, she was Miss Hamilton no longer. She was now Mrs. Shelton.

"It will be delightful," she said with a sigh. "Two married ladies and their husbands, and not a sister in sight to tell me that the eldest should marry first." She giggled softly. "Would it not be a lark indeed if I were to marry before Felicity?"

Philomena mewed her agreement before snuggling in for a sleep while Grace stroked her fur and dreamed of handsome gentlemen who only had her with whom to flirt.

Chapter 2

"I do not see why Grace had to come with us."

Walter Blakesley peeked over his morning paper to see the source of the comment. She was a fair-looking young lady with a pleasing figure and a dignified carriage. Not his sort. Such an air of grandeur was more likely than not accompanied by fits of temper when the chit did not get her way. He turned his attention back to the news from last night's soirees.

"And leave her at home?"

Walter chuckled. The mother sounded shocked, but he reckoned that an opinionated young miss spouting her opinions should not come as a surprise to the young lady's mother. He held his paper in place as if he were reading it but turned his attention to what he was certain was going to be an interesting conversation between mother and daughter as they strolled past where he sat in the Sydney Gardens.

"She has enough gowns for the number of soirees she will be attending. There is no need for her to follow us around from shop to shop."

"I do not believe we are in a shop."

He peeked around his paper so he could match a face with the voice of the young lady, most likely the aforementioned Grace, who had just spoken. His lips curled up with pleasure. Grace had all the beauty of the first young lady with none of the regal air. However, she looked as if she possessed a good dose of pertness.

"We will be," the first young lady retorted. "And then you will be bored and saddened." She wore a forlorn expression. "I am only thinking of your comfort, my dear sister."

"Are you, indeed?" Grace's tone spoke of uncertainty, but the manner in which her lashes fluttered spoke of her being wise to the true intent of her sister.

Walter turned his attention back to the sister. She pursed her lips and shrugged.

"I suppose it will be good preparation for when you have a season next year, but do not blame me if you weary of all that needs to be done long before it is complete."

"Come now, Felicity," the mother cajoled. "You will be happy to have Grace's opinion on how well you look. I know you will. She has very good taste."

Felicity gave Grace an appraising look. "I suppose so," she agreed and then smiled broadly. "I do hope we see Mr. Ramsey today. I told him we were to go shopping when he asked if he might take me for a drive again this afternoon, but with so much to do before we visit the Upper Rooms tomorrow, I assured him it would not be possible."

She leaned toward her mother and lowered her voice so that Walter had to strain to hear her.

"He made me promise him the first set."

"Oh, that is delightful!" her mother cried.

The Upper Rooms. Tomorrow. Walter made a mental note of the detail. He would most certainly like to see who this Mr. Ramsey was, for he seemed an excellent choice from how the mother was going on about him at present. He lowered his paper and folded it. Looking up, he caught Grace watching him.

He smiled and nodded. To his great amusement, she flashed a quick smile and then turned away as if she had not seen a thing, only to glance back at him after they had turned down a path away from where he sat. With any luck, tomorrow's outing to the Upper Rooms would be one of the soirees which Grace would attend.

"What are you about, Blakesley?"

"Just reading my paper and taking in the view, Mr. Norman. Do you have the morning free from patients?"

Mr. Norman was one of the many physicians who made a good living off of the people who came to Bath to take the waters and improve their health.

"I do not need to see anyone for another hour." Mr. Norman took a seat next to Walter. "The view from here is not without its pleasant aspects." He cut a sly look at his friend.

"Indeed, it is not. However, I do not think that the mother of those two is looking for a physician either for herself or her daughters."

Mr. Norman chuckled. "They look a bit young for my liking."

"Still set on finding a spinster?"

Mr. Norman nodded. "As long as she is not older than thirty or younger than twenty-seven. I think a gap in age of at least four years but not more than seven is ideal."

"You have very odd notions," Walter countered. "I dare say that both of those ladies are more than seven years younger than me."

"A gap of more than seven years is perfectly fine for you. It just is not for me."

"I do believe the infirmities of your patients have addled your brain. How can it be one thing for you and another for me?" Walter said as he rose.

"Are you visiting tenants or just taking your ease today?" Mr. Norman asked as he also rose.

"I have a couple of things that need my attention, but then, I am free."

"Good, good. Then you can keep me company for an hour."

"I just said I had things that needed attention."

"Yes," the good doctor said, taking out his watch, "but only a couple, which is not more than two. I am certain you will have time to complete all that needs doing if you start an hour later than now. In fact, it will not even be an hour." He snapped the cover of his watch closed. "I will need to return to my office in half an hour to prepare for my next visit."

"Oh, very well, then. You may accompany me on my way."

"That sounds like an excellent plan. Where are we off to first?"

"To see a man about a jacket."

"Another jacket? Do you not have enough already?" Mr. Norman hurried after Walter.

"This one is more generously proportioned." Several of his jackets were no longer comfortable to wear for anything more than sitting still while having a portrait painted. Not that he had any plans for commissioning portraits of himself – let alone having one done of him in an ill-fitting jacket.

Mr. Norman chuckled. "Did I not tell you that too many Sally Lunns would do that?"

Walter shook his head. "It is not the Sally Lunns. I have taken up pugilism." He made a fist and bent his arm. The fabric over his upper arm strained against the muscles flexing beneath it. "I believe it was you who recommended physical activity once when you were watching me eat a Sally Lunn." His lips curled into a smirk. "By all rights, I should be sending you the bill for the wardrobe improvements your advice has necessitated."

"I did not specifically say you should take up boxing. Dancing and walking would not require new clothing."

"I walk enough as it is. I wish for something more if I am to exercise."

"Fencing is another option."

"It is a great sport. I must agree. However, I have done that for years – even before your recommendation – and before you suggest it, I also ride. Pugilism seemed the one remaining sport of interest that required a great deal of exertion."

"Yes, well, I am not paying for your jackets. Your pockets are far deeper than mine," Mr. Norman said with a laugh.

"Put it on my account, and at the first sign of gout, I will collect what I am owed in service."

Mr. Norman continued laughing. "If I were a surgeon, you'd likely have better luck at collecting the cost of your coats. How many stitches have you had so far?"

"Counting this one," he pointed to a small scar above his left eye, "three. I am not fond of having my head knocked about. I spend most of my time hitting things that cannot hit back. Sacks of grain, saplings, and the like."

"You hit trees?" Mr. Norman cried. "I am surprised your hands are not in worse shape than they are."

"An old rug softens the blow. You do not expect me to put any of the trees in the orchards at risk, now do you?"

"I suppose I do not, but just the same, it must cause some injury."

Walter removed the glove from his right hand. "A bruise or two." He showed his friend the yellowish-green bruise that a tree had inflicted upon him.

"It looks as if it is healing well, but I will still caution you about such things. A body can only survive a beating so many times before it begins to take a toll."

Walter was just putting his glove back on and about to enter his tailor's shop when a carriage came to a stop a few feet from where he stood.

"Your view has followed you," Mr. Norman whispered as the occupants of the carriage began to disembark.

"Why can you not wear the pair of gloves you purchased in London?" the mother asked.

"There is a hole in the right one."

"I am sure it can be fixed," her mother offered.

"But to wear a damaged pair of gloves to a ball, Mama? What will the gentlemen think of me?"

"Do you really think Mr. Ramsey will mind?" Grace asked.

"I will not only be dancing with Mr. Ramsey," Felicity replied. "I cannot. It would be scandalous to dance every set with the same gentleman."

"But is he not the one gentleman whom you wish to have think well of you?" Grace asked as she followed behind her mother and her sister toward the store just two doors down from Walter's tailor.

"Oh, indeed!" Felicity cried. "But to gain his favour, I must not lose the favor of everyone else. Who would wish to marry a lady who was thought too poor to have a fine pair of gloves?"

"Who indeed?" Walter said to Mr. Norman.

"I am sure I cannot say," Grace answered her sister in a tone that spoke of her wishing very much to say something other than what she had said.

"You may wear my old pair. I am certain it will not harm your chances at all."

"That's a pleasant one," Mr. Norman whispered

as he opened the door to the tailor shop. "If only every lady had such a generous sister."

"Your tongue is as sharp as your knife," Walter quipped. Giving one last look toward the shop just two doors down, he caught the eye of Grace, who once again smiled but turned away quickly and looked as if she had seen nothing. It was a very odd thing. Most young women would smile and then duck their heads before peeking at a fellow again – his thought was interrupted as Grace once again turned her eyes towards him and smiled before stepping into the store into which her mother and sister had already disappeared.

"Did you see that?" he asked Mr. Norman.

"See what?"

"The way that young lady keeps secretly smiling at me?"

Mr. Norman peeked down the street. "I cannot say I noticed."

"She did it in the gardens as well."

"Then, I would venture to guess you have an admirer."

"But why is she so secretive?"

Mr. Norman shook his head. "I am certain that even I am not capable of understanding the working of the female brain, especially the young female brain. If I were, I might not be looking for a spinster. Do you know that not one of the ladies whose care I have taken on has a companion that is less than forty? It is rather odd."

Odd seemed to be the word of the day when it came to ladies. Walter took one more look down the street at where Grace had been. He should not think about her. She was an oddity, the sort of lady which a gentleman of proper standing and great responsibility such as himself should avoid. He really should not think about her, but, unfortunately, his insatiable curiosity had already latched onto the pretty riddle named Grace.

Chapter 3

"Beatrice!" Mrs. Love cried when her niece entered the sitting room. "It has been this age since we have seen you."

"Yes, nearly a year," Mr. Love added. "Mr. Clayton," he added with a bow. "It is a pleasure to see you both."

"And it is a pleasure to see you both as well."

Grace was not certain that Mr. Clayton was speaking truthfully. He seemed to be holding himself rather stiffly, and Bea seemed to have a firm grip on his arm. Grace could not blame him. Felicity had treated his brother abominably.

"My sister is still abed," Grace offered to Bea. "She will be sorry to have missed you, but when one spends a great deal of time dancing into the night, one simply cannot be roused too early in the morning. Or so I hear."

Mrs. Love made a small clicking sound that spoke of disapproval nearly as much as the look Grace's father wore did.

"Is it not true?" Grace asked in her most startled voice in an attempt to cover the jibe she had made about her current, lack-of-a-season circumstances.

"Yes, it is true," her mother said.

"Oh! I am glad. I thought for a moment I had misspoken," Grace said with a little laugh. Her mother looked mollified while her father seemed skeptical, but then, he had always been harder to fool than her mother.

"Please, have a seat. Would you care for some tea or perhaps a glass of port?" Mr. Love asked.

"No, we cannot stay long," Beatrice replied as Graeme helped her to take a seat.

He was so attentive. He had even been so before he married Beatrice. Grace had not been unaware of the care he gave her cousin when she had been at Heathcote last year. The hand on Bea's elbow accompanied by the whispered "Are you well?" made Grace wish to sigh, but she refrained and merely smiled at the sight. One day, she would have a gentleman who would be so thoughtful and caring.

"Mr. and Mrs. Shelton are expecting us to return quickly so that we can make plans for today and tomorrow," Bea continued.

"Do you not just love Miss Hamilton — I mean Mrs. Shelton?" Grace asked eagerly.

Bea smiled softly as she often did. There was such a sweet, gentleness about her. Grace had not admired it so very much until now. It was in complete contrast to Felicity.

"She is lovely," Bea assured Grace. "I understand you became friends at a house party?"

Grace nodded eagerly. "We did. Mr. Shelton, Mrs. Shelton, Mrs. Berkley — that is Mr. Shelton's sister — and myself. I have not made such good friends in some time. I truly have missed them, though Mrs. Shelton writes to me regularly." Excitement bubbled up inside her. Soon, very soon, she would be reunited with friends – true friends. And then, she would begin her quest to become friends with Bea instead of just being cousins.

Mr. Clayton chuckled. "Even Shelton seems eager to have you visit. If Mrs. Shelton had been feeling better this morning, they likely would have joined us." He looked at Mrs. Love. "Yesterday's travel fatigued her."

"I am surprised it has not fatigued Bea as well," Mrs. Love cried. "She has always been so delicate."

"She would not have missed seeing you for the world," Mr. Clayton replied.

"Indeed, I would not," Bea agreed.

"Are you certain you do not wish for tea?" Mr. Love offered once again.

"A cup would be welcome," Bea answered. "If it is not too much trouble that is."

"My husband has been wishing for a cup of tea for this past half hour. You do him a great service by accepting his offer. Does she not, my dear?" Mrs. Love said.

"It is quite a noble service you render me, Bea." His lips curled into an amused smile. "I am still allowed to call you Bea even though you are a married lady, am I not?"

Bea laughed. "Of course. Only my last name has changed. You are still my uncle."

Grace's father sobered somewhat. "I had hoped that you would still claim me as such even after all that has passed." His eyes focused on Mr. Clayton, who nodded.

"Yes, well," Mrs. Love said uneasily, "we are hopeful." She shrugged and sighed.

"As are we," Mr. Clayton replied.

Grace longed to ask about Mr. Everett Clayton, but, knowing how that might upset everyone, she did what was prudent instead of what was wished and held her tongue.

"Your drive was good? The weather seemed perfect for it, yesterday," Mr. Love continued the conversation with only a small amount of unease in his voice.

Grace's father had been most displeased to hear about how his eldest daughter had treated Mr. Everett Clayton. Grace was certain he felt the folly of Felicity's actions much more than her mother did, for Mama tended to move on easily from a disappointment with a hopeful optimism about the future while Papa was more prone to ponder and stew.

"It was most pleasant yesterday," Mrs. Love agreed. "Felicity, Grace, and I even took a walk in the Gardens before we visited the shops. Dry paths and roads. Almost no clouds in the sky, and you could just feel spring in the air. It was delightful. Simply delightful."

"Our drive was just as it should be," Bea assured her. "We could not have ordered better weather than what we were given."

She likely would have said the same if it was raining. Bea rarely complained about anything – not even a cousin who connived to steal the attention of a friend from her. Grace sighed.

"Is something amiss," her father asked.

Grace shook her head. "No, I... I was just thinking about Philomena." Her cheeks warmed at the lie. She was doing nothing of the sort. She was regretting how she had helped Felicity charm Mr. Everett Clayton, but she could not say that!

"Who is Philomena?" Mr. Clayton asked.

"My cat."

"Will she be joining us?" he added with a smile.

He was offering to let her cat accompany her?

"I had not thought it proper to ask if she could." Though she had considered asking for some time before deciding it would be too forward to do so.

"I understand Mrs. Shelton was required to leave her cat at home," Mr. Clayton continued. "It might be a welcome surprise if your Philomena is not averse to ladies other than yourself doting on her."

"That cat will not turn down attention," Mr. Love said with a laugh before rubbing his hands together in satisfaction as the tea tray arrived. "Much like I will not refuse a tea cake and a cup of tea."

For the next several minutes, the conversation revolved around pets, sweets, and the weather. The whole event only took twenty minutes according to the clock in the corner, but to Grace who was eager to be off, it seemed a great deal longer. However, as is almost always the case, time did march forward and soon all Grace's things had been tied to Mr. Clayton's carriage, and she and Philomena were seated across from Bea and Mr. Clayton while the vehicle began its journey to the house where Mr. and Mrs. Shelton awaited her arrival.

Grace held the leash she had affixed to Philomena's collar in one hand while stroking her with her other hand. She blew out a breath and pulled in a deep, fresh one.

"I take it you are happy to be away from home." Mr. Clayton said.

"I am happy to be away from Felicity," Grace answered honestly. "I cannot apologize enough for her behaviour. Your poor brother." She looked down at the cat beside her. "Is he well? I have worried about him."

"He will be."

"Is he in town?"

"No."

"He is not in Bath, is he?" Grace asked in surprise.

Mr. Clayton chuckled. "No, he is at home. He will go to town for a time perhaps in a month or so."

"That is too bad."

"I am not sure I see why it is a bad thing that he is at home and not in Bath. Was there a reason you wished he was here?"

Grace's eyes grew wide, and she shook her head as mortification spread like a fire across her cheeks. "I had not intended to say that aloud."

"Ah, but you have, and so now you must explain it."

"Graeme," Bea said softly, "I do not think it is necessary."

"No, no. He is right. I would be tormented with curiosity if I were him," Grace assured her cousin. There was no way she was going to be the cause of an argument between Bea and Mr. Clayton. "It is disgraceful to admit it."

"Then, you do not need to," Mr. Clayton assured her.

Grace shook her head. "You have been very gracious in not breaking with my family over how shabbily my sister treated your brother. I shall admit what I was thinking so that you can know where I stand in relation to the whole horrid affair."

"I think I can tell as it is," Mr. Clayton said. "Mr. Shelton has told me about your disapproval of what your sister did."

Of course, Mr. Shelton did. Best friends did not keep secrets. Her cheeks warmed even further. "Did he tell you that I found your brother attractive when I first arrived at Heathcote?"

Mr. Clayton shook his head.

Hmm. It seemed gentlemen did keep some secrets from their best friends. She would have to remember that. She ran a hand along Philomena's fur.

"Well, I did," she said, "but that is not the disgraceful thing I must admit. While I am happy that Mr. Everett Clayton is not going to have to see my sister and be reminded of her duplicity, I almost wish he were here to tell his tale and ruin my sister's chances in Bath." She looked from one startled face across from her to the other. "I told you it was disgraceful. It is not at all what a lady should wish for her sister, and yet I do."

If it were not for the wheels turning along the road and the clipping and clopping of horse's hooves, the carriage would have been entirely silent for several minutes.

"We are hopeful that she will make a match with Mr. Ramsey, for if she does not, I fear I will never get a season."

"I do not understand," Mr. Clayton said.

"The hope of my sister's success comes at the cost of my season."

"You are not here for the season?" Mr. Clayton asked in surprise.

Grace shook her head. "Not my own season. I was to be allowed to attend a few soirees, but the focus must be my sister, you see."

Across from her, Mr. Clayton smiled broadly.

"I do not see how that is a happy thing," she said.

"He is not happy about your situation," Bea assured her. "He is happy for Mr. Shelton."

Grace's brow furrowed. She had no idea what her lack of a season had to do with Mr. Shelton.

"Shelton imagines himself somewhat of a matchmaker," Mr. Clayton said, "and since you were unsuccessful at the house party, he was hoping for a second chance to prove himself."

How wonderful! Grace clapped her hand in delight!

"I take it you are not distressed by this news?" Bea questioned cautiously.

"Not at all!" Grace assured her. "I shall welcome the adventure."

She settled back against the squabs and sighed. How the state of one's life could change in an instant from dreary to hopeful! It was remarkable. Would it not make Felicity jealous to see her sister on the arm of some handsome beau? Oh, the thought was nearly too delicious to consider without giggling until...

She gasped and shrank into herself a little as the thought struck her. Her sister must not know of any possible matches for if she did... well, that was how she had discovered both Mr. Everett Clayton and Mr. Ramsey.

And, in the blink of an eye, life was back to dreary.

Chapter 4

"I was sorry to have missed you yesterday, Blakesley."

Walter turned away from studying the couples lining up for the first dance and toward the gentleman who had greeted him.

"Mr. Clayton." He gave him a shallow bow. "It was unfortunate that I could not greet you at Erondale, though I suspect it was poor planning on my part. I should have waited another day before calling. However, I was anxious to make sure that all was well and as you expected it should be."

"I understand you had to replace your housekeeper rather suddenly, so I can understand your anxiety about things."

"Apoplexy is not just a scourge of the wealthy. Of course, my friend, Mr. Norman could tell you more about that." Walter motioned to the fellow next to him. "Mr. Clayton, if I may, this is Mr. Norman, one of the many physicians here in Bath, and in my opinion, one of the best. Mr. Norman, Mr. Clayton."

"It is a pleasure to meet you. I had hoped to gain an introduction to a man of medicine from Blakesley. I knew that if anyone knew precisely who I should meet, it would be him." Graeme leaned forward. "I think that was the one thing at which he excelled in most in college – knowing who was who and what was what."

"He does have an ear for such things," Mr. Norman agreed.

"Someone needs to," Walter inserted. "Mr. Clayton's wife has a delicate constitution," he added in a whisper.

Graeme smiled broadly. "More so now than most times, though no one is to know that."

"And you have brought her to Bath in spite of her condition?" Walter asked in surprise.

"She would not have it any other way. Her constitution might be delicate, but her will is not."

Walter chuckled. "I would assume that is a good thing since she is married to you."

Graeme only shrugged and smiled in response.

"I will introduce her to you as soon as I can pry her away from Mr. and Mrs. Shelton and Miss Love."

Walter's eyes roved over the crowd as best they could. "You should come earlier so that you might get seats in the gallery," he said in passing to Mr. Clayton.

"It is rather a crush," Graeme agreed. "I think if my wife had known it would be so, she might have allowed me to persuade her to stay at Stratsbury Park."

"Not a fan of large groups of people, is she?"

"Not normally, but there are inducements to enduring it now, you see."

"Such as?" Mr. Norman inquired.

"She has never had a season and thinks that it is best to experience one before she becomes a mother so that she can be prepared for what her child will experience in seventeen years or so."

Walter chuckled.

"Bea likes to be prepared for all eventualities," Graeme offered.

"Different sides of the same coin, then," Mr. Norman muttered.

"Quite," Graeme agreed.

"It seemed to me that such is also true of Shelton

and his wife." Walter's lips tipped up as he finally found for whom he was looking. Mr. Shelton was bending to hear what a very pretty young lady named Grace was saying. Miss Love was it? "Is that your guest with Mr. Shelton?" he asked Graeme.

"Yes, that is Miss Love. Would you care for an introduction?"

Yes, yes, he would very much like to meet the secretive Miss Love. "If it is not a bother," he replied with an air of indifference before following Graeme across the room.

"How do you know her?" he asked as they moved through the gathered throng.

"She is my wife's cousin."

"Ah, I see. Mr. Shelton said that you were collecting her in Bath, does she have family here?"

"Yes and no. Her mother, father, and sister are here for the season."

"An unmarried sister?" Walter asked as if he did not already know such a thing to be true.

"Yes, and not worth your time." There was a cold bitterness to Graeme's tone that was curious.

"Then, you shall have to point her out to me so that I might avoid her." A thing which he had already intended to do. He had both seen and heard enough from the other Miss Love to inform him that a wide berth around her would be best.

"Gladly," Graeme replied.

There must a story of great interest behind such an emphatic response. Perhaps over time, Walter would discover it, but for now, he was about to meet the mysterious Grace – after he met Mrs. Clayton, that is. Blasted propriety that stood in the way of satiating curiosity!

"Oh!" Grace cried upon being introduced to Walter. "I believe I saw you yesterday in the gardens."

"I believe you are correct. You do look familiar and that must be where I saw you."

"And then you visited a tailor," Grace added. "Felicity – that's my sister – was in need of a new pair of gloves," she explained to the group.

"Did she find what she needed?" Walter asked. This young lady was as delightfully entertaining as her secret smiles had told him she might be.

"Felicity always finds what she wants," Grace said with a flutter of her lashes.

"Even if someone else has it," Roger Shelton muttered, earning a glare from his wife.

"You are not wrong," Grace assured him. "However, I was fortunate enough to claim her old pair." She held out her hands for inspection. "I should not tell you this, but there was the tiniest tear right here." She pointed to a spot just above her left wrist. "But I dare anyone to know that it is there."

"Your needlework is exemplary, Miss Love. I would not have thought that those rosebuds hid a blemish. It is very well done." Walter was not prevaricating. She had done a marvelous job of disguising the tear and making the gloves even more lovely than they originally had been. She was a clever young woman.

"It is, is it not?" she agreed with a pleased smile.

Clever, and not unwilling to claim such a thing.

"Would you allow me the privilege of a dance?" he asked. Her eyes grew wide at the offer and her head shook ever so slightly. She was refusing him?

"I am sorry," she said softly, "but I was hoping for someone else to claim my hand for the next dance." Her cheeks grew rosy.

"No one has asked you," Shelton muttered.

"No, but if I give this dance to Mr. Blakesley then I will not be free if another arrives to ask."

Roger Shelton's brow furrowed. "You did not mention this before."

"Because I did not know the gentleman's name. One must not speak of a hope to dance with someone to whom she has not been introduced." She cast a glance in Mr. Norman's direction. "However, that is no longer a problem."

"Norman?" the question flew out of Walter's mouth.

Grace's head bobbed up and down. "Though it is forward to even admit to it."

Forward was not the word Walter would use for it. "Well, then, Norman, do not keep the lady waiting." Walter knew his tone was less than gracious.

Grace put a hand on his arm but then withdrew it quickly. "Do not be discouraged, Mr. Blakesley. It is not that I do not wish to dance with you. It is just that I had hoped to speak to Mr. Norman."

"You had?" Roger echoed the question in Walter's mind.

"Yes, I would like some advice." Her hands were twisting in a nervous sort of fashion. "About a condition."

What was she about?

"You wish to speak to him because he is a physician?" Mrs. Shelton's tone was incredulous.

Grace's head bobbed up and down as she pulled

her lower lip between her teeth. Walter would put ten pounds on it that the chit was lying.

"You did not know he was a physician until just now," Mrs. Clayton said.

"But he looked like one," Grace declared.

"He looked like one?" Skepticism filled Roger's question. Apparently, no one else quite believed Miss Love's story any more than Walter did.

"And what is your condition?" Mr. Clayton asked, earning him a disapproving "Graeme" from his wife.

"Oh, it is merely a curiosity, really."

"About what?" Graeme pressed.

Grace tapped her chest.

"Your heart?" Walter said. "Are you not a trifle young for such a thing?"

Grace fluttered her lashes at him. "Did I say it was my heart?"

"It seemed as if you did," Roger inserted.

"Well, it might be, or it might not be. If you would all just allow Mr. Norman to ask me to dance, then after I have spoken to him, he can share what he knows with his friend and I will tell you all about it on our ride home." Her brow furrowed. "I am not intentionally being rude to Mr.

Blakesley." She huffed. "Do not look at me as if I am my sister."

The last comment raised several eyebrows, including Walters, for it was spoken with great vehemence.

"Mr. Norman." Walter gave his friend a nudge. "The rest of us are counting on you to discover what we would like to know."

"Miss Love, might I have the pleasure of this dance?" Mr. Norman asked.

"I thought you would never ask." Grace put her hand in his but instead of allowing him to lead her directly to the dance floor, she stopped so that she was standing shoulder to shoulder with Walter, though she was looking toward the dancers and he was looking away. "Please, do not dance with my sister," she whispered and then allowed herself to be swept into the group of dancers.

"That was odd."

"You have never been more correct about anything, Shelton," Graeme agreed.

"What did she say to you just now, Blakesley?" Roger asked.

Walter shook his head in bewilderment. "She

told me not to dance with her sister. I'm beginning to think that Miss Love's sister is akin to poison."

"Very like it," Graeme assured him. He blew out a breath. "She broke my brother's heart," he whispered.

Ah. Things were beginning to fall into place. "My condolences," he muttered.

"It was done in a rather spectacular fashion," Roger added. "You would do well to heed Grace's advice."

Even Shelton was warning him away from the other Miss Love? That added to the weight of caution greatly. Graeme Clayton had never been quite as devil-may-care about things as Roger Shelton had been. Therefore, a warning from Graeme was to be heeded, but, when it was paired with rousing support from Roger, the danger of ignoring such advice would be foolish in the extreme, and Walter was no fool.

"Then, I shall take myself to the card room and await Mr. Norman there."

"You are not dancing?" Mrs. Shelton asked in surprise.

Walter smirked. "It seems the safest way to avoid Miss Love's sister, and I have already suffered rejection once. I am not entirely certain I can survive it a second time, although perhaps if I were to ask a young lady while Norman is occupied and not at my side." He chuckled and shook his head.

If not for the way Miss Love had used a begging sort of tone when she had whispered *please* to him just now, he might have truly felt her rejection far more than he presently did. The word was as tantalizing as her secret smiles, which she flashed at him once again when he looked her direction as she lined up across from Norman. The taunting tease of a woman!

"If you find you change your mind," Mrs. Shelton said, "I am not opposed to dancing and, as much as my husband would rather that I dance every set with him, it is not how things are done. I would not refuse your offer."

"I shall keep that in mind," Walter said with a nod of his head before making his way out of the room to find a table at which to sit and watch others play cards while he and a glass of port contemplated the secrets held by the lovely Miss Grace Love.

Chapter 5

"I saw you dancing."

Grace pasted a smile on her lips. She had been doing her best to not meet up with her mother, for doing so would inevitably lead to having to speak with her sister. And, she was not wrong, for Felicity was at her mother's side, looking all eagerness.

"He was very nice looking and exceptionally light on his feet," Mrs. Love continued.

"Oh, indeed!" Felicity cried. "He might be one of the best dancers here."

"Even better than Mr. Ramsey?" Grace asked. Her sister should be thinking only of Mr. Ramsey, but, of course, she was not.

"Yes, I do believe so, though I would not for all the world tell him so," her sister replied.

"What was his name?" her mother asked eagerly.

"Mr. Norman," Grace replied. "He is a physician."

Her mother gasped and blinked. "A physician? He has no estate?"

A wicked thought captured Grace's imagination. "None of which I know, but he has a home here in Bath. Some rooms somewhere. I really do not know where." Nor did she really know in what sort of accommodation Mr. Norman lived, but rooms had seemed like they would be the most revolting residence. "There is still so much to learn about Bath."

"Rooms?" Felicity repeated. "Not even a townhouse?"

Yes, it was fun to see them both so aghast at her choice of a dance partner. She was certain Felicity would not even attempt to steal Mr. Norman away from her — not even if he was light on his feet, which he was.

"He does not have one yet," Grace quite possibly lied, making a mental note to discuss this with Mr. Norman at some point, "but once he is better established, I am certain he will have a townhouse." If he did not already have one that is. "He seems very intelligent. I have every faith in his ability to become quite successful in his career." She should also likely find out how successful he was at present. They had spoken a little about themselves while dancing, but long drawn out discussions were not meant for the dance floor. Therefore, the focus of their conversation had been about Felicity and Mr. Blakesley.

"Yes, yes. I am sure he will be," her mother muttered.

Grace straightened her glove as she allowed her less than commendable thought from earlier to make itself fully known. "I have given him leave to call on me tomorrow."

"You have not!" her mother cried. "A physician? Grace!"

Grace batted her lashes and looked at her mother in feigned surprise. "Is there something wrong with that?"

"Of course, there is," Felicity snapped. "One does not participate in a season to secure a physician as a husband. One strives for a higher connection."

Grace smiled at her sister. "But I am not here for the season. You are. I am only here because there was nowhere else to send me."

"That is not true." Her mother's whisper was harsh. "We had hoped you would get a partial season and find some success."

"Is that true, Felicity?" Grace asked in as sweet a confused tone as she could.

Her sister looked at their mother in surprise before turning her attention back to her sister. "Of course, it is."

"Then, you will not fault me for wishing to have some success in getting to know Mr. Norman? He is excessively handsome, and from what I hear, he comes from a wealthy family. He was just not born first or even second or third. Sadly, he was fourth, which was a grave oversight on his part. However, he seems quite happy in his chosen occupation, and, from the greetings he received from several people, I would venture a guess that he is well-respected." She looked over her shoulder and then leaned toward her sister and mother as she lowered her voice. "I believe Mr. Clayton will keep him in mind for Bea if there should be a need. I am not certain how she will tolerate Bath. She is not used to so many people, you know."

Mrs. Love looked startled by that revelation. "Is she unwell?"

"No," Grace assured her with all haste. "It is just a precaution. You know how Bea can be. Frankly, I think it is sweet how well Mr. Clayton cares for her." She sighed. "I would not have to worry about good care if I were to decide on Mr. Norman. I do think he would see to the well-being of his wife quite well. You can see his caring nature in his eyes. They are a lovely shade of brown."

She had no intention of ever becoming Mrs. Norman, no matter how kind and compassionate she truly found Mr. Norman. However, neither her sister nor her mother needed to know that.

"Do be serious," Felicity scolded. "He would not have the means to see you set up as you would desire. How many fine dresses could a lady expect to have on a physician's income?"

"Oh, at least, as many as I have now," Grace assured her but then sighed. "Of course, I do not have many at present."

Mrs. Love grasped Grace's hand. "You are a very good sister to give up so much on our sister's behalf. Is she not, Felicity?"

"Yes, very good," Felicity replied.

It would have been a more convincing agreement if Felicity had looked even a smidgeon guilty for what her sister was giving up because of her.

"Oh!" Felicity cried. "I have worn this dress three times now to various functions. I am certain I cannot be seen in it again. So, I will send it to you. With a few alterations, it will be very flattering on you." She ran the ribbon at the waist of her dress between her fingers. "I would change out the embellishments if I were you. That would make it look less like my dress and more as if it has always been yours."

"That is a very generous thing!" Their mother cried. "I will send some lace and ribbon with it."

Right. How very generous. Grace thought ruefully. That dress was supposed to have been hers before it was snatched away for her sister's use.

"However," her mother added in a whisper, "I would caution you against settling on the first gentleman who asks you to dance."

Grace laughed lightly. "Really, Mama. I must find someone to refuse before I can find someone to wed. Mr. Norman seems the perfect sort of gentleman to sustain such a blow. Would you not agree, Felicity? I am certain just by being seen with him, I will become much more sought after."

Their mother scowled. "One does not select gentlemen for the sole purpose of refusing them or increasing one's appeal to others."

Grace blinked. "Oh, I thought we did." She fluttered her lashes at Felicity, who scowled.

"I did not select Mr. Everett Clayton for such a reason," Felicity whispered. "I am certain I would have been quite happy to be Mrs. Everett Clayton had I not met my dear Mr. Ramsey."

"Hmmm." Grace pretended to consider her sister's words. "Then, I suppose, I shall have to spend the rest of the night considering if I would be happy to be Mrs. Norman since I have given the gentleman permission to call on me."

"Truly, Grace," Felicity scoffed, "you are such a simpleton. Have you not learned anything from school or me about securing a good match?"

"Apparently, not. Though I thought I had." She felt the smile she wore down to her toes. Pretending to be interested in Mr. Norman and provoking her sister was delightfully amusing.

~*~*~

"Why did your mother caution me about allowing Mr. Norman to call on you?" Graeme asked as he settled into the carriage later that night.

"Is Mr. Norman calling on you?" Mr. Shelton asked in surprise from the bench across from where Grace sat next to Bea.

"He most certainly is if he can find the time in his schedule," Grace replied. "It is only polite to do so, you know. He did dance with me after all."

"Because you asked him to," Roger returned.

"No, I only said I hoped he would ask me. I did not ask him. The two are very different things."

"I am not certain my sister would agree," Roger said.

Grace could hear the scowl in his words. Her plans had not included angering her friends.

"It was necessary," she said softly. "Your sister is all that is good. Mine is quite the opposite."

"I will not argue that," Roger assured her in a more friendly tone.

"Why just imagine if Felicity thought I found Mr. Blakesley attractive. I just know she would try to snatch him away since that is what she did with Mr. Everett Clayton and Mr. Ramsey."

"Mr. Ramsey, too?" Bea asked in surprise.

Grace nodded. "But Felicity will not bother attempting to snatch away a gentleman who is a physician, even if he has lovely brown eyes and can dance better than anyone I have met. He would be too far beneath her notice." She smiled, still rather amused with herself.

"She also thinks such a gentleman should be beneath my notice." She looked around Bea to Graeme. "As does my mother, which is why she has cautioned you. However, you need not worry. I have no intention of entertaining the idea of becoming Mrs. Norman, and Mr. Norman knows he is only calling on me as a ruse. Everything is perfectly well."

She leaned back against the squabs before popping forward again. "Oh, I forgot to tell you. Felicity is sending me a dress and my mother is including some lace and ribbon. It is the dress she was wearing tonight. The very one which was originally ordered for me before Mama decided we must put all our efforts toward Felicity's happy future."

Victoria Shelton laughed softly. "She is sending you *your* dress?"

"Yes. She has worn it three times and simply cannot be seen in it again." Grace sighed. Sadness washed over her. "Dresses, gentlemen, it seems it is all the same to my sister. What I am supposed to have or what I like must be hers. She really is a self-ish creature. I only wish I had come to that realization sooner."

"Just because she is selfish now, does not mean she will always be so." Bea's voice was soft and soothing.

"Perhaps," Grace agreed. "I cannot believe I spent so many years trying to be just like her. Oh! The unpleasantness of which I have been an unwitting part! It is most shameful to consider. We were not at all nice to you, Bea. I am most grievously sorry for my part in that. Mr. Everett Clayton would have done better—"

"No, he would not have," Graeme interrupted forcefully. "My brother is an idiot. He always has been. While the fault in his unhappiness rests in a large part on your sister's behaviour, he is not blameless. He was led astray by a pretty face and a lively spirit, but he did not go unwillingly. And, while I harbour some ill-feelings toward your sister for the way in which she treated him at the house party, I am not sorry Everett is a daft fool, for it did result in my finding the most perfect bride." He lifted Bea's hand and kissed it.

Grace sighed. "I hope one day to be as happy as you all are."

"You will be," Roger assured her. "I shall see to it."

He was a good friend!

"While you are seeing to it," she said after thanking Roger for his concern, "could you do so in such a fashion that my sister will not know?"

"I am not certain how that is possible," Roger replied.

"We could have a dinner party," Graeme cried. "Your sister would not be at a dinner party, for I would not invite her."

Across from her, Roger nodded his head. "That is an excellent idea."

"Just a small one," Bea begged.

"Yes, yes, nothing too large, my love," Graeme assured her.

"And if I am seen with several gentlemen and not just one in particular –"

"Your sister would think you were not serious about any of them," Roger concluded Grace's thought.

"But what do we do if one gentleman, in particular, catches Grace's fancy and wishes to court her?"

Victoria asked. "Will he not be put out by all the other swains buzzing about his prize? How is that any different from what Miss Love was doing at the Abernathy's house party?"

"That is simple," Roger answered. "By then, the said gentleman will be so far under Grace's spell that not even her trollop of a sister could pry him away from her." He shrugged. "Besides, maybe by then Ramsey will have gained Miss Love's promise or forced her hand."

No, Grace thought as Mr. and Mrs. Shelton continued to argue over whether it was polite to say such a thing about Mr. Ramsey's intentions, *the difference was that the gentleman she fancied would never be amongst the hopeful swains*. At least, he would not be if Mr. Norman played his part well.

Chapter 6

This was foolish.

Walter glanced toward Erondale and then looked at his watch before tucking it back into the pocket of his waistcoat. It was five minutes past the time Mr. Norman had said to be exactly where Walter was. If he was not such a curious sort of fellow, he would have told his friend that there was no way he was taking part in a scheme to meet a lady in such a clandestine fashion. Curiosity he had in great quantity. Patience was in shorter supply in normal circumstances and in extreme want when his curiosity had been excited.

He punched the rug which was wrapped around the tree next to him. If he was to be left standing like a fool in an orchard, he might as well get some benefit from it even if a cravat and waistcoat were not a usual part of his exercise costume. He sighed and hit the tree again before bobbing to the side as if the tree had thrown a punch in return.

Blowing out a breath, he gave Erondale one last glance before turning his focus to punishing the rug and tree and attempting to ignore the prick of impatience which taunted him to satiate his curiosity without waiting a moment longer.

For three jabs and just as many bobs to the side, Walter ignored the pleas of impatience. However, its demands could not be pushed to the side for longer than that. Therefore, after just three punches to the tree, he stopped and donned his jacket.

This was foolishness. He had waited at the spot as required for a quarter of an hour now, and Grace had not met him here as she said she would.

He was going to Erondale. It was his property after all, and those within its walls were his tenants. There was nothing to keep him from calling on them, and it was not as if it was an exceptionally warm day. The breeze had a bitterness to it despite the sky being nearly free from clouds, and he could not just wait under a tree forever.

With his jacket buttoned, straightened, and made as presentable as could possibly be done without the use of a mirror, he put on his greatcoat and hat before untying the rug from the tree and storing it in his gig as he normally did – folded and tucked in the boot.

A quarter of an hour and two days was a long enough wait to find out who the mysterious Grace Love was. Her secret smile had taunted and tantalized him since he first saw it in the park. He would be put off no longer. And so, he urged his horse to traverse the short distance between orchard and house as swiftly as possible.

"Why are you here?" Mr. Norman whispered to Walter when Walter took a seat next to him in the sitting room at Erondale.

"You were late."

"It could not be helped," Norman returned.

"So could not my arrival here." He turned a smile on his hosts who were looking at the two gentlemen curiously. "I beg your indulgence of my poor manners. My friend is somewhat startled to see me as I was supposed to have been engaged elsewhere. However, plans change."

"I hope it was not anything unpleasant which caused your change in plans." Grace was looking at him with concern.

"A prodigious lack of patience," Mr. Norman muttered.

Walter chuckled. "My friend is correct. I seem to be incapable of waiting very long for anything." He looked pointedly at Grace. "Especially if the longed-for item is of great intrigue."

"Oh!" she said with a small gasp and then a smile. "I could not agree more, Mr. Blakesley. I, myself, am frightfully impatient at times when I am anxious for something to happen or a journey to start."

"Miss Grace and I were about to take a drive." Norman lifted an eyebrow as he gave Walter a look of pure displeasure.

If Grace were a spinster, Walter might have been concerned by such a glare. However, he knew that Miss Grace was far too young to meet his friend's requirements for a lady. He also knew that his friend was only playing a part and the lovely lady who was supposed to take a drive with Norman was not actually interested in Norman at all but was rather intrigued by Walter, himself. Such knowledge gave him a great deal more confidence today than he had had last night when Grace had refused him in preference for his friend.

"Well, do not let me keep you from it." Walter waved his hand toward the door.

"We cannot leave now!" Grace cried.

"And why is that?" Mr. Shelton, who was settled very cozily on a settee next to his wife, was smirking at Walter.

If anyone was to figure out that a game was afoot first, it would be a master of games such as Shelton. Of course, he might just be enjoying the prospect of two gents having a tiff over a pretty lady.

"A guest has just arrived, of course," Grace replied.

"But will not Mr. Norman feel..." Shelton furrowed his brow, "how shall I say this? Put out? Perhaps that is it. Will not Mr. Norman feel put out to be made to wait to take you on a drive?"

Grace's mouth popped open but then closed just as quickly, and for the first time since Walter had seen her in the park two days ago, the lady looked befuddled. She had been frustrated and annoyed at the Assembly Rooms when questioned about her desire to dance with Mr. Norman, but she had not looked perplexed as she did now.

She turned wide eyes to Norman. "Will you?"

Norman sighed and shook his head. "Not overly much."

"Mr. Norman likes to keep to a schedule, you see," Walter added.

Grace's head bobbed up and down, though her puzzled expression had not left her face. "But I should not like to be the cause of disappointment."

Walter believed every word of that for she looked rather grieved at the thought.

"I truly did not think you would be put out at all," she added as she reached down to pick up the orange ball of fur at her feet. "I am not very good at this," she muttered as she stroked the cat she now held.

Between her look of sorrow and Norman's look of concern, Walter was beginning to curse his impatience.

"Would you like to walk in the garden instead?" Mrs. Clayton asked. "It is not a drive, but it is a change of place."

Norman shook his head. "I am well. Thank you."

"Are you certain?" Grace asked.

"Yes, I am just sorry –" He did not finish his sentence but shifted his eyes from her to Walter.

Grace sighed. "This is foolish, and precisely why

these sorts of things should not be attempted. Is that not right, Philomena?" The cat meowed at her mistress as if it had understood the question.

"Perhaps you could explain what is foolish." Mr. Clayton was looking for all the world like a displeased and suspicious father or older brother. If it were not for the fact that he was part of the reason for that particular expression on his friend's face, Walter might have chuckled at seeing someone of Graeme's reputation – at least, what it was in college – looking as he did.

"I can explain part," Walter offered.

Graeme's eyes narrowed as he turned them towards Walter.

"At her request, given to me by Mr. Norman, I was to meet Miss Grace in the orchard three-quarters of an hour ago," he snapped his watch closed.

Graeme had now crossed his arms and was looking at Grace with raised brows.

"I only wished to meet him without anyone knowing." Grace leaned forward and whispered, "He is very handsome," to Graeme, which caused Roger to chuckle and Graeme's brow to furrow while Walter could only smile. It was not so dreadful a thing to be called handsome by an intriguing lady like Grace.

"Why could you not meet him here?" Mrs. Shelton asked, and then closed her eyes and shook her head.

"Are you well?" Roger sat forward and looked at his wife.

She shook her head once again and, rising quickly left the room in great haste, followed by her husband.

"Oh, goodness!" Grace cried. "Have I caused her to be ill?"

Mr. Norman shook his head. "It is not you."

"How do you know?" Grace demanded.

"I am a physician and privy to details others might not know."

"What do you mean?" Grace asked.

"I cannot say. I just know that you are not the cause of her illness."

Walter nodded and settled back in his chair. "A bit of tea and toast might help."

"How do you know that?" Grace cried. "You are not a physician."

Graeme shook his head and chuckled.

"Blakesley has an annoying habit of knowing more than he should."

"I am very confused," Grace said. And she looked it.

For all her alluring and secretive actions, Miss Grace Love appeared to be an innocent.

"While we wait for Roger and Victoria to return," Mrs. Clayton said, "perhaps we can hear Grace's reason for arranging a secret meeting with Mr. Blakesley?"

Grace's cheeks flushed very prettily as she ducked her head. "I wished to see if he might wish to be..." she peeked at him, "my secret beau."

"Explain," Graeme demanded.

"I had hoped that we might get to know one another without anyone, most especially my sister, knowing."

"Why?" Walter asked.

"She is horrid," Norman answered for Grace. "That is what I was told," he added, holding up his hands in defense against Walter's shocked expression.

Grace nodded in agreement. "She will attempt to steal you from me. She has done it twice in the last year."

Walter tipped his head and studied Grace. Her hands were busy stroking her cat, but her eyes spoke of the truth of her fear. "Twice, you say?"

She nodded.

Apparently, it was not just gloves and gowns that Miss Love dangled over her sister then.

"Why me?"

Grace shrugged. "You returned my smile in the park."

A returned smile? That was her reason for selecting him? That seemed a rather foolish way to select a suitor.

She ducked her head again. "And you are handsome."

Well, that did make some sense, he supposed. "You know nothing about me. I could be an adventurer who would only toy with your heart."

Her eyes grew wide. "Are you?"

"No," Graeme answered. "At least, he was not when I knew him in college."

Grace smiled. "I thought from speaking with Mr. Norman that you could not be a scoundrel, for Mr. Norman does not seem the sort to keep company with such people."

"I agreed to meet with you in secret," he cautioned.

"Yes, I have not forgotten that," Graeme grumbled.

"You would not do me harm with Mr. Norman at my side," Grace protested.

"Norman could be a murderer cleverly disguised as a physician. Who would suspect him of such gruesome acts when he is pledged to heal and not harm?" Walter was not sure why he was taking so much pleasure in attempting to dissuade Grace from thinking of him as an upstanding individual who posed little risk to a beautiful young woman. He was, of course, honorable, but she could not have known that from a smile in a garden.

"You are not, are you?" she asked Mr. Norman.

"Would he tell you if he was?" Walter countered.

She looked positively ill as she shook her head. He should stop.

"He is not. At least, as far as I know, he is not, and he has had ample opportunities to do me harm and as you can see, I am well."

Her hand was resting on her heart. "But you are not a lady," she whispered.

"Oh, for the love of all that is good!" Mr. Norman cried. "I am not a murderer! If I were, I would be far more likely to harm Blakesley than anyone else after being treated as I have been today."

Walter laughed. "I apologize, Norman. You are the least likely to do harm to another. Other than to make them drink some horrid concoction designed to improve their health."

"But that is just the sort of person who would be a murderer in a novel," Grace whispered. Her hand was still on her heart, and she was still looking a trifle ill.

"We do not live in a novel," he assured her.

"But do you not think that the ideas found in a novel might have their roots in reality?" she asked in all seriousness.

"In some cases, yes. But not in this one. Mr. Norman is not capable of harming anyone without great provocation. I assure you this is not the first time I have taunted him beyond what is either polite or reasonable, and the worst he does to me is badger me not to eat too many buns and to take some air for my health."

"You are certain?"

"Yes!" Norman cried after giving an exasperated huff.

"The point remains, however," Walter said, "that he could have been, and you could have made an agreement with death. At the risk of sounding far too much like a stern old man, it is an ill-advised thing to be too secretive when you have only just met someone." He smiled at her look of contrition. "That does not mean, however, that we cannot be somewhat secretive in how I call on you."

Her eyes grew wide as a smile spread across her face. "Do you really wish to?"

He sighed. If she kept looking at him as she was, he'd do just about anything for her. Heavens but she was bewitching! "I do, for I am a very curious person, and you, my dear, fascinate me."

Chapter 7

"No, do not turn your head," Mr. Blakesley scolded as he once again sat in the drawing room at Erondale two days later — this time without Mr. Norman and with a screen and drawing paper in front of him.

"But I wish to see what you are doing," Grace replied.

"I am taking your likeness, and I am not very accomplished. Therefore, I beg of you, stay still, or I shall not be responsible for your face looking more like an apple that has been trampled by a herd of pigs than the pretty shape that it is."

"Are you truly so bad?" Grace peeked around the screen.

Truth be told, she did not care what the drawing on the paper looked like. She was far more interested in seeing his face while he sketched, and if that screen was not in the way, she could also see how his mouth moved and eyes narrowed as he shifted his head while studying her. The thought of a gentleman such as Mr. Blakesley studying her likeness so intently was both unsettling in a nervous sort of fashion and exhilarating in a rapid heartbeat that made one smile and sigh sort of fashion.

"You have ruined it." Mr. Blakesley favoured her with a scowl. She was certain she had never met a gentleman who looked so dashing when he scowled.

"It does not look ruined at all," Grace said. Of course, it could be a squiggly mess of knotted lines, and she would think it lovely merely because he had done it. "I shall just put my head back where it was."

She turned and sat as she had been. Or where she thought she had been.

"That is not precisely where you were."

Grace jumped when he poked the back of her head, but thankfully, she did not squeal in fright. That would have been most embarrassing. As it was, Mr. Shelton, who had been designated the chaperone while his wife was resting, was finding the whole process excessively amusing. He rose from his seat and came to where Mr. Blakesley was.

"It will work far better if you were to move her head with both your hands while I study the grid and guide you," he said. "Pushing her head with one hand while trying to keep an eye on these lines will only make things worse."

Grace sucked in a breath as she waited for Mr. Blakesley to place one hand on each side of her head and guide it into position. She might have to peek around the screen again if this were to be the result. She had wondered what his hands must feel like, and until just now, she had not yet been able to discover the answer.

She sucked in a second breath when that for which she had been waiting finally took place, and he actually held her head between his hands. His grip was firm and sure, much as she suspected. A gentleman who practiced boxing trees had to have hands which were as strong as the rest of his person. That is what she had thought, and that was what appeared to be true. If only he could just hold her head and Mr. Shelton could sketch her likeness.

"Now, stay still," he whispered next to her ear

when Mr. Shelton had, at last, said she was in position.

"I am not excessively patient," she replied.

"Do not look at me when you talk." He once again straightened her head.

"I will do my best, but I do like seeing to whom I am speaking."

"Especially when he is so handsome," Mr. Shelton teased.

Grace smiled as Mr. Blakesley muttered a less than polite rejoinder to Mr. Shelton. But, it was true. It was far more interesting to look at a handsome gentleman than a not so handsome one.

Mr. Shelton looked out the window toward the drive. "I will return," he said.

"Is someone here?" Grace asked. Hopefully, it was not her father or her mother coming to call on her.

"Mr. Norman," Mr. Shelton said as he exited the room.

"Why do you suppose Mr. Norman is here?"

"Keep your head still," Mr. Blakesley growled.

"I apologize. It is just such a habit to turn my head when speaking. Do you wish to stop? I do not mind if you do."

He peeked around the screen at her and smiled. "No, I wish to have a likeness of you to put in a frame in my sitting room so that when I have callers and they ask me who that is, I can say it is the image of a mysterious angel whose name is known only to me."

Oh! That was lovely. Grace sighed. Being a mysterious angel was quite a wonderful thing to be.

"And then, they shall beg me to reveal that name, but I shall deny them."

"Would you?"

He nodded. "However, if you cannot remain still, I will not have the chance to refuse to tell them your name."

"Are you teasing me so that you might scold me into sitting still?" That would not be a nice thing to do at all.

He shrugged. "Not entirely."

He ducked back behind the screen, taking away Grace's lovely view and returning her to looking at the empty chair in the corner.

"I do think it would be delightful to have something with which to taunt people. Such a thing likely reflects poorly on my character, but truth be told, I have few who visit me for a social call."

"Do you not have friends?" How did one not have many callers? When she was home, their sitting room was in use constantly for visits from this or that neighbour.

"I have several friends, but I find most of my callers visit me regarding business matters, or to play a game of billiards or drink a bit of port. And none of that happens in my sitting room."

"But a game of billiards is still a social call," Grace protested.

"I suppose it is," he agreed.

"Where do you drink port with your friends?"

"The same place I do business," he replied, "in my study."

"Well, then, that is just where you should place my likeness." She nearly turned her head to smile at him through the screen which would have been stupid since there was no way for him to see anything more than a shadow through the screen.

"That is an excellent idea," he agreed. "I have just your neck left, and I must say it is as lovely a neck as I have ever seen – neither too long, nor too short, and not at all too wide. Quite refined."

A refined neck? Grace stroked down her throat. It did not feel refined. It just felt normal to her.

If she were to be honest, she had never thought a great deal about the appearance of one neck compared to another. She stroked her fingers down her neck again.

"That is very distracting." Mr. Blakesley's voice sounded a bit strained.

"You mean this?" She brushed her fingers down the length of her neck for a third time.

"Yes." He peeked around the screen at her. His eyes swept from her eyes to her neck and then upward to her mouth. "I am almost done," he assured her. "Your lips are as lovely as your neck," he said with a wink before ducking behind the screen once again.

"Should I worry about you attempting to seduce me, Mr. Blakesley?"

His head popped back around to look at her. "No. Not even if I should wish to. I am not that sort of fellow."

"That is good to know." Or, at least, she imagined it was a good thing. "Do you want to?"

"I am quite certain that is not a proper thing to ask," came the response from behind the screen.

"Of that, I am fully aware," Grace assured him. "And, though you cannot see them, I assure you my cheeks are burning at having done so. However, I was merely curious if you were refusing to seduce me only because your character is upstanding or if you were refusing because you do not find me...um..." She was not quite certain how to word what she wanted to say without being even more improper than she had already been.

"You are beautiful," he replied. "I am refusing just because seducing a young lady such as yourself would be wrong, not because you are not tempting."

"Then you are not rakish at all?"

"Not at all."

"Have you ever been?"

Mr. Blakesley chuckled. "Never. Believe it or not, I have never even called on anyone as a possible suitor before."

Grace's brow furrowed and her mouth opened but then closed without making a sound. He had never called on a lady as a suitor before? A gentleman as handsome as he? "Are you teasing?"

"No." He moved his chair so he could see her. "I am done." He held up his handiwork. "It is not as good as it could be, but then, it is my first attempt at doing this since I was a boy and forced to do it for my sisters."

"Truly?"

He nodded.

"I see I have confused you."

"Indeed, you have," she admitted. "Surely, you must be popular at all the balls. Who would not wish to dance with you?"

"Oh, I dance. I am never in want of a partner, and I do make the required calls afterward as is polite and all that. However, I have never singled out one lady on whom to call and become better acquainted."

The door to the drawing room opened, allowing Mr. Shelton and Mr. Norman to enter.

"You look perplexed," Mr. Shelton said to Grace.

She was. "How old are you, Mr. Blakesley?"

"Twenty-seven, nearly twenty-eight, much like Shelton."

Her eyes shifted to Mr. Shelton. "Did you attend college together?"

Mr. Shelton nodded. "We did not always circulate together, but we were well-acquainted and good friends. Blakesley was more apt to be found studying than either Clayton or I were."

"I had a fortune to amass," Mr. Blakesley explained. "Erondale is not a large property, and the estate in Surrey will go to my brother."

"Surrey?" He was not from here?

"Yes, that is where I grew up. This was my mother's father's home."

"And you are here in Bath because of Erondale?"

He nodded. "Mostly. It also seemed a good place to establish myself in property investments since it is a place where people are often looking for accommodations, and I prefer it to London." He smiled and shrugged when her mouth popped open. "There are far fewer orchards in London, which would make my study of pugilism a trifle more challenging."

Well, that did make sense, and Grace had to admit that Bath and Erondale were both beautiful.

"We have sat long enough," he said, rising. "Would you accompany me on a stroll around the garden before I take my leave? If that is acceptable to Mr. Shelton, that is."

"May I?" Grace asked eagerly. She was in no

hurry to have Mr. Blakesley leave. He was not only handsome. He was also interesting.

"Mr. Norman, do you care for a turn of the garden?" Mr. Shelton asked.

Mr. Norman shook his head. "No, I believe I shall wait to speak with Mr. and Mrs. Clayton."

Mr. Shelton leaned back in his chair. "I think I shall wait for Victoria to join me." He chuckled. "Do not look so forlorn, Miss Grace. I shall not keep you from your walk. You may go without me."

Chapter 8

"Which path shall we take today? There were a few flowers emerging from the soil in the side garden last week when I was here. Have you made an inspection of the beds there today?" Walter asked as he and Grace stepped out the garden door. They had made a short circuit of the garden each day when he had called – even yesterday when the clouds were heavy and a mist hung close.

"There are crocuses about to set their blooms."

"Then you have inspected the side garden today?"

Grace nodded. "This morning before breakfast." She pulled in a breath and released it. It was a sound filled with contentment. Grace seemed to enjoy nature as much as he did.

"Gardens are wonderful are they not?" she asked.

"I could not agree more. About the side garden..." He watched as worry etched its way across her face, causing her to pull in her bottom lip and creating a furrow between her eyes. "It is too visible from the drive." He was certain that was what she was thinking, and he was proven right when her head bobbed up and down.

"I wish I could show you the blossoms I have seen, but if my mother should come to call." She shrugged. "One cannot have a secret beau if everyone knows about him."

"This is true," he agreed with a smile. "Then, the back garden it is, and this time we will pass through the gate and take one of the paths beyond the hedge."

Her face lit with excitement. In the short time he had known her, Walter had found that it was never terribly difficult to discover what Grace was feeling as her features were often painted with whatever emotion grasped her in a particular moment. He had seen her playful secret smile, her frustration in attempting to hide her intentions, and her delight, such as was displayed now, when a scheme met with her satisfaction. Those were but a few of her charming expressions.

However, her most beguiling look, which would likely haunt him from today forward, was the look of longing she had worn when he had poked his head around the screen in the sitting room. It had matched his own feeling in that moment, though he sincerely doubted that she knew such a feeling had been on display to him, for she did not seem to be aware of those sorts of things — not that she did not have an understanding or knowledge of them. He suspected she had a general idea, as evidenced by her questions about whether he was rakish or not, but beyond that, he imagined she was relatively innocent. She was not the kind of lady to toy with a gentleman and lead him down a merry path. Where she led, she wished to travel with him, and he was feeling surprisingly content to follow.

"You are very quiet," she said, interrupting his thoughts.

"My apologies, Miss Love."

"Could you call me either Grace or Miss Grace? I find that Miss Love reminds me too much of my sister."

"Very well, I shall call you Grace when we are alone as we are now and Miss Grace when we are in company. Will that satisfy?" It would be no trial for him, for he had been thinking of her as Grace since first setting eyes on her in the garden almost a week ago.

"That would be wonderful." Her whole being seemed to relax into a place of great comfort, the peacefulness of which, in turn, spilled over onto him.

"And will you insist upon calling me Mr. Blakesley or will you favor me with Blakesley or Walter?"

They took three silent steps before she made her reply. "Is there one you prefer above another?"

"No, I cannot say that there is," Walter answered, "I shall leave the selection up to you."

"That is most unusual, is it not?"

He held the gate open for her. "I am not certain I understand the question."

"Does not everyone have a preferred name they wish to be called?"

He shook his head. "Not everyone. For I do not." He secured the gate behind her. "Or perhaps I do, but since I have never played the part of a suitor before, I do not know what it is that I should like a pretty lady, such as yourself, to call me. However, I must say I do enjoy hearing you say Mr. Blakesley."

In truth, his name had never sounded so sweet as it did falling from her lips, which were currently tipped up in a small becoming smile that danced in her eyes.

"That seems sensible. Therefore, I shall try them both, and we shall, together, see which seems best."

He extended his arm to her again. "I think that is a marvelous plan."

"You truly have never courted any other lady?"

He shook his head. "Never."

"Did you wish to?"

Again, he shook his head. "Not particularly. Most ladies I have met are... well... not to be impolite, but they have all been rather dull. Not a one of them has ever refused a dance in favour of my friend." Her hand gripped his arm more tightly. "I understand your reasoning. There is no need to apologize."

"How did you know I was going to apologize?"

He shrugged. "You have a caring heart. I do not think you could knowingly harm another person."

"But I have!" she cried. "I was dreadful to Bea when I was at Heathcote."

"Knowingly dreadful?"

She nodded. "I felt it was not entirely right, and yet, I assisted Felicity in separating Bea from Mr. Everett Clayton."

"Why?"

"What do you mean?"

"Why did you persist in behaving as you were despite your misgivings?"

"Well, because Felicity assured me that I was being foolish to worry about such things, of course. She said it was how things were done, and that everyone understood that. That is exactly what she told me. That, and that she loved Mr. Everett Clayton most dearly – which she did not."

"You trusted your sister to guide you. There is nothing wrong in that."

Grace shook her head. "I will not allow it to be so. I should have listened to my heart and not my sister. I see that so clearly now."

"Seeing what has been is always easier than seeing what is."

Beside him, she sighed and very naturally, as if walking arm in arm with her closest friend, she squeezed his arm tight, which had the lovely effect of bringing a great deal more of her person in contact with him.

"You are very wise," she said.

Walter chuckled. "On occasion, but only on occasion. I reserve the right to be foolish and nonsensical when needed." The comment had the desired effect of eliciting a lovely laugh from her.

"When is it necessary to be nonsensical?" Grace asked between giggles.

"I really do not know, but I am certain there must be times when foolishness is preferable to being prudent." He leaned closer to her. "I will let you know when I discover such a time."

Again, the comment had the desired effect of causing her to continue to giggle.

"Shall we sit on this bench for a few minutes before we return and I must leave?"

They had come to the part of the garden where the path either circled back around toward the house or continued up a small set of stone steps and out into a portion of the garden that had been left quite rustic and natural. Here at the foot of those steps was a stone bench, tucked neatly off the path between two hedges and overshadowed by a tree, which when it bore leaves was a welcome respite from the sun. The bench itself was made of two stacks of stone, comprising the legs, and a large slab, spanning the distance between them. The slab, or seat, was well-worn from the many people who had sat upon it over the years.

"Do you know," Walter continued as Grace took a seat on the bench, "that this was my favourite place when I was just a lad and came to visit my grandparents."

"Was it really?" Grace smiled and ran a hand over the bit of slab next to her where he was about to sit. "It is a lovely bench, and the aspect from here is delightful." She leaned toward him when he finally took a seat. "I am particularly fond of arched garden gates, and you can see the gate between the hedges quite perfectly from here. I imagine that the gate is even more delightful when all the flowers are in bloom."

"It is," Walter agreed. "And when the tree behind us is laden with leaves, there is something very cozy feeling about this place, almost as if one could hide here, which I must say, I have."

"You have hidden here?"

Walter nodded. "When I was just a boy of about six, I used to curl into a ball under this very bench when playing hide-and-go-seek. Every time." He gave her a sheepish grin. "I would not advise using the same hiding place over and over if one has been found in it. It is the surest way to lose a game."

She giggled. He did so love hearing her do so. It was enough to make any of the uneasiness he felt at admitting such foolishness fade away.

"As I said, I am not always wise."

"No one is when he is six," she assured him. "Do you still hide here? Not under the bench. You would surely not fit there now, but by sitting here?"

He nodded. "I do not know if I would say I hide here now, but it is one of my favourite spots in all of the garden."

She turned toward him, angling her body so that she was not just turning her head. In doing so, her knee rested against the side of his leg. The action did not seem to bother her in the least. She seemed exceptionally comfortable with him. He, on the other hand, found it to be unexpectedly distracting in a very pleasant sort of fashion. So distracting in fact, that he shifted his leg away from her so that he might keep his mind where it should be.

"Why do you not live here? Erondale is your house, is it not?"

"It is," he replied as he shifted to look more fully at her but taking care to keep from touching her. "I am only one person. What do I need with so large a house?"

"But you could sit here every day if you lived here."

"True, but I can command a higher rent for Erondale than I can for my townhouse, and currently, I would rather have more money and live in my townhouse where I am steps from all that there is to do in Bath. I fear I would find spending my evenings at Erondale to be dreadfully boring with only myself to keep me company."

She looked toward the house. "It would be a difficult thing to choose between the beauty here and the excitement of town," she agreed. "What will you do when you marry?" She was looking at him again and her cheeks bore a rosy hue while she attempted to looked serene, though she was doing a very poor job of it.

"I will likely rent out my townhouse and take up residence here. That is, of course, unless my wife wishes to live in town. However, after there are children, this garden would be just the thing for them." He tipped his head and studied her face for a moment. "What would you do? If you were the owner of Erondale and a townhouse in Bath?"

"I would have to know what the townhouse looks like to make an accurate decision, but if it is as nice or nicer than the one which Father has rented, I would be tempted to stay in town for a time — although I do love Erondale and this garden, and the shops are not too far a drive away."

"But it all hinges on the townhouse?" He was quite certain she would like his home in town. He had not taken some small place that suited his needs as an unmarried gentleman. He had taken a townhouse that was both in a desirable location and had rooms enough for a family, for he knew that one day he would be renting it out and so, he had invested accordingly.

She nodded.

"Well, then," he said as he rose and held out his hand to assist her in rising, "you shall have to visit me in town at some point."

Her eyes grew wide as she stood before him. Close enough that if he put his arm out — just so. He could wrap it around her back and pull her to him – like that.

"In case," he said, looking down into her eyes and seeing once again that delectable look of longing, "in case, somewhere along the way during this courtship, we decide we suit."

Her tongue flicked out, moistening her lips, while she nodded mutely. It was nearly an invitation he could not resist. Nearly.

"Forgive me," he whispered as he released her from his embrace. "I have taken liberties where I should not have."

Her disappointment was written clearly on her face. "Please, I..." She shrugged as if she was not certain what she wanted to say. "You may kiss me," she offered quietly. Her chest was lifting and lowering with deliberate breaths just as his was.

"Not yet," he said above the hammering of his heart in his ears. When had holding a lady ever caused his heart to thud so loudly? When had he ever desired a kiss so much as he did at this moment?

"When?" she whispered.

He lifted her hand to his lips and kissed it. "Perhaps, one day," he said as he tucked the hand he had kissed into the crook of his arm. "Perhaps, one day."

Chapter 9

A full day and several hours later, the lingering effects of an almost first kiss had not worn off. Such an intimate moment was a heady thing, and Grace could not put the memory of such wonderfulness by without giving it the full amount of respect it was due. This, of course, required a wistful sigh upon each remembrance. Since Mr. Blakesley had departed Erondale yesterday, it had honestly been a struggle of nearly herculean proportions for Grace to think of much else besides how it had felt to be held by him. Oh, it had been most delightful! How did one feel such perfectness in the arms of a gentleman and still entertain thoughts of others? Grace simply could not fathom how her sister could do so. Felicity really was beyond understanding.

"What is that sigh?" Victoria whispered. "I have

heard it several times both yesterday and today. Is all well?"

"Yes, all is perfect. Can you believe we are here? This room is so lovely, and I just know the music will be divine, do you not think so?" And Mr. Blakesley would join them – along with Mr. Norman, of course. But even if he was to be a full chair away from her, she would get to see him and speak with him. Turning from Victoria to survey the room once more and peek yet again at the doorway in hopes of seeing Mr. Blakesley arrive, she was surprised to find that very gentleman standing behind his friend near the empty seats beside her.

"You look lovely this evening," Mr. Norman said. "May I sit with you?" He looked past her to Graeme, who nodded.

"Good evening, Mr. Norman and Mr. Blakesley." Grace tried to keep her eyes mostly on Mr. Norman, but it was excessively difficult to ignore Mr. Blakesley. This scheme was going to be most trying for that very reason.

"Good evening, Miss Grace," Mr. Blakesley replied. "Mr. Norman insisted I join him in attending tonight's concert. I hope you do not mind the imposition?" Small crinkles formed near his eyes which were filled with amusement.

Grace had never thought that lines around one's eyes could be so lovely as they were when he smiled at her. "I do not mind in the least. It is a grand thing to have a large group of friends to keep one company. Would you not agree, Mr. Norman?"

"Yes, yes. Quite so." He leaned forward. "And how are you this evening, Mrs. Shelton?"

"I am well, thank you. As is Mrs. Clayton."

"That is good news."

Mr. Norman's smile was relaxed and easy. He truly did care about the wellbeing of others. Grace looked around the room as he continued to speak to Mr. and Mrs. Shelton about their day and the weather and a few other things. Surely, in this vast array of people, there must be one lady who would like to marry a handsome and kind physician.

"Grace!"

Her eyes closed as the wonderfulness of the evening was sucked from her with that one word.

"Mama, look. It is Grace."

"Indeed, it is, and Beatrice and Mr. Clayton," Mrs. Love replied. "And several others I have yet to meet," she added with a quick glance at Mr. Norman and a raised eyebrow for Grace.

"I am well," Grace replied, causing her mother to look somewhat chagrinned.

"I am delighted to hear that. I was just about to inquire after your health and that of dear Bea." With a few *pardon me*'s, Mrs. Love and Felicity, followed by Mr. Love and Mr. Ramsey, squeezed past those already seated in the row in front of Grace so that they could sit just in front of Mr. and Mrs. Shelton and Mr. and Mrs. Clayton.

Having gained her seat, Mrs. Love turned to Bea. "How are you, my dear? I have been concerned about you. There is so much commotion in Bath and all that."

"I am no worse than normal," Bea answered. "Tonight will wear on me, but tomorrow is to be devoted to quiet pursuits."

Grace was not certain if what Bea said was true. It had seemed to her that Bea was finding it impossible to make it through a single day without retiring for a rest. She had never done so at Heathcote last year.

"As long as the times of reprieve outweigh the

times of exertion, no ill will befall her," Mr. Clayton said.

Could any gentleman look more pleased with his wife than Mr. Clayton did right now? It was enough to elicit one more small sigh from Grace, which in turn earned Grace a furrowed, worried brow look from Victoria.

"He is just so good to her," Grace whispered.

Victoria smiled and patted Grace's hand in way of agreement.

"It is a relief to hear it, is it not, Mr. Love?" Grace's mother said.

"A great relief," Mr. Love said with a wink for Bea. "Now, if my wife is done, perhaps we can have some introductions."

And so, the Sheltons, as well as Mr. Norman and Mr. Blakesley were introduced by Graeme to the Loves and Mr. Ramsey. And, in turn, Mr. Ramsey was introduced by Mr. Love to the Claytons and Mr. Norman and Mr. Blakesley, since he was already known by the Sheltons.

"A man of medicine?" Mrs. Love asked as if she had never heard of such a thing about Mr. Norman before. "That is a handy friend to have." She smiled at Bea.

"Oh, he is more than handy," Mr. Blakesley said. "He is one of the most loyal friends a fellow could find. He has done me more than one good turn for very little in return."

"And he is very well-liked," Grace added. "I am certain you did not make it into the room without being stopped by several people eager to wish you a good evening." She looked expectantly at Mr. Norman whose brow furrowed for a moment.

"We spoke to four individuals and their parties before we had even reached the door to this room," Mr. Blakesley said, much to Grace's relief. Thankfully, it seemed one of her companions understood the need to praise Mr. Norman to her mother.

"I suppose I am so used to being stopped that I did not even consider it as something about which to keep account," Mr. Norman added. "It is a hazard of my profession, I suppose."

"I shall have to disagree," Mr. Blakesley said. "Norman here would have just as many well-wishers no matter his profession. He is just the sort of fellow who makes friends with ease."

"He does seem so," Grace agreed.

"The same could be said about Blakesley," Roger

inserted. "Therefore, it makes sense that you should be such good friends."

"And how do you know Mr. Shelton?" Grace's father asked of Mr. Blakesley.

"We attended school together," Graeme answered. "The three of us."

No more was able to be said as the concert was set to begin. At least, no words were able to be spoken. However, Mrs. Love could not refrain from sending a speaking glance Grace's direction several times during the performance. Therefore, when the music had stopped and the crowds began to mill about and make their way out of the room, albeit slowly, Grace was not surprised at all to find her mother at her elbow.

"Does Mr. Blakesley have an estate?" she whispered.

"Yes, it is the one Mr. Clayton and Mr. Shelton have leased."

"And is it large?"

Grace shook her head. "Not overly so. It is quite perfectly proportioned. The gardens are well-designed, and the house does not want for care."

"He is handsome."

The hopeful note in her mother's tone caused

Grace's stomach to tumble. "But what of Mr. Ramsey?" she asked, putting her anxious thoughts into words.

"Oh, I am not inquiring for Felicity." Her mother looked at her expectantly. "An estate owner is a better choice than a physician," she added when Grace said nothing.

Grace had not held her tongue purposefully. Her mind was whirling, attempting to keep her scheme in her control rather than having it overtaken by any of her mother's matchmaking attempts. It would not matter if their mother had arranged things to Grace's advantage. Grace could see how Felicity even now, while standing with her hand on Mr. Ramsey's arm was assessing Mr. Blakesley, and Grace would not allow Mr. Blakesley to be snatched from her like Mr. Everett Clayton and Mr. Ramsey had been.

"He is not unattached," she whispered to her mother. Her heart thudded, heavy and fast within her chest. "There is a lady who has captured Mr. Blakesley's attention.

"I do not see anyone on his arm," her mother countered.

"That is because she is not here. She is not even in Bath."

"She is not?" There was a great deal of interest mixed with surprise in the question. "If she is not here, then, where is she?"

Grace's brow furrowed. Where was this imaginary lady from? "Um, I think..." A smile curled her lips as the perfect reply became obvious. Surely, any gentleman who had nearly kissed a lady must have had his attention captured by that lady. "I think she is from Kent."

"Near us?" her mother asked, casting a furtive look in Mr. Blakesley's direction.

"I could not say." Because the lady was very, very near their estate in Kent. In fact, she was a resident at that estate. However, her mother could not know that.

"What is her name?"

Grace shook her head. "I am sure I could not tell you. I have only heard bits and pieces, and I did not think it polite to ask."

Her mother looked disappointed. "I suppose that is true, unfortunately." She sighed. "Do you know if he is betrothed?"

"I do not believe he is." *Oh! That was the wrong*

thing to say, Grace scolded herself as her mother's face brightened.

"If he is not betrothed, then there could be no harm in a wee mite of flirting."

"Mama, I am not Felicity."

Her mother gasped and looked affronted.

"I will not attempt to steal a gentleman from another," Grace clarified.

"I was not saying you should, of course. I was just thinking that if you were to flirt with him a trifle, we might find out how attached he is to this young woman."

"That sounds a great deal like attempting to steal him from another," Grace answered. "I will not do it."

"Oh, very well. I suppose you are correct. But an estate owner is so much better than a physician."

"Mr. Norman is a very kind man, Mama."

Mrs. Love sighed. "But kindness does not put food on the table."

"It is far more likely that kindness will before unkindness does."

"Oh, Grace," her mother chided. "You know what I mean. I cannot say your father will approve of such a match."

"Please, Mother, could we speak of something else?" Anything else. There were two older ladies who were watching them closely. With any luck, they would both be hard of hearing and would not have heard a word of her discussion with her mother.

"Mr. Blakesley," her mother said as she pulled Grace forward. "Grace was telling me that you have a young lady waiting for you in Kent, and since we are from Kent, I do hope that you will call on us when you are there."

Grace's eyes grew wide. Her mother was not supposed to mention this imaginary lady to Mr. Blakesley!

"You are from Kent?" he replied with all the calm of a gentleman surveying a billiard table. There was a calculating look to his expression and small quizzical lift to his left eyebrow when he glanced at Grace.

"Yes, has Grace not told you?"

"I am afraid we have not had a great deal of time to discuss such things."

Grace pressed her lips together to keep from smiling. That was a bald-faced lie, and though she did not normally approve of such things, presently, she found it very well done.

"Well, then," her mother said with a coy smile of her own, "I would not be opposed to a call so that we can learn more about one another. It would be a great boon to have another person from Kent to count as a friend."

"I am not from Kent, nor will I ever be," Mr. Blakesley interrupted.

"Yes, yes, but your young lady. I would be delighted to know about her and her family."

Mr. Blakesley opened his mouth to protest further but Mrs. Love, rather pointedly, paid him no mind and continued on.

"Of course, if you do not wish to call on me to discuss such things, I am certain Grace would be able to do an admirable job of acquainting you with our family. You could accompany your friend, Mr. Norman, when he calls on Grace." Her lashes fluttered twice.

Embarrassment washed over Grace. "Mama," she whispered. Could her mother be any less circumspect about her motives?

Mr. Blakesley's lips tipped up ever so slightly. "I suppose that will be entirely up to Mr. Norman, madame. However, I dare say even his kind nature will not allow me to interfere with his purpose regarding your daughter." He looked at Grace. "I know I would not let anyone, whether gentleman or lady, divide me from such a lovely prize if I were Mr. Norman." His gaze held hers for the briefest of moments, but long enough to inform her that he was not speaking in hypothetical terms. "And speaking of that good friend, I am going to have to snatch him away from Mr. Shelton, since we travelled together, for I have an early day tomorrow and would like to find my pillow quite soon. Good night, ladies. It has been a pleasure." He bowed first over Mrs. Love's hand and then, Grace's, giving her fingers the tiniest of squeezes as he did.

"He is a lovely young man," Mrs. Love said longingly as she watched him leave.

And for once, Grace had to admit that her mother was perfectly correct.

Chapter 10

"Mr. Blakesley, what a delightful surprise to see you here."

Walter, who had risen quickly and found himself a seat other than beside Grace when it was noted that Mrs. Love had arrived, bowed and extended his welcome.

"Is Mr. Norman with you?" Mrs. Love glanced around the room.

"He was, but then he was called away," Grace answered.

"Yes, there was a patient in need of an urgent consultation," Walter added. "He has promised to return to collect me before night falls." Not that Walter cared one bit if he was forced to spend the night at his own estate. There were certain inducements which would make it quite pleasurable. Not only did he have friends and a well-stocked larder and wine cellar here at Erondale, there was also Grace.

Mrs. Love tsked. "Such a life. To be always at someone's beck and call." She gave her daughter a pointed look. Apparently, Grace had not exaggerated her mother's disdain for a physician as a possible husband for her daughter.

"I believe he enjoys it, Mama," Grace replied. "For he did not look put out in the least. I can imagine that being so very knowledgeable about all things pertaining to health and knowing that you might bring relief and help to another is quite fulfilling. Why if I were to be in possession of such knowledge, I am certain I would not mind one bit being asked to provide aide to another. As it is, you know how much I enjoy visiting those who are less fortunate."

"You do?" There was no little amount of shock in Mrs. Love's tone, which pricked Walter's curiosity.

He could see Grace being quite good at visiting those in need and lending her aide.

"I do." Grace smoothed her skirt. "I have just decided it."

Grace was also very good at vexing her mother.

Walter relaxed into his chair to watch the scene between mother and daughter unfold before him.

"You have?" Her mother still looked as if she were floundering in the sea without a hope of help.

"Yes. I find Mr. Norman to be very inspiring. If we were not in Bath, I would seek out the parson and discover if there is someone to whom I might be of service for an hour or two."

"You find Mr. Norman inspiring?"

"Very."

Walter bit back a grin at the look of utter delight Grace wore, which was in stark contrast to the ashen hue of her mother's face.

"But," Grace continued, "I suppose, I might find that I do not like being of service to the less fortunate as much as I imagine I might, and that would be dreadful in the extreme." Her brow furrowed. "I wonder if Mr. Norman would find me wanting if such were the case?"

"Yes, yes, I think he might," her mother hurried to assure her.

"Is Felicity not with you?"

Mrs. Love blinked at Grace's sudden shift of topics. "She was expecting a call from Mr. Ramsey."

"And you are letting her receive him without

yourself being present?" Graeme asked in astonishment.

Mrs. Love smiled slyly. "Her father is there, and I think Mr. Ramsey might wish to see Mr. Love rather than me."

Grace's face lit with excitement. "Do you really think he is going to offer for her?"

Something of great interest on the hem of Mrs. Love's glove captured her attention as she replied, "It is quite likely."

"And will she accept him?" From the wideness of Grace's eyes, Graeme's question surprised her as much as her mother.

"I do believe she will," Mrs. Love replied. "At least, we are hopeful."

"Will she marry in Bath? How quickly do you think it could be accomplished?" Grace asked eagerly.

Mrs. Love laughed. "I think we shall leave some of those details up to the happy couple to decide."

"But to be married in the Abbey would be something worthy of note to all Felicity's friends. Do you not think?" Grace bit her lip anxiously.

Walter had known Grace was eager to have her

sister settled, but he had not thought her quite so eager as she appeared at this moment.

"It would be noteworthy," her mother agreed. "But there is no rush."

Grace's shoulders slumped. "Can my season begin before she is Mrs. Ramsey? Or must I wait until after she marries."

"She will still need to be seen in company, and I do not see why she cannot enjoy a few more festivities as Miss Love before she becomes Mrs. anyone."

Grace sighed and slumped down in her seat. "I should like to have a season before I marry," she said softly.

"Ah, but if you marry Mr. Norman," Mr. Blakesley said, "you will have the delights of Bath at your door. Your life can be a continual season. That would be a definite advantage to having a husband who lives in Bath."

Mrs. Love looked at him in horror, and he thought for a moment that Grace was going to giggle. However, she refrained. Roger did not. He chuckled while his wife discreetly captured his hand and, most likely, gave it a squeeze to remind the fellow that he was not to find the conversation so entertaining.

"I suppose it is." Grace sighed loudly. "Then, Felicity may marry whenever she wishes."

"A wedding in the Abbey would be noteworthy," her mother said, this time with a great deal more conviction than she had the first time.

"A double ceremony would be even more noteworthy," Roger said as he shot a quick glance in Walter's direction.

It was a thought worthy of consideration. He tilted his head and studied Grace. Grace Blakesley? It had a pleasing ring to it. However, the double ceremony would never happen. Grace deserved her own day, far removed from her sister. She had lived in that shadow long enough.

"No, no," Mrs. Love said, "one wedding at a time will be trying enough. And I am certain Grace is not yet ready to marry."

"I might be," Grace said.

"It is not a thing to be rushed into," Mrs. Clayton said softly.

"Oh, goodness, no!" Grace agreed.

"However, if one meets the right gentleman and falls in love with him and he with her, then is it rushing?" Walter asked, keeping his eyes on Mrs.

Clayton and not allowing them to roam to Grace as they wished to do.

"I would say no," Graeme answered.

"I would agree," Roger said.

"What of the ladies? What do you think on this matter?" Walter asked.

"This imaginary couple is truly in love?" Mrs. Shelton asked.

Walter nodded. "They would give all they had to see the other happy."

"Then, no, if they are certain they are in love and do not just fancy themselves so, I would say it is not rushing."

"I think I would agree if that is the case," Mrs. Clayton said.

Walter turned to Mrs. Love.

"I do not think I wish to answer that," she said, lifting her chin. "I shall leave it up to Mr. Love to decide if it is rushing."

Walter had to admit that hers was the perfect answer, for if she had said she did not think it was rushing, it would have given her daughter, whom she feared thought herself enamoured with the unacceptable Mr. Norman, freedom to run pell-mell into marriage with the fellow. However, by deferring to her husband, who was not present, she allowed room for the delay of an untenable marriage and avoided any present argument with her daughter.

"He would give all he had to see her happy?" Grace asked when Walter turned to her for her answer.

Walter nodded. "And she would do the same for him."

"Even if it led to misery?"

"Or death," Walter added.

"Oh, my."

He had never seen Grace look so very serious.

"Is that how you feel about your husbands?" Her eyes shifted to Mrs. Shelton and Mrs. Clayton, who both nodded. "And you about your wives?" she asked Graeme and Roger, who also nodded. Her brow furrowed, and she turned to her mother. "And that is how you feel about Father?"

Mrs. Love glanced around the room, her cheeks growing the faintest bit rosy. "Well, that is rather dramatic, and I am not one to be dramatic."

Walter doubted that. He had seen her daughters, and both appeared to him to be perfectly capable of dramatics.

"However," she continued, "I suppose that is how I feel about your father."

"The question remains, Miss Grace," Walter pressed. Her answer was the most important one in the room. "If those were the conditions, do you think it would be rushing to marry in haste?"

She sat quietly for a moment before her lips curled upward. "I suppose that would depend on what the gentleman who loved me thought, for if I am willing to live in misery on his behalf, then if waiting to marry, which might prove miserable, is what would make him happy, I would have no option but to defer to his desire. If I did otherwise, would that not prove I did not love him as deeply as I should?"

That was not an answer he had expected her to give. "I had not thought of it so," he admitted.

"But does this gentleman know that making you wait would make you miserable?" Roger asked. "Would that not then call his own devotion to you into question?"

A pained expression created a great furrow between Grace's eyes. "Then, how is one ever to know if one is in love enough to marry?"

"That is an excellent question," Roger replied,

turning to Walter. "Do you have an explanation? You always had some reply when we pondered such impossible things in school."

Walter shook his head. "I am afraid my answer will not be satisfying, for I think that love is not something which can be dissected into bits and pieces to be analyzed for proof of existence. Not that it cannot be examined and found to exist."

"I am terribly confused," Grace said.

Walter smiled at her. "I think that one just simply knows, and that, for each person, the item of proof differs despite some similarities in all cases."

"You are very wise," Mrs. Love inserted.

"Thank you," Walter answered, though his eyes did not leave her daughter.

"And have you found that measure of proof with your lady?" Mrs. Love prodded.

Had he? Was it not too soon to have discovered such a thing? He had not known Grace for more than a handful of days, though he had known *of* her for a few days before that. He shrugged. "I am not entirely certain."

"You are not?" Mrs. Love sounded eager as if she was hoping he would give up this lady whom she did not know was her daughter.

"No, I am not. Though," his heart beat a bit faster as he considered giving Grace up to another gentleman, "I dare say I could not be persuaded away from choosing her." And within the walls of that thought lay the truth. His heart belonged to his mysterious angel – even if it did feel a bit as if he was rushing into something – something which, he suspected, would be quite wonderful.

Chapter 11

"We could sit under this tree." Grace suggested when she, Bea and Victoria were taking a stroll through Sydney Gardens two days later.

Bea was looking rather tired, causing Grace to worry about her. She would hate for her cousin to become ill, and not just because it would mean they would have to forego their plans for the evening. She was finding it quite delightful to have friends such as Bea and Victoria, and she desired to demonstrate her care for them as much as they seemed willing to do for her.

Graeme and Roger had left the three of them to take a walk while they went to see a tailor about a... Grace's face scrunched. They had gone to see the tailor about something, but for the life of her, she could not recall what it was. That was likely because she had been too occupied with looking at

Mr. Blakesley...Walter... She sighed as she thought his name. She still had not decided what she would call him in private, but she did enjoy using his Christian name when thinking about him.

"If we sit there, we could indulge in our buns," Victoria agreed. "I find I am once again hungry and being hungry does not bode well for my ability to keep my stomach right side up."

"Are you also unwell?" Grace turned her attention from her cousin, who was beginning to look pale, to her friend who did not look at all unwell. However, both her friend and her cousin had been ill several times over the past few days. It was odd really. No one else had become ill, and the illness had not settled in, forcing either lady to take to her bed for an extended period of time.

"No, not at present," Victoria said to Grace before turning to smile at Bea. "We should sit. It would most certainly not be the thing for you to cast up our accounts or swoon in the garden."

"Oh, not at all!" Grace cried.

"Graeme would never allow me out of the house or his sight again if he were to learn of it," Bea said.

Victoria laughed. "I was more concerned with being a spectacle, but I think my husband would be the same." She took a seat on the ground and smoothed her skirts. "And being confined to the house would be no way to experience Bath."

"Is the ground dry?" Grace asked. She did not wish to ruin the skirt of her dress as she had only just received this one from Felicity who had been seen enough times wearing it on walks.

"Yes, and it is not too very cold either since it has had the sun to warm it this morning," Victoria assured her.

There was still a bit of sun shining on the ground, though the sun was beginning to find its way to the other side of the tree under which they sat.

"This must be a lovely place for a picnic when the leaves are all out," Grace commented as she took a seat.

"Perhaps one day you will be so fortunate as to have a picnic here," Bea said with a smile. "Mr. Blakesley is a wonderful match, and I do believe he is intent on convincing you of that very thing."

"I do hope so," the words popped out of Grace's mouth before she had a moment to think about them. "Or, at least, I think I do," she corrected.

"You do not need to pretend with us," Victoria assured her.

"I am not pretending," Grace replied. "I am not certain if I should hope for such an eventuality or not." She shook her head. "No, that is not it. I am quite certain I could like Mr. Blakesley very well for the rest of my life. However, I am not certain if I should know if I could or not just yet." She looked at the confused faces of her companions and added, "I do not know if I would give up everything for him. I have been considering it since his call two days ago, and I think that I would. However, how can I know for sure unless I have been faced with the possibility?"

Victoria laughed. "I think the fact that you are thinking about it so carefully likely proves that it is not too soon to hope to be Mrs. Blakesley at some point."

"He is as upstanding as he appears," Bea added. "Graeme has been doing some investigating," she whispered.

"He has?" That was surprising.

"He would not want you to be taken in by a scoundrel," Bea answered. "He is taking his role of guardian to you while in our company quite seriously." She rested a hand on her stomach. "He will be a good father to our children – which, of course, I knew, but of which I am happy to be reminded."

Grace's brow furrowed. Was Bea hinting at what she thought Bea was hinting? She glanced at the hand on Bea's stomach.

"Yes," Bea whispered, her cheeks growing a tad rosy.

"You are going to have a baby?"

"You cannot tell anyone," Bea cautioned. "Not yet. Not until things are more firmly undeniable. I have yet to feel any movement, and I will feel much better sharing the news with one and all once that has occurred."

"I think with how ill you and I have been, there is little doubt that we are pregnant."

"You, too!" Grace cried, turning toward Victoria, who nodded. "This is why you have been tired and unwell?"

Again, Victoria nodded.

"And why you have seen Mr. Norman so often?"

"Yes," Bea said. "Graeme is far more concerned about my health than is necessary, but it is sweet."

"He is so solicitous." Grace clapped her hands together once but then, put them in her lap rather than clapping more as she wished to do. She had just been trusted with a great secret. Therefore, she was not about to draw attention to them by being overly exuberant. "This is such good news! When is the happy event to take place?" She tried to keep her tone interested but not excited.

"The end of summer," Victoria said. "For both of us, according to Mr. Norman's calculations."

"How exciting! You will have children who will be the same age. They will be such good friends, just as Mr. Shelton and Mr. Clayton are and how the two of you are as well." They would no doubt spend a great deal of time visiting one another for Grace could not imagine Graeme and Roger being separated for too overly long a period of time.

"It is a lovely thought," Bea said. "And one which I hold close."

"It is wonderful, simply wonderful," Grace said as she broke off a piece of her bun. "These are enormous," she muttered.

"And delicious," Victoria added.

Victoria was not wrong. Having tasted her first bite of a Sally Lunn, it was obvious to Grace why Walter liked them so well. In fact, it was he who had brought the delectable treats to them today.

If she were to marry him, these delectable treats could be a frequent visitor to her table. She closed her eyes and savoured the taste of her bun and the thought of being Mrs. Blakesley.

"This is quite the lovely sight."

Grace opened her eyes to see Mr. Blakesley standing before her.

"Indeed, it is," Roger agreed.

Grace pulled her eyes away from Walter long enough to see that both Roger and Graeme had returned.

"You may join us," Grace offered. "There is plenty of this bun for sharing. I am certain I should not eat the full thing."

"And why should you not?" Walter did not wait to be convinced to take a seat next to her. He rather swiftly claimed the bit of ground to her right and accepted the portion of bun she gave him. "They are delicious."

"Oh, indeed, they are," Grace assured him. "However, if I were to eat an entire bun every day – as I quite wish to do – I would have to be rolled through the garden since I would likely grow very round."

The responding laughter from Walter was delightfully pleasing.

"You are sounding a bit like Mr. Norman," he cautioned.

"How so?" Grace asked.

"He is forever telling me that I should not indulge in these as often as I do." He popped a second morsel of the sweet roll into his mouth.

Warmth spread across Grace's cheeks as she envied the fingers from which he kissed away every trace of bun. That was most improper. She focused her eyes on the bun she held. "Do you eat them very often then?"

"As often as I can, which is nearly every day."

"The whole thing? Every day?" How did he not grow fat? Her mother had always scolded that indulging in sweets of any sort rather than vegetables and meat only lead to being fat and gouty.

He nodded as his fortunate fingers once again were kissed free of any morsels of sweetness. "That is why I walk far more often than I ride, and why I have taken up pugilism. Exercise balances the indulgence – or so Mr. Norman assures me. Therefore, if you were to say, dance a set or two with me this evening, that should compensate for the extravagance of this treat."

"I cannot dance with you." As much as she would like to do just that.

"One dance would not cause any stir. Your mother knows we are acquainted. In fact, to not dance with you would seem suspiciously rude."

"He has a point," Roger inserted.

"But my sister –"

"Will never pose an issue," Walter said.

"You do not know that," Grace argued.

"I think I do." He held her gaze most intently.

Oh, she wanted to dance with him! She truly did. She also wanted to believe that Felicity would never come between them, but at present, she was not certain she could trust her sister at all. Why just think of how Felicity had treated her!

"Trust me," he whispered. "Please."

"One set?" How could she refuse him when he looked so desirous of her granting him his wish?

He nodded.

"Not the first. That one should really go to Mr. Norman if he is there."

"Does that mean I may have one of the other sets?" Pleasure danced in his eyes.

"Yes, but only one set and only as a friend of a friend."

"If that is how you wish it to be. I will remind you, however, that your sister will never sway me to pay her any particular attention."

"I cannot trust her," Grace said softly.

"You do not have to. You need only trust me."

"One set," she replied. "We would not wish for your lady in Kent to hear of more than that and become jealous."

He chuckled. "She has no need to fear being made jealous."

"Right, well," Graeme interrupted. "If we are to get to the Assembly Rooms at all today, we must finish our walk and make certain these ladies have had ample time to rest and recover before preparing for a ball."

"Which is no small feat," Roger agreed with a laugh.

"Are you ready to go on?" Grace whispered to Bea who was on her left.

"Has she been unwell?" Graeme asked.

"No, no," Grace rushed to assure him. "She was a bit tired and... hungry," she added after taking note of Bea's half-eaten bun.

"Are you certain?" Graeme asked.

Grace nodded vigorously as Bea assured her husband that she was well. There was no way Grace wanted to miss either that dance with Walter or the dinner party which had been cunningly arranged so that she could see his townhouse.

"There are rooms at my home just waiting to be filled," Walter said as he rose and extended his hand to Grace. "The maids will be perfectly put out if they went to the bother to prepare them, and then they are not used. And Norman will be joining us later if there is a need for any tonics or tinctures. Although," he continued as he helped Grace to her feet and slipped her hand into the crook of his arm, "I have some peppermint leaves from which we can make a tea – not too strong, mind you – and then when it is cooled, you can try it for any relief it might impart. Or I have some oil which you can use for a headache."

Roger chuckled. "You sound very little like a bachelor, and more like a mother hen."

"Ah, the dangers of having Mr. Norman for a friend, I am afraid," Walter answered with a laugh. "I have learned much from him – some of it willingly even." Again, he laughed. "In all seriousness, a gentleman could not find a better friend than Norman." He glanced down at Grace. "Unless, of course, he gets two sets while I only have one."

"I must make a show of being enamoured with him," Grace argued. That was the crux of the plan. She was to pretend to wish for Mr. Norman's attentions while in truth it was Mr. Blakesley who was her true beau.

"I do not believe you do."

Grace sighed. "But that is the plan."

"Plans can change," Walter retorted.

"I know they can," Grace agreed. And she knew that someday her plan would need to change, but today was not that day, no matter how much Mr. Blakesley argued it should be. While she might be able to trust him, Felicity, the reason for the plan in the first place, was another matter altogether.

Chapter 12

"This is it," Walter said as Graeme's carriage drew to a stop in front of a town house in the middle of a row of houses standing on the eastern side of a square. "It is not overly grand," he said as he stood on the walkway that crossed over to the door. "However, it is of ample size for a small family."

"It is lovely," Victoria said.

"Yes, very," Grace agreed.

Walter could tell by the way she scanned the front of the building, tipping her head to see up it as high as possible, while smiling broadly, that she was duly impressed.

"If you look below us, there is a small courtyard and some storage with an entrance to the servants' quarters, as well as the kitchen and such."

"How do they get down there to enter?" Grace asked.

"There is a true entry at the rear of the house. I suppose I should have more accurately stated that there is an exit from the servants' quarters for access to the courtyard and storage."

"Ah," she said with a nod of her head as she continued to look at the courtyard and then once again moved her gaze to the façade of the house. "It is not very old, is it?"

He shook his head. "No, it not much older than you."

"Indeed? Is it very modern within?"

"I shall let you determine that." He waved his hand toward the door which stood, waiting for them to enter. He smiled at her exclamation upon entering just ahead of him.

"I believe she likes it," Graeme muttered behind him.

"I would say you are correct." And Walter was as delighted by that fact as Grace was by the flooring and the second door that separated the foyer from the interior of the house. He had hoped she would like his house, for he was beginning to hope quite seriously that it would one day also be hers.

They passed through the second door and stood in front of the staircase with two doors to the right of them and a third past the staircase and down the hall. It was through this door that a footman was disappearing with the various articles of outerwear he had gathered from Walter's guest.

"Your maid will be given what she needs," he said softly to Grace who was watching the footman.

"Oh, I have no doubt of that."

The smile she turned on him caused him to forget for a moment what he had intended to show them next. Thankfully, his mind did not fail him for long – only long enough for Roger to cough.

It was all well and good for him to be laughing at Walter's expense. The man was married and utterly besotted with his wife. It was not as if Walter was acting the part of a smitten swain on his own. It was just that he did not have the assurance that the object of his affection would always be at his side as both Roger and Graeme did.

He raised an eyebrow and gave Roger a challenging look that was met with a smirk and a nod of acceptance. Both of the men with him knew how important this evening was to Walter. He had made certain they knew on their walk to the tailor.

"Through here," Walter opened the first door to

his right, "we have the dining room. You may peek in, but since we will be spending time there later, there really is no need to enter. We do not wish to be underfoot," he added.

Within, one maid was using a small brush to sweep the chairs while another was placing a cloth on a table that stood near the table and would receive many of the serving utensils.

"And this door," he had moved to the second door which was only separated from the first by the space of a wall, "leads to my study." He stepped inside and the others followed.

"It is as organized as I would have expected," Roger said. "Blakesley was not the sort to ever have anything out of place in his lodgings," he explained. "You could ask him for anything and within a few moments, he would have it for you for he knew just where it should be."

"That seems like an excellent way to be," Bea said.

"Clayton and Shelton were also fairly well organized. Clayton more so than Shelton."

"I could see that," Grace said.

"You could?" Roger said.

Grace nodded. "You are a trifle more carefree

than Mr. Clayton. He is not stodgy, mind you, but he does have a more fatherly air about him." She shrugged. "Or so it seemed to me when I was at Heathcote, but then, I might just be thinking so from the way he was always scolding his brother and asking after Bea's wellbeing."

"My brother is an idiot," Graeme retorted. "If he were not, there would be no need to scold."

"I do not find him to be an idiot," Grace retorted and then shrugged. "If I did, I would also have to call myself one since I was just as duped as he was by my sister, and frankly, I do not wish to even think that word about myself. I will allow that we were both foolish."

"I did not mean to imply that you were an idiot," Graeme apologized. "But trust me, there have been many things over the years which Everett has done to earn the moniker."

"That is because he is your brother," Bea inserted. "To the rest of us, he is not so bad as he is to you."

"He treated you very ill," Graeme retorted.

"And look where that has led," Roger said.

And that one statement was all that was needed to silence Graeme about the idiocy of his brother.

In fact, much to Walter's amusement, before they had left the study, Graeme had begun to think that perhaps his brother's lack of sense was one of his best qualities.

"Has anyone asked you about the picture on our desk yet?" Grace asked as they climbed the stairs to the first floor.

She had stood behind his desk, picked up the framed silhouette he had drawn, smiled her secret smile at it and then him, and then returned it to its place.

"Not yet," he replied. "I only just got it back with the frame yesterday. I have not yet had time to have anyone ask."

"Are we not stopping on this floor?" she asked when he turned toward the second flight of stairs.

"We will return to it."

She stood at the bottom of the stairs and looked at him as if that was the most foolish thing she had ever heard.

"The drawing room and billiards room is on this floor. We will return to it after I have seen you settled in your accommodations."

Her brow furrowed and her lips puckered with displeasure.

"I promise."

"Very well," she said with a small huff. "But I am a curious creature."

"As am I," he assured her when she had reached the step on which he stood. "This next floor is mine. There is my bedchamber, a sitting room, and a dressing room. Do you wish to see it?"

"I think we can do without," Graeme said.

Walter chuckled. Grace was correct about Graeme having a fatherly air about him. "I assure you I have no intention of doing more than showing the rooms to Miss Grace." That lady gasped, while Roger chuckled, and Graeme cleared his throat and glared at Walter.

"Our rooms?" Graeme said.

"Are on the next floor. There are two rooms of substantial size and two smaller rooms. I have instructed that the larger rooms be readied for you and Shelton, while one of the smaller rooms has been made ready for Miss Grace." He opened doors and assigned people to each room. Then, he made to leave them. "I will be in the drawing room or my study if you should need me."

Grace turned to enter her room, but not before sharing one more of her secret smiles with him. If he had deduced things correctly, Grace would not be long in finding her way to the drawing room which she had not been allowed to see.

And he was not wrong. No more than twenty minutes later, Grace stepped quietly into the drawing room. Alone.

He discarded the book he had been reading. "We have no chaperone," he cautioned.

"Am I not to trust you?" Her eyes danced with impertinence.

"I had hoped you would, but you seem hesitant to do so."

Her mouth popped open and then closed as her brow furrowed. "Do you mean about our scheme and not just now?"

"I do." He rose and motioned toward the windows. "The view of the park is excellent from here."

The comment drew her across the room to him.

"Oh, it is!"

"Those trees will one day be much larger, but there are several different specimens which add to the beauty of the autumn when the leaves show all their glory." He stood directly behind her. Almost of their own accord, his arms wrapped around her.

It was almost of their own accord because he had paused for a fraction of a moment to consider the action before undertaking it. True, it had not been long enough of a pause to consider much more than how wonderful it would be to hold her. To his delight, she did not jump or squeal, but instead, sighed and leaned back against him.

"This is not proper," she said.

"Indeed, it is not, and I am risking the ire of Clayton."

She nodded.

"He might even force me to offer for you if we are found thusly." He was not sure if his caution was for her or his own mind, which had begun to wonder how her neck might taste.

"What would you do if he did?" The question was barely more than a whisper.

"I would offer for you now, rather than later." He felt her sharp intake of breath. "I have come to the conclusion that I should very much like to offer for you at some point if you will allow it." His heart hammered against his ribs as if it was asking to be freed from the confines of his body. This was not part of how he had planned this evening to go. He was rushing forward when he should be holding back and giving her time to come to trust him enough to be seen with him in public without the ruse of being merely a friend before making any sort of offer. He swallowed and, despite his trepidation, pressed on. "Do I have a hope of ever being allowed?"

Her hands covered his where they were clasped against her stomach. She rubbed them gently as the silence following his question grew longer. Finally, she spoke.

"I want to say yes."

His heart sank. She was rejecting him.

"However, I am not certain." She turned in his arms to look at him. "I have only just learned what love is. I had not thought it so all-consuming as it appears to be." She tilted her head. "Could I give up my happiness for yours?" She shrugged. "I should like to think so, but..." She shook her head.

"You are uncertain?"

She nodded. "And I would hate myself forever if I were to promise you my heart only to discover later that I was mistaken." Her eyes glistened. "I have seen the harm such a thing can do, and I could never harm you in such a fashion."

His heart thrilled at her admission. She was not

rejecting him out of hand. In fact, her words proved that, unbeknownst to her, she was well on her way to being in love with him. He ran the back of his right hand along her jaw, and then passed a finger over her tempting lips. How he long to kiss them! However, they were not his to claim just yet.

"Then, I suppose we should not be caught standing as we are, for I would not wish to be the cause of your unhappiness." He passed his finger over her lips once more before pressing a kiss to her forehead and then releasing her before he allowed himself to do more.

"Do you like to read?" He turned from her, smiling at her disappointed sigh. "Or, I could teach you to play billiards."

"Could you really?" she asked eagerly.

He crossed to the door which joined the drawing room to the billiards room and opened it. Billiards would be far better than reading. He had told Grace that he was not the sort of gentleman to seduce a lady, and until this moment, he had not been. However, as her face lit with delight, he had to admit to himself that he most certainly planned to seduce Grace. Not so he could have the momentary pleasure of having her in his bed just once, but so he could win her heart and, in so doing, have her always in his bed, in his drawing room, at his table, as his dance partner for as many sets as he wished, in his arms as they stood looking over the park or admiring his garden at Erondale, and forever as his wife.

Chapter 13

"You make a charming couple," Mrs. Love whispered.

Grace sighed. There were many interesting places where her mother could see and be seen and hear any number of tantalizing tales, but instead of choosing one of those places to be, her mother had decided that the empty seat beside Grace was the perfect place to sit while Felicity danced.

"Have we any happy news?" Grace completely ignored her mother's comment about Mr. Blakesley, who had just danced the first set with Grace, and attempted to steer the conversation in a better direction.

Mrs. Love clucked her tongue. "Not yet, and I cannot imagine what is keeping him from coming to the point."

"He knows about Mr. Everett Clayton, you

know," Grace ducked her head close to her mother's ear. "Perhaps he is just being cautious?"

"How can he doubt her regard? Look at her." Mrs. Love motioned toward the floor with her fan. "She is smitten, simply smitten. Can you not see it in how she looks at him?"

Grace squinted her eyes and studied, really studied, her older sister but to no avail. She had seen Felicity look at Mr. Everett Clayton in that same way.

"One does not look so at a suitor unless one is hoping for an offer," Mrs. Love added.

One did if one was Felicity. No, that was not entirely true, Grace corrected. Her sister had wished for an offer from Mr. Everett Clayton until she had found something more to her liking.

"How do you know it is not just an act?"

"An act?" her mother repeated in surprise.

"Need I remind you that Felicity was smitten at Heathcote and remained so until the second day of the Abernathy's house party when Mr. Ramsey spoke to her."

The statement was met with a great exhalation of breath from Mrs. Love. "A mother knows," she answered.

Grace schooled her eyebrows to remain immobile rather than arching skeptically as they wished to do. "How precisely does a mother know?"

"I am certain I cannot distill it, but there is feeling." She laid her hand on her heart. "Your sister is more attached this time. I just know she is. There was a hesitance about Mr. Everett Clayton. I never once saw her smile wistfully while stitching as if she was thinking of Mr. Everett Clayton, but she does now. And when I asked her about it just yesterday, she sighed and said, 'Is he not the most perfect gentleman?'"

Grace was not completely convinced, but she was willing, upon hearing such a story, to allow that it might be possible for her sister to be, at long last, irrevocably attached to a gentleman. However, for herself, she would only be satisfied when she saw Felicity standing at the altar repeating her vows.

"I dare say you would not say Mr. Ramsey is the perfect gentleman."

Grace looked at her mother in feigned astonishment. "How do you mean?"

"Oh, come now, Grace. I would venture that Mr. Blakesley is a trifle more perfect in your estimation.

You were looking very content to be dancing with him."

"He is a friend. How could one not feel content while dancing with a friend?"

Her mother tipped her head and pursed her lips. It was a sure sign that she did not believe a word Grace was saying. And that was not good for Grace's scheme. Therefore, without much thought beyond needing to keep her ruse going and Mr. Blakesley safe from Felicity, she continued, "However, I do see your meaning now, and I would have to agree."

Her mother smiled smugly.

"Mr. Norman is far superior to Mr. Ramsey." She sighed for effect. "It really is too bad he was not here to dance the first set as he had promised. But one cannot predict, with any great deal of accuracy, when someone is going to fall ill."

"Mr. –" Her mother huffed as if she could not even bear to speak Mr. Norman's name. "Really, Grace. You cannot be serious. I do not know why you insist upon pursuing such a fellow. He seems an honorable sort of gentleman, I will give you that. But, Grace, your father and I did not send you to school to become a physician's wife! You will cease this foolishness."

"It is not foolishness," Grace insisted but her mother would not hear any explanation.

Instead, she rose. "I will find your father. See that your sister does not come to ruin in my absence."

Grace grabbed her mother's hand before she could leave. "You do not need to get Father. I admire Mr. Norman greatly, but I am not yet set on him."

Her mother looked down at Grace. "You are not?"

Grace shook her head. "I have not even entered this season yet. I am only participating in soirees at my hosts' behest. How could I be settled on a gentleman when I am not truly partaking in the season?"

Her mother did not look convinced. Grace held her breath, waiting to know what her mother would do. Telling fibs to her mother was one thing – one easily done thing – but telling even the smallest untruth to her father was excessively challenging, especially if one wished for him to believe the falsehood. Her father was more astute than her mother. An explanation such as she had just given to her mother would likely be met with a...

"*You had a season last year. However, that is neither here nor there for one does not have to be part of any season ever to marry. It is not as if parliament has amended the marriage act to include the necessity of a season.*"

And he would be right. She did not need a season to tell her where she hoped her heart lay. And that was precisely why she needed her mother to not get her father. None of her family needed to know that her heart was quite likely more attached to a gentleman than Felicity's would ever be. The thought of Mr. Blakesley preferring Felicity was an annoying thought to Grace at the start of her scheme. However, at this very moment, such a thought caused her heart to ache and tears to gather.

"I wish to hear naught else about him," her mother demanded.

"I cannot not speak about a friend. He calls on my hosts. I must be allowed to speak about him."

Her mother's eyes narrowed. "There will be no sighing over him or talk about being his wife."

Grace's brow furrowed. How was she going to dissuade her mother from pushing her at Mr.

Blakesley if she did not have Mr. Norman to play his part in pretending to court her?

"But what if I find I truly do wish to be his wife. It is possible."

"You will not. It is not allowed."

"You cannot decree where a heart will find its desire," Grace argued.

"I believe I just did," her mother replied in that tone which said that to say anything other than "Yes, Mother" would be met with some sort of punishment.

"Yes, Mother," Grace dutifully replied. "I will do my best not to sigh over Mr. Norman or think of him as a suitor, though he will be greatly disappointed, and I do so hate to be the cause of disappointment. It is too bad there are no convents to which I could be sent for I fear if disappointing gentlemen is to be part of gaining a husband, I am not sure I wish to find a husband."

Her mother huffed. "Do not be dramatic, Grace. Dramatics are your sister's domain."

"It is true, though. I do not like being a disappointment."

"Then, do not set your cap at Mr. Norman and

consider Mr. Blakesley instead, and you shall not disappoint me."

"Mr. Blakesley is not free," Grace protested.

"He does not appear very attached to his lady. He has done a great deal of watching you."

"Mother," Grace scolded.

"Just be polite and charming and allow him to chose for himself. I am not asking that you fling yourself at him."

"I will be his friend. I will not do more."

Her mother's smile was self-satisfied. "That should suffice."

And with that, she left Grace sitting alone on her bench until a lady, who had been standing behind them, took the seat vacated by Grace's mother.

"I did not know Mr. Blakesley had a lady," Grace's new bench mate said. "Indeed, I have never seen him with any lady in particular in all the time I have been in Bath."

"Oh, she is not from Bath." Grace's stomach twisted at the idea of spreading gossip about Walter.

"I do not see how she could not be. I do not believe Mr. Blakesley has been gone from Bath for these past six months." She leaned a bit closer to Grace. "Not even at Christmas time. His parents came here." She clucked her tongue. "If he has told you he has a lady somewhere other than in Bath, he has not been honest with you." She sighed. "And I find it difficult to believe he would be so deceptive."

Grace turned startled eyes toward her companion who seemed to know Walter quite well.

"Mrs. King," the lady said by way of introduction and then waited for Grace to introduce herself before continuing. "Mr. Blakesley helped me find a home in Bath last summer, and he introduced me to Mr. Norman, who has taken prodigiously good care of me." She patted Grace's knee. "You would not go wrong setting your cap at such a fine fellow. Mr. Blakesley and I are good friends. He visits me at least once a week." Again, she leaned close to Grace and said softly. "I suspect it is for my cook's apple cake, but I like to think it is my company which brings him to my door."

"Oh, I am sure it is your company. He would never be so crass as to visit you only for sweets," Grace rushed to assure the lady at her side.

Mrs. King laughed lightly. "Which, Miss Grace,

is precisely why he cannot have a lady anywhere but in Bath."

"Could he not have met someone here and kept up a correspondence?"

"It is possible, but I do think I would have heard about her."

Grace did not know how to respond to such a thing. "Have you met my friends?" Changing the topic of conversation would likely be a good thing.

Mrs. King looked past her to where Bea sat. "No, I have not."

"Mrs. King, this is Mrs. Clayton. She is my cousin with whom I am staying. Her husband, who is next to her, is a friend of Mr. Blakesley. Bea, this is Mrs. King, whom I have just met."

"Ah!" Mrs. King clapped her hands in delight. "You have leased Erondale, have you not?"

"Yes," Bea replied.

"And have you found it to your liking?"

"Very much so."

"I have heard about you. Such a lovely man Mr. Blakesley is." She leaned close to Grace. "You'd not go wrong setting your cap at him. Your mother is not wrong about that."

"Mr. and Mrs. Shelton are also staying at Erondale," Grace added, for she did not know what else to say. "They are currently dancing."

"As is my niece. See her there – in the light blue with Mr. Baily — the short blond gentleman?"

Grace turned her eyes toward the dancers and sought out a lady in light blue who was dancing with a short fellow. It took a minute or two as the partners were separated and then reunited by the dance.

"She is very pretty." A trifle older looking than most of the ladies who were dancing. In fact, she looked at least as old as Mr. Baily.

"She has come to keep me company since she has not yet taken."

"Oh." She was a companion?

"However, I will not call her my companion," Mrs. King whispered. "Her father would, but my brother has never been good with words or a lady's feelings. He is more of a facts and figures sort of person."

Mrs. King was certainly a talkative sort of woman, but she seemed rather nice despite that fact. After all, Mr. Blakesley was her friend.

"Is your niece very old then?" Grace whispered.

"Seven and twenty."

Grace gasped.

"She is rather firmly on the shelf if I cannot find her a match." Mrs. King chuckled. "I think that is truly why her father sent her to me. I have been known to make some very good matches." She looked Grace up and down. "You really should consider Mr. Blakesley. I do believe you would suit quite nicely. As for Mr. Norman?" She shook her head. "You need someone more attentive."

"Oh, but he is attentive."

Mrs. King's brows rose. "When he is present, he is, but how often is he not present?"

Grace shrugged.

"You would grow lonely. That would never be the case with Mr. Blakesley." She winked at Grace. "Do not be afraid to consider it. I promise I will not say a word to your mother." She chuckled. "I remember when my mother was pushing me at this gentleman and that." She smoothed her skirt. "In fact, there was this one time..."

Grace could see why Walter only visited Mrs. King once a week. The woman was an excellent storyteller, and as the second song of the set began, meaning that Mrs. King's niece would not be coming to collect her any time soon, Grace had to admit that a cup of tea and a slice of apple cake would be a rather perfect complement to her story.

Chapter 14

"Are you watching my sister?"

Walter turned toward Felicity with the idea to put her off with a partially truthful answer, but he had no more than opened his mouth than her mother was answering for him.

"I dare say he is. Why would he not be?"

"Actually, I was noticing that Mrs. King has made an appearance at tonight's soiree, which means her niece must have arrived. She does not attend assemblies on her own account. She is more of a theatre or concert-going lady."

"Who is Mrs. King?" Mrs. Love inquired.

"She is the lady sitting with Miss Grace." Walter's answer earned him a pleased smile from Grace's mother. "I should go give her my greetings since we are good friends."

"Are you certain that is the reason you wish to

go over there?" There was a note of teasing in Mrs. Love's question.

"Yes." It was one reason he wished to cross the room. The other reason had to do with preferring to be with Grace rather than her sister.

"Are you engaged for the next dance?" Mrs. Love asked as Felicity batted her lashes.

"No," Walter replied, "nor do I plan to be. There is a cardroom which is, no doubt, missing my presence, although I may have to do my duty in regard to Mrs. King's niece as I did promise to dance with her at least once after her arrival. It seemed the least I could do to help the girl settle into her new surroundings." As he smiled at a somewhat affronted looking Felicity, his eye caught Grace's attention on him.

"If you will excuse me." He gave Felicity and her mother a bow and made his escape.

"I say, Blakesley," Roger said as Walter joined him and his wife, who had just completed their set, "Miss Love is looking daggers at you."

"Yes, I suppose she is."

Roger leaned toward him. "What did you do?"

"It is what I did not do," Walter replied. "I did

not ask her to dance as she and her mother seemed to wish for me to do."

"Indeed?" A pleased smirk settled on Roger's mouth. "Is that all?"

"No," Walter replied. "I also mentioned needing to do my duty in standing up with Mrs. King's niece despite my desire to find the card room."

Roger let out a low whistle.

Walter shrugged. "I do not intend on ever dancing with Miss Love."

"Is there a reason?" Mrs. Shelton asked.

Walter nodded. "The evening when I first met Miss Grace, she asked me not to dance with her sister."

Mrs. Shelton sighed just a bit as a smile lit her face.

He took two steps away from the Sheltons. "Mrs. King," he greeted.

"Mr. Blakesley. How good it is to see you! I was just beginning to despair that you might be too tangled up in willing young dance partners to see me."

"What? Never say you thought so," Walter replied in the same playful fashion in which Mrs. King's comment was made. She was wearing her teasing grin – the one she always wore when mentioning his lack of a wife and her desire to help him remedy such a blight.

"I have made a new friend in your absence." Her brows waggled at him. "She was telling me that you have a lady of whom you have not told me."

Mortification settled over Grace's features.

"Well," Walter said, "that is because it is a new arrangement."

Mrs. King's eye narrowed with suspicion.

"And I did not know until very recently how such a thing might progress. Therefore, I could not tell you about it."

Mrs. King looked slightly mollified. "I should hope you intended to tell me."

"Oh, most certainly." He would tell anyone who would listen, as soon as Grace came to trust him enough to allow him to openly court her.

"I understand she is not from Bath."

"No, she is not," Walter answered truthfully. "She is from Kent, though she is not there at present as her family is travelling." He was pleased to see amusement in Grace's eyes.

"It would be lovely if they were to come to Bath,"

Mrs. King said, giving Walter a pointed look, "so that I might meet her."

"That would be lovely," Walter agreed before adding, "I think you would like her."

"Well, if she is anything like Miss Grace, here, I know I would. I would suggest you ask my new friend to dance, but I understand you have already done so." Her lips curled up into that teasing smile again. "However there is no law or stricture saying you cannot ask Miss Grace for a second dance."

Walter chuckled and shifted his gaze to Grace. "I fear Miss Grace would not wish for me to do so, for then she would have to refuse me."

"Refuse you?" Mrs. King looked at Grace as if there was something wrong with the girl.

"Because a second dance would signify marked attention," Walter answered. He would like nothing better than to make such a declaration, but he would not push Grace beyond where she had so far willing allowed him to lead her.

"Paw, such nonsense!"

"And, if you would allow me, I should like to request a set of your niece."

Mrs. King tipped her head and lifted an eyebrow as if she thought it was not at all sensible to be refusing Grace to offer for her niece, who had just joined them.

"Thank you, Mr. Bailey." Mrs. King's niece dipped a curtsey as her partner left her with her aunt.

"Annabelle," Mrs. King began, "I would like you to meet Mr. Blakesley. Mr. Blakesley, this is my niece, Miss Annabelle Chapman."

"Miss Chapman, it is a pleasure to finally put a face to the name I have heard so many times."

"Likewise," Miss Chapman replied with a wide and welcoming smile. She did not seem the sort to be retiring or off-putting. Indeed, she was very pretty and radiated pleasantness.

"Would I be able to convince you, on such short acquaintance, to dance with me?" Walter offered.

Miss Chapman laughed softly. "I believe, Mr. Blakesley, that though we have only just met, we are likely well-acquainted. My aunt is not known for her retiring nature or for her lack of stories to share."

Mrs. King huffed and clucked her tongue before saying, "Such impertinence!" To which, Miss Chapman's only reply to her aunt was a smile.

"I would be pleased to dance with you," she said to Walter.

"Excellent," Walter answered. "Perhaps you can tell me a few stories about your aunt."

Again, Mrs. King huffed.

"Miss Grace, I must apologize for not being here earlier." Norman was straightening a sleeve as he hurried up to them. He opened his mouth to speak but snapped it shut again upon seeing Mrs. King and her niece. Oddly, his friend seemed at a loss for how to proceed. Even more odd was the fact that Mrs. King did not attempt to introduce him to her niece, and that niece seemed to be embarrassed.

Grace gave a quick glance around the group and then, said, "There is nothing to forgive. One cannot schedule emergencies around a dance card."

"Oh, indeed," Norman managed to say.

"I am free for this dance," Grace prompted.

Norman nodded. "That would be wonderful." He extended his hand to her. "Might we walk a bit before we take our places?"

Grace looked to Graeme, who nodded his consent. Then, she put her hand in Norman's and rose.

Walter watched Grace leave with his friend.

"They are all wrong for each other," Mrs. King

muttered. "And I have told Miss Grace that very thing." She took her niece's hand and winked at her when Annabelle looked her direction. "Mr. Norman, who I have taken on as my physician, requires a different sort of lady, and Miss Grace requires a different sort of gentleman."

"Mr. Norman is your physician?"

Was there a touch of horror mixed with the surprise in Miss Chapman's tone?

"Yes, Mr. Blakesley recommended him upon my settling into my house," Mrs. King replied.

"But—"

Mrs. King shook her head ever so slightly, keeping her niece from saying anything further. "Mr. Norman is excellent at his profession and well-respected."

"Then, I am happy you have found him." She turned from her aunt to Walter. "Our set will begin soon."

"Of course." Walter offered her his arm and led her onto the dance floor. "Are you well?"

Miss Chapman nodded. "It is nearly overwhelming finding one's footing in a new town."

"It can be," Walter agreed. "Have you found Bath to your liking so far?"

"Oh, yes! It is beautiful, and my aunt is delightful. We have always gotten on exceptionally well." Miss Chapman leaned a bit closer to him. "She has long been my confidant." One shoulder lifted and lowered in a shrug. "My mother has more than just me with whom to be concerned. There were six of us. Three boys, and three girls."

"Six children?" That was a sizable family.

She nodded. "I am the oldest and least likely to marry, so I have been sent to stay with my aunt."

"Least –?" Walter looked at her in shock unable to complete his question. She did not seem unmarriageable to him.

"My ideas about who would make a good husband do not mesh with those of my father," she said in explanation. "Therefore, I shall not marry."

"Oh." He took his place across from her in line.

"Father is very traditional and unyielding."

The first notes of the song began, and Walter prepared to remember his steps while attempting not to spend too much time pondering Miss Chapman's predicament. However, as it turned out, he was not the only curious person in their set who was attempting to put things together.

"I think Mr. Norman knows her," Grace whispered to Walter when the steps of the song brought them together. "He is very flustered."

Yes, Walter could see that. Usually, his friend was the picture of serenity. Not much unsettled him, which was a very good quality for a physician to have. Walter hopped from his right foot to his left foot and, taking his partner's hands, circled.

Miss Chapman smiled at him, and he returned it. She was aptly named for she was indeed a beauty – not in the strict classical sense, but in a fashion which was heightened by her smile and the sparkle in her eye – and belle did mean... He nearly faltered in his steps. Belle. This was Belle. The Belle. The lady whom Norman sought each year to replace and never found any who could take her place.

"He says she is a friend from long ago," Grace shared with him when once again they were brought together.

"A very good friend, I believe," Walter replied with a speaking look.

"Oh! Is it a tragic story?" she asked.

Walter only had time to nod before they were separated again. According to Norman, he and Belle had been immediately taken with one another. However, they were never allowed to even converse if it could be prevented. Being young and in love, they attempted at every turn to thwart the intervention of her parents and the brother who was closest to Miss Chapman in age.

It was this brother who had turned Norman away for good. A few well-placed disparaging hints regarding his ability to do his duty as a physician with any degree of skill had made it challenging for him to find a place to practice his profession, and so Norman had left his home county to make a new start of things in Bath.

"Does your brother know that Mr. Norman is your aunt's physician?" he asked when the song was over and he was leading Miss Chapman back to her aunt.

Her eyes grew wide. "You know about that?"

"Mr. Norman and I are good friends. I put the pieces together. Does he know?"

She shook her head. "My brother died."

"My condolences."

"Thank you. It was a year and a half ago now, so the shock of it is gone."

And his friend was, at least, safe from her brother's machinations. However, his friend did not know that.

"Thank you for the dance, Mr. Blakesley," Miss Chapman said as they reached her aunt.

"The pleasure was all mine," he assured her, and then made his excuses about needing to visit the card room. However, the card room was not where he was truly going. Mr. Norman had left the room, and there was an important bit of information Walter needed to share with him.

Chapter 15

"Come with me." Felicity took Grace by the arm when Grace's set of dances had ended and she and Mr. Norman were leaving the floor in the direction of the Claytons and Mrs. King.

"But Mr. Norman –"

"I have need of my sister's assistance, Mr. Norman." Felicity directed one of her most charming smiles at him. It was the one Grace had seen her use many times on various gentlemen to get her way. "You would not keep me from my sister, would you?"

"But..." Grace once again attempted to extract herself from her sister's grasp. "Bea and Mr. Clayton will be expecting me to return to them."

"Mr. Norman can relay a message." Felicity's eyelashes fluttered as her hold on her sister tightened.

She might feign innocence, but Grace knew better. There was some scheme brewing in her sister's mind, and it was most likely a scheme in which Grace did not wish to take part. Of course, that would not matter to Felicity. She rarely cared about what Grace did or did not want.

"I will inform them of your being with your sister," Mr. Norman said quickly.

It was almost as if the man wanted to run from Grace's presence, but she knew that could not be true. In fact, she suspected that it was the presence of another young lady from which Mr. Norman wished to flee, and Grace had hoped to discover somewhat more about that particular young lady. Being drawn away from her goal by her sister was most distressful.

"What do you want?" Grace demanded as Mr. Norman scurried over to the Claytons. "I have friends with whom I wish to sit."

"I do not know why you are so disagreeable," Felicity said as she drew Grace toward the door. "You have been barely civil to me since you went to stay with the Claytons. I am not certain they are the best friends to have if they are going to make you so prickly."

Grace drew a calming breath through her nose

and released it. "Have you ever considered that it is not the influence of my hosts but rather your behaviour which makes me cross?"

"My behaviour?" Felicity questioned with some surprise. "I do not see how I could be the cause of your foul humor."

"You seriously do not see how?"

"Do keep your voice down, Grace," Felicity scolded. "Yes, I do not see how I could be the cause."

Grace knew in these sorts of moments when her displeasure was stirred as it was now that, unless she could bite her tongue hard enough to keep it from wagging, she should turn and walk away. However, what she knew and what she did were not of the same level of wisdom. Frustration at her sister's behaviour bubbled over as Grace straightened her gloves while attempting to keep her composure. It was the sight of her well-stitched and pretty repair to Felicity's gloves which overruled her good sense. She drew her sister into the corridor and toward the vestibule of the Assembly rooms instead of allowing herself to be steered to the tearoom.

"Have you no recollection of Mr. Everett Clayton?" Grace hissed as they stepped to the side to avoid walking into a cluster of people.

"Of course, I remember him," Felicity said. "I truly cared for him."

"Cared for him?" Grace parroted with no little amount of astonishment. "You flaunted Mr. Ramsey in front of the poor man."

"I did not flaunt Mr. Ramsey."

Grace rolled her eyes and shook her head. Her sister was completely lost to all good sense if she could not see such a thing!

"You flaunted. Most distastefully," Grace retorted. "Do you know why I am wearing these gloves?" Grace thrust her hand in front of her sister's face.

"Because gloves are the thing."

"No, because you could not be bothered to repair these, so you cast them aside to your poor sister who did not need them since she was not to have a season. And do you know why your unfortunate sister was not to have a season?" She waited for a full half-second for Felicity to respond before answering in her stead. "Because you flaunted Mr. Ramsey and deserted Mr. Clayton, and now, you are in danger of never being wed if your season is not successful and Mr. Ramsey is led along and then rejected just as Mr. Clayton was."

Felicity's mouth, which had gaped during Grace's diatribe, snapped shut. "I wished to tell you that I think Mr. Ramsey is going to offer for me tomorrow. He has just asked if he could call on me privately, and Father agreed."

"Oh." That was not what Grace had expected to hear.

"I love him, Grace."

Grace's brow furrowed.

"I know I thought I loved Mr. Clayton, but this time is different."

"How so? Is it because he has a larger estate?"

Her sister shrugged. "I will not deny that his estate is an inducement to think well of him, although it is not as prosperous as it should be, and my dowry will be needed to make any improvements I should desire."

"He wishes to marry you for your money?"

Felicity shook her head. "He is not a fortune hunter, for he has been honest with me about the state of his finances. He has even discussed them with Father and taken notes on the advice Father has given him. He loves me, and I love him."

Grace was not certain her sister knew what love was. "If his estate were to be taken from him, would you still wish to marry him?"

"Yes."

"If he was told he had to chose between his estate – his future inheritance which would provide for him and his family for generations to come – and marrying you, would you let him choose you to his detriment?"

"Why would I not?" Confusion etched a furrow between her eyebrows.

"You would allow him to do that which would harm him? Do you not care for his happiness?"

"Of course, I care for his happiness, and I know he would not be happy without me. He has said so many times."

Grace was not convinced. "What if you did not have a sizable dowry? Would he still have chosen you?"

Felicity blinked. "I do not know for certain, but I believe he would have."

"Ask him."

The suggestion was met with rolling eyes.

"I would want to know," Grace added in explanation.

"Do you not trust him?"

"I trust very few." She trusted Bea and Mr. Clayton, as well as Mr. and Mrs. Shelton, and of course, Mr. Norman and – she nearly sighed – Walter. Perhaps it was more accurate to say she trusted all save her sister and anyone who appeared to love her sister. However, that would be rather rude to say, though the thought was tempting.

"No, you trust everyone," Felicity countered. "You always have."

Grace shook her head. "Not any longer."

"What do you mean?"

"I trusted you. I helped you win Mr. Everett Clayton from Bea when we both knew she liked him. Not that she was the only one who admired him. I told you that I did, do you remember that? And what did you tell me?"

"That I was the oldest and should marry first."

Grace nodded. "So, I trusted your wisdom and allowed you to pursue Mr. Everett Clayton. No, that is not entirely true, I helped you pursue him. My heart was not attached, but you claimed yours was." Her lips pursed in displeasure. "As it turns out your attachment was less than mine."

They had nearly reached the portico and stood

just where they could see the entrances for those arriving in carriages. A few people were strolling along the corridors but one couple was not strolling and was instead standing very close to each other. The gentleman looked rather familiar to Grace.

"I thought I was firmly attached to him. Truly, I did," Felicity was saying just as the gentleman Grace was watching turned enough for her to see his face.

She sucked in a quick breath. "We should return to the ballroom. Mother will worry." She turned her sister toward the interior of the building.

"I do not believe we have concluded this discussion," Felicity protested. "I have not finished pleading my case."

"You cannot convince me of that which I do not wish to be convinced," Grace retorted.

Felicity pulled away from Grace. "Why do you keep looking down that corridor."

"For no reason," Grace lied as she attempted to turn her sister back toward the interior of the building, but to no avail.

"I love Mr. Blakesley," she blurted.

That arrested her sister's motions and spun her around.

"Mr. Blakesley? Truly? Not Mr. Norman?"

"I do not love Mr. Norman. I love Mr. Blakesley – or I am almost certain I do." Her heart raced. On the list of all the people who were not to know about Mr. Blakesley, her sister sat at the top. She should not have made such an admission, but she also could not allow her sister to see Mr. Ramsey with whomever it was that had her hands on the gentleman's jacket, straightening the buttons. As much as she did not trust her sister and was excessively unhappy with her for the way she had treated Mr. Everett Clayton, she could not bring herself to knowingly allow her sister to be harmed and humiliated publicly. Oh, she knew some would disagree with her – Roger, for one – but she was just not able to knowingly cause harm to her sister.

Her hand flew to her heart. He was right. Walter was right. She did have a caring heart. She needed to find him and tell him that their charade could come to an end. If he was right about her having a caring heart, he was likely also right about not needing to trust her sister but to only trust him.

"What did Mr. Blakesley talk to you about earlier tonight?" Grace asked.

Felicity blinked. "I will tell you if you will tell me why you have been playing with Mr. Norman's affections." She crossed her arms and scowled at Grace. "And all the while you were berating me for how I treated Mr. Everett Clayton, you have been doing no better."

Grace huffed as she pushed her sister forward and deeper into the building. "About what did you talk to Mr. Blakesley?"

"I attempted to get him to ask me to dance – after I teased him about watching you, that is." She sighed. "He refused."

"He did?" Grace smiled. Oh, she had been such a fool to think Walter was the sort to fall for her sister's charming manners. Of course, he was not the sort! He was not like any other gentleman she had met.

"Oh, he made it very clear that he did not wish to dance with me."

The bitter edge to Felicity's tone made Grace smile just a bit more broadly.

"Mother will be delighted to hear she does not need to worry about Mr. Norman."

Grace gasped. "No! You must not tell her. Not yet."

"Why ever not?"

"I have to tell Walter first."

Felicity's eyes grew wide. "Walter? Has he given you leave to call him by his Christian name?"

She would have to give herself a very stern lecture later about thinking before speaking. "Yes, but only in private."

"Oh," her sister cried eagerly, "there is so much you must tell me."

"No, there is not. I have told you all I am going to tell you."

"I am afraid, dear sister, that, if you do not wish for me to tell Mother about your declaration, there is more you must share with me."

Grace closed her eyes and sighed. She should have known Felicity would dangle that in front of her. Felicity was, after all, very adept at getting what she wanted.

"Very well, I will tell you a bit more, but not right now. I must speak to Mr. Blakesley first."

"I believe Mother wished to call at Erondale tomorrow, perhaps I will join her."

"What about Mr. Ramsey's private call?"

Her sister's lips pursed with displeasure while Grace felt rather smug for having thwarted Felicity's plan. Of course, there might not be a need for a private conversation between Felicity and Mr. Ramsey once Mr. Ramsey's duplicity was revealed — later. Much later. Not here. Not now. For here and now, she would pretend that she had not seen what she saw.

Chapter 16

Walter took a turn of the cardroom before proceeding out of it and toward the entryway. Ahead of him, Grace seemed to be pulling her sister along, and from the expression on Grace's face, it was not because she was excited to show something of interest to her sister. It looked very much as if Grace was excessively put out with Felicity.

Despite the tantalizing intrigue posed by Grace and her sister, he ducked into the tearoom to see if his friend was there.

As fortune would have it, he was. Norman was sitting at a far table, doing his best not to be pulled into any conversation.

Norman glanced up as Walter joined him. "I cannot leave Bath. I will not. However, I must find someone to recommend to Mrs. King in my stead."

"I do not think you need to do either."

Norman leaned forward. "Her niece is Belle."

Walter nodded. "I know. I figured that out."

"Then, you know precisely why I must not continue my care of Mrs. King."

"No, I do not know."

Was Norman actually glowering at him? This was not the calm, rarely-ruffled-until-Walter-had-pushed-him-too-far friend with whom Walter was acquainted. But then, loss of love and having that loss tossed in front of a gentleman unawares would likely have an unnerving effect on anyone.

"Miss Chapman is lovely."

"I know." The words rumbled from his friend, causing Walter's eyebrows to lift.

"We had a very pleasant, if short and somewhat halting, discussion during our dance."

The comment was met with a small huff and narrowed eyes.

"It seems her family is not so large as it used to be."

There. Surprise and curiosity. Those were much more welcome expressions on Norman's face.

"A certain brother died."

Norman blinked. "Died?"

Walter nodded. "I believe she said it was a bit

more than a year ago, and from the sounds of things, it was sudden."

"It matters not. Her father will still not approve of someone like me. Was it an accident?"

Walter shrugged. "I did not ask. My apologies."

Norman shook his head. "I do not need to know. It changes nothing."

"She is seven and twenty. She does not need her father's approval." He held Norman's gaze and watched his friend wilt from anger to sadness.

"I cannot."

"Why?"

"It would create a gulf between her and her family. I cannot do that."

"You do not know that." Walter held up a hand to stop Norman's protest. "You think you know that, but until you talk to the lady, you cannot know that."

"I am not you, Blakesley."

"And a good thing that is. I am not sure that Bath could survive as well as it does without your unique ability to care for one and all."

"You care for people, too. Do not even attempt to tell me that you do not have a fondness for half the people in Bath. How many of them know you by name and sing your praises?"

"Nearly as many as know and praise you."

"That is not the point," Norman protested.

"I believe it is."

Norman pushed up from his seat. "Miss Grace, Miss Love, is all well?"

"Perfectly well." Miss Love's eyes seemed to be dancing with merriment. Walter was uncertain if that was a good thing or as dreadful as he imagined it might be. "I believe my sister was looking for you, Mr. Blakesley."

Grace's eyes closed, and she shook her head but only just. Did she not wish to see him?

"Then, she is in luck as you have found me – not that I was hiding, of course." He rose and offered a chair to Miss Love.

"No, no. I will sit beside Mr. Norman."

There was a gleefulness to the comment that unsettled him.

"I was on my way to see Mr. and Mrs. Clayton." Grace looked pointedly at her sister while Walter helped her with her chair.

"And we are still on our way, but there is that bit of information I so wish to know."

"I am not telling you here."

"Oh, well, of course not. We would take a turn of the corridor."

"I meant here in this building."

It seemed as if Grace was still put out by her sister.

"We could all take a stroll," Felicity suggested.

"No!" Grace snapped.

"I would not be opposed to it," Walter said softly.

"I would be."

"You would?" Did she need to be so adamant in her attempt to make it appear as if she cared for no one but Norman?

"Yes, I would. I should like very much to be returned to my party."

"I will not detain you." If she was in such a hurry to be away from him, then he was not going to stop her.

She melted a bit, her shoulders slumping forward while her head drooped.

"It is not that I do not wish to speak with you. It is just that I do not wish for my cousin to worry."

The corner of her lower lip was drawn between her teeth. Something was not right with her.

Walter stood. "I insist. I am in need of some air, and do not wish to escort myself."

She turned wide eyes to him and shook her head ever so slightly.

"If you will not accompany me, then perhaps your sister would?" He smiled at Felicity.

"If I must." Felicity batted her lashes, but not at him. The expression was directed at her sister.

"Oh, very well." Grace stood. "I will accompany Mr. Blakesley for a short stroll of the corridor. However, I am still not telling you anything tonight," she added to her sister.

Miss Love did not look as if she believed what Grace had said, but she was delighted when Walter offered Grace his arm and it was accepted.

"I will be right here with Mr. Norman," Felicity said as they were leaving the table.

"I would rather that she would go back to my mother," Grace grumbled.

"I take it you are displeased with your sister?"

"Not as much as I am with myself and Mr. Ramsey."

That was not the response he had expected. But then, Grace was a rather interesting and surprising young woman. "What have you and Mr. Ramsey done?"

"I saw Mr. Ramsey with some lady down the passage that leads to the carriages, and so I told my sister I love you. I could not let her see Mr. Ramsey, after all."

Walter stopped walking. "I am not certain I heard that correctly."

"Mr. Ramsey was down there –" She waved her hand toward the carriage entrance.

"Not that part," Walter stopped her. "Though I am curious about that. You love me?"

"Yes, and my sister knows. Therefore, our scheme is at an end, for I am certain she is incapable of keeping such a thing hidden from my mother and once my mother knows..." She sighed. "Everyone will know."

"And why is this a problem?" Her lip was between her teeth again and her eyes were lowered.

"I will not have you all to myself."

He had to lean towards her to hear what she said.

"I do not wish to have our secret discovered. It is so lovely and private when just we and a few others knew."

"Do you still fear that I will fall prey to your sister's charms?" Was that the real reason why she did not wish to have others know?

She shook her head. "You did not dance with her tonight. She said she attempted to get you to ask her."

"Of course, I did not dance with her. You asked me not to," he replied. Why could she not have declared her love for him when they were at his townhouse playing billiards? Why did it have to be in a busy corridor at the Upper Rooms?

"I did?"

He nodded. "When we first met and you refused to dance with me in favor of dancing with Norman."

She blinked. "I did, did I not?"

"Yes, and I do not break my promises."

"But you did not promise me that you would not dance with her." Her brow was furrowed.

"Did I not nod and smile at you when you were lining up with Mr. Norman?"

Her lips pursed as she thought. "You did!"

"That was my promise," he said. "And I will never break a promise I have made to you. Even if I found your sister charming – which I do not — I would not break it."

How he wanted to take her in his arms. She was wearing that compelling look of longing she had worn the day he had traced her silhouette at Erondale.

"Now, about Mr. Ramsey." A change of subject might make things a trifle easier. Or so he hoped.

"You really do not find Felicity charming?"

Walter shook his head.

Her lashes fluttered as delight overtook her features. "That may be the thing I love most about you, Mr. Blakesley."

"About Mr. Ramsey," Walter tried again. As much as he wished to stand here and discuss her love for him, here was not a safe place to do so. For such a conversation would make it a great deal more challenging to not kiss her, and, as it was, he was struggling with wanting to do just that.

"He was in the corridor with a lady. They were standing very close – closer than we are – and her hands were on his jacket." She glanced to her right and then back at him. "If we were in the garden at Erondale, I would show you."

He was beginning to understand why Grace was so despondent about their scheme being found out. It would be likely that such secret and intimate moments would be a thing of the past for some time – at least until he could marry her.

"I do not know who that lady was. I have never seen her at any of the soirees I have attended, but then, I have not attended very many."

"I should speak to your father."

"About Mr. Ramsey?"

Walter shook his head. "I apologize. I was thinking about being alone in the garden with you and not fully attending to what you were saying."

Her smile was enchanting. The sooner he spoke to her father the better.

"We should likely take you back and save Mr. Norman from your sister, and then, I will take a roam around the place and see if I can find out anything about Mr. Ramsey and his mysterious lady."

"Will you?"

"For you, I will." He barely refrained from lifting her fingers to his lips.

"Oh, Miss Grace."

Walter turned to find Mrs. King approaching them.

"What a delight to find you here and with Mr. Blakesley." There was that teasing note to her voice once again. "Annabelle and I were just getting some air and contemplating going home."

"So soon?" Grace asked.

"It seems the evening has lost its sheen."

"That is unfortunate."

"Indeed, it is, Mr. Blakesley. I have not even had the opportunity to question you about your secret courtship with some lady from – where was she from?"

"She is from Kent," Walter answered. "My secret angel is from Kent. And," he added, "now that I am at liberty to do so, I will tell you all about her someday when I call."

"I should hope you will. I had not thought you so secretive."

"Normally, I am not. However, the young lady asked me to be, and I can deny her nothing."

Mrs. King tilted her head and smiled at him as a proud mother might gaze upon a child who had done something of merit.

"Now, see, Miss Grace, this is why I thought you should set your cap at him instead of Mr. Norman." She shrugged. "But, it seems you were correct, and he is not free."

No, he was not free. His heart was irrevocably gone both now and forever.

"I still would not have you set your cap at Mr. Norman," Mrs. King was instructing Grace as Miss Chapman looked ill beside her aunt.

"I do not plan to," Grace assured her, and Miss Chapman expelled a breath as if she was relieved.

It seemed there was a great deal of hope for Norman to finally gain the lady as his own — if Norman could be made to see reason, that is.

"I believe we would be more than delighted to have you call on us, Miss Grace. My Annabelle is in need of some good friends."

"I would like nothing better."

Walter could hear the excitement in Grace's voice and knew that she was more than delighted by the idea of calling on Mrs. King and her niece. "We could call together," he suggested. "If your cousin would join us, that is, Miss Grace."

Mrs. King's head pulled back in surprise. "But would that not make your lady uneasy to hear you are making calls with a lady as pretty as Miss Grace?"

"I think she could tolerate it."

Mrs. King did not look convinced. Therefore,

after he had excused himself to see Grace back to her party but before he had actually removed himself completely from Mrs. King's presence, he leaned near her ear as he passed her and whispered, "Miss Grace is from Kent."

Chapter 17

"Grace. Grace. You must wake up."

Was that her mother? Grace popped one eye open just far enough to see her mother sitting on the side of the bed with Bea standing in her robe behind her.

Grace yawned. "What time is it?" Had she slept until calling hours? Last night had been tiring in a wonderful sort of way so it was possible that she had slept far longer than was her normal wont, though she did feel a great deal more tired than she would expect to feel if it was late enough for calling hours.

"It is six o'clock," Bea answered.

No, she had not slept late. It was indeed as early as it felt. She closed her eyes.

"Why are you here, Mama?"

"Something has happened. It is most dreadful. I

do not know how I have managed not to succumb to the horror of it, but I knew I must get you before I could think about myself."

Drowsiness fled and Grace propped herself up on her elbows. "What has happened? Is someone ill?"

"We must go home immediately."

Grace sat up. Her heart was racing. "Why? What has happened? Tell me what has happened."

Mrs. Love wrung her hands together – which Grace noticed were not gloved. Her mother never left her house without a pair of gloves on her hands. Something was most certainly wrong.

"Mr. Ramsey has..." She leaned toward Grace and lowered her voice. "He has quit Bath and abandoned your sister."

No! He could not have. She could not believe it. Not after what Felicity had told her. "But he asked Father to speak to Felicity in private."

"Yes, yes, he did. We were all so certain he was going to make her an offer, but then..." She covered her mouth with her hand and shook her head. "When we arrived home from the ball, there was a note awaiting us which said he would not be able to call tomorrow. Well, Felicity wished to know why, as is natural — I am sure I wished to know, too — so, your sister sent a note to him asking for his reason. However, no reply was forthcoming. The messenger was told that the master was not available to give a reply. Your father and I figured it was because of the lateness of the hour, and we would discover what we needed to know on the morrow." She rose from her perch on the bed. "Your sister was not satisfied, and after we all went to bed, she... Oh, it is too dreadful."

"May I get you a glass of wine?" Bea offered as she led Mrs. Love to a chair.

"No, no. I will be well as soon as we are gone from this dreadful place. I shall never wish to see Bath again. Oh, what are we to do?"

"Shall I call for your husband?" Bea asked.

Mrs. Love shook her head. "It is a mother's job to speak of these things."

Grace was out of bed and kneeling beside her mother. "You are frightening me, Mama. Please, tell me what has happened. What did Felicity do?"

"You know how impatient your sister can be."

Yes, Grace was well aware of Felicity's desire to have or know things immediately.

"Oh, she is ruined!" Mrs. Love cried.

"How is she ruined?" Grace begged. Her mother could be so trying at times!

"She went to the rooms he is renting."

Was Felicity mad?

"By herself?" Grace asked.

Her mother nodded.

Of all the stupid things to do!

"In the middle of the night?" Grace asked.

Again, her mother nodded. "It seems it was not the first time she has done so."

Dread settled around Grace's heart. She was all too familiar with her sister's propensity to sneak away and behave inappropriately. "Where is she now?"

"Downstairs with your father and Mr. Clayton."

That was a relief. Had Felicity been left to her own devices, she might have attempted to follow Mr. Ramsey.

"And where is Mr. Ramsey?" Bea asked before Grace could.

"No one knows. He has not returned to his rooms."

"But his things, Mama." Grace grasped her mother's hand attempting to capture her mother's quickly deteriorating attention. "He will have to return for his things or have them sent. Surely, someone will soon know where he is. We only need to wait and be patient. He could be anywhere doing anything. We do not know that he has quit Bath."

"But he has! He has quit Bath, for that is what Felicity was told when she inquired of the gentleman who keeps the room below Mr. Ramsey's."

"She spoke to someone?" Oh, that was not good. Sneaking in and out was always best done when no one discovered the activity.

Mrs. Love nodded as tears began to spill down her cheeks. "She may be with child."

Grace's stomach attempted to tie itself in a knot. How could Felicity do such a thing as that? Kissing a gentleman was one thing but to allow him to bed her? Oh, it was unthinkable!

"Do you know this for certain?" Bea asked.

"Her father quizzed her most thoroughly. It is a very real possibility."

"Then, it is imperative that we remain in Bath until we discover where Mr. Ramsey has gone." He must be made to marry her, if not for her sister's sake, at least, for the sake of the child. If her stomach was not so knotted, Grace was nearly certain she would have cast up her accounts at the thought of such wickedness as a gentleman abandoning a lady, whom he claimed to love and had seduced, as well as his child.

"He quit Bath with another lady. He has used your sister very ill."

The image of the lady in the corridor at the Upper Rooms sprang to mind. "Oh, dear. Did this lady have blond hair?"

"I really do not know. Why do you ask such a thing?"

"Because I saw him with some blond-haired lady last night at the assembly in the passageway to the carriages. They looked very cozy, and I thought it strange. I was going to tell you about it tomorrow – I mean today – before Felicity had her private interview with Mr. Ramsey." She was not about to allow her sister to accept such a fellow without telling her of what had been seen, and she had hoped to know more about who the lady was once Walter called on her this morning.

"It is too late now. Your father insists that you prepare to depart as soon as can be. We cannot stay here any longer. The shame is too much. It shall surely taint you as well."

"But I did nothing wrong!" Grace cried.

"That may be, but to be the sister of such a wanton woman! Oh, you are ruined."

Grace sat backwards on the floor. "No, no. I will not leave."

"You have no choice in this matter. If we can leave quietly and find a place for your sister..." Her mother's voice trailed off as she began to weep.

"I will help you," Bea offered. "As soon as I see that your mother has been safely returned to your father."

"I cannot leave."

"It is best," Bea said. "The less gossip there is, the better."

No! No, it was not best. She could not and would not leave Walter. How could her mother ask her to give up her happiness because of her sister? True, her mother did not know about her attachment to Mr. Blakesley, but that did not matter. It was still horribly unfair to be asked to leave Bath and her friends just because her sister was stupid.

"Oh, what gentleman would want to be tied to such a family? We are doomed," her mother wailed.

Her mother's words fell heavily on Grace. Would being married to her cause Walter harm?

Would his business endeavors suffer? Would she be shunned by his family? And would that, in turn, bring even more misery to him?

As Bea helped Mrs. Love from the room, question upon dreadful question tumbled and tangled in Grace's mind, and her heart crumbled into a thousand jagged pieces as she realized what she must do because she loved him. She could not ask him to face a life of unhappiness because of her. It was too selfish by half.

A cold deeper than the dampest, most frigid winter's day settled over her as she rose from the floor and sought a piece of paper and a pen. It was best to dissolve their scheme and end their relationship while it still remained a secret.

We have been called home unexpectedly, she wrote and paused.

No, that would not do. She tore that part of the paper off and began again.

Thank you for indulging me in my scheme and being my secret beau. I have had the most delightful time and shall cherish my memories of you. Please know that my heart shall never forget you. I wish you well and a life of happiness.

Forever your secret angel.

G-

She wiped tears from her cheek with the sleeve of her nightgown. Then, she folded the missive and wrote *Mr. Walter Blakesley* on the front before sealing it and leaving it on the desk. If Bea did not see that it was given to Mr. Blakesley, he would find it when he came to check on his house after the Claytons and Sheltons had left.

She imagined him sitting at the desk, reading her words, and smiling fondly as he remembered her. Would he find another angel? How could he not? He was handsome and had a fortune. Added to that, he was amiable and sweet. He was perfect. Absolutely, utterly perfect. Any lady would be an utter fool not to fall in love with him.

She sank down onto the bed and wiped away more tears with her sleeve.

What would his new lady be like? Who would share this house with him? Would they have loads of children or just two? Each new and troubling contemplation tore the pieces of her heart into smaller and smaller bits, leaving a vast and painful void where her heart had once been.

"Your mother is safe at your father's side. My husband has seen to getting her some wine."

Grace drew in a deep breath and released it before turning toward Bea and beginning the chore of packing.

Half an hour later, with help from Bea and her maid, Grace was appropriately dressed for travel and her trunk was ready to be tied to the carriage which would travel ahead of them to Kent.

"You did not mean to leave without a proper goodbye, did you?" Roger stood in the entry with his wife at his side. "Victoria is going to miss Philomena almost as much as she will miss you." He scratched behind Philomena's ear and then grasped Grace's hand firmly and lifted it to his lips. "Your absence will be felt by many."

Grace glanced at her mother and then leaning forward whispered. "I left him a note in my room." She simply could not leave it to chance that Walter got her message.

"I will see that it is taken care of," Roger assured her. "I wish you could stay, and I know I am not alone in such sentiments."

"No, you are not," she agreed. She wished with every fiber of her being that she could remain right her with her friends, where Walter would find her.

Victoria embraced her warmly and muttered her

sorrow at having to part and then added that she would write faithfully. Bea did the same, and then Graeme saw them all to their carriage and, after handing Philomena to Grace, gave her his wishes for a safe journey.

"You are certain he is not returning to Bath?" Grace whispered as they pulled away from Erondale. The agony in her soul deepened with each turn of the wheel down the drive.

"I think we are," her father answered.

"Could we not chase after him?"

"Chase him to where? We do not know where he has gone. And, there is no need to draw undue attention to a situation which might otherwise be dispelled of quietly."

"Felicity could have gone home, and I could have just said she was ill." She sighed as Erondale was no longer visible through the carriage window.

"I know this is not easy for you," her father replied. "You have endured a great deal."

"Far more than you know," Grace muttered. Thankfully, Felicity seemed too distraught to be a danger in revealing what she knew about Mr. Blakesley. With any luck, the strain of her current ordeal would wipe the memory of Mr. Blakesley from Felicity's mind. It was best if that part of Grace's stay in Bath remained secret.

"Come sit with me," her father said. "Your mother can sit with Felicity."

The exchange was made, and Mr. Love wrapped an arm around his youngest daughter's shoulders, kissing her forehead, and muttering his sorrow for what she must suffer. Grace snuggled into her father's side, and while stroking Philomena's fur, allowed her tears to fall unfettered, for once again, though she had not charmed him away, her sister had stolen a gentleman from Grace. Only this time, in doing so, Felicity had not crushed a gentleman's heart, but that of her own sister.

Chapter 18

Walter rubbed his neck. Sleeping on a rug on the ground even for a few hours was bound to make a gentleman stiff and sore, or, at least, that is how it was for him. The sun, which was just beginning to climb above the horizon and wake the world, was starting to warm him some as he started down the road towards home. That small amount of warmth would have to suffice until he got home and could climb into a steaming bath.

His stomach rumbled. He should have brought more food with him. However, he had not expected to be out all night trying to discover where Ramsey and his companion had gone. He had followed them to a tavern ten miles back, but from there, he could not find their trail anywhere. Who Ramsey's mystery lady was remained a mystery. No one seemed able to identify her. Of course, most of the men in the tavern had not been completely sober, and the barmaids had been too interested in flirting with him to tell him anything about some lady whom they considered a rival.

He would have to present himself empty-handed to Grace, and that fact did not sit well with him. He had promised to discover what he could, and he had done exactly that. Yet, the fact that all he could discover was nothing did not seem a fitting way to keep such a promise. Grace would want to know more. She was a curious, caring sort. In his opinion, she owed her sister little, but Grace's heart would not see it that way. No matter how much she disagreed with or disapproved of her sister, Grace would do what she could to protect her sister from harm.

He chuckled, causing his horse's ears to twitch in his direction.

"I was just thinking about your new mistress," he said to his horse. "She is a unique lady."

The horse blew a breath through its lips.

"I tell you she is. You will understand once you meet her."

Maybe today she would allow him to take her for a drive now that she was willing to reveal their secret relationship. Today, he would begin court-ing Miss Grace Love publicly, and next week, he would speak to her father. Well, he would speak to her father next week if he could be patient enough to wait until then.

His failure to obtain the information Grace sought was a small cloud on his very happy future. If he were not so stiff and sore from spending a few hours sleeping beside the road, and if his boots did not smell like the ale which an inebriated patron at that tavern had managed to spill on them, he would drive directly to Erondale. But as he was, going home to make himself presentable was the best option.

Tomorrow, he would attempt to take her with him when he called on Mrs. King, and together, they could decide how best to encourage Norman and Miss Chapmen to re-establish their friendship. Grace would likely find that to be an amusing scheme.

Again, he chuckled.

His horse blew through its lips in response.

"You are excessively cranky today, Lady," Walter called forward. "I promise you will get a good meal before we visit Miss Grace. That should set you up to be properly friendly, but if it does not, it is no matter. Miss Grace will charm you into a better mood."

From the replying snort, his horse did not seem to agree with his master's assessment, but then, Lady had not met Grace. If she had, then she'd know it to be true. Grace was ebullient. Her smile sparkled, and her eyes twinkled. Joy seemed to bubble just beneath the surface on most occasions. Even when she was repressing her enthusiasm for life and adventures, her joy seemed to need to find its release in small sighs.

And all that exuberance was soon to be his – as soon as he could talk to her father and then make his offer to her. How fortunate could one gentleman be?

~*~*~

"You seem exceptionally cheerful," Norman said to him later as Walter poured his friend a cup of tea.

"Do you wish for some?" Walter sliced a Sally Lunn in half.

"Just a quarter," Norman replied.

How the man survived on such scant meals was

beyond Walter's ability to comprehend. "Do your patients feed you?" That was likely it.

"On occasion."

"And did you see many patients this morning?"

"Two. Both with excellent cooks." Norman smiled over the rim of his cup.

Ah, so that was it. The man only ate small bits at every stop so that he could indulge in all that was offered. It was a good way of doing things. Many of the elderly women upon whom Norman called would likely find it an offense if their hospitality was refused. Mrs. King was that way.

"Did you call on Mrs. King?"

Norman shook his head. "No. Nor do I plan to call on her. I have sent a note withdrawing my services."

"You have done what?" Walter lowered his cup without taking a sip. "Have you lost all sense?"

"It would be folly for me to continue," Norman snapped.

The man was testy!

"Do you love her? And I do not mean Mrs. King." Walter finally took a sip of his tea while waiting for Norman to slowly chew a bit of his bun.

"I never stopped loving Belle, which is why I cannot pursue her."

Walter said nothing in response. Not that he did not wish to say something. He very much wanted to say several somethings, but he was not the sort to pontificate over his friend. The heart was a delicate organ. It was capable of great things such as holding onto love for an entire lifetime, but it was also easily damaged and difficult to repair when love was unrequited or worse — stolen.

"I would speak to her," was the only comment Walter allowed himself to share.

Norman simply shook his head and tore another bite off his bun.

"Mrs. King knows about Grace."

Norman looked at Walter in surprise. "How?"

"I told her – not in so many words, but I hinted quite blatantly."

"When? Did you do this last night?"

Walter nodded. "When Grace and I were taking a turn of the corridor, she and her niece found us." Walter smiled at the memory. "She loves me."

"Miss Grace?"

Once again, Walter nodded. "She told me last night." He expelled a great sigh. "I am planning to speak to her father soon. I realize we have not been acquainted long, but I see no need to wait." Not when his heart was so irrevocably lost to Grace.

"Indeed? That is excellent news!"

"Miss Chapman seemed relieved to know that Grace was not pursuing you in earnest." Walter shrugged when Norman looked at him skeptically. "You know Mrs. King and her opinions on who should be matched with whom."

Norman chuckled.

Mrs. King was excessively interested in the lives of young lovers. How many times had she suggested ladies to him only to be disappointed in his assessment that whichever lady was presented was not up to his standards? She had even lectured him a time or two on his expectations being too far-reaching. He tipped his head and studied his friend.

"Has Mrs. King tried to match you with anyone?"

Norman shook his head. "Not as of late. I believe she gave up her quest sometime in the autumn if not before."

"Hmmm. Interesting." If he was remembering correctly, that was also right around the time when she began speaking more and more about her niece who was to join her in Bath.

"How so?"

"She is not the sort to give up on seeing someone well-matched. Heaven knows I have tried to get her to leave off matching me."

"That does make it interesting, but I am sure there was a reason."

Most likely, the reason was now living in one of Mrs. King's guest rooms, but he would not say as much to Norman. He would just bide his time while watching and listening – and scheming with Grace. He smiled.

"You do look exceptionally happy today," Norman commented. "But I guess knowing the lady you love returns that love will have that effect on a gentleman."

"Indeed, it will. I am going to Erondale as soon as I am through here. I thought it best not to arrive in my travelling clothes and famished." He swallowed the last of his tea. "Are you going to visit either Mrs. Shelton or Mrs. Clayton today?"

"I had not intended to do so, but I am free for the afternoon. A social call would not be out of the question."

"Then allow me to offer you a ride, though I do hope to convince Grace to go driving with me while you are occupied with the Claytons and Sheltons. So, I will not be available to cart you back to town for an emergency should one come calling."

"I am certain I can be free from being called away for a few hours, and if not, perhaps Clayton would do me the service of conveying me back to town." He rose from his place at the table. "And while you are driving me to Erondale, perhaps, you can tell me why you were in travelling clothes."

~*~*~

"I had hoped that what I had heard was not true," Norman said as they approached Erondale and Walter had finished telling him his tale of chasing after Ramsey once he had discovered that the man had left the Upper Rooms.

"What did you hear?"

"Just that Ramsey was seen with some pretty lady who was not the same pretty lady he had been dancing with at the ball, and that it seemed he was playing Miss Love false."

That was what it most certainly looked as if

Ramsey was doing. Walter shook his head and sighed. "Gossip travels quickly."

"Excessively," Norman agreed. "I do not carry it myself, but I am often privy to a great many interesting tidbits." He blew out a breath. "If there is one festering pustule that I would like to see eradicated, it would be the wagging tongue. Far too much damage can be done by one exposure to it. However, to this point, no one has discovered a tincture, tonic, or extraction procedure to rid society of the dread disease."

He was, of course, speaking from experience – grievously miserable experience. It almost made it understandable that the man would not wish to risk another exposure to such ruinous viciousness again even for a chance to gain the lady he loved.

Walter jumped down from the gig and waited for Norman to join him before proceeding to Erondale's door.

"We have been waiting for you," Roger said as he opened the door.

Where was the butler? Walter peeked behind Roger and saw Graeme.

"Is something amiss?"

Roger's grimace was enough of an answer to set Walter's heart racing.

"What is it?" he asked as he stepped inside the house.

"This." Roger held out a letter. "I told her that I would see you received it."

Her? With great trepidation, he took the missive from Roger. On the front was his name, very prettily written with a feminine flourish.

"Come. Have a seat before you read it," Graeme suggested.

"Is she gone?"

Graeme's nodded. "Have a seat. Read the letter. And then, we can tell you what we know."

Walter shook his head. "Where did she go?"

"Home," Roger answered.

"How long ago?"

"It was about seven this morning when they left."

Walter turned toward the door. "There is still daylight." He could cover a good bit of ground before it was dark if he left now. He might even be able to overtake them on the road if he travelled through the night.

Graeme grabbed his arm and steered him into

the sitting room. "Did you discover anything about Ramsey?"

Walter shook his head. Why did they want to know that now? There were more pressing matters needing attention. The woman whom he loved and who had said she loved him had left, and he needed to be away.

"Blakesley," Norman said, "please, take a seat."

"But Grace –"

"Left you a missive she wishes for you to read," Mrs. Clayton inserted. "There were a good number of tears that went into its writing. It would be a shame not to read it."

"And you cannot leave until you know where to look," Roger added when Walter hesitated and looked once more toward the door.

That was true.

"And we will not tell you that bit of information until you have had the rest of it."

Walter scowled at Roger and, then, took a seat as close to the door as possible. "Tell me what I need to know."

"Ramsey has left Bath," Graeme said.

"I know that. I followed him as far as I could."

"Did you know that Miss Love sneaked out of her house to go see Ramsey?" Graeme asked.

Walter's brow knit. "How would I know that?" He unfolded the letter he had been given. His curiosity would wait no longer to be satiated.

"You would not unless we told you, which is why you need to take a moment before running after Grace," Roger said. "We are not attempting to keep you from her."

Walter sank back in his chair as he read what Grace had written. "She meant to break off with me?"

"No," Mrs. Clayton said quietly. "She thought she was doing the proper thing."

Walter looked at her in confusion. "How is it the proper thing?"

Mrs. Clayton glanced at her companions. "Her sister might be with child."

"Ramsey's child?" Only Graeme did not look as surprised as Walter was at the news.

Mrs. Clayton nodded. "Why would any gentleman such as yourself wish to be tainted by such a scandal as Felicity has created?"

"Because he loves Felicity's sister."

Mrs. Clayton nodded again. "Love is also

Grace's reason, for because she loves you so much, she could not fathom allowing you to be discredited or harmed in any way."

"But her leaving me is the harm," Walter protested. A few whispers were nothing to him. It was not as if he had gotten Miss Love with child. That was Ramsey's cross to bear. "I will not allow her sister to take yet another gentleman from her – especially not one who loves her as fiercely as I do." He rose. "I need to know where I am going."

Chapter 19

Chickens fluttered their wings and squawked in the small patch of fenced-in garden next to a hen house while shouts from one servant to another lifted above the clatter of the courtyard below. Grace sighed and rested her head against the back of the rocker she had drawn from the corner of the room to the window.

It was lovely to be off the road again, and this inn was a touch nicer than yesterday's, but none of that truly soothed her as it would have on her trip to Bath. Several days on the road when anticipating adventure were much easier to endure than the same number of days spent travelling while one's heart was breaking.

She closed her eyes. A tear slid down her cheek, and she brushed it away quickly.

"Are you still so disappointed?" her mother

asked from where she sat at a table with her needle-work spread out. Felicity was flopped across the bed, and their father was below stairs, likely talking with some gentlemen at the bar.

Grace shrugged and nodded. She did not want to speak about it. She wanted to be miserable and alone. However, as it was, she was only allowed to be miserable. One was never alone when travelling for one was either in a carriage with her family or in a rented room with at least a sister.

She turned her head to the right until she could just see Felicity. She felt dreadful for her sister, of course, but she also could not bring herself to the point of completely forgiving her for her stupidity. Sneaking out to kiss a gentleman in a garden was one thing. Sneaking out to allow him to take you to bed was another altogether. It really did not matter to Grace how much her sister protested that Mr. Ramsey had proclaimed his love for her or how he had spoken of marrying. It was foolish. She would never sneak out to visit Walter at his home in such a fashion. Not even if she enjoyed his kisses and caresses — which she would never know as he had never kissed her.

She closed her eyes and tried to remember what

it felt like to be held by him as she had been at his townhouse with his strong arms encircling her while she rested against his firm chest.

Another tear slid down her cheek. How she missed him!

"We will have to begin planning for your season as soon as... well... soon." Her mother smiled tightly. What was to become of Felicity had been a topic of discussion today in the carriage. If all was well — meaning she was not with child –it might be reasonable to allow her to participate in some of the season's activities. Their mother was certain that some gentleman would be willing to take her on. There was no way for a gentleman to know that she was not a maiden as long as gossip did not follow her.

That was the biggest concern, for it seemed Felicity was incapable of not being followed by gossip. And if it did not follow her, she seemed to create it wherever she was. At school, she had been the topic of several stories that had circulated. Those had been mostly innocent. Miss Amelia Abernathy was a great lover of posing dares, and Felicity was all too willing to prove herself as fearless. However, those dares had been just for fun.

Nothing more than a day or two of discipline by the headmistress had been at stake.

"I do not want a season," Grace said.

"Not want a season? That cannot be. You will miss your friends for now, but, in a few months, you will forget the time with them which you were made to miss and will be eager to be on your way once again."

Grace shook her head. "I shall never forget." There was so much to miss!

Bea and Victoria had not yet told anyone else about their babies. Only Grace had been privy to their conversations about becoming mothers. Only she had heard their excitement and apprehension. She would miss that. It would not happen again.

And then, there was Walter. She did not need a season, for she had no heart left to give to any gentleman. Ever. She had not lied when she had written to him that her heart would never forget him. She sighed. Being in love was not so amusing as she had expected it to be. It was dashed hard to not put her own desires ahead of what would be best for him.

And that was why she was having a horrid time of forgiving her sister.

Her mother looked up from her work as she pulled her needle through the fabric. "You are not pining over Mr. Norman, are you?" There was a hint of a scold in her tone. "There will be far better choices in town next year."

"She does not love Mr. Norman," Felicity said from the bed.

Oh, dear! She had thought Felicity was asleep.

"Well, I am happy to hear that," her mother said. "He was a lovely fellow, but he was not for you."

"Yes, Mother. He did not own land," Grace replied flatly.

"There is that," her mother agreed. "But he was not right for you. You need someone far more... Oh, I do not know what the proper word is for it. You just need someone who is more... Well, to put a fine point on it, you need someone more like Mr. Blakesley. He is amiable and lively. I dare say you'd not want for enjoyment if you were to marry him."

There was more to her mother's complaint about Mr. Norman than just that he was a physician? Grace was surprised. It would have been nice if her mother had made such a thing known before now.

"Mrs. King said the same thing," Grace admitted. "I think that Mrs. King would like Mr. Norman to marry her niece. It was not said, but I think they would make a good match."

"Then, you are truly not attached to the man?" her mother asked.

"She loves Mr. Blakesley."

Grace froze in her chair. Perhaps if she sat very still her mother would not remember she was there, or perhaps someone could knock at the door and distract her mother. She wanted to peek at her mother for she was so silent, but she dared not.

"Mr. Blakesley?" Unfortunately, her mother had found her voice and no knock at the door had distracted her.

"She calls him Walter."

Felicity had barely spoken a word in the two days since leaving Bath. Could she not remain silent for just a bit longer?

"Does she?" Their mother sounded quite excited. Still, Grace sat perfectly still, not daring to make a noise or movement.

"I do not think she was ever truly being courted by Mr. Norman."

Oh, wonderful. Not only was Felicity not going to remain silent she was going to become astute.

"Was she not?"

From the sounds Grace heard, she imagined Felicity had propped herself up on the bed.

"Why would she pretend that Mr. Norman was her suitor?" her mother asked.

"I am sure I do not know," Felicity replied. "Why would you do that, Grace?"

"Do what?" Grace asked.

"Do not play stupid," Felicity retorted.

How she wanted to retort that it was not she but Felicity who was stupid, but that would not be kind nor would it aid her cause at the moment. She did not need her mother to be put out before she needed to be.

"Why would you pretend that Mr. Norman was courting you?" Their mother asked. "Turn your chair so we can see you."

Grace rose and did as instructed.

"Now, tell us why," her mother commanded once Grace had taken a seat.

"Because of Felicity." That was the entire reason

as shocking as it appeared to be to her sister, though it should not be.

"I do not understand," her mother said. "How could Felicity be the reason for your subterfuge?"

Grace sighed. "Felicity is always the reason. She is why I was not allowed to flirt with Mr. Everett Clayton. She was the reason why I was not to even consider Mr. Ramsey at the Abernathy's house party." She felt a pang of regret at having mentioned his name when her sister closed her eyes. "And she was the reason I had no season. She either gets or takes everything." Grace blew out a breath. "Therefore, I thought it best to keep Mr. Blakesley a secret from her so that she would not take him from me." She closed her eyes. "But as it turns out, she has taken him anyway." Tears once again slid down her cheeks while she attempted to dash them away before they were seen.

"Oh." Her mother seemed lost for words beyond that one word.

"I did not take him from you," Felicity protested.

Grace shook her head. "You are right. You took me from him. I suppose there is a difference, though the result is the same."

"How have I taken you from him? Because we

are going home? And you are no longer in Bath?" Felicity looked honestly confused. "Surely, he can call on you at home."

"In Kent? That seems a rather long drive for a call, do you not think?"

"I did not mean he would drive it all in one day. He could come for a visit. Father can invite him."

"No, he cannot. I have broken off with him."

"Why?" Felicity cried.

"Do you truly not know what you have done?" Was her sister really that senseless?

"No one knows what I have done," Felicity said through clenched teeth. "They only know that I was treated poorly by Mr. Ramsey."

"You were seen at his apartment. It does not take a great mind to decipher why you would be there." She blew out a breath. "And if there is a child..." She shrugged. "I could not ask Walter to be tied to such a scandal. His home is in Bath you know. He will not get to drive away from any gossip." Her words were cutting, and she knew it.

Felicity looked horrified. "Surely, you are being far more dramatic than the situation warrants."

"Not all families would approve of a connection to ours at present," her mother said. "Perhaps after the air has cleared for a time, then we can invite Mr. Blakesley to Kent." She gasped. "Kent! You said he had a lady in Kent." She gasped again. "You were speaking of yourself! Oh, you, sly girl!"

Grace had expected her mother to be more irritated and less pleased about having been duped. However, it was likely good to have one parent who was not utterly put out with her. Her father would not be as amused.

"You love him?" her mother asked.

Grace nodded. With all her heart.

"And does he love you?"

Grace thought once again about how he had held her in the drawing-room at his townhouse and how he had told her that he hoped to one day be able to offer for her. She thought about how delighted he had been when she told him she loved him in the corridor at the Upper Rooms, and how he mentioned speaking to her father. And then, he had told Mrs. King that she was from Kent. She smiled despite the pain each memory brought her.

He loved her. She was absolutely certain of that.

However, there was a knock at the door before Grace could push her memories of Walter away and answer her mother.

"I have brought a visitor," her father said as he pushed the door open slowly.

"Walter?" Grace cried. Were her eyes deceiving her? The gentleman behind her father looked a great deal like Mr. Blakesley.

"Mr. Blakesley and I have had a very interesting discussion."

It was him. He had come for her. She just knew he had.

"Grace." Her father's tone and look were stern. "I am not an advocate of deception, though I do think I understand the faulty reasoning behind it." He tipped his head and smiled at her. "Your deep disappointment in leaving Bath makes a great deal more sense now." He held out his hand to her. "I think Mr. Blakesley would like to have a private discussion with you, or, at least, as private as a discussion can be in the yard of an inn."

He wanted to speak to her privately! Her heart was surely going to burst from joy.

"Mr. Blakesley, I am entrusting you to make certain no other scandal befalls my family."

"I would never do anything to harm your daughter or her family," Walter said.

Grace sighed. He was so noble, so good, and so...

well... everything. Was there another man in all of England as perfect has Mr. Blakesley? She was certain there was not.

Mr. Love placed Grace's hand in Walter's. "I am excessively pleased to hear that." He winked at Grace. "I will wait here with your mother for the happy news." Then, he shooed them from the room and closed the door, leaving them standing in the hallway of the inn.

Chapter 20

Walter looked up the hall and then down. Seeing it was empty, he pulled Grace into his arms for a quick embrace – not long enough by half but enough to assure himself that she was truly there with him. Two days of travelling and stopping at inns in search of her had been two very long days.

"Do not ever leave me again," he whispered before releasing her. He grasped her face between his hands. "Promise me, you will not leave me." He pressed a quick kiss to her lips. Again, it was far from how he wished to kiss her.

"How can I promise that?"

There was a twinkle in her eye that spoke of her understanding full-well what he meant. However, there were also tears clinging to her lower lids. It was an apt picture of how he felt – a tumultuous mix of lingering pain from separation and sheer delight at having found her.

"Marry me. We can live at Erondale or in town. I do not care as long as you are with me." Her smile was welcoming. "Please, will you be my wife?"

Her lips parted as if she was going to speak and then they closed as she cast a look at the door in front of which they still stood. He took her hand and, tucking it into the crook of his arm, led her the short distance to the stairs which would take them to the public rooms below. He was certain he knew what or, more precisely, who was causing her to hesitate.

"I know about your sister. Your cousin told me." He drew her close and spoke in low tones. Not everyone in the establishment needed to hear what he was saying. But she did.

It was not a very far journey from the bottom of the stairs to the door. However, they did have to wait twice – once for a maid to enter a room with a tray laden with dishes and once for a fellow who required a cane to assist his bent form in walking.

"Then, you know why I left," she whispered after the man with the crooked back had passed them.

"Partly. Your parents required you to leave Erondale. However, they did not require you to leave me. That was your decision." He let her exit before him. The air outside was a bit fresher than it was within, but it was still not without its own blend of aromas – food being cooked mingled with dirt and dust, as well as the scent of animals. It was not where he would have chosen to speak to her about serious matters, but it was the best they were going to be afforded.

"There is a tree with a bench just behind the hen house," she offered

"Is there?"

She nodded. "I have been looking out the window for some time wishing to be anywhere but in my room and had thought of asking to go sit there. It is not as lovely as the bench in your garden, but it reminded me of that... and you." She rested her head against his shoulder for a moment but then with a gasp, she straightened. "I forgot," she whispered.

"I think we could withstand a few curious glances. I would venture to guess that most do not know we are only courting. I do not think it will cause a scandal."

She sighed. "But my sister has."

"Most likely."

"She will be the talk of Bath when the gentleman who lives below Mr. Ramsey shares his story."

"He will not be sharing anything." When Mrs. Clayton had shared that bit of the tale with him before he left Erondale, he had decided to delay his journey by an hour so that he might have a frank discussion with the fellow.

"How do you know?"

"As it turns out, he has been looking to rent a nicer set of rooms. Ones which could be found in one of my establishments and which will be his if he keeps his silence."

He had told the fellow that he was looking for a new tenant since he was planning to marry and wished to prop up his coffers by filling a vacancy. When the chap had discovered who it was that Walter was marrying, he had smirked and said something a trifle out of step. He would not make that mistake again, or he would be out of a fine set of rooms and be required to meet Walter for an early morning boxing match. Neither were things for which the fellow wished.

"You did that for Felicity?" Grace's eyes were wide with surprise and filled with delight.

"No, I did it for you. I only care what happens to your sister as it pertains to how it affects you. She is not my responsibility."

If it were not for how her sister's actions might harm Grace, he'd not have cared if the gentleman shared his story with everyone he met. However, Walter could imagine just how grievously that would distress a kind heart such as Grace possessed.

He took a seat next to her on the bench beneath the tree.

"My window is that one on the right."

He looked to where she was pointing.

"Do you suppose we are being watched?" he asked in a whisper.

She giggled. "I suppose we are."

He lifted her hand to his lips.

"Mr. Blakesley, we are not to create a scandal!"

He chuckled. "We will not. I have only kissed your knuckles." He kissed her hand once again. "Now, you were telling me why you decided to leave me."

She tipped her head and looked at him. Once

again, tears filled her eyes. Mrs. Clayton had said the note was not easily written, and it appeared that even thinking about having written it was painful.

"I could not allow you to be harmed." She blew out a breath. "What would your family think of your marrying someone with a sister such as mine?"

"Frankly, I do not care what they think. You are not your sister, and they will come to understand that."

"But what about the people in Bath? You need to retain a certain reputation to be able to continue to do business as you have been." She grasped both of his hands and looked at him very seriously. "While sitting out a dance or two, I have heard how much you are admired. I should hate to be the cause of that changing."

"They will also admire you. How could they not?"

She smiled. "You are impossible! It is entirely probable that many would hold my sister's actions against me. That is how it works. If one daughter is a wanton seductress, then her sister is assumed to be the same."

He shook his head. "Not always."

"But often." She punctuated her words with an exasperated huff.

He loved how she revealed all of her emotions to him. He doubted she did so with her sister or her mother. He had seen her affect expressions in their presence. He had never seen her do so with him.

"I will give you that there are some who think as you have suggested, but anyone who is too blind to see the goodness in you, my dear, is not worth my time." For such a person was likely either intolerably stupid or thought far too well of themselves. Neither were the sorts of people with whom he enjoyed doing business, though sometimes it was required.

"You have also been seen with Mr. Norman," he continued, "and he is highly regarded. I think you are worrying unnecessarily." Her mouth popped open. "However," he hastened to say, "I would rather bear a thousand heinous whispers than one more day without you. Please, say you will marry me."

"But –"

"My life will only be miserable without you in it. I love you, Grace. More than life itself."

Her lips trembled. "And I love you the same. These past two days have been wretched. I knew I must not put myself first, but how I wished to do just that and demand to be returned to Erondale."

"Will you marry me, Grace?" She was taking an interminable amount of time to answer a simple question, but then, she had been trying his patience since before they met. It was one of the things about her which, while driving him to distraction, he loved.

Her head bobbed up and down. "If it will ensure your happiness, I will."

"And what of your happiness, my love?"

"It will be greater than one person is likely supposed to be granted."

He lifted her hand to his lips again. "I wish we were not being watched."

She sighed. "That is too bad, is it not?" Her eyes rested on his lips. "We did just become betrothed."

"I gave my word to your father."

She sighed but then brightened and, leaning forward, kissed him. "I did not give my word to my father, and he is likely put out with me as it is."

Walter shook his head.

"It is not how I wish to kiss you," she whispered.

"We are in agreement there." He stood and offered his hand to her. They should return to her parents before he found it impossible to keep his word to her father. "I will send an express to my father if your father will allow it. I should like for you to meet my family."

"I would like that." She once again rested her head on his shoulder for a very brief moment as they walked back to the door to the inn. "But are you not returning to Bath?"

"Not unless you are. I was not jesting when I said I had no desire to be separated from you again."

"But you have business, do you not?"

"Nothing of a pressing nature. Norman has agreed to be my go-between if one is needed, and even Shelton offered assistance. He seemed very eager to see me on my way to claim you as my own. Do you know why?" he added when she giggled at that bit of information.

"He has been attempting to help me make a match since the house party we attended last summer." She smiled up at him. "It seems he has finally done it."

"Since when did he become a matchmaker?"

"Oh, he helped Mr. Clayton make a match with Bea."

"He did?"

Grace nodded as she climbed the stairs ahead of him. "He paid Bea marked attention while he was at Stratsbury Park, and that is all it took for Mr. Clayton to realize how much he loved my cousin."

Walter shook his head and chuckled. He was not certain that causing another gentleman to be jealous was precisely being a matchmaker, but it did seem like something Roger would do.

"And then, while attempting to find a match for me, he found a match for Victoria."

The match had been himself! Again, Walter was not certain he would place that under the auspices of being a matchmaker.

"And now," Grace said as she gained the landing, "he has helped me find you." Her brow furrowed. "Actually, I found you on my own. He just helped me keep you a secret."

Roger had been a wonderfully negligent chaperone. Walter could not fault the fellow for that since it had worked so well in his favour. He offered Grace his arm, and together they walked down the corridor. Before knocking on the door to the

Love's set of rooms, he once again looked up and down the hallway, and, seeing they were alone, pulled Grace into his arms for a brief embrace and far-too-chaste kiss.

"How long until you would like to marry and return to Bath with me?"

She sighed as he lifted his hand to knock on the door. "We should likely ask Mother. She has not yet had the opportunity to host a wedding breakfast, and mine might be her only chance."

"Then," he replied with a smile, "we will let your mother decide, though I will not be pushed to wait longer than three weeks. I will eventually have to return to Bath." He knocked and waited for someone to answer rather than allowing Grace to open the door for him. "And," he whispered just before the door opened, "I will not, for any reason, allow your sister to come between us. Not for a dance nor for the distance between Kent and Bath."

Chapter 21

Three and a half weeks later, Grace found herself once again settling into a strange room. However, this room and all the others below and above her would soon become familiar for they were to be her new home until the summer when she and her husband – she paused a moment and sighed at the wonderful thought – would take up residence at Erondale.

She put the last item for her toilette on her dressing table and took one more happy look around the modest-sized room which was fitted with wardrobes and dressers, as well as her dressing table and a lovely yellow sofa and footstool.

How wonderful it was that she had been forced to come to Bath on her sister's account! She chuckled to herself. Things had certainly changed in the time since she had first arrived in Bath with her family.

"Are you finished?" Walter poked his head into their dressing room. "It most certainly looks as if you are."

"Everything is as it should be." Grace rose and crossed to the door which joined this room to the master chamber.

"I could not agree with you more." Walter pulled her into his embrace and captured her lips for a kiss.

Grace sighed and melded to him. She was married – excessively, delightfully married in every way – and to the most wonderful man in all of creation. Her heart threatened to rupture with its joy at the knowledge. Walter was hers and hers alone.

"We have guests," Walter whispered when finally, he broke away from their ardent kiss. "And as much as they are the understanding sort, I dare say they would not be pleased to wait for an hour for us to join them, even if I wish to be locked away in this room with you for at least that long." He gave her a quick kiss.

"How do we have guests?" Grace asked as she checked her appearance in the mirror while Walter straightened and fidgeted with his clothing. "I did not think anyone would know we had arrived back in town until tomorrow."

In the mirror, she could see his grin. "What have you done?"

He shrugged and shook his head. "It is a secret," he whispered.

Grace giggled and hurried to follow him out of the room. Catching up to him, she wound her arm around his, pulling herself close enough that a good portion of her body touched his upper arm. She would affect a proper distance when they reached the bottom of the stairs, but for now, she wished to be as close to him as she possibly could be. However, when they reached the bottom of the stairs before she could affect her proper distance, he set her aside.

"Stay right here. Do not move, and do not peek."

"Shall I put my fingers in my ears and close my eyes?"

"If you wish."

She smiled. "I do love surprises. Well, happy surprises, not the sort that took me back to –" His finger on her lips stopped her from talking, and she put her fingers in her ears and squeezed her eyes closed.

He removed his finger from her lips and replaced it with a kiss. "Stay right here," he whispered, pulling one finger away from her ear so that she could hear him. "Do you know how lovely you are?" He kissed her lips again after she shook her head.

She popped one eye open to look at him.

"I will tell you about it later," he promised.

Grace closed her eye and counted silently in her head as if she was playing hide and go seek. She had gotten all the way to one hundred and nineteen before she jumped when a hand was placed on her arm and once again, one finger was pulled away from her ear.

"We are ready," Walter said.

"Ready for what?" Grace batted her lashes at him innocently, causing him to chuckle.

"Feigned innocence will not work with me, Mrs. Blakesley. I know you are very good a scheming. The only way to discover this secret is to follow me."

"Anywhere."

"I could be leading you into danger," he cautioned.

Grace rolled her eyes. "You would never do that."

"Are you certain?"

She nodded. There was no one, absolutely no one, whom she trusted more than the man standing before her. "I trust you." She ran her hand down his arm before placing it in his hand.

His fingers twined with hers, and the two of them proceeded from the stairway to the dining room.

"Oh, my!" Grace cried when the door was flung open to reveal a room decorated for a party.

The table was laid with flowers and candles in the center and the finest china and glassware at each place. The sideboard was laden with several covered dishes, as well as serving bowls and decanters of wine. A footman and a maid stood one on each end of the sideboard, smiling in an understated fashion at their new mistress. And gathered around the table were the Sheltons, the Claytons, Mrs. King and Miss Chapman, and, of course, dear, dear Mr. Norman.

"I wrote to Norman," Walter explained when

the cheers and hardy congratulations, which had greeted them, had died down and everyone was taking their seats. "And he arranged it all."

"You are a very good friend," Grace said to Mr. Norman.

"Better than I likely should be," Mr. Norman replied with a grin.

"And not a killer at all," Roger inserted, causing Graeme to chuckle and Walter to explain their first secret meeting to Mrs. King and her niece.

Mrs. King looked shocked at first, but then, smiled. "I knew you were the perfect match for Mr. Blakesley from the moment I met you." She leaned toward the table and to her right, lowering her voice just a touch as if sharing a secret across the table with Grace. "He needed a lively wife. I have always thought so."

"And yet, all the ladies you presented to me were not lively," Walter accused.

"They were as lively as I could find. It is not my fault that they were not intriguing enough for the likes of you."

"There is likely not another lady in all of England as intriguing as Grace," Walter replied. "At least, there is not to me."

"That is as it should be," Roger said. "Now, my wife is interested in knowing all the details about your wedding."

"I am interested? I think it is my husband who is interested," Victoria said. "Not that I do not wish to hear it," she added with a smile. "We truly could not be happier for you."

"Here. Here," Graeme cried as the first dish of stew began making its tour of the table and finding itself relieved of its contents.

"Your parents must have been surprised when Mr. Blakesley appeared at your door," Bea said.

"Oh, very!" Grace replied. "My father was not pleased with my subterfuge but was understanding once I explained all that Felicity had done." It had saddened her father to hear about it. He knew that his eldest daughter could be demanding and prone to getting her way, but he had not known those tendencies had devolved into taking advantage of her sister's gentler temperament.

"What had Felicity done?" Mrs. King asked with interest.

"Oh! I should likely not say, but since I forgot that you did not know, I suppose I must tell at least a portion." Grace looked at Walter who nodded.

"Mrs. King will keep it to herself." He gave the lady a pointed look. "She would not wish to have any harm come to you."

"It goes without saying, does it not, Annabelle?"

"Most certainly," Miss Chapman agreed. Her eyes darted toward Mr. Norman, who, Grace noticed, was doing a fine job of ignoring the lady. "Gossip is dangerous, and I would never wish to be the source of harm to another."

Mr. Norman's jaw clenched, and his head shifted just a bit as if the words were a blow to him.

"I am happy to hear it," Grace said while giving both Mrs. King and Miss Chapman a reassuring smile. "I think we shall be great friends, and that might require sharing secrets with one another. It often does."

"Very true," Roger muttered with a chuckle.

"My Grace is fond of secrets," Walter added.

"Only secrets of the best kind!" Grace protested. "I do not like those which would damage." Her hands were resting on her lap and her chair was placed just right to allow her to bump her husband's foot with her own, and for her to touch his knee without being noticed, which made him smile. After sharing a secret look with Walter, she turned back to her guests.

"My sister is fond of courting." That seemed a polite and kind way to say it. "And it is her belief that the elder should marry before the younger sister." She pulled her bottom lip between her teeth to keep from smiling too broadly. While that might have been Felicity's belief, it had not been what had happened.

"I will assume that such things have caused a gentleman or two to have been snatched up by your sister when you might have been interested in them," Mrs. King said. "I am not without siblings with strong opinions either." She winked at Grace.

"Yes, she has snatched a few," Grace answered simply. There was not much else to say. Felicity had stolen a couple of gentlemen from Grace but not the one who mattered, the one who held her heart and had covered her hand, which lay on his knee, with his own.

"Well, it seems it has all worked out for the best," Mrs. King added.

"Indeed, it has," Walter said. "My parents and brother were happy to meet Grace and her family. We stopped there on our way to Kent."

He continued to ramble on about the estate and the improvements being made to the garden while Grace half-listened. She had enjoyed meeting his family. She could see where Walter had gotten his drive to do well. His father was similar to him in that way, as well as in appearance. His older brother was, Grace had discovered, only older by a few minutes, and while he was nearly an exact image of Walter, his personality was quite different. He was the quieter of the two.

Felicity had found Walter's brother to be a great source of entertainment. It appeared that to Felicity the surest way to get over a broken heart was to flirt with an unattached gentleman. However, Grace knew from the tears Felicity shed each night before sleep that what appeared to be true was not the truth. Her sister's heart was well and truly broken. No gentleman was going to fix it. Time would have to do that.

She sighed as she took a sip of her wine. She would likely get a letter in a few weeks informing her if Felicity was to have a season or a child. The thought was enough to pull a grey cloud over the festivities around her. She knew that what Felicity suffered was of her own doing, but it was still not easy to contemplate that her sister might be less than happy for the rest of her life.

"Has –" she stopped. She could not ask that.

"What is that, my love?"

She shook her head. "I was just contemplating someone I had seen several times at several soirees and had thought to inquire after him. It is nothing."

Graeme caught her eye and shook his head. So, Mr. Ramsey had not returned? That was sad indeed. How did a gentleman declare his love and promise marriage one day and run away from it all the next?

"Mrs. Love is an excellent hostess," Walter said, thankfully, drawing the conversation back to a safer subject. "The wedding breakfast will be the talk of Kent for some time, I should think."

It would be unless Felicity was with child. Then, that would be the focus of gossip. Their father had declared that he would not cover it up. There might be a time away during the summer at the seaside for the family, but his daughter, who had gotten herself into such a predicament by being secretive, would be required to deal with the whispers and looks if it came to that. The announcement had been met with tears from nearly everyone, including her father. It was only Walter who had not found it necessary to cry over the ordeal. That is not to say he was not sensible to the tragedy. He was. He was just not the sort to shed tears over such a thing, or so he said, though his eyes had glistened when holding Grace's hand and attempting to comfort her after that meeting. He truly was the best of men!

"Oh, yes! The cake was delicious. I have requested the receipt from my mother so that I can add it to my collection," Grace inserted when Walter began discussing the food which was served.

"And the bride was – is – beautiful, so all was as it should be," Walter concluded.

Their discussion fell to the news of the area after that and continued with plans for the future as they all looked forward to the summer.

"Well, Mrs. Blakesley, shall we take a walk in the square now that we have eaten?" Walter swallowed the last of his wine.

"Only if our guests wish to join us."

"Oh, we are not staying beyond the meal," Bea said softly, a faint pink staining her cheeks.

"No, indeed!" Mrs. King agreed. "Newlyweds do

not need a house full of guests on their first evening in their home." Again, she winked at Grace, who blushed but was happy to hear she would be alone with Walter.

"I do not see why you could not take a walk with us before departing," Walter inserted.

"Would you even know we were there?" Roger quipped.

"I might remember it when you took your leave," Walter replied.

"Bea is tired," Graeme inserted. "We took a stroll through the gardens earlier, so I think it is best to take her home for a quiet evening. I also happen to know that there is a book, which she is eager to read, waiting for her at Erondale."

Walter rose. "Do not let it be said that I shooed you out of my house without offering to be hospitable."

"Who would believe such a thing?" Mrs. King asked with a chuckle. "You will both come call on me soon, will you not? My cook has a fresh supply of apple cake." Her eyebrows waggled. "I do hope it is still enough to tempt you to join me on occasion for tea."

"We would come even without the offer of

cake," Walter assured her. "However, the cake is greatly appreciated."

One by one, their guests joined them in the corridor and said their farewells. Walter promised each that he and his wife would call on them soon. He was eager to be seen in society with Grace on his arm.

"You are well?" Grace whispered to Bea as her cousin gave her a hug before departing.

"Quite. I find I am still tired but far less likely to cast up my accounts. However, I am hungry. Constantly hungry. I doubt my dresses will conceal my expanding belly much longer."

"My brother might come for a visit," Graeme said when departing. "He is not enjoying his time in London so very much, so I invited him and Max to join us for a few weeks."

"That would be wonderful!" Grace cried.

"Yes, it should give my husband something to do." Victoria's eyes shone with merriment. "You know he is claiming he helped you make a match."

Of course, he was.

"He was a help," Grace said. "If he had not kept my secret, who knows how things would have turned out."

"I suspect," Victoria said with a glance toward Walter, "that the results would not be so very different from how they are now." She embraced Grace before her husband said his farewells, and then the house was quiet. Very quiet.

"Shall we take that walk in the square?"

Grace shook her head. "Maybe tomorrow."

"Then what do you suggest we do, my love?"

"There is a lovely view of the square from the sitting room if a remember correctly."

"There is."

"I think I should like to view it just as I did the first time." She moved toward the stairs but only took two steps up them before turning around to face Walter. "Only this time," she said in a whisper, "I should like you to kiss me while we are there just as I hoped you would last time."

"Would you now?" Walter's eyes were filled with amusement and desire.

Grace placed a hand on his heart and then slid it slowly up to his shoulder. "Very much." She moved her hand around to his neck and leaned toward him. "But that does not mean you cannot kiss me now as well."

"But everyone will know that you like me," he teased.

She shook her head. "I do not like you, Mr. Blakesley. I love you with every inch of my being from my head down to my soul, and I do not care who knows."

"That is just how I feel about you, my angel."

"Then kiss me."

And he did kiss her – on that step and each of the others up to the floor where their chambers were located.

"But the square," Grace protested weakly.

"It will still be there tomorrow." Walter opened the door to the bedroom and pulled her inside, where, once he made certain the door was locked, he spent the rest of the evening ensuring that all thoughts of squares or balls or sisters or anything other than her wonderful good fortune in being loved by him were impossible.

As the moon grew brighter while the shadows of the night deepened, Grace sighed and rested her head on her husband's chest above his heart and allowed her eyes to flutter closed, drifting off into blissful sleep, here in the safe embrace of the gentleman who had once happily agreed to be her secret beau.

Before You Go

If you enjoyed this book, be sure to let others
know by leaving a review.

~*~*~

Want to know when other books in this series
will be available?

You can always know what's new with my
books by subscribing to my mailing list.

(There will, of course, be a thank you gift for
joining because I think my readers are awesome!)

Book News from Leenie Brown

(bit.ly/LeenieBBookNews)

~*~*~

Turn the page to read an excerpt of another one
of Leenie's books

His Irreplaceable
Belle Excerpt

[Now that Belle has once again stumbled into Mr. Norman's life, what is he going to do about it? His Irreplaceable Belle, book 4 in the Touches of Austen series, is Mr. Norman's story.]

Chapter 1

Fredrick "Fritz" Norman had just picked up his pen and begun to record his observations about his most recent patient when the door to his surgery opened. He looked up, intending to give a nod of greeting to his visitor before returning to his writing. But the sight of the person who had stepped inside his office caused his pen to stutter on the page.

She was not supposed to be here. In fact, at present, if he had to choose one patient he did not wish to have enter his surgery, it would be her, for he was attempting to avoid her.

Quickly, he placed his pen in its holder before he could make a further mess of his notes. There would be no returning to recording his thoughts while Mrs. King was present. She was a lovely woman, but she was demanding and did not like to wait.

"Mrs. King, I had not thought to see you." He pushed up from his desk.

Mrs. King was not one of the patients who called on him at his surgery. She did not need to pay him in feed for his horse or eggs for his breakfast. She kept him on a retainer and expected him to call on her once a week to hear about whatever ache or pain was plaguing her at that moment. She was in good health and had no dire need of medical attention. All she really needed was for him to assure her that she was not ill.

"You have not called in two weeks."

That had been purposefully done, though he was not about to admit that to her.

She removed her reticule from where it hung on her wrist before skewering him with a critical look.

"I could have died in that time, and you would not have seen me at all."

"You are not dying. You are amongst my healthiest patients." He motioned for her to take a seat in the chair that was in front of his desk. It was turned at an angle so that he might approach his patients from the front, but, if need be, with a turn of the head, a patient could also hold a conversation with him while he sat and wrote notes.

"I will not be in such good health if you continue to ignore me." She sat as indicated, and her lips pursed and her brows rose as a look of great displeasure settled over her features.

"I have not ignored you." Avoiding was not the same as ignoring. "I have sent Mr. Spencer in my place. I assure you that he is an excellent assistant and his reports are most thorough."

"I will not see him. I wish for a physician, not a surgeon. It matters not to me how fine Mr. Spencer is."

Fritz blew out a breath. He had had a suspicion that his assistant being sent away completely yesterday without even gaining entrance to Mrs. King's residence was a sign that he would need to find someone else entirely to take on her care.

"I have a couple of meetings arranged with other physicians. Mr. Spencer was just a temporary measure to see that you were well while I found you an appropriate replacement for my services."

Mrs. King's gaze roamed over Fritz's face. Then, she shook her head. "That will not do. I shall see you or no one at all. Do you wish to be the cause of my deteriorating health?"

"You are in excellent health, Mrs. King. I am certain you could sustain a period of time without weekly calls by a physician."

She adjusted the hem of the glove on her right hand. "But I do not wish to go without those calls, and I will have no one but you. I shall raise my payment by ten percent." She opened her reticule and drew out a banknote. "Do you wish for me to leave this with you or your man of business?"

"I have no man of business." Which she knew for they had discussed that very thing not more than a month ago, and Mrs. King's memory was as sharp as any he had seen.

"Then, I shall leave this with you, and you can call on me tomorrow."

"I cannot do that." For that would mean seeing her niece, and he truly could not bear that.

She studied him again for a long silent minute. "Why?"

"I just think it would be best if you were under the care of another." It would most certainly be best for his peace of mind.

Her expression told him that she did not think it would be better. "Is this new physician I am to see better than you?"

"Perhaps." He was not so arrogant as to think there could not be a better physician than he, but he also was not so self-abasing that he would refrain from declaring his skills as finely honed.

"Can you guarantee that he is? For, from what I have been told by Mr. Blakesley, there is none better in Bath than you."

The praise of a friend was supposed to be something for which one should feel grateful. However, at the moment, grateful was not the feeling coursing through Fritz's veins. Dread, fear, the feeling of being backed into a corner and held at gunpoint – all of those were much closer to the way he was currently feeling.

"No, I cannot guarantee that. While I do believe my friend puts greater faith in my abilities than even I do, he is not wrong in saying that I am good at what I do."

Mrs. King smiled rather triumphantly. "Well, if that is the case, then, I should like a reasonable explanation as to why I should be placed in inferior care when I am paying for the best. If you cannot give me one acceptable reason to quit me, then you must remain as you have been – my physician." She placed the banknote she held on his desk. "With a ten percent increase in your fee."

He picked up the banknote and held it out to her. "I can neither give you a good reason, nor can I accept this."

She shook her head. "You can and you will accept it. I will have it no other way, and you surely must know that a disappointment at my age is a perilous thing. It would not do at all for me to take to my bed with malaise when I have a niece who needs to visit the Upper Rooms and the theatre." She stood.

"And how," she added with a charming smile – she must have been a very popular lady in her youth – "when I am bedridden, am I to take a walk in the Gardens to take in the air and enjoy the brightness of the day? It does so much good for one's health, or so I have been told by the best physician in Bath."

It was just like her to use his words against him. She was like Blakesley in that regard – both were prodigiously good to him until they wanted something, and then, they would sway him by repeating his own wisdom to him. He shook his head. There was no way he was going to be allowed to quit his place as her physician.

"I will have an apple cake," she said with a smile and a waggle of her eyebrows. "Cook is making it first thing tomorrow as I expect Mr. and Mrs. Blakesley to call."

Very carefully, she placed her reticule back on her arm. "I should think that if you were to call half an hour before regular calling hours begin, you would be able to take tea and eat cake with your friends. I find it is always a better time when there are several good friends gathered." She stopped at the door to his surgery which he opened for her. "And I do consider you a friend, Mr. Norman."

"I thank you for your consideration."

"No thanks is needed. One does not befriend another to receive thanks." She shook her head as if it was the daftest thing she had ever heard.

"Now, Annabelle," she said to the pretty lady who had risen from the chair in the hall outside his surgery, "we have a garden to visit. Do not dawdle. A brisk walk is best for one's constitution. It makes the heart hardy and hale and gives vibrance to the cheeks. Is that not what you tell me?"

Apparently, he was not the only one to have his words of wisdom tossed back at him by Mrs. King when she wished to have her way.

"Yes, Aunt. Thank you for seeing my aunt without an appointment, Mr. Norman." She gave her aunt a pointed look.

"Mr. Norman is a friend. One calls on a friend as one feels led. I needed no appointment." Her smile slipped into a smirk. "Besides, his appointments were concluded for the day. I was not delaying him from another."

"How did you know that?" Fritz asked.

"I saw Mr. Spencer leaving upon my arrival."

Oh! She was cunning.

"From the sounds of your niece's advice, Mrs. King, you do not need my care. I think you would do well enough without me."

"And not have a handsome young man to simper

TOUCHES OF AUSTEN, BOOKS 1-3

over me?" She chuckled. "I think not. Come along, Annabelle."

"Thank you," Belle whispered once more before adding, "your attention means a lot to her."

"So it would seem," Fritz muttered.

"I am very glad to see that you have done so well." She gave a sweeping look around the hall and through the door to his surgery before scurrying away when her aunt called to her from the door to Fritz's townhouse.

He watched her exit, and then returned to his surgery to finish making the notes he had been writing when Mrs. King entered. However, he did not cross immediately to his desk. Instead, he chose to peek out the window and watch Mrs. King and her niece make their way down the road.

As he watched them, Belle looked back. Fearful of being caught watching, he stepped back but did not give up his observation of her. How could he? His heart was as drawn to her now as it had been six years ago. He sighed and allowed himself to feel the agony of a longing which would never be satisfied. Then, when he could see them no longer, he continued to his desk and dropped into his chair.

His pen was waiting for him, and he knew he

needed to finish his notes. Yet, his mind was not ready to return to the improvement of Mr. Weller's leg pain when exercise and rest were taken in proper measure. There was no room to contemplate the role proper meals and limited sweets had played in Mr. Weller's improvement. There was not even space to chuckle over the consternation expressed by Mr. Weller over the grievous lack of sweets in his home.

Fritz's mind was filled to overflowing with thoughts of Mrs. King's beautiful niece and the puzzle of how he was going to be able to call on Mrs. King and not feel his heart constricting each time he had to sit and take tea with Belle.

He dropped his head into his hands. Surviving such a call while Belle remained unattached would be painful enough, but what would he do when she had callers? How would he be able to tolerate seeing other fellows fawn and flatter her? And he knew they would. How could they not? Belle was as pretty now as she had been when he last saw her six years ago. She was much sought-after then, and he was certain she would be just as sought-after now.

He expelled a slow breath in an attempt to alleviate some of the deep ache in his heart. The thought of another gentleman courting Belle was as disagreeable now as it had been every time it had crossed his mind over the past six years.

He needed a remedy, some sort of prescription.

He leaned back and looked up at the ceiling. What would cure a broken heart? There were tonics on the apothecary's shelf or in the liquor cabinet in his home which could dull the pain, but none of those would cure it.

He tapped his fingers on the arm of his chair.

Love.

That seemed the only thing which might do it. But where would one find such a tonic? Fritz had not met one lady of what he considered the proper age who captured his attention. And he had looked. Every season, with each new influx of temporary residents, he had looked.

He scrubbed his face. He knew that if a patient were ill and if the right tincture was not available and could not be created, he would look to other solutions even if they were new and had not been rigorously tested.

He blew out a breath. That was what he would have to do since the perfect remedy for his heart –

someone who was as old as Belle, as pretty as Belle, and as practical as Belle – was not something that was available to him. He would have to look to a newer remedy.

He scrubbed his face again.

"A younger lady," he told himself. "You must consider a younger lady." Surely, there would be one who was not squeamish and given to fainting if he forgot himself and brought up a topic considered less than delicate.

Belle had never been one to look faint or horrified if he mentioned some particular experiment which he had witnessed while assisting Dr. Darby in town. She had always found even the most gruesome bits to be of great interest. For all her beauty – and she had a great deal of it, even now when her bloom should be fading – it had not been her beauty alone which had captivated Fritz.

What had called to him was her mind. It was inquisitive and quick. She would ponder the things he had told her about his studies and would often come back to him with some remedy which she had learned at the side of Mrs. Codling, a trusted servant in the Chapman house and the one on whom her mother would call first when one of her children became ill.

There would never be another so perfect as Belle. He knew it in his heart. However, he also knew that such perfection was not to be his, for he could not take her away from her mother.

He did not care if she never saw her father again. That gentleman was a fool of the highest order and did not understand Belle's intelligence. In fact, Fritz had heard him caution her on more than one occasion to keep her knowledge to herself so that she would not frighten away a good prospect by being labeled a bluestocking.

However, Belle and her mother had always been close, and it was only the fear of never being allowed to return to her home and see her mother that had kept Belle from running away to Scotland with him. He could have just as easily set up a practice in the north where no one would know of the rumor's Belle's brother Andrew had started which had labeled Fritz as inept and had kept him from finding a new position when his time with Dr. Darby had come to an end.

He blew out a breath in resignation. Perfect or no, a replacement for Belle must be sought, so that his heart might, after all these years, finally find some measure of peace.

About the Author

Leenie Brown has always been a girl with an active imagination, which, while growing up, was both an asset, providing many hours of fun as she played out stories, and a liability, when her older sister and aunt would tell her frightening tales. At one time, they had her convinced Dracula lived in the trunk at the end of the bed she slept in when visiting her grandparents!

Although it has been years since she cowered in her bed in her grandparents' basement, she still has an imagination which occasionally runs away with her, and she feeds it now as she did then — by reading!

Her heroes, when growing up, were authors, and the worlds they painted with words were (and still are) her favourite playgrounds! Now, as an adult, she spends much of her time in the Regency world, playing with the characters from her favourite Jane Austen novels and those of her own creation.

When she is not traipsing down a trail in an attempt to keep up with her imagination, Leenie resides in the beautiful province of Nova Scotia with her two sons and her very own Mr. Brown (a wonderful mix of all the best of Darcy, Bingley, and Edmund with a healthy dose of the teasing Mr. Tilney and just a dash of the scolding Mr. Knightley).

Other Leenie B Books

You can find all of Leenie's books at this link
bit.ly/LeenieBBooks
where you can explore the collections below

~*~

Other Pens

~*~

Touches of Austen Collection

~*~

Nature's Fury and Delights, Novelette Anthologies

~*~

Sweet Possibilities and Sweet Extras

~*~

Dash of Darcy and Companions Collection

~*~

Marrying Elizabeth Series

~*~

Willow Hall Romances

~*~

The Choices Series

~*~

Darcy Family Holidays

~*~

Teatime Tales Novelettes Collection

~*~

Darcy and... An Austen-Inspired Collection

Connect with Leenie

E-mail:

LeenieBrownAuthor@gmail.com

Facebook:

www.facebook.com/LeenieBrownAuthor

Blog:

leeniebrown.com

Patreon:

https://www.patreon.com/LeenieBrown

Subscribe to Leenie's Mailing List:

Book News from Leenie Brown

(bit.ly/LeenieBBookNews)